**Select praise for author
Reese Ryan**

"[These relationships] have plenty of heat and heart."
—*Library Journal* on *A Valentine for Christmas*

"A story that deals with issues such as autism
and learning disabilities in a sensitive and simple
way without overshadowing the essence of
Harlequin Desire books, the sexy romance."
—*Harlequin Junkie* on *The Bad Boy Experiment*

"Reese Ryan has written another enjoyable
character driven romance and I'll be looking
for the next on her release list!"
—*Harlequin Junkie* on *Seduced by Second Chances*

"I'm so glad I picked this one up,
and I highly recommend it for those who love
seeing couples work through their issues
to find real love and commitment."
—*Harlequin Junkie* on *The Billionaire's Legacy*

"Ryan's style is as crystal as a flowing stream,
her characters are like rapids drawing you in
but giving you enough bumps in the road to
make life interesting and her plot is seriously
realistic enough to jump off the page."
—*Harlequin Junkie* on *Savannah's Secrets*

"I've enjoyed all the stories in the series
and look forward to more from this author!"
—*Harlequin Junkie* on *Waking Up Married*
and the Bourbon Brothers series"

REESE RYAN

&

USA TODAY BESTSELLING AUTHOR

JULES BENNETT

BREAKING THE BAD BOY'S RULES
&
THEIR WHITE-HOT CHRISTMAS

HARLEQUIN

DESIRE

Recycling programs
for this product may
not exist in your area.

ISBN-13: 978-1-335-45789-9

Breaking the Bad Boy's Rules & Their White-Hot Christmas

Copyright © 2023 by Harlequin Enterprises ULC

Breaking the Bad Boy's Rules
Copyright © 2023 by Roxanne Ravenel

Their White-Hot Christmas
Copyright © 2023 by Jules Bennett

For questions and comments about the quality of this book,
please contact us at CustomerService@Harlequin.com.

Harlequin Enterprises ULC
22 Adelaide St. West, 41st Floor
Toronto, Ontario M5H 4E3, Canada
www.Harlequin.com

Printed in U.S.A.

CONTENTS

Reese Ryan writes sexy, emotional stories featuring thirty-plus-somethings finding love while navigating career crises and family drama.

Reese is the author of the award-winning Bourbon Brothers series and an advocate for the romance genre and diversity in fiction.

Connect with Reese via Facebook, Twitter, Instagram, TikTok or at reeseryan.com. Join her VIP Readers Lounge at bit.ly/VIPReadersLounge. Check out her YouTube show, where she chats with fellow authors, at bit.ly/ReeseRyanChannel.

Books by Reese Ryan

Harlequin Desire

The Bourbon Brothers

Savannah's Secrets
The Billionaire's Legacy
Engaging the Enemy
A Reunion of Rivals
Waking Up Married
The Bad Boy Experiment

Dynasties: Willowvale

Working with Her Crush
Breaking the Bad Boy's Rules

Visit the Author Profile page
at Harlequin.com for more titles.

You can also find Reese Ryan on Facebook,
along with other Harlequin Desire authors,
at Facebook.com/HarlequinDesireAuthors!

Dear Reader,

It's been so much fun creating the world of Willowvale Springs, Wyoming, with the amazing Jules Bennett. In *Working with Her Crush*, we met Andraya Walker, who was devastated when she discovered that the horse ranch she hoped to inherit had been left to her former friend. Thankfully, she had her best friend, Alejandra "Allie" Price, to help her through the ups and downs. In *Breaking the Bad Boy's Rules*, we get Allie's love story.

When bad boy rocker Vaughn Reed returns to Willowvale Springs to renovate the old resort he inherited from Hank Carson, he hires his friend's family-owned construction company. He can hardly believe that the gorgeous interior designer managing the project is his friend's little sister Allie, who is all grown up. But dating his best friend's little sister is what led to the breakup of his rock band. So it's a mistake he doesn't plan to make twice. But Allie Price is determined to take her shot with her celebrity crush, and she's too tempting for Vaughn to resist.

For book news, giveaways and more, be sure to visit reeseryan.com/desirereaders and join my newsletter list.

Until our next adventure!

Reese Ryan

BREAKING THE
BAD BOY'S RULES

Reese Ryan

To reader Vilma Fitzpatrick Akins:

Thank you so much for coming up with the name for Vaughn's rock band, Sin & Glory. And thank you so much for being a supportive longtime reader.

To Jules Bennett:

Thank you for inviting me to join you on this project and for being both incredibly creative and unbelievably accommodating. It was a joy to work with you.

To my family:

Thank you for your love, patience and support.

To K. Sterling and Leigh Carron:

Thank you for keeping me company and keeping me sane as I finished this book. Love you both!

To our readers:

I hope you have as much fun reading Dynasties: Willowvale as Jules and I had creating the series. Thank you for joining us for the ride!

One

Vaughn Reed stepped off of the private plane that had flown him from Dublin to LA. He said his good-byes to the other members of the session band that had traveled the globe with a pop star whose talent lay primarily in being photogenic and an excellent dancer with a huge social media following.

Not the best gig he'd ever had, but not the worst, either.

More importantly, the gig paid well, and it kept him relevant—a waning commodity since his legendary rock band Sin & Glory had broken up four years ago.

Vaughn had been the reason the band—which had been together for fifteen years—imploded. The reason his personal and professional life had spiraled.

It was a mistake he wouldn't make again. To ensure that he didn't, he'd devised a set of rules for himself.

First: Don't think with your dick. *Period.* Second: *Never* get involved with your best friend's sister. Third: *Always* consider your career first. Fourth: *Never* fall in love.

For the past four years, those four rules had served him well. No more awkward or sticky situations. No career-destroying revelations. No public meltdowns. After all, he would be forty on his next birthday. If he didn't get his shit together now, he probably never would.

Vaughn hopped into his matte black Lamborghini Aventador. Then he made his way onto Hollywood Boulevard toward the empty house in the Hollywood Hills that awaited him.

Vaughn pulled into the three-car garage of the magnificent home that had previously belonged to one of his rock idols. The beautiful home boasted contemporary architecture and gorgeous views of the iconic Sunset Strip, the ocean and the LA Basin. But the house held too many bad memories.

Now that he planned to spend the next few months in LA, maybe he'd finally have time to do a few updates and put the property up for sale.

He'd barely turned off the engine when his phone rang. It was his assistant, Cherry Bingham.

"What's up, Cherry?" Vaughn tried not to be short with her despite his exhaustion after the grueling eleven-hour flight and disappointment after reading the latest message from his agent. "If this is about Hannah's email... I already read it. The label isn't interested in funding a comeback album or tour for Sin & Glory without Steven."

Vaughn gritted his teeth. Steven Iverson was Sin & Glory's former lead singer and Vaughn's former best friend. And he'd made the mistake of dating, marrying and eventually divorcing the man's younger sister. The breakup of the marriage led to the end of their friendship and the dissolution of the band. Now, Steven was enjoying a mildly successful solo career, and Vaughn and the rest of the band were fighting for a place in the industry.

"Sorry. I know how hard you've been working to revive the band. Should I send Steven another certified letter?" Keys clacked in the background.

"He'll just ignore it like the others." Vaughn got out of the Lamborghini and unlocked his garage door and entered the kitchen. The house was pristine and smelled like lemons and fresh flowers. "The place looks great."

"Alonzo cleaned the pool yesterday, groceries were delivered this morning and Anita cleaned the house and put away the groceries earlier today," Cherry said. "Which brings me to the reason I called—"

"Don't tell me Anita broke something again?" Vaughn slipped the band from his dark, wavy hair pulled atop his head in a man bun his parents would've hated. His hair—long overdue for a haircut—fell to his shoulders with a gentle shake of his head.

"No, this time I'm the one who screwed up." Cherry's voice suddenly sounded small. "Anita found an envelope underneath the console table in the entry hall. It must've slipped off the pile when I set your mail down there before sorting it. The postmark is from two months ago. I'm *really* sorry, Vaughn."

"It's okay, Cher." Vaughn set his luggage just inside his bedroom, then massaged his stiff neck and circled his tight shoulders. "Who was it from?"

"A law office in your hometown of Willowvale Springs." She seemed to be holding her breath.

What could that possibly be about?

"If the delay resulted in any kind of fees or loss, I'll explain what happened, that it's all my—"

"Relax, Cher," Vaughn said calmly, hoping to allay her anxiety. "I'm sure it'll be fine. Where is it?"

"Your mail is sorted and stacked on the desk in your office."

"Great. Now back to this thing with Steven... I was hoping we could get everyone on board, but Matt suggested that we move forward without him." Vaughn rubbed his chin and sighed as he stood at the glass wall in his bedroom overlooking the city. "Steven and I were best friends when we started Sin & Glory. Just a couple of broke-ass kids with big dreams." He shrugged. "Maybe his reaction to the end of my relationship with his sister was unfair. But it still feels wrong to do this without him."

"Plenty of other groups have moved on without their iconic lead singers, Vaughn," Cherry said gently. "Besides, there's a ton of talent out there. You'll find someone else."

"The guys are definitely open to it. But I'm not sure how our fans would take it. Especially since Steven is doing his own music now."

"The fans just really miss hearing the old Sin & Glory songs. I think you'd be surprised by how happy most of them would be to hear that the group is even considering a reunion tour." There was the clacking of more keys. "There are three petitions going right now requesting a reunion tour. They have a combined total of fifty thousand signatures and counting."

It was nice that the fans cared that much. Still…

"That still doesn't address the issue of funding," he reminded her.

He was doing quite well due to his generally frugal nature—thanks to a modest upbringing. The house in the Hills and the Lamborghini had been among his few splurges. He saved and invested wisely, more acutely aware of the realities of poverty and homelessness than the other band members, some of whom had come from wealthy families. But as much as he wanted to make this Sin & Glory reunion album and tour happen, it would be unwise to use his personal finances to bankroll the venture.

"Fan-funding is an option," Cherry stated.

"What if it flops? We'll lose whatever credibility the band has left."

Cherry didn't argue the point. "You could try to get a few investors to bankroll the project. Or maybe start playing the lottery."

"I'll consider it." Vaughn chuckled.

He toed off his black-and-white Vans Old Skool

Classic Skate Shoes—his preferred footwear for performing. He'd owned just about every color they'd ever made because they were both comfortable and functional when working the foot pedals of his drums.

"But right now, I just want to take a long soak in a hot bath while I enjoy the view, and then crash for a couple days. Could you order the calamari and rigatoni carbonara for me and then whatever you want? Have mine delivered in an hour," he said. "Then we can meet over breakfast tomorrow."

"All right, but don't forget to open that envelope!" Cherry reminded him as he ended the call.

Vaughn groaned. He'd hoped to put off anything other than a hot bath and a warm meal until tomorrow. But Cherry would be stressed about her blunder with the envelope until she knew everything was okay.

He shoved his phone into the back pocket of his jeans, then made his way to the kitchen. Vaughn retrieved his favorite blend of freshly squeezed juice, guzzling from the glass bottle. He sighed contentedly. Every road trip reminded him of the simple joys of being at home.

Then he went to his office to retrieve the envelope.

Vaughn held the brown, craft paper in his hand, and for a moment, he froze. There was something surreal about seeing the words *Willowvale Springs* in print. He'd lived in Los Angeles for nearly twenty years. Yet, deep down, Willowvale Springs would always be the place that was truly *home*.

He'd lived there with his adoptive parents from the age of twelve to nineteen when his mother died barely a year after they'd lost his father. He still owned the old farmhouse his parents had left to him because he couldn't bring himself to sell the place. But he couldn't bear the idea of the old place sitting abandoned and unloved, either. So he'd been listing it on home rental sites for the past several years.

Vaughn roughly set down the small bottle on his desk, then settled in his chair. He sliced into the envelope with a letter opener and slid the thick document and an accompanying flash drive onto his desk. Then he read the letter paper clipped on top.

Holy shit.

Vaughn went back and slowly read the note from Phil Walker, whom he'd known growing up. Phil had apparently become a lawyer and had his own practice back home. He'd written to inform Vaughn that old Hank Carson—the godfather of Willowvale Springs—had died and left him the old resort ranch.

"This has to be a joke," Vaughn muttered the words beneath his breath.

Hank wasn't a relative. In fact, he and Ms. Edith never had children. Nor had they been particularly close. Vaughn had simply worked for Hank as a bellboy and all-around seasonal help at the rustic old ranch for a few summers as a teen. He and the old man had had the occasional conversation. And when he'd given Hank his resignation and expressed his desire to move to Los Angeles to start a rock band, the old man hadn't been pleased. Still, he'd sincerely wished him the best of luck. A gesture Vaughn had appreciated.

Vaughn opened the flash drive, stuck it into the hub of his desktop computer, then opened the lone file. A video of the old man appeared on the screen, invoking a pained smile.

The man who had always loomed in his memory larger than life had grown thin and frail, ravaged by the effects of age and perhaps illness. Hank went into a hacking cough, then quickly recovered, wiping his mouth with a handkerchief.

"Hello there, Vaughn. I wish we were chatting under better circumstances, son. And that we were having this conversation in person. But I couldn't leave this earth without telling you how damn proud I am of you. You said you were going to start your own rock band and become famous. Sell out arenas all over the world. I applauded your gumption and your effort. But I honestly didn't think you had a chance in hell of making that happen." The old man chuckled, prompting another coughing fit. "But my Edith believed in you. And you did it, son. Made fools out of every one of us that ever doubted you. I only wish your parents had lived long enough to see it. They would've been damn proud, Vaughn."

The words seemed to catch in Hank's throat, and he dabbed his eyes with his hanky.

Vaughn was stunned.

Hank Carson had never been given to displays of emotion—though his adoration for his wife had been quite clear. So his words—uttered with such deep respect and heartfelt affection—made Vaughn's eyes sting and his throat burn. Especially the kind words about his parents. Arthur and Carolyn Reed had been well into their fifties when they'd rescued him from the foster system and decided to take him in and raise him as their own.

He'd been lucky to have had two sets of parents who'd truly loved him. But he'd also had the unenviable distinction of burying both sets before the age of twenty.

"You know Edith and I never had kids of our own," the old man continued. "But the children of Willowvale Springs were our family. A few of you made quite an impression on us. So as I face the time for me to leave this world, I'd like to leave each of you something. And to you, I leave the Willowvale Springs Resort. You were much more than a bellboy or a stable hand. You were a hard worker. Conscientious. Cared about the guests and the animals. It never felt like it was just a job to you, son. I've seen how you held on to your parents' farmhouse and how you've cared for the old place—even from a distance. So I'm leaving you the resort to do with as you please. I know you'll make the right decision, Vaughn. Good luck, son."

The screen went black, leaving Vaughn staring at the blank space, stunned. So many emotions churned in his chest. All the words he'd never get to say to Hank ran through his head. He was grateful for Hank's thoughtful gift and his belief in him. But he had no idea what he would do with the old resort. He didn't even want the farmhouse he currently owned in Willowvale Springs. He simply hadn't had the heart to let go of the old place. Not even when he'd been struggling to make it in LA before his career had taken off.

Vaughn dragged a hand down his face and headed to the luxurious bathroom that afforded views of the entire LA basin while offering him privacy. He ran water in the tub and sprinkled in the lemongrass and lavender bath salt his housekeeper made for him because it helped him sleep. Then he stripped out of the clothing he'd been wearing for nearly twenty hours. He submerged himself beneath the warm, foamy liquid, soaking his hair before reemerging.

He wiped the water from his face, leaned against the cushioned headrest and squeezed his eyes shut, truly relaxing for the first time in weeks.

Vaughn had nearly drifted to sleep. Then his eyes shot open and he bolted upright, splashing water onto the white-and-gray Carrera marble tile floor.

Maybe he didn't need to play the lottery to fund a comeback album for the band. Hank Carson had seen to that.

Within minutes, he'd dried off, gotten dressed and called Cherry to make arrangements for him to meet Phil in Willowvale Springs. Then he called his childhood best friend, Reynaldo Price, whose family owned Price Construction. Because if the Willowvale Springs Resort was anything like he remembered, it would require a complete overhaul if it was going to generate the money he needed to get Sin & Glory's next album made.

Vaughn pulled his rented Audi Q7 SUV into the drive of the Willowvale Springs Resort at the edge of town. He'd spent summers working there as a teen. Then after high school, he'd worked at the resort full time. He hadn't seen the place in twenty years. And when he'd scanned the photos on the bare-bones website, it looked like the lodge had been stuck in a time capsule.

He exited the truck, slid his bôhten shades atop his head, and surveyed the main building. The tired photos had actually been quite generous. Not only had the place not been updated since he'd worked there nearly two decades before, it clearly hadn't been maintained for at least the past five years.

When he'd worked there, the old man was a stickler about ensuring regular maintenance was done. No wonder the resort was barely hanging on. It appeared about three steps from being condemned.

Just how long had Hank been ill?

Vaughn climbed the rickety old steps that led to the large, front porch. The old porch swings were still there but needed a fresh coat of paint and new chains. The decor framing the door looked the same as when he'd been there.

Vaughn stepped inside and made his way to the front desk. He'd been thinking that the old place looked as if it was in some kind of twilight zone where time had stood still.

He was wrong.

Instead, it felt as if he'd been transported back to the sixties...*the 1860s*. If he didn't know better, he'd think he was on the set of his parents' favorite old show, *Bonanza*. That Ben Cartwright, Adam, Hoss and Little Joe would appear at any moment.

"Vaughn Reed?" An older woman glanced up from the front desk, her head cocked. "My word! I haven't seen you since...since your mama's funeral. My gosh, that has to be ten or fifteen—"

"Twenty years ago," he said. "It's good to see you again, Mrs. Halston."

The woman had been working the front desk at the ranch for as long as Vaughn could remember. She'd been Willowvale Springs very own version of Dolly Parton. Her blond hair was now gray and her sparkling blue eyes weren't quite as clear as they'd been when he'd had a killer crush on her as a teen. But she still had an amazing figure and dressed like she'd stepped out of a fashion magazine.

"It's Mrs. Weinstein now." She chuckled with a glint in her eyes. "Barry died about five years ago. God rest his soul." She glanced up at the ceiling. "But call me Barbara. And my goodness, let me give you a hug."

Barbara came around the desk and enveloped him in a bear hug before releasing him. "What brings you here, sweetheart?"

"I'm the new owner of the resort." Vaughn practically held his breath as he said the words.

Barbara had been running the ranch for twenty

or thirty years. Surely, she would've expected Hank to leave the place to her.

"Thank goodness!" Barbara pressed her hand to her chest, flashing her bejeweled nails. "Been terrified that the old buzzard was gonna leave this place to me like he left the general store to Mabel Miller. Mabel wanted the store, mind you. Me? Not so much."

"Why not? I mean…you've probably worked here longer than anyone." He should just be grateful Barbara wasn't upset about Hank leaving him the place.

"I'm a grandmother now." She smiled proudly. "Got three grandkids and one on the way. Plus three bonus grandkids from Barry's kids. I like getting out of the house and doing things. But these days, I'm wanting to spend more time with the grandkids and travel. I've been waiting to find out who the owner is so I can—"

"You're quitting?"

"Not quitting…*retiring*." She patted his arm. "But don't you worry none, sugarplum. I won't leave you high and dry. I'll stay on as long as you need me to get you acclimated and to train my replacement. In fact, I've got time if you'd like a tour of the old place right now."

Vaughn was still trying to process the information that he needed to staff the place and oversee things until he could find a good replacement for Barbara.

He glanced down at his watch. "I have about fifteen minutes before I'm meeting with a designer and a construction project manager to discuss renovations."

"Well, hallelujah!" Barbara did praise hands and quickly scanned the room. "Lord knows this place could use it."

Vaughn chuckled, glad the woman didn't oppose taking a wrecking ball to the outdated floor plan and antiquated decor.

"Think we'll have time to squeeze a quick tour in before they get here?" he asked.

"No, I don't." Barbara nodded toward the door.

Vaughn followed the woman's gaze to a pair of sexy, tan-and-black leather booties with a stacked heel and side buckles stepping through the door attached to a pair of shapely legs. The creamy brown skin shimmered and glowed.

Dayum.

Vaughn hadn't returned to Willowvale Springs to find a hookup. But the woman who sashayed toward him—hips swaying in a black, midthigh-length blazer dress that perfectly accented her Coke bottle shape and thick thighs—could *definitely* get it.

"It's good to see you again, Vaughn." The woman placed a palm on his chest and leaned in and kissed his whiskered cheek. Her voice was slightly husky and oddly familiar. Her vibrant scent—like pomegranate, lilies and something spicy—lingered as she pulled away.

"I'm sorry but do I know..." His voice trailed off as he studied the woman's gorgeous face, taking in the familiar mischievous dark eyes, button nose and cheeky grin. "No...no way." Vaughn covered his mouth and shook his head. He turned toward Barbara who was more than amused by the exchange. "There is no way that this is *little* Allie Price."

"It is. Only our little mischievous squirt had the audacity to grow into a lovely and incredibly talented young woman." Barbara beamed as if she'd raised Allie herself.

Then again, in Willowvale Springs, you didn't just belong to your parents. You were claimed by the whole damn town.

"Well, I can certainly see that." Vaughn laughed. He held out his arms to give his childhood best friend's little sister a proper hug. "It really is great to see you again, Allie."

He hugged her, trying his best to shut down his dick, which stirred in response to Allie's buttery soft curves cradled against him.

Refer to Rules #1 and #2. Not gonna happen, bruh. Not in a bajillion years. So calm the fuck down.

Vaughn pulled out of Allie's lingering hug, cleared his throat and shoved a hand into the pocket of his rag & bone jeans. He diverted his gaze slightly, so as to at least give the pretense he was making eye contact with the stunningly gorgeous Afro-Latina woman who'd once been that adorable little snaggle-toothed girl who'd had an innocent crush on him. Because the thoughts he was having about her now were anything but innocent.

"So are you here to introduce me to the designer and the project manager?" Vaughn rubbed his chin.

"That explains why you wanted to take pictures of this old place." Barbara shook a finger at the younger woman, her eyes twinkling as if Allie was a naughty teenager who'd played a trick on her. "Vaughn hired your family to handle the renovations. Well, we simply couldn't be in better hands. Been watching the work you've been doing over at the horse stables where I board my Molly. Your family does some amazing work."

"Thank you, Ms. Barb." Allie sifted her manicured fingers through her shiny, curly, shoulder-length tresses, tugging them over one shoulder.

Vaughn squeezed his free hand into a fist, aching to run his fingers through her hair. His eyes met Allie's again. It had been accidental. Yet, he couldn't tear his gaze away from hers.

The phone rang, and it seemed to shake them both from the awkward moment.

"I'd better get that," Barb said. "If either of you needs anything, just give me a holler."

"Will do. Thank you, Barbara," Vaughn said. He shifted his attention back to Allie. "So…the designer and the project manager…"

"You're looking at her." Allie held her hands out, the way she often did when she'd put on some sort of show for them as a kid.

"So *you're* the interior designer?" Vaughn frowned as he folded his arms, resting his chin on a closed fist as he studied her.

"Yes." Her reply was less cheery with a hint of indignation this time.

"Okay. *Great,*" Vaughn said, only slightly sarcastically. "What about the project manager?"

"Again…you're looking at her."

"Wait…" Vaughn dropped his arms at his sides and stood to his full height. He wasn't particularly tall, but he was at least half a foot taller than her. "You're handling both jobs?"

He realized that he was a local boy and no longer a member of one of the world's bestselling bands. But he expected to get at least a little star treatment.

Rey knew that this job was important to him, that he needed the place to look its absolute best, and that he was on a tight turnaround. And what did he do? He'd sent his little sister to play both designer and project manager.

Well, he was going to have a few choice words with his childhood best friend as soon as he sent little Allie packing.

"Look, I appreciate your time, and I don't mean to be rude. But I made it clear to Rey just how important this job was and that I'm on a *really* tight schedule. So if he's not taking this seriously—"

"That's it." Allie cursed in Spanish and slapped a nearby high-top table. She set down her colorful tote bag. Allie folded one arm over her chest and massaged her temple with the other. "Why is it that every good-looking man has to go and open his big fat mouth and *completely* kill the illusion?" she muttered. "This is pretty disappointing behavior from a man who has written some truly empowering ballads for female artists. Not to mention that you actually referred to yourself as a feminist in that *Rolling Stone* article."

That article interview had been at least ten years ago. Did she really remember that?

Vaughn wouldn't let Rey's gorgeous little sister with her killer body and glowing brown skin sidetrack him. Maybe he'd been a little brusque, but he was still the customer, wasn't he?

"If this is how Price Construction treats their clients, maybe it's better if I go with another firm."

Allie snorted and cocked one hip. Which wasn't helping his attempts to not notice the delicious curves she'd acquired over the years. His cheeks and forehead felt as though they'd suddenly burst into flames.

"Suit yourself, pal." Allie snatched her bag off the table and glared at him. "But good luck finding anyone else around here to handle this project on such short notice. There's been a construction boom in the area. All of the other contractors in the region are just as slammed as we are. Rey sent me because I'm the best person to handle the design job. I'm also handling the project management because we are *completely* booked. If you're too sexist, pigheaded and generally chauvinistic to recognize that you are incredibly lucky to get to work with me, then you don't deserve the designs I've been working on day and night for the past three days. I'd say good luck, but we'd both know I don't really mean it."

Allie turned on her heel and strutted her fine ass toward the front door.

Vaughn groaned and cursed under his breath. "Allie…wait!" He followed her, grasping her hand before she could escape.

He could swear a bolt of electricity traveled up his arm and exploded in his chest. It was the kind of instant attraction he hadn't experienced in a long time. A feeling that this jaded old rocker suspected he was incapable of anymore. But those butterflies eventually led to heartbreak and worse, they'd blown up his career.

Maybe you couldn't teach an old dog new tricks, but he was damn well going to try. He had no intention of making the same mistake twice.

Allie swiveled around, her dark eyes filled with fire as she glared at him expectantly.

Little Allie Price had grown up to be fucking beautiful, smelled like heaven, and had full, lush lips that sent erotic fantasies about their feel and taste spiraling through his brain.

But gorgeous or not, friend or not, Vaughn needed this job *done fast* and *done right*. And whatever happened, he most definitely would not make a move on the still annoying little brat who'd apparently morphed into an incredible goddess.

Two

"Is there a particular reason that you stopped me, or do you just *really* enjoy holding my hand?" Allie leaned in and whispered loudly.

Vaughn dropped her hand and stumbled backward, nearly toppling over a table that went out of style around the same time silent movies had. Allie grabbed his arm, steadying him.

The deep olive skin of Vaughn's cheeks and forehead flushed as he recovered from his near fall.

"Thanks," he mumbled, shoving his hands in his pockets.

Allie tried her best not to grin. She'd sent a clear message to her brother Rey's old friend: *Do not try me*.

Allie clutched the tote bag, which held the tools of her trade, to her chest as she sized up Vaughn—

who had the decency to look contrite for having un-
derestimated her. The folder contained three days'
worth of blood, sweat, tears and lost sleep. Vaughn
Reed might be a world-famous rock star. But there
was no way she was going to let him just waltz in
there and discount her hard work, precious time and
brilliant designs.

She was the lone woman working in their family-
owned construction company consisting of her father,
who still called her *princess*, and four brothers—
all alpha males, like their father—with a misguided
sense of overprotectiveness. It had been an ongoing
struggle to get them to take her seriously.

It had taken some time, but they'd agreed to add
an interior design component to the company. A decision they'd likely considered an indulgence when
Allie had refused to join the firm as either the office
manager or bookkeeper. Both were fine jobs; they
just weren't right for her.

In addition to studying interior design, Allie had
taken the same contractor courses her father had
insisted that her brothers take. And as soon as she
qualified, she applied for and obtained her general
contractor license. Allie made it her business to become well-versed and damn good in both disciplines.

"This is not my first go-round, you know." Allie
stared down the man she'd had a killer crush on as
a young girl and throughout her teens. "I've handled
design and project management simultaneously on
other projects."

Very small projects. But Vaughn didn't need to know that.

"I'm an award-winning designer and a card-carrying member of ASID—the American Society of Interior Designers," Allie explained, shoving one of her manicured nails in his direction. "And if you want to give this place a glam, modern makeover that will attract celebrities and put this place on the map, I'm your best bet."

Her father and brothers respected her abilities—as long as she produced more of the same safe, cozy farmhouse interior designs.

Allie appreciated a neutral palette, comfy, oversize furniture, shiplap, barn doors and exposed wood beams as much as the next designer. But she also loved playing with bold colors and unexpected textures; the crispness of a sleek, contemporary space; Asian and Scandinavian-inspired interior design; and applying elements of feng shui. And she'd been trying to convince her family for the past few years that they could tap into the luxury market if they would be a little more open-minded with their design offerings.

Her father thought her ideas were too "jarring" for their customer base. So he'd always vetoed any designs leaning in that direction.

Allie got it. Every region had its own flavor, and people liked what they liked. But sometimes, people didn't know they wanted something different until you showed it to them.

Price Construction could be at the forefront rather

than chasing the trend once someone else kicked it off. And this project for Vaughn—who would be accustomed to and likely appreciate a more glamorous, contemporary design—was the perfect opportunity for her to show her family exactly what she was capable of.

"Who said anything about going after celebrities?" Vaughn hiked an eyebrow and rubbed his bearded chin.

Something about the innocent motion set fireworks off inside of her.

She cleared her throat.

"Vaughn, you're a badass, world-famous drummer who was a founding member of one of the best rock bands *ever*. Why wouldn't you tap into the clout you've earned by trying to attract clientele who can afford to pay top prices?" Allie shrugged, glad the large, colorful, Classic Dezi Consuela tote bag shielded her body's reaction to him. "Besides, from what Rey said, I got the feeling that you planned to hold on to the property, just like Kahlil and Mason have. And if so, naturally you want the resort to be a place worthy of having your name associated with it."

When Hank Carson had died, he'd left his horse ranch to Kahlil Anderson and his farmhouse to Mason Clark. Both men were locals who'd worked for Hank on the respective properties as teens.

Vaughn was still rubbing his chin as he took a few steps, glancing around the space as if seeing it for the first time. His eyes lit up, and Allie was sure she saw dollar signs in them.

She had Vaughn Reed right where she wanted him.

Okay, where she really wanted him was in bed beneath her while she rode him hard, like a prize-winning stallion. But lapping up her design ideas, poised to write her family's company a big, fat deposit check would definitely be a close second.

Get your mind out of the gutter, girl. Vaughn Reed is a client, and you do not sleep with clients.

Vaughn turned to her. "You really think we can turn this old place into a posh resort? Maybe even a wellness spa?"

Now Allie's eyes lit up. She was going high-end, but Vaughn was going even higher.

Cha-ching.

Cue the cash register opening and money shooting out of it like a fountain—cartoon style.

"I like the way you think, Vaughn Reed." Allie shook a finger, her smile widening as she envisioned the space. "I'd incorporated space for yoga and meditation rooms and potential space for a salon and a few massage rooms. But I could easily upgrade the plans to include a true spa. We'd have to do some additional building on the property to make that happen. But if you're targeting high-end clientele, you'll be in a position to recoup those costs relatively quickly."

The wheels were turning in Allie's head, and she liked where this train was going.

"All right, let's see what you've got, nena." Vaughn gestured for Allie to have a seat at the nearby high-top table.

Had Vaughn been a stranger, Allie would've told

him off for calling her *baby girl*. The term was used affectionately between romantic partners but could also be used as a term of endearment for a little girl. Hence, her parents, brothers, and Vaughn had often called her nena—or the English equivalent: baby girl. In fact, her father often still did. Still, it seemed weird to hear him refer to her as nena now. It confirmed that Vaughn still saw her as that mischievous little girl with a fiery tongue. Not as a grown woman who was extremely attracted to him. And he clearly wasn't attracted to her.

It was just as well. He'd only be in town long enough to hire a construction firm, and she didn't date clients. So why was Allie's ego bruised over Vaughn's lack of interest?

Not everyone has good taste. Pull it together.

Allie stood taller, turned up the wattage on her smile and set her bag on the table. She climbed onto the high barstool chair as gracefully as possible given her height of five-two. It took her by surprise when Vaughn pushed in her chair. His enticing scent—likely some insanely expensive European cologne—was subtle. Yet, it surrounded her like a warm, soothing hug. She just wanted to wrap herself in it—and him.

"Let's begin with the plans I've already developed. Then we'll go into the additional changes and costs required to turn the resort into a full-scale wellness spa, and to do it as quickly as possible."

Allie pulled her tablet from her bag and turned it so that they both could see the plans she'd created in her 3-D modeling design software. The moment she'd opened the first page, Vaughn made an audible gasp.

"Wow. That's *incredible*, Allie," Vaughn said once she'd taken him through the entire plan that she'd laid out for the resort. She'd handed her tablet to him so he could scroll back through various portions of the design. "You can really do this and have it up and running in a couple of months?"

"We can have the designs, as they've been laid out, completed by Christmas," she clarified. "If you choose to go with the more entailed option of turning the resort into a wellness spa, it's going to require us to build additional structures. We can handle that, of course. And we'll complete the job as quickly and efficiently as possible. But a project like this… I always allot enough time to ensure that everything is done right. So if you're pressed to reopen the resort as quickly as possible, we could always handle the project in phases. This would be phase one—" She indicated the designs Vaughn was still marveling over. "Then phase two would be the additional buildings, which would house key elements of the wellness spa."

"I love that idea." Vaughn stroked his chin, and Allie's hand involuntarily closed into fists as she wondered about the feel of his beard—dark brown and laced with gray—abrading her skin.

She shut her eyes momentarily and tried to shake the thought from her head.

"That'd give me a chance to see how things develop in the initial phase of the project and then decide whether it'll be worthwhile to move forward." Vaughn seemed to be thinking aloud more than speaking directly to her.

Allie jumped in anyway. "It will *definitely* be worthwhile to continue with phase two of the project. Give me a week, and I'll design the wellness center of your dreams," she assured him.

"Allie Price, you are as confident as ever."

A small smile curved one corner of Vaughn's sexy mouth. Her heart fluttered in response, and there were butterflies in her stomach.

"I remember how serious you were about designing your little dollhouses back in the day. You even had your mom make little slipcovers for the furniture out of your old clothes." Vaughn chuckled fondly, his dark brown eyes flickering in the sunlight streaming through one of the few windows in the dark space. "I once asked you what you wanted to be when you grew up," he continued. "You said you were going to be a builder, like your dad. But that you were going to build the most glamorous houses anyone has ever seen."

"I said that?" Allie honestly didn't remember that conversation.

She did, however, recall asking Vaughn to marry her when she was about ten years old. She'd overheard her parents talking after the death of Vaughn's adoptive dad. They'd mentioned how he'd already lost so much. He only had his adoptive mother left, who was also sick. Beyond that, he didn't have any other family.

Allie had decided to fix that by asking Vaughn to marry her. That way, he'd become an official member of the Price family.

Vaughn had been shocked by her question, but he'd handled her request graciously. He'd said that she was the little sister he'd never had, and he wouldn't want to ruin that.

Allie had shrugged, said okay, then returned to playing with her dolls.

"You did." Vaughn handed the tablet back to Allie. "Even at ten, you were a girl who knew exactly what you wanted. And I'm glad to see that you've been able to make your dreams a reality."

"Thank you, Vaughn." Allie tucked a few strands of her hair behind her ear and smiled sheepishly. "I was thrilled to see that you became a world-famous drummer, just like you set off to do when you left Willowvale Springs. But then again, I never doubted you would. You were one of the most focused, determined teenage boys I'd ever met."

There was a quiet moment between them that was sweet and familiar, yet painfully *awkward*.

"I'd love to claim that focus as some admirable character trait I was born with," Vaughn said. "But the truth is that losing so much when you're young and then being cast in a situation where you feel you need to fend for yourself…it forces you to grow up faster than you should." Vaughn shrugged.

"Well, how you chose to direct that focus was

a conscious choice, Vaughn." Allie placed a gentle hand on his wrist and smiled. "So don't ever discount your achievements. You've worked damn hard for the career and life that you have. You cofounded Sin & Glory. You've been featured on some groundbreaking albums and record-breaking tours. Then there's your songwriting career that's really starting to take off."

"Wow…" Vaughn rubbed his chin. "I didn't think anyone back home followed me like that." He regarded her curiously.

Oops! She'd gone from playing it cool to stalker vibes in two seconds flat.

"I…uh…well, I've always loved a variety of music. Besides, you were my brother's best friend and you're one of Willowvale Spring's very own homegrown celebs. It's not like we have a ton of those." Now it was her turn to shrug. "You've done well for yourself, Vaughn. Folks around here are proud to consider you one of us."

Allie let go of his wrist, cleared her throat and tried to ignore the warmth that had trailed up her arm when she'd placed her hand on his skin.

"So it sounds like you're prepared to move forward with what we're now calling phase one of the remodel." She tapped on the keys of her laptop, updating the parameters of the renovation and the corresponding figures.

Allie used the resort's antiquated printer to print out the contract. She circled the projected completion date and the estimated cost. "This is the estimated price tag for the project."

Vaughn whistled in response.

"Sticker shock?" Allie teased, laughing when he nodded. "You want a high-end finished product, you've got to use high-end supplies. Besides, just imagine how much this project would cost you in LA."

Vaughn groaned quietly and accepted the pricey fountain pen she extended toward him. "True."

They went over the paperwork and executed the necessary documentation. Allie climbed down from the stool and gathered her things. She tucked Vaughn's retainer check into her portfolio along with the signed contract, then slipped them into her bag.

"My team and I will be out here on Monday," Allie said. "In the meantime, I'll be drawing up plans for phase two of the project. We can start as soon as we're done with phase one. Or, if you'd prefer, we can begin the second phase at a later date. But once you see how we transform this space—" Allie glanced around, excited about the prospect "—you won't be able to sign that second contract fast enough."

"After what I've seen… I don't doubt it." Vaughn stood, too. He pulled her into a hug. This one was far less awkward than their first. "Sorry if I came off as kind of a—"

"Divo?" Allie couldn't help laughing at the way his eyes widened in response to her referring to him as the male version of a diva.

"I was thinking asshole, actually. But…fair." Vaughn rubbed his chin and smiled sheepishly. "I'm feeling more pressure to get this job done than I thought. Thanks for fitting th project in and for saving me from tumbling over that old table. I could've broken something."

"No problem." Allie hitched her bag onto her shoulder and grinned. "Besides, I had to protect the hand that'll be writing the checks."

They both broke into laughter and it felt...*nice*.

"See you on Monday, kid." It was another nickname he'd frequently used when she was little.

Allie said her goodbyes to Vaughn and Barb, then got into her car. She couldn't wait to tell her father and brothers that she'd secured the project and that this time, they'd be doing things her way.

On the drive back to the office, she couldn't stop thinking of Vaughn and how the man had aged like fine wine. But their relationship was a business one coupled with an old friendship, and it would never be anything more.

It was for the best. Yet, Allie harbored a hint of disappointment that she'd never fulfill her long-held fantasy of being with the man she'd adored long before he'd become a famous rock star.

Three

Vaughn woke up early on Monday after a late-night flight in from LA and a two-hour drive from the Casper-Natrona County International Airport. He'd gone to LA to attend a couple of important meetings. The first was with a studio exec he and his agent were trying to convince to give Sin & Glory an album deal. The second was a singer from the UK whose star was on the rise internationally. She'd gushed that her parents always listened to Sin & Glory so she'd be "honored" to work with him to write songs for her highly-anticipated second album.

He'd scuttled the first deal since the studio was offering an insultingly crappy advance unless he could convince his former brother-in-law—Sin & Glory's lead singer Steven Iverson—to rejoin the band. The second he'd accepted because the studio was offering a lucrative deal for him to cowrite songs for the young artist, whom they were sure would be the next big thing.

Vaughn was honored that she'd been genuinely eager to work with him, but damn if his conversation with the bubbly, optimistic twenty-year-old singer hadn't made him feel like a rock and roll relic.

His parents' house was booked solid through the fall and the holidays via a popular vacation home rental app. So he'd had no choice but to move into one of the unoccupied cabins on the property during the renovation of the resort. The one-bedroom cabin was a stone's throw from the main house and not far from the outdoor pool. It was private and cozy, but like the rest of the resort, the cabin was in serious need of updating.

Renovating the individual cabins would be the latter part of phase one. Today, Allie and her crew would begin work on the main house.

Allie.

Vaughn groaned quietly, then abandoned all hope of sleeping in. Despite his long travel day and late arrival, he'd barely gotten any sleep. His thoughts kept returning to the gorgeous, talented, fiery-tongued Allie Price.

How had he not recognized her from the moment she'd sashayed into the room? In many ways, Allie was much the same as she'd been as a kid. She was sweet and adorable as long as you were nice to her. But mess with her or one of her friends, and the littlest thing on the playground converted into a fire-breathing dragon with a stinger for a tail.

Vaughn had been like another big brother to Allie. But the handful of times he'd been prepared to step in to protect her from some larger bully, she'd either played the dozens, trading barbed insults that practically brought the bully to tears, or she'd demonstrated the meaning of fuck around and find out long before it was a popular hashtag.

Vaughn chuckled, recalling the time he'd had to haul Allie off of a bully about twice her size. Her legs were kicking and her arms were flailing as she cursed in English and Spanish at the older boy she'd gifted with a busted lip and a black eye. Vaughn rubbed his jaw at the memory of the pain from when he'd accidentally caught one of those flying elbows in the chin.

He climbed out of bed, headed for the bathroom, then hopped into the shower.

Vaughn was nine years older than Allie, which would make her thirty now. In the larger scheme of things, their age gap didn't make much of a difference anymore. They were both adults. But he doubted that Allie's four older brothers would see things that way. His childhood best friend Rey, particularly.

Before arriving back in Willowvale Springs a few days ago, he'd never thought of Allie as anything but an annoying little pseudo-sister. But since he'd laid eyes on the woman who'd given him a well-deserved dressing down, he hadn't been able to stop thinking of her.

It was lust: pure and simple. And there was no way in hell he was going to blow up another friendship by getting involved with his best friend's sister. He'd been there, done that, and had the souvenir T-shirt, emotional scars and stalled-out career to prove it.

Don't be a dumbass twice, man. Learn from your mistakes.

Maybe working out would burn off his anxiety about the start of the renovations and take his mind off of the gorgeous woman Allie Price had grown into.

Vaughn slipped on a pair of charcoal gray sweatpants, an old white-and-black Sin & Glory T-shirt, and his socks and sneakers. Then he grabbed a towel from the bathroom and headed for the gym in the main building. Maybe he'd even have time to make himself something quick for breakfast before demolition on the kitchen started.

He'd be in and out before Allie and the crew arrived. And the way he'd been obsessing over her the past few days, he'd decided it would be best if he minimized the number of times he and Allie crossed paths.

Then what are you doing here in Willowvale Springs? Why aren't you in LA? It's not like you ain't got shit to do.

The voice in the back of his head sounded a lot like Allie, and like her, it wasn't afraid to call him out on his bullshit.

He popped in his wireless earbuds and cranked

up the music to drown out the pain-in-the-ass voice of reason that demanded an answer. It was already set to one of his workout playlists. This one leaned heavily toward Queen and kicked off with "Somebody to Love."

Vaughn locked up the cabin and jogged toward the main house.

Why was he here in Willowvale Springs when he had so many other things he needed to be doing right now? He could've just engaged the Prices' construction company to handle the renovations, then flown back to LA and kept in touch with Allie via phone. But his brain wasn't built that way. He was a perfectionist who wanted things just the way he wanted them—especially if his name was going to be attached to the project.

This renovation was important to Vaughn. Not just because he was using the unexpected inheritance to fund the making of Sin & Glory's new album if they didn't get a better offer from one of the recording studios. The resort was an incredibly thoughtful gift from a man who meant a lot to him. Hank wasn't a man of many words. But the words he'd uttered had meant a lot to Vaughn. Especially after the loss of a second set of parents before he'd reached the age of twenty.

Hank had promised Vaughn that if he stayed, he and Ms. Edith would take care of him. Treat him as if he was their very own flesh and blood. He wondered if the old man truly understood just how much he'd appreciated his offer.

Still, Vaughn needed to go out into the world and make his own way and go after his dreams. And he was glad that he had. But as he made his way toward the main house he was overcome with feelings of guilt. Yes, chasing his dreams was an important pursuit. But he should've made time to see about Hank, Ms. Edith and the Prices. They'd been family to him as much as the parents he'd been born to and the ones who'd adopted him.

That's why he was determined to ensure that the renovated resort would be worthy of the town he'd always have a soft spot for. And of Hank's magnanimous gesture. And he wouldn't do anything stupid—like making a move on Allie. He wouldn't ruin his relationship with the only family he had left.

Allie parked her Tango Red Audi A5 Sportback, opened up the back hatch, removed the collapsible wagon and set it up before loading it with a tray of breakfast sandwiches, a fruit tray, a box of doughnuts, two boxes of coffee and all of the necessary accouterments.

Getting the wagon up the steps without tipping everything over was tricky, but she managed. She punched in the lockbox code and entered the empty building.

There had only been a handful of reservations through the end of the year. So Vaughn had opted to cancel them with his deepest apologies and the promise that he'd honor their booking price when they rebooked at the newly renovated resort. Then he gave Barb paid time off while they completed the initial phase of renovating the main house, so Allie's crew could get the work done as quickly as possible.

She washed her hands, then got started setting up everything so the mini feast she liked to treat her crew to on the first day of a job would be ready before the first worker walked in the door.

"Something certainly smells good."

"Vaughn?" Allie turned suddenly, nearly toppling over the jugs of cranberry and orange juice she'd gone back out to the car to get. She steadied the teetering containers and Vaughn hurried over to help her.

"Sorry, Al. I didn't mean to startle you." Vaughn placed a solid hand on her shoulder, and Allie could swear she felt a tiny zap of electricity.

Then again, it was late fall in Wyoming. With the dry air, static electric shock wasn't uncommon. But dammit if the man wasn't glistening with sweat and wearing a pair of fitted, charcoal gray sweatpants and no shirt.

Despite his slim build, the man was surprisingly fit, and his muscles were toned. The fine hair on his chest trailed down over his washboard abs and disappeared beneath the waistband of his pants.

Allie swallowed hard, her heart beating wildly and the sound of her pulse echoing in her ears.

"No worries. I just didn't expect you to be here." Allie smoothed down the front of her shirt.

"I thought I'd get a quick workout in and connect with the old place one last time before your crew starts tearing into the walls." He glanced around the space reverently.

Allie's gaze dropped to the bulge in the front of his dark gray sweatpants. The bulge that was practically saying, "Hello, how you doin'?" in its best Madea voice. Or maybe that was all in her head.

She cleared her throat and raised her gaze, just in time to meet his once he turned back to face her again. "That's nice, but I meant I didn't expect you to be here in Wyoming. I thought you flew back to LA the day after our meeting."

"I did," Vaughn acknowledged. He slipped on the black T-shirt that had been hanging over his shoulder. "But this project is really important to me and to my future plans for Sin & Glory. I figured I should remain onsite and accessible." He shrugged.

Great. Another client who'd be looking over her shoulder the entire project.

"When it's time to select paint colors, flooring, furniture and any other design choices, we can easily collaborate via video conference or text message." She checked her watch, then returned to setting up the table.

"Actually, I'm more of a hands-on kind of guy."

Allie froze. The unintended double entendre shot straight to her sex and tweaked her nipples...*hard*. She cleared her throat, keeping her back to him and wishing she'd worn a padded bra.

"But you already signed off on the design." Allie glanced over her shoulder. "Do you not trust my judgment?"

"Of course I do, Allie. I wouldn't have hired you if I didn't. But I've always been a very visual, tactile kind of person. It's how I best absorb the necessary information to make a decision."

Allie opened the bottles of juice and then set them near the upside-down stack of red cups—the kind used in every backyard barbecue she'd ever attended. She turned around with her arms folded over her chest.

"You said this project was important to the future of the band. I didn't realize the band had a future," Allie said tentatively. It was a touchy subject, and she didn't want to piss off her biggest client to date. "I mean, you guys broke up what…four or five years ago. And in every interview of Steven Iverson's that I've seen or read he's always pretty adamant that there would *never* be a reunion for Sin & Glory."

Vaughn winced. Whatever memories were going through his head were clearly painful. She instantly regretted having brought up Steven's apparent animosity toward the band.

"I'm sorry, Vaughn. I didn't mean to—"

"It's fine." He forced a smile, seemingly more concerned about any discomfort the conversation might be causing her.

That was the Vaughn Reed she'd always known. Sweet, thoughtful and accommodating. Emotionally intelligent. Conscious of the feelings of the people around him.

No wonder she'd fallen head over heels for him as a girl.

"You're right. Steven isn't interested in doing a reunion album or a reunion tour. But the rest of the band is, and I'm not going to let him hold the rest of us hostage especially when his animosity toward me and the rest of the band is—"

"Based on a lie?" Allie searched Vaughn's eyes, needing his confirmation.

The thing that had broken her heart more than learning that Vaughn was marrying Steven Iverson's sister was the news that Vaughn supposedly cheating on her was what had caused their divorce and the dissolution of Sin & Glory.

She hadn't believed it. Couldn't believe it. Because it wasn't in keeping with the personality of the man she'd revered growing up. But the tabloid and gossip blogs were adamant about it and the stories seemed so convincing. Still, a tiny sliver of her heart held out hope that it wasn't true.

"That's right." Vaughn scratched at the stubble on his chin. "Eva has always had Steve and her parents wrapped around her little finger. So he wouldn't listen to anything I had to say. And he was just as angry at the rest of the guys when they tried to defend me. I'm convinced it was all a part of the plan. Eva had been pushing Steve to go solo for a while. I wouldn't put all of the fallout that happened past being part of her design to maneuver her brother into a solo career."

"How would that have benefited her?" Allie didn't doubt Vaughn's assessment. She just didn't quite understand it.

"She'd become his agent a couple years before that," he said. "At the time, Steve was her only client. After he went solo, she picked up a few more clients. Most of them were part of bands but had aspirations of going solo, too."

"Wow. Your ex was a piece of work, wasn't she?" Allie muttered the words beneath her breath, more to herself than to him.

"That she was." Vaughn heaved a quiet sigh. "But I've spent enough time being angry with her for lying and Steve for not even being willing to hear my side of the story." He shrugged. "And despite all of that, I still tried to make amends with the guy. To see if he'd be open to listening now that some time had passed and he had a chance to reassess the situation. But he hasn't budged on his position. So now we're moving forward."

"But Steven was the voice of Sin & Glory," Allie reminded him. "And he has a distinctive, gritty tone that's easily recognized. How do you replace a unique talent like that?"

"I've been worried about that, too," Vaughn admitted. "But my team assures me that the Sin & Glory fan base is hungry for a reunion, even if it means doing so without Steve."

"Wow." Allie was fascinated by the drama behind the scenes of the Sin & Glory breakup. She blamed her mother's obsession with telenovelas when Allie was a kid. "Coffee?" She filled one of the disposable coffee cups.

"Please." Vaughn approached the table, his eyes

sweeping the spread as if he'd been waiting for her to ask. "And maybe one of those raspberry Danishes, too?"

"Of course." Allie slipped a sleeve onto the hot cup and handed it to Vaughn. "The sugar, cream and stirrers are there. As for anything else... Help yourself to anything you'd like." Allie gestured to the breakfast spread.

But when she raised her gaze to meet Vaughn's again, he wasn't looking at the food. His eyes scanned her body—as if *it* was the only feast he was interested in partaking of. There was a deep longing in his soulful, brown eyes that sent a wave of desire through her chest and nearly took her breath away. She swallowed hard in response to the shiver that ran down her spine.

"Thanks." Vaughn tipped his chin, his eyes assessing hers. He used a napkin to grab a raspberry Danish.

Allie's heart thudded with the realization that— for the first time in twenty-five years—maybe this crazy crush she'd always had on Vaughn Reed wasn't a one-way affair anymore. But of course, it would happen at the one moment she couldn't act on it.

Vaughn was a client. She didn't date clients or any of the contractors they worked with. It had been a hard, fast rule that her father had instituted before he'd finally given her the reins to handle projects like this one on her own, without one of her brothers lurking around. Until now, it had been a rule she'd always agreed with.

Allie had gleefully recited the rule to creepy clients or contractors who'd gotten overly familiar. If that hadn't been clear enough, she'd gone what her brothers often referred to as "full Allie" on them. Even if it meant losing the job or the contractor relationship. But this was Vaughn.

What she'd discovered upon his return was that the crush she'd had on him—the crush she'd been so sure she was over—was still in full effect. Only now, she wasn't a silly little girl with a crush on a much older boy. She was a grown woman and Vaughn's equal.

Except for the whole client thing.

Allie huffed quietly as she watched Vaughn make a small plate of fresh fruit. She should let Vaughn go on his merry way doing whatever it was rock stars—typically nocturnal creatures—did whenever they were awake at this time of the morning. But another part of her couldn't resist the opportunity to spend some time with him.

She glanced at the time on her wrist, then cleared her throat.

"I've got about fifteen minutes before the guys begin arriving," Allie said hurriedly, her pulse racing. "Wanna have breakfast with me?"

A smile slid across Vaughn's handsome face. He nodded. "Sure. Is it okay if we eat at the high-top table?" Vaughn indicated the table where she'd first shown him her plans for the renovation of the resort.

"That'd be perfect." She grinned as she hastily made herself a plate so she could have breakfast with Vaughn.

Four

Vaughn sat at the Roland FP-90X Digital Piano he'd brought back with him when he'd returned from LA and played a few of the notes he'd written the other night. He'd spent the week since his return trying to write songs for Extreme Overload—a band that had opened for Sin & Glory back at the height of their career. But now Extreme Overload was the big-ticket act selling out stadiums and reigning supreme on the rock charts.

He'd written a couple of songs for the group before. But the band's bass player and chief songwriter had died in a car crash that summer. So this time, they wanted to collab with Vaughn on writing their entire album. He'd taken the gig because his old friends needed the help, and after such a huge loss, they wouldn't be ready to head back into the recording studio for a while. But the date he'd promised to deliver a handful of songs to get the creative process started was looming, and he had yet to write a song that was worth the paper it was written on.

Maybe he'd been a little burned out after touring and the session work, but he'd been struggling with a serious creative block the past few months. And if he didn't get over it soon, he'd lose his credibility as a songwriter—an element of his career he planned to expand further.

He'd tried reading, listening to music, going for long walks in the mountain terrain and working out daily. Nothing seemed to work.

He played a few chords he'd written the other night.

While he did his songwriting on the keyboard, it was when he was seated on the throne behind his drum set—his feet working the pedals and his sticks connecting with the snare, high hat, toms, and cymbals—that he felt free and allowed himself to get out of his head and let go of whatever was bothering him.

Playing didn't fix everything. But it wouldn't hurt to give it a try. Besides, in a moment of gear acquisition syndrome, he'd ordered himself a new custom Yamaha drum kit. It'd been delivered the day before, and he'd spent the morning setting everything up just the way he liked it. Why not try working out some of his frustrations on the drums?

Vaughn slipped onto the leather drum throne and settled in behind his new drum set. He put on his isolation headphones, cranked up his favorite Extreme Overload album, and picked up his sticks. He took a deep breath, closed his eyes, and then exhaled deeply, trying to push out all of the noise in his head right along with it.

He twirled the stick in his right hand, then dove in, playing in time with the music. With every rimshot, stroke, crash, and groove his mind felt freer. Playing the drums alleviated the stress that had been agitating him. His concerns about the future of Sin & Glory. Worries over whether he'd taken on more than he could handle with this wellness spa. His anxiety over not being able to write these past few months. And the guilt over his growing attraction to the one woman he couldn't have: Allie.

After nearly an hour of playing, Vaughn had shed his T-shirt, sweat dripped down his back and forehead, and his hair—which had come loose from the top knot—was flying with every movement. He made one final cathartic crash the cymbals in time with the last note of the album but was startled by movement and the sound of applause.

Vaughn jerked his head around and was greeted by the gorgeous face and bright smile of the woman he'd found himself so preoccupied with.

"Allie?" Vaughn stilled the cymbals, then dragged his fingers through his sweat-dampened hair. "How did you—"

"I knocked, but there was no answer," Allie said.

"The front door was open and I heard you playing, so I let myself in."

"What brings you by?" he stammered.

"I brought way too much food for me to eat alone but not enough to share with the crew." Allie smiled sheepishly. Her dark brown eyes glistened in the sunlight streaming through the cabin window. "I was hoping I could interest you in having a bite to eat with me while I update you on the project. The private concert and male revue show…" Her gaze glided over his sweat-slickened skin, and Vaughn could swear his skin tingled in the wake of it. "Well… those were bonuses I definitely wasn't expecting."

Vaughn's cheeks heated. He cleared his throat, silently congratulating himself for at least wearing pants. "That'd be great. I could definitely eat."

"Great." She glanced at the set of drums, then at him. "Nice drum set. But that doesn't look like the setup you usually play with."

"It isn't. Just had this delivered yesterday. But how'd you know…"

"I've seen you in concert a few times with Sin & Glory and a few other artists over the years. Then there's those drum tutorials you did on YouTube." She shrugged.

"You came to our concerts? If I'd known, I would've gotten you tickets and backstage passes." Vaughn got up from his drum throne and retrieved the shirt he'd tossed when he'd gotten too damn hot.

Thoughts of Allie had commandeered his brain as he drummed along with a song about falling for the girl you'd least expect. Allie appearing at the cabin unannounced definitely wasn't making it better. Still, he was glad to see her.

"We hadn't seen each other since I was a kid. I didn't want to be that person who only reaches out because they're begging for free concert tickets." She propped a hand on her hip as she looked around. "What happened to the dining room set that was in here?"

"I had the movers put it in the storage shed at the back of the property." Vaughn toweled off his damp skin and hair, then slipped his shirt back on. "Figured it didn't go with the new aesthetic anyway. But don't worry, it's undamaged in case some museum is interested in it." He winked, and Allie laughed—a sound he'd come to love.

"Well, I need to heat these in the oven." Allie held up a fancy, fabric lunch bag.

"Please do." Vaughn gestured toward the kitchen. He excused himself to freshen up, wash his hands, and change into a fresh T-shirt. When he returned, he settled onto one of the stools at the breakfast bar.

Vaughn tried his best not to notice how well the one-piece, beige jumpsuit Allie was wearing clung to her shapely figure as she moved about the kitchen. The belted waistline showed off her full breasts and curvy bottom. The brown leather booties she wore gave her a few inches of height and looked perfect peeking from beneath the wide legs of the pants.

Ignoring his growing attraction to Allie Price had

become a daily exercise. And he was pretty sure he was getting worse at hiding it.

Since their impromptu breakfast on demo day, he and Allie had had breakfast, coffee, or at least a quick chat nearly every day he was on-site because he'd insisted on being kept up-to-date on the project.

She'd caught Vaughn up on all the goings on in Willowvale Springs over the past two decades. They'd talked about who'd gotten married and had kids, who'd moved away, who'd returned to town, and which members of the community had passed away.

Price Construction had a hand in building the new residential communities on the edge of town and a new shopping center. They'd also been instrumental in the apparent construction boom since Hank's death. Each of the men whom Hank had mentored as teens and subsequently bequeathed one of his prize properties had returned to town and upgraded the property.

Tech entrepreneur Kahlil Anderson and retired pro baseball player Mason Clark had decided to make Willowvale Springs home again. His life was in LA and on the road, so he wouldn't be putting down roots here again. But it was just as important to him to uphold Hank's legacy and create a facility that would benefit the town that had nurtured and raised him.

Of course, Kahl's and Mason's decisions to stay had more to do with them falling for the women who'd been their childhood best friends: Andraya

Walker and Darcy Stephens, respectively. Since his best childhood friend was Rey Price—who was married and whom Vaughn was pretty sure had never nursed a flame for him—he felt safe in stating that the same wouldn't be happening for him. Still, if seeing their old friends again had been anything like his reaction to reconnecting with Allie again—Vaughn could understand how things had progressed so quickly for both men.

He and Allie hadn't had nearly as close a relationship.

Yet, since returning to town, he'd enjoyed getting to know her, and he looked forward to their frequent interactions. Vaughn was so damn proud of the woman Allie had become. She hadn't let her parents or older brothers coerce her into a career she had no interest in for the sake of the business.

Vaughn had been wanting to say as much to Allie, but he didn't want her to think he was being condescending. He admired Allie, and he was glad she was flourishing in a career clearly meant for her. Vaughn would forever be indebted to his adoptive parents for buying him that first drum kit as a gift for his sixteenth birthday. But he honestly didn't know if he would've pursued his dreams of being a professional musician if either of his adoptive parents had still been alive.

He'd been so grateful to them for taking him in and raising him as their own. So he'd been obsessed with trying to be the perfect son to the older couple who hadn't been able to have children of their own.

He wouldn't have been able to walk away from either of his parents who were older and infirm. They'd needed him as much as he'd needed them the day they'd visited that foster home and recognized just how unhappy and alone he was.

"So…" Vaughn tried to shake his rumination about the possible taste of the shimmering, peach lip gloss rimmed with a brown lip liner on Allie's lips. "What's for lunch?"

"It's a surprise." Allie plopped onto the seat beside him.

Her bright smile was contagious and her soft, floral and fruit scent tickled his nose. Vaughn fought the urge to lean in and get a deeper whiff.

"But while the oven is warming, I have a few things to go over with you. It isn't great news, I'm afraid." She frowned, shifting effortlessly from the playful woman who always knew how to make him smile to the businesswoman who demanded to be taken seriously by her father and brothers as well as her clients and contractors.

"Been holding my breath and waiting for the other shoe to drop. There's bound to be some unplanned disaster when renovating older structures." Vaughn sighed. "So let's hear it. What's wrong and what's the blow to my budget?"

Allie showed Vaughn photos of water damage and rotting wood as well as leaky old water pipes. It was a definite hit to the budget, but they were still well below the contingency they'd built into the budget. Hopefully, it would stay that way.

As they discussed the issues that had arisen during the renovation, Allie removed a foil-covered item from her lunch bag, loosened the foil a bit, then set it on a cookie sheet. She placed the food in the oven.

"Anything else?" Vaughn asked.

"Actually, yes. The lumberyard where I like to get my flooring is having a big sale in the coming week. If you like one of the options they offer, we can recoup some of that additional cost."

"Well, that's good news," Vaughn said.

"Great. I'll pull up the website. You can review the options and let me know if anything stands out."

Allie pulled out her tablet, opened the website and then handed it to him already on the page for the flooring on sale."

He thumbed through them. But without being able to see them in person and touch them, it was hard to gauge how much he liked any of the options.

Allie wandered over toward the keyboard set up on the opposite side of the living space. She pointed at it. "I forgot you also play both the piano and the guitar. Since you found your success as a drummer, I didn't realize you still play the piano."

"I use the keyboard or the guitar when I'm writing songs," Vaughn explained.

"Are you writing something now?" she asked. When he indicated that he was, she sat on one end of the bench and patted the other. "I'd love to hear what you're working on. Would you play it for me?"

Vaughn had planned to decline because the song wasn't anywhere near finished. But with such excitement in Allie's voice and a genuine glint in her dark eyes, he couldn't refuse her. He moved over to the keyboard and sat on the other end of the bench, painfully aware of her subtle teasing scent and the warmth emanating from her golden brown skin.

"I've had a lot going on the past few months." He was already apologizing. "So I've been in sort of a creative slump," he admitted. "I'm not quite sure what to do with it, but this melody came to me the other night. Right now, it isn't much. Just a piece of the puzzle."

"So the song is raw and unfinished. Sort of like my renovations to your place." Allie's smile was sweet and reassuring. "I get it. You saw my vision. I'd like to see yours."

Vaughn stared into the penetrating eyes that gazed up at him with affection and admiration. Heat emanated from where Allie's shoulder leaned into him, and warmth spread through his skin.

Alejandra Price was like a bright burst of light capable of illuminating even the darkest night sky. She was a breath of fresh air, and his world instantly felt better and the weight on his shoulders lighter whenever he was around her.

Vaughn shook out his wrists and stretched his fingers. He drew in a deep breath, then started to play. He'd intended to play those same few chords that had been playing over and over in his head. But as he sat there beside Allie, the next chords came to him, and the next.

"That's beautiful, Vaughn. And I definitely wouldn't describe it as 'not much,'" she chided.

"I promise you that these last few chords came to me just now." He grabbed a pencil and started to jot the notes down. "I've been working on this for the past few days and I was getting absolutely nowhere. Then you ask me to sit down with you and play the song and the next notes just came to me."

"Does that make me your muse?" Allie broke into laughter at his surprised expression. "I'm teasing you, Vaughn. You would've come up with the rest of the song whether I was here or not. But it was amazing to witness your creative process firsthand."

Vaughn stared at Allie as they sat shoulder to shoulder. There'd always been something *special* about Allie. He'd never really been sure what it was. He just knew that the feisty kid always seemed to have an inner glow. Even on his worst days, she'd found a way to do something that would make him smile or just feel a little less sad. That inner light hadn't dimmed. If anything, it had gotten stronger. It surrounded her like a force field. As Vaughn sat beside Allie, her warmth penetrated his skin, and her teasing smile filled his chest with a deep affection he hadn't experienced in so long. It felt as if he'd been drawn into her light.

He was captivated by it, and by her.

But Allie was just a friend. More importantly, she was his oldest friend's younger sister. And she was his interior designer. All good reasons not to entertain thoughts of her as anything more. So why couldn't he tear his gaze away from those tantalizingly plump lips of hers.

"Empanadas," he said suddenly. "That's what's in the oven—your mother's empanadas."

"You remembered." Allie's delighted smile lit her dark eyes. "Impressive."

They sat there, neither of them moving as their eyes met and only a few inches of space separated them. Vaughn swallowed hard, his gaze dropping involuntarily to her mouth again.

He gripped the edge of the bench and resisted the urge to cup her cheek and lean in for a taste of her sensual lips.

Suddenly, Allie's phone rang over on the breakfast bar.

"I'd better get that," Allie said after a beat.

Had she been hoping he'd lean in to kiss her?

Vaughn closed his eyes and sighed. He should be grateful for the interruption. It had prevented him from making a huge mistake by kissing Allie.

He needed the distraction. Something to keep his brain from imagining how good it would feel to take Allie into his arms and trail kisses down her neck.

Vaughn played the notes again, including the ones he'd first played sitting there with Allie. The notes kept coming. Like finding the key piece to a puzzle that made it clear what came next and what came after that. For the first time in weeks, it felt as if his creativity had been unleashed. He jotted down the music notes and a few lyrics that came to him. When he glanced over at Allie, she appeared to be having an animated conversation. He'd been too absorbed in his sudden burst of creativity to hear what the heated conversation was about.

Maybe Allie was right about being his muse. At the very least she'd provided inspiration and helped him get unstuck.

That was a gift he wouldn't squander.

Allie indicated that she was going to take the call out on the porch, then stepped outside in the crisp fall air, wishing she'd thought to grab a jacket. But between the heat running through her body after stumbling upon the enthralling vision of Vaughn Reed playing the drums, half-dressed and hair flying, and the irritation she felt at her brother, she barely noticed the chill in the air.

"Reynaldo Price, who the hell do you think you're talking to?" Allie asked in a harsh whisper. "I may be your baby sister, but I am *not* a child. So *do not* talk to me like I'm one."

Her brother huffed. "Look, I'm not trying to treat you like a kid, Al. But you will always be my kid sister. I won't apologize for looking out for you."

Allie sighed, and the rage in her belly died down. When she'd told her brother that she was at Vaughn's cabin and they were going over a few pressing items over lunch he'd proceeded to lecture her about "being smart" and "staying safe."

"I appreciate that you love me and want to protect me, Rey," Allie said. "But I'm not a little girl anymore. I'm as invested in this business as you are.

I'm aware that there are inherently more concerns for my safety, and I act accordingly," she assured him.

Rey snorted in response, but she chose to ignore it.

"This is Vaughn we're talking about for God's sake. He was as protective of me as you all were. Are you really saying that you don't trust your best friend?" Allie continued.

Vaughn was still working on the song he'd played a sample of for her. It was soft and emotional. A stark contrast to his vibrant, kinetic drum playing. And the notes seemed to come to him more easily now. She smiled, hoping he was having a much-needed breakthrough.

The fact that Vaughn had purchased a drum set and had it delivered to his cabin made Allie hopeful that Vaughn planned to spend more time in Willowvale Springs. It was the perfect respite to escape the hustle and bustle of LA and find some peace and solace. Perhaps the lovely plains, the pristine river, the nearby hot springs and the majestic mountains would spur Vaughn's creativity.

"Al!" Rey called her name, impatiently.

"Yes?" Allie stared at Vaughn through the window. His fingers were flying over the keys and he was singing to himself, then he'd stopped to write down a few notes.

"Vaughn and I haven't been close in a really long time. I love the guy. Always will. But money and power change people. Make them think they can have whatever they want whenever they want it. Never forget that, Allie."

"Has Vaughn given you the slightest indication that he's changed in any significant way?" Allie turned her back to the window and propped a fist on her hip.

"No," Rey admitted. "But the old Vaughn wouldn't have insisted on priority treatment on such short notice."

"Which he was willing to pay handsomely for," Allie reminded him. "You and Dad pull your weight with vendors all the time. So what?"

"Didn't say anything was wrong with it." Rey chuckled. "Just said the old Vaughn would never have done it."

Allie peeked over her shoulder through the window at Vaughn. She could faintly hear the timer going off. Before she could tap on the window to ask him to remove the empanadas from the oven, he was on his feet donning oven mitts so he could take the pan out. He inhaled the smell of the savory meat pies and a soft smile spread across his face.

She smiled too.

"Look, Rey. Vaughn loves you, too. He loves our family and the town of Willowvale Springs. He would never do anything to jeopardize his place in any of that. The guy is all alone. No family. No band. We're the only family he has left. Maybe think of that next time we're seated at our family feast and you're surrounded by your wife and kids, parents and siblings, nieces and nephews," Allie said. "He'll be here at this run-down little cabin trying to decide whether to order in pizza or heat a frozen meal."

"Shit. Never thought of it like that." Rey sounded remorseful for having intimated that being alone with Vaughn might put her in jeopardy. "I should ask Mom and Dad if it's okay for me to invite him to dinner on Sunday."

Allie smiled, her heart dancing a little.

Little Sister 101. How to manipulate your older brother like a marionette on a string.

If she'd invited Vaughn to dinner, it might've raised eyebrows. But she'd gotten her brother to do it instead.

"The way he's in there inhaling the scent of those empanadas, I'm pretty sure he'd gladly accept your invitation." Allie laughed and her brother did, too. "I realize that my last serious relationship blew up big time. Yes, it shook my confidence a little and my desire to get involved seriously with anyone again. But I'll never learn to start trusting myself again if you all are always second-guessing everything I do and policing my interactions with every man on the planet."

Rey sighed quietly but didn't respond. So Allie continued.

"If I need you to interfere on my behalf for any reason, I won't hesitate to ask. But you've gotta give me room to breathe, make my own mistakes and live my life. All right?"

There was a long pause. Finally, Rey groaned. "All right."

"Thank you. And don't forget to tell the others. I do not want to have this conversation five more times."

"You've got it." Rey chuckled. "Love you, kid."

"Love you too, knucklehead. See you on Sunday."

Allie smiled, her heart full. As annoyingly suffocating as her older brothers and parents could sometimes be, she couldn't imagine not having them in her life.

She stepped back inside the cabin and rubbed her arms. Allie glanced toward the kitchen, but Vaughn wasn't there.

Movement in the living space drew her attention. Vaughn rose to his feet, holding his hands out to the fire in front of him.

"Thought you might be chilly after being out there without a coat. I considered bringing you one, but you were in a pretty intense conversation." He paused, as if hoping she'd provide details. When she didn't, he continued. "So I didn't want to interrupt."

"You built a fire for me?" Allie walked over to stand beside Vaughn. She wasn't about to divulge that the time she was spending with him was the topic of her heated phone conversation with her brother. "That was incredibly sweet of you."

"Well, you did bring me empanadas." Vaughn shrugged. "Which reminds me… You ready to eat? I didn't realize it before you arrived, but now I'm ravenous." His eyes trailed down her body momentarily, and he sank his teeth into his lower lip before returning his gaze to the fire in front of them.

Allie's skin tingled with awareness, and a warmth trailed down through her chest and made her sex feel damp and heavy.

He was talking about the food. Pull it together.

"I'm starving, too." Any chill she'd felt from being outside without a jacket was long gone. "I need to heat up the arroz con pollo in the microwave and take out the salsa verde anyway. So grab a seat whenever you're ready, and I'll make our plates."

"Please tell me it's your mom's homemade salsa verde." Vaughn held praying hands up in front of his chest and briefly closed his eyes.

He was absolutely adorable.

As much as she loved her work in construction and interior design, there were few things that gave her more pleasure than cooking for the people she cared about and watching them enjoy her food.

"Of course, it's homemade." Allie grinned, moving toward the kitchen. She washed her hands again, then put the bowl filled with chicken and rice in the microwave. She pulled out the container of homemade salsa verde. "Seems like you're making some progress on that song."

"I am." Vaughn shifted his gaze from hers and jammed his hands into his jean pockets. "Maybe this place is good for me, after all."

"Then maybe you should stay." Allie glanced back at Vaughn momentarily before grabbing plates for them. "I realize this will be one of the top rental units once renovations are complete and that you'd need something bigger than your parents' place. But you could always build your own place like Andraya and Kahlil are doing."

Allie couldn't be happier for her best friend despite the fact that they saw much less of each other since she and Kahl had gotten together.

"That sounds more appealing than you might realize." Vaughn's gaze was on her again, and its heat was unsettling. Yet, she couldn't turn away from it. "But my life…the industry…most of it is based in LA or New York."

"True. But lots of celebrities have chosen smaller, more laidback communities as their home base. Places like Austin or Jackson Hole, just a few hours away from here," Allie noted.

Maybe she was being a little selfish in trying to convince Vaughn that he should build a house in Willowvale Springs. Because A: she'd love to design and build a home for famous Sin & Glory drummer, Vaughn Reed. And B: she liked having Vaughn around. But there was a more important reason she was pushing Vaughn to consider relocating to Willowvale Springs. He was more at ease than he'd been when he'd first rolled into town. She was suggesting that Vaughn stay because it seemed to be in the best interest of his mental and emotional health.

"I'd forgotten how beautiful and peaceful it is here." Vaughn sat at the breakfast bar and rubbed his chin. "It's kind of weird just being alone with the sounds of nature and my own thoughts." He chuckled. "Relocating to Willowvale Springs wouldn't be impossible, but it would be pretty damn inconvenient. Especially once we start recording the next album or whenever I'm called on to do session work," he noted.

"Getting session gigs is as much about availability as it is my talent or name recognition."

Allie tried her best not to pout about Vaughn gently shooting down her idea.

"You don't actually believe that a studio or artist would rather have some rando drummer just because he lives nearby when they could have Vaughn Reed of Sin & Glory, do you?" Allie asked incredulously.

When Vaughn didn't respond, she continued.

"Aside from that, Willowvale Springs is obviously inspiring you." She gestured toward the keyboard setup in the other room. "And it's a place where you'd get to spend time with the folks who've always felt like family. So would living here be less convenient? Maybe. But the trade-off would be totally worth it."

Vaughn chuckled and shook his head as he leaned forward on his elbows at the counter.

"You're as determined and persuasive as ever." Amusement lit his dark eyes as he watched her apportion the food onto their plates, then set them in place.

"You say that like it's a bad thing." Allie added ice to their glasses, then filled them with pineapple juice produced from her seemingly bottomless lunch bag.

"Never said it was bad." Vaughn chuckled. "It's just completely on brand for a Price."

Allie climbed onto her stool, then they dug into their food and Vaughn murmured with pleasure.

"Your mom is an amazing cook," Vaughn muttered through a mouthful of food. "Her food is better than I remember."

"Mamá is a phenomenal cook," Allie agreed, taking another bite of her food. "But I made the empanadas and the arroz con pollo."

"Wow." Vaughn's eyes widened as he shoveled more of the arroz con pollo into his mouth. "All those years you spent underfoot in the kitchen with your mom certainly paid off."

"I suppose they did." Allie couldn't help smiling. There was something about seeing someone she really cared about enjoying the food she'd prepared for them. But this wasn't a date. It was a working lunch with an old friend. She wasn't auditioning to become Vaughn Reed's latest flame, so she should really pull it together. "About those flooring choices. I assume you didn't get the chance to look at them. I'll send you the link to the warehouse so you can take your time and study the options. I know you said that you're very visual and more tactile. So if there's something you'd like a sample of, I can grab it while I'm there. I'm going to make the drive in a couple of days to pick out some flooring for another job."

"I should just go with you." Light flickered in Vaughn's brown eyes.

"The warehouse is an hour and a half away in Cody," Allie noted.

"I don't mind." Vaughn shrugged, shoveling more rice into his mouth. "Unless you do...sorry." He set down his fork. "I shouldn't have invited myself. You might be planning to meet another client. Or maybe make it a road trip with your boyfriend or something."

Is he asking if I'm seeing someone?

"I'm not meeting another client. I'm just placing her order. And I wanted to go in person so I can shop the sale, see what options might work for the resort, and stock up on samples." Allie turned on the stool and tried her best to rein in a smile. "And no, I'm not seeing anyone. How about you?"

"No. Me neither." Vaughn picked up his second empanada and bit into it. Steam rose from the flaky, hand-rolled crust filled with minced beef; boiled, diced potatoes; onions; bell pepper; and garlic in a savory tomato sauce.

"If you'd like to ride with me to the warehouse… great." Allie finally spoke again, filling the awkward silence between them. "But I'm leaving at seven sharp on Friday."

"In the morning?" Vaughn frowned, then held up a hand and laughed when Allie raised an eyebrow. "All right, fine. I'm the one who's crashing your party, so seven it is."

Allie nodded, then they resumed eating and went back to chatting. They had a lovely lunch together. She'd honestly meant to just have a quick meal with Vaughn then dash out to run some errands. But they were having such a great time, two hours had passed before she'd even realized it.

When the plumber called to see if Allie could come over and take a look at something, she held on to her smile for Vaughn's benefit, promised to be right over and hoped to God this wouldn't mean another huge hit to their renovation budget.

It was Vaughn's money, not hers. Still, she was

conscientious of how she spent her client's money just as her father had taught her to be. That applied whether she was doing a bare-bones renovation or a high-end one like the revamping of the old resort into a new-age wellness spa.

"Gotta run." Allie grabbed her purse and slipped on her jacket. "But I'll see you on Friday at 7:00 a.m. sharp." She pointed a finger.

"What about your lunch bag and the rest of the leftovers?" Vaughn followed her to the door.

"You could use some real food," she said. She'd noted that his fridge, freezer, and trash can were evidence of all the fast food and convenience foods he'd been subsisting on since his return. "Help yourself. I'll grab the lunch bag and my glass storage containers when I pick you up on Friday at—"

"Seven sharp," Vaughn said in an exaggerated tone meant to mimic her voice. He even rocked his head from side-to-side for added effect.

"Watch it, sucka." She punched Vaughn in the arm, playfully.

He broke into a belly laugh. "Not you going full Aunt Esther on me."

She'd loved *Sanford & Son* as a kid and had often used the retort on her brothers, Vaughn, and any classmate who was on the verge of seeing the flip side of her usually sweet disposition. It was the equivalent of a warning shot.

"Hey, if it ain't broke, why fix it?" Allie shrugged innocently. "I'd better go before someone puts an APB out on me. Try eating something that doesn't come from a fast food joint or out of a freezer box every now and again, huh?"

Allie hugged him, then lifted onto her toes and dropped a kiss on his whiskered cheek. When she pulled away, their eyes met for a moment. Her belly flipped and her pulse raced. There seemed to be a crackle of energy in the air between them.

She tucked her hair behind her ear and smiled. Then she turned to leave. Just as Allie rounded the corner toward the main building, she glanced back and caught a glimpse of Vaughn. He was standing on the porch staring after her, his hand pressed to where she'd kissed his cheek.

Allie tried to calm the fluttering in her belly. But there was something happening between her and Vaughn.

Whether it was desire, simple curiosity, or the potential for something more, Allie was intrigued by her growing interest in Vaughn Reed. And once this job was over, she planned to find out exactly which one it was.

Five

Vaughn sat on a rickety, metal stool and sifted through samples of wood flooring at the warehouse. It helped to be able to see and touch the flooring options. But it was hard to concentrate while he was watching Allie out of his peripheral vision. She was several yards away talking with one of the salesmen. The older man seemed as taken with Allie as Vaughn was.

He couldn't blame him.

Allie was dressed simply. Minimal makeup. A pair of black skinny jeans. An oversize cream-colored top tucked into the front of her pants but not the back. A knee-length camel duster coat. Matching camel booties. A pair of oversize, tortoiseshell shades. Yet, she looked effortlessly cool and more glamorous than any of the actresses or fellow musicians who'd accompanied him on the red carpet over the course of his career.

Her shiny, shoulder-length, loose, natural curls had smelled like honey and pomegranate when she'd sailed into the store past him with the elegance of an angel floating on a cloud. Vaughn could swear that every pair of eyes within a sightline of that door had focused on Allie. And while he knew he didn't have the right to, he'd instantly felt a twinge of jealousy.

It was ridiculous. He and Allie weren't involved; couldn't get involved. And even if they were, there was no quicker way to lose a woman like Allie Price than by behaving like an insecure simpleton.

He tried to tell himself that he was just being a protective older brother figure to her. But there was no point in lying to himself. Because the truth was that he'd been enamored with Allie since the day he'd returned to town. The more time they'd spent together, the fonder he'd become of her.

Allie was a gifted interior designer. She had a clear vision for the project and impeccable organizational skills. She had a warm, affable personality that drew people in and made them fall over themselves to please her and earn her praise. Yet, she was assertive when she needed to be. And she wasn't afraid to call out the men she worked with on their bullshit, even if they towered over her in size.

He'd never really considered that he might have a *type*. But getting to know the all-grown-up version of Allie Price, he was pretty sure that she was everything he ever wanted in one tidy little package wrapped up neatly in a bow.

"Find what you're looking for?" Allie was staring at him from where she stood, and now so was her companion.

The man didn't look happy that Allie had interrupted his inept attempt at flirting with her to check on Vaughn.

"I don't know." Vaughn dragged his hand through his hair and heaved a sigh. "I've seen so many samples at this point. They're all beginning to look alike."

The man rolled his eyes and folded his arms.

"I know it's a lot to take in. That's why I suggested you allow me to whittle down the choices and bring you a few select samples." Allie smiled at him sympathetically. "But no worries. I'll be there in a sec, and we'll figure it out."

Vaughn nodded, a sense of relief washing over him. Maybe he was being too hands-on with this project. But the wellness spa needed to be profitable for him, a valuable addition to the town *and* a space worthy of Hank Carson's legacy.

"Thanks, Allie."

Maybe Vaughn was being needy. But at least he'd been mature enough not to flip off the old man, who seemed irritated that Allie was abandoning their conversation to take care of him.

"I need to see about my client, Bill. But if we need anything else, I'll be sure to let you know." Allie placed a hand on the man's arm and offered a warm smile before joining him at the table.

Allie climbed onto the stool beside him and set her large, trapezium-shaped, black leather tote bag on the counter. She slid her shades on top of her head, grabbed one of the sample books and flipped through the various types of wood flooring.

"Sorry, I didn't mean to break up your conversation with your friend over there," he said, his eyes on the sample book.

"It's no trouble, Vaughn. That's why we're here." She flipped another page.

"Pretty sure your friend would disagree." He glanced up at the man. Bill was glaring back at him.

Allie tried her best not to laugh. Who would have thought that her reluctant smirk could be even sexier than her million-watt grin? It honestly should be illegal to possess the ability to render a man speechless with the slightest hint of a smile.

"Bill is the second-generation owner of the flooring warehouse. He's harmless," Allie assured him. She turned another page. "And he'll be fine. There are plenty of other customers for him to chop it up with."

"But none as beautiful as you," he noted.

Allie flashed a shy smile that made Vaughn's heart feel like it might explode in his chest.

"It isn't like that," Allie said.

"You sure? 'Cause the guy is staring at me like he's planning a covert attack." Vaughn was only half-joking, but he wouldn't be turning his back on the man any time soon. He flipped a page.

Allie chuckled quietly. "I'm pretty sure he's trying

to figure out where he's seen you before. Don't celebs usually leave the house in a baseball cap and dark glasses when they don't want to be recognized?"

"Never been much for hats," Vaughn responded. "And I'm having a hard enough time telling the difference in these samples. I don't think dark shades would help my cause." He leaned closer to Allie.

Both of them broke into subdued laughter, not wanting to make it obvious to Bill that he was the topic of their conversation.

"Fair." Allie turned toward him on her stool, and her knee brushed his thigh.

God, she smells amazing.

He turned to face her, too. With Allie seated this close, he was pretty sure that his pulse rate had doubled. He mentally chastised himself for briefly imagining what it would feel like to lean in and get a taste of her shimmering, gloss-covered lips.

Vaughn swallowed hard, then met Allie's gaze again. A knowing grin spread across her gorgeous face as she raked her hair over one shoulder. Neither of them spoke as she studied him. It was as if she was daring him to lean in and kiss her. Something he wouldn't put past the bold, audacious woman who'd gotten into her share of misadventures as a girl

"Maybe we should order lunch. Got a feeling we're going to be here a while," Vaughn said.

"Actually… I was thinking that we should go with one of these three options." She arranged three samples of tongue and groove hardwood flooring in front of him: a warm, golden hickory; a khaki-colored oak; and a light gray Canadian Ash.

"They're all nice." Vaughn ran his hand over each sample. "But very different."

"True. It would probably help if you saw the flooring with my ideas for the paint color and the kitchen and bathroom tile. That will require a trip just up the road. If you're okay with us selecting one of these three options, we can head there now," she said.

Vaughn studied them. He'd been sitting there for nearly an hour and Allie had floated in and selected three perfect options in a matter of minutes. She not only knew her craft, but she also had a good sense of what he liked.

"It's between these two for sure." Vaughn indicated the hickory and oak samples. "I prefer the soothing, warm tones of those to the cooler gray tone."

"Excellent. We'll get samples of these two that we can take to the granite yard, and I already have samples of the paint." Allie hopped down from the stool and beckoned Bill over. She asked him to pull together a list of items.

"Yes, ma'am." Bill scribbled on a pad he'd produced from his back pocket, along with a pen. He called over a younger man and asked him to pull the order together. Bill cocked his head and folded his arms as he studied Vaughn. "Pretty sure I've seen you somewhere before, young fella."

Young fella? Seriously?

Vaughn scratched at the wiry gray strands in his

beard. He hadn't been called a young fella since he was in his twenties.

"I get that a lot. Got one of those familiar faces, I suppose." Vaughn shrugged and tried his best to hold back a smile despite Allie's snicker.

"That you do," Bill said.

"There was something else I meant to ask you, Bill." Allie shot Vaughn a pointed look as she grabbed her purse. Then she led the way toward another section of the warehouse. She called to him over her shoulder, "I'll meet you in the car in a few."

Vaughn took his cue and disappeared into the parking lot, glad he'd insisted on driving. He slipped into the rental luxury SUV and waited for Allie to emerge. The entire time, his wayward brain obsessed about whether Bill had Allie cornered somewhere in the store or if he was hugging her again, as he had when they'd first arrived and Allie had handed him a container from her trunk, presumably filled with some sort of food.

Finally, Allie appeared with the young store employee in tow, who loaded two boxes into the back of the SUV.

Allie climbed inside and studied him for a moment before shaking her head and smiling.

"What?" Vaughn couldn't help laughing. There was something about the woman's smile that instantly put him at ease and brought him a sense of peace.

"'Got one of those familiar faces, I suppose'?" she said, mimicking the tone and cadence of his voice with a shake of her head as she secured her seat belt. "I thought celebrities lived for being recognized."

"Not all of us live for the spotlight, Allie," Vaughn noted. "For most of us, it's more about doing the thing that we love. Yes, there are definitely some perks to fame and notoriety, but it also comes with a price. Ceding any notion of privacy and anonymity is a part of the cost, but very few of us live for fame or recognition. The folks who do? Those are the ones who either self-destruct or take the biggest emotional dive once the fame comes to an end. And it almost always does," he added.

Vaughn heaved a quiet sigh, then forced a smile, feeling like he'd brought down the mood. He wasn't chastising Allie. He was just being honest. Too honest, maybe. Her radiant smile disappeared.

"I never thought about it that way. Sorry if I—"

"There's nothing to apologize for, Al." Vaughn placed a hand over her forearm, propped on the center console. "Maybe I shouldn't have responded quite so honestly."

"I like getting to know the real you," A smile slid across Allie's face. "You were a staple at our house. But now I realize that there's a lot I didn't know about you. And what I did know… It's all kind of hazy, being sifted through the rose-colored glasses of a little girl with a huge crush on her older brother's best friend."

Allie's smile deepened as she met his gaze again. "Besides, that was a long time ago. It's nice getting to know the man you are now as opposed to the enigmatic boy I once knew or the man portrayed in the media."

"I appreciate that you recognize that there's a difference," Vaughn said.

It was common for people to assume they knew exactly who he was based on the media portrayal of him as the "bad boy drummer of Sin & Glory." It fit a predetermined narrative and was based on mistakes he'd made as a young adult living on his own in LA and navigating a near-meteoric rise to fame before he had the foresight and experience needed to handle it.

"And I feel the same. It's been great getting to know you too, Allie. The industry can be crazy, so it's nice…stabilizing even…to have friends outside of the industry. People who are there to remind you that some of the fucked-up shit we've come to accept living in this world isn't exactly healthy," Vaughn said.

"I'm glad you consider me a friend now, and not just Rey's little sister." Allie's eyes glinted in the midday sunlight.

For a moment, Vaughn felt disoriented, as if he'd fallen into the inky depths of those dark eyes, narrowed by her impish smile.

When she'd been a kid, that smile had put her brothers on alert that she'd had some devious plan or was congratulating herself for playing a practical joke on one of them—hiding their favorite pair of sneakers or worse…filling them with half a can of shaving cream. But that was a million years ago. Now, he couldn't look into those eyes without his heart racing and his pulse pounding.

No, he definitely didn't see her as Rey's kid sister anymore. And while he saw Allie in a completely different light now, he doubted that Rey's protective stance had much changed. So he needed to act accordingly.

Vaughn removed his hand from Allie's arm and cleared his throat. "As your *friend*—" he emphasized the word as a reminder to them that this was a friendship and nothing more, regardless of the tightness in his groin or the zing of electricity that zipped up and down his spine "—I would've been happy to carry your things out to the car," Vaughn told her.

"I would never ask a *client*—" she emphasized her chosen noun to describe their relationship "—to schlep around stuff for me." Allie slid her shades back on, then glanced at the time on her phone. "We should get over to the granite yard before it gets too busy."

"Which way are we headed?"

"About five miles up the road in that direction." Allie pointed.

Vaughn started the car and they drove for a few minutes in silence before she spoke again.

"You weren't jealous of Bill, were you?" Allie kept her gaze on the terrain passing by the window.

"Jealous of Bill?" He said it as if it were a preposterous notion despite it being true. "I don't even know the guy, Al. Besides, it's not like you're *with* him."

"I'm with you," Allie was saying simultaneously.

"Right," Vaughn agreed. "You're not into him, and you're not *with* me. So why would I be jealous?"

"Solid logic." Allie nodded. "But then, one might

wonder why you were glaring at the man and making him uncomfortable?" She cocked her head and hiked an eyebrow before returning her attention to the road ahead. "You're worse than my dad and brothers. Do I need to leave you in the car when we get to the granite yard?"

"No, of course not," he said. "And I'm sorry if I was acting—"

"Territorial?" She looked at him again.

"I was thinking overly protective," Vaughn said. "But okay, we can go with what you said." He heaved a quiet sigh. "I just wanted to make sure the guy wasn't being creepy and invading your space. Is that so wrong?"

"You never were a good liar." Allie shook her head, then laughed at his expression of outrage. She turned toward him again. "I laugh at a few of his jokes and occasionally bring the guy some pastelitos or queso fundido with chorizo and he keeps me in the loop about new products and offers us a great price." She shrugged. "Everyone goes home happy."

"Ouch. I thought I was special." Vaughn placed a hand over his heart.

"You are. That's for damn sure." Allie shook her head and laughed. "But if you must know, *friend*, Bill's wife died a few years ago after a long and brutal terminal illness. He was so heartbroken. I know a little home cooking and friendly conversation won't ever replace what he lost. But I like to think that my visits bring a tiny bit of happiness to him and his son."

"That was his son?" Vaughn groaned, thinking of the emo kid who'd hauled Allie's stuff out to the car. "Shit. Now I feel like a complete asshole."

"Good." Allie scrolled through her phone. "'Cause you kind of were."

She wasn't wrong. And though he should feel insulted by Allie's direct hit, he didn't. Because she was right. He loved that she didn't hold back the truth to boost his ego or spare his feelings. But rather than creating the distance between them that he should, he was even more drawn to her.

Allie almost felt bad about the guilt she'd just laid on Vaughn for behaving like a jealous lover over her chat with Bill. But the last thing she needed was another man who behaved as if he'd been personally assigned as her guard dog.

She already had a family full of alpha males who thought it was their job to protect her from any man who came sniffing around. Particularly since her last long-term relationship had flamed out so spectacularly and very, *very* publicly. She didn't need Vaughn joining the crew.

Aside from their working relationship, all she wanted from him was friendship. Because the more time they spent together, the more she'd gotten to know the man Vaughn Reed had become instead of the boy she'd adored or the rocker she'd idolized as a teen. She was getting to know what felt like the real Vaughn.

In many ways, he was much as he ever was.

Thoughtful. Kind. More cerebral than her brothers had been at that age. But then again, Vaughn had lived many lives before he'd arrived in Willowvale Springs, hadn't he?

"Can I ask you something, Vaughn?"

"Of course. Ask me anything."

Allie resumed walking among the slabs of marble and granite, and Vaughn fell into step beside her. "You were once such a big part of our lives. Yet, I feel like I know everything and nothing about you."

"What do you mean?" Lines furrowed Vaughn's forehead as he studied her face.

"You never discuss your life before you came to Willowvale Springs."

Allie stopped walking when she realized that Vaughn was no longer beside her.

When she turned to look back at him, he stood frozen with a pained look etched on his handsome face. Allie's heart ached for him, and she immediately regretted having given in to her curious nature which her brothers preferred to call plain old nosy.

"I'm sorry. I should've taken the hint." Allie walked back toward Vaughn, the words tripping over her tongue and her cheeks feeling flushed. "You obviously don't talk about that time in your life because you don't want to. Just forget that I—"

"No." He rubbed his chin and started to move forward again. "We were talking about building a friendship as adults, right? So it's a fair question." Vaughn shoved his hands through his chin-length brown hair, which he'd worn loose.

The movement exposed the gray hair at his temples, which gave him a sexy grown-man look that she was particularly drawn to. Then he shoved his hands into the pockets of his rock-star-worthy skinny jeans. Slim enough to qualify as skinny without being tight enough to show everything.

"You're right. I don't talk about it because it was a really tough time for me. My birth dad was in the military and died before I really have much of a memory of him." Vaughn clutched at the jeweled pendant of the sun and moon hanging around his neck. He swallowed hard, his Adam's apple working. "My birth mom was…*amazing.*" A soft smile lifted one corner of his mouth and exposed crinkles around his eyes. "But she and my dad were both only children, and we didn't have any other family. So when she got really sick with leukemia, the time came when she realized that she didn't have much longer. She wanted to be sure I'd go to a good home and had me placed in foster care. She didn't want me to be there for the end with no one to support me. So she did everything she could to ensure I ended up in a good situation."

"And were you placed in a good situation?" Allie asked, despite being reasonably sure she knew the answer.

Vaughn stopped and his shoulders tightened. He ran a hand down a gorgeous, polished slab of light gray quartz marbled with darker tones of gray. He seemed to need a breather from telling the painful story, so she'd wait until he was ready to continue.

"That's pretty. It's a good option for the bathrooms," Allie said.

Vaughn nodded his agreement, then continued down the row.

"Things aren't always as they appear," Vaughn said, finally. "My mother believed she was putting me in a good situation. I'd like to believe that the caseworker did, too. But the couple I was placed with…they weren't the same when it was just us and them. So no, it wasn't a particularly good situation." Vaughn flexed and tightened one fist, then shook it.

There were a million questions Allie wanted to ask, but she wouldn't push Vaughn or cause him further pain. So rather than asking any of the questions racing through her brain, she pointed out a lovely slab of travertine in a creamy, golden hue punctuated by hints of brown and gray.

Vaughn nodded his approval, indicating that they should add it to the list of possibilities. Allie made note of it in the leather-bound, black traveler's notebook engraved with her full name, her constant companion on these sorts of exploratory shopping trips with clients.

"I was an angry, sullen kid. I was mad that my mom had dropped me there instead of permitting me to stay with her. I knew she was sick, but I was so fixated on the idea that she would eventually get better. So I didn't really understand that she'd done what she felt was best for me. It wasn't until my adoptive mother was sick and we talked about it that I realized what a heart-wrenching choice that must've been for my mom. It must've been agonizing for her to leave this world knowing she was leaving her only child behind and having no idea if I'd be okay."

His voice felt distant and his eyes were filled with unshed tears.

Allie swallowed hard, her heart breaking for both Vaughn and his birth parents who had never gotten to discover who he'd become. She regretted putting her shades atop her head again. Fat tears clouded her vision and spilled down her cheeks before she could stop them.

"I'm so sorry, Vaughn."

When he turned toward her, Allie lunged forward and hugged him tight.

He froze, his muscles stiffening beneath her palms. Then he released a quiet sigh as he rested his chin atop her head and wrapped his arms around her.

"There's no need to be sorry, baby girl." Vaughn's deep voice was reassuring. "In fact, thank you for asking about my parents. For a long time, I buried my memories of my birth parents out of the misguided belief that missing them was being unappreciative of my adoptive parents. Besides, thinking of them just hurt too damn much. So it was easier not to, but then I'd feel guilty about acting as if they'd never existed."

They stood like that—him comforting her as much as she was trying to comfort him. Finally, she slipped out of his arms and wiped carefully beneath her teary eyes, thankful she'd chosen to wear waterproof mascara.

There were times when he'd looked so pensive as

a teen. She'd wondered what had been going on inside that head of his. And now she knew.

"I'm glad you found your way to the Reeds and to Willowvale Springs." She offered a small but sincere smile. "According to my mom, becoming your parents changed their lives. It was a dream come true for them."

"A dream come true?" Vaughn huffed as they resumed their walk among the large stabs of expensive stone. "That's a bit of a stretch."

"No, it isn't," Allie insisted. "I once overheard your mom tell mine how lucky they were to have such an amazing son. She said you were almost too perfect."

"I definitely wasn't perfect," Vaughn said. "Then or now. But I can understand why my mom might've felt that way. Especially in comparison to your brothers who were always getting into shit."

They both laughed because Vaughn wasn't wrong. The Price brothers were always up to some sort of mischief or other. Especially the older three.

"Compared to Manny, Reynaldo, and Rafael, you were an angel." She guided him toward a row of travertine slabs with much bolder designs and coloring."

"Maybe." Vaughn chuckled. "But it wasn't because I was some inherently angelic child. Everything I did or didn't do was a calculated decision. From making my bed in the morning and volunteering to do the dishes or passing on whatever wild scheme your brothers were contemplating... It was all a part of this desperate need I had to be a *good* kid."

It felt as if a light bulb had lit up over Allie's head. She stopped suddenly, and Vaughn stopped, too. She turned to study the handsome face that was now more weathered with age and a life she couldn't even begin to imagine.

"When I heard your mother singing your praises that day, I remember being jealous that your mom thought you were perfect when mine was always telling me I wasn't being ladylike enough, that my skirt was wrinkled, my face was dirty, or that I wasn't crimping the edges of the empanadas correctly," Allie admitted. "But you weren't trying to be a Goody Two-shoes. You were trying to be the perfect kid because you were afraid of upsetting your parents. That maybe they wouldn't want you anymore if you were anything less than perfect."

Vaughn nodded solemnly. He looked relieved. As if someone had taken a weight off his shoulders.

"The families that you were in before…did they…" Allie swallowed hard, not wanting to say the words aloud.

Did they hurt you if they thought you were being bad?

Vaughn stretched his hand and flexed his fingers—something he'd done earlier when she'd asked about his life in foster care. But this time he gazed down at his hand as he did it. Finally, he looked up at her again.

"At that first foster home, the guy shoved me hard because he said I was being unappreciative. I tumbled down the stairs and broke this arm." He flexed his hand again. "His wife, who was actually really nice, convinced me to tell the social worker that I'd slipped and fallen down the stairs. I did it because she convinced me that if I told the truth, I could end up somewhere much worse. And that the other kids—who were younger than me—might, too."

Allie slipped her hand into the one he'd been flexing mindlessly as he spoke. Vaughn stilled.

"You did what you needed to do to survive and to protect the other children there," Allie said quietly, conscious of the other people wandering around the granite yard. "Don't feel guilty about it. You were just a kid, and that couple...*they* were supposed to be protecting *you.*"

Vaughn lifted the back of her hand to his mouth, pressing a brief kiss there before releasing it.

"In my head, I know that's true." Vaughn tapped two fingers to his temple. "But in my heart—" he placed his palm over his chest "—it feels like I should've done a lot more."

Allie couldn't begin to imagine the mental anguish Vaughn had suffered because of that experience. Just considering it put every childhood complaint she'd ever had into perspective.

"But it's nice to hear someone else say it." Vaughn started walking again. "Believe me, I paid my therapist a hell of a lot of money for just that."

He laughed bitterly, the pain and resentment evident.

"How about this?" Allie pointed to a slab of travertine in a khaki color with bold ribbons of deep browns and slate gray running through it.

"This is the one." Vaughn ran his large palm over the surface of the stone reverently. "It's perfect."

Allie couldn't help wishing it was her skin Vaughn was fondling so admiringly.

"Excellent choice." She pushed the thought from her head. "This is the one I had in mind. Glad to know we're on the same page. I'll let them know we want this one."

"Seems you would've done just fine on this trip without me," Vaughn said.

"There are still plenty of chances for me to be completely wrong about what you want."

Vaughn's gaze met hers, and for a moment, time seemed to slow and there was no one in the world but the two of them. The heat in his eyes seemed to liquefy her insides and make her legs suddenly feel unsteady. Her pulse sped up and she tried her best to ignore the jolt of electricity that ran down her spine and reminded her just how close she was standing to the man she'd fantasized about regularly as a teenager.

"I definitely know what I want when I see it." Vaughn's tone was breathy and full of meaning as his gaze trailed down her body momentarily. He cleared his throat and took a step back. "But you obviously know exactly what I want, too." He folded his arms over his chest. "So the floor tile is this way?"

Allie nodded blankly, rendered speechless momentarily. Her heart beat like a drum as she met Vaughn's gaze.

"Great." Vaughn placed a hand on her low back

as he guided her toward the sign that denoted the location of the tile section. "After this, I'm taking you to lunch."

"You don't need to—"

"I know…you would never allow a client to pay for lunch," he said the words before she could finish them. "But as an old friend, I appreciate everything you've done, and I insist on treating you. After all, you're not just my interior decorator, Allie. Seems you were onto something with that whole muse thing."

It'd been a couple of days since she'd brought Vaughn lunch and he'd played her a few bars of the song he'd been working on.

"Wait…did you finish your song?" she asked excitedly.

"I did." Vaughn nodded proudly. "It was the first song I've finished in months. And I was so inspired that I was able to write a couple more."

"That's fantastic, Vaughn. What happens next?"

"Since these songs are for another group, I wanted to make sure I was headed in the right direction. I called a few of the group members up and played them a little of each of the songs."

"And?" Allie was wholeheartedly invested in whether the group liked the song she'd somehow inspired Vaughn to write.

"They loved all three songs and gave me the go-ahead." Vaughn beamed. "So the least I can do is spring for lunch."

"Wow. Interior decorator. Contractor. Rock muse…"

"Don't forget badass goddess and empanada

fairy." Vaughn's eyes danced as his handsome face split with a grin. "You're going to need a longer business card."

"Is professional muse even a thing?" Allie asked. "If so, what exactly is the going pay for it these days?"

They both broke into laughter and an older couple gave them a pointed look.

"Another Price trying to get me in trouble," Vaughn teased.

"You love it." She elbowed him in the side.

"Damn right I do." Vaughn's smile deepened, and there was something in his eyes that made her chest expand.

Vaughn's phone beeped with a message, and he pulled it from his back pocket and looked at the screen. He chuckled. "Speak of the devil. It's a text message from Rey."

"My brother's ears must've been burning." Allie ran her hand over a marble tile in an elongated hexagon design. "What does he want?"

"He invited me to your parents' place for dinner." Vaughn didn't seem as pleased by the invite as she'd hoped.

"You don't want to come to dinner?" She tried not to sound too disappointed.

"That's not it. Tomorrow, I'm headed back to LA for a few days. So I can't come this Sunday."

"Oh." Allie tried not to sound disappointed that Vaughn was heading back to LA. "Then come the following Sunday."

Vaughn still seemed hesitant.

"Is there something else?" she asked.

"I know your parents are just being polite. They probably still think of me as that twice-orphaned kid they need to look out for."

"If you think that my parents are just being polite, I should tell you that Mamá is upset that you haven't been by to visit her yet." Allie raised a brow. "So I suggest you bring her a big bouquet of flowers. White roses are her favorite."

"Yes, ma'am." Vaughn chuckled. He typed out a quick reply to her brother's text message. The phone quickly dinged again with Reynaldo's response. Vaughn held up the phone. "He says next Sunday will be fine. So guess who's coming to dinner?"

Allie couldn't help laughing thinking of the movie *Guess Who*, where Zoe Saldana's character had surprised her parents by bringing home her fiancé portrayed by Ashton Kutcher. A remake in reverse of the brilliant Sidney Poitier movie *Guess Who's Coming to Dinner?*

Vaughn's eyes widened and he looked panic-stricken. "Not that I'd be coming as your—"

"Fiancé?" Allie elbowed him. "Relax, Vaughn. I think I'd know if we were engaged," she stage-whispered behind her open palm. They both laughed, and the tension in Vaughn's shoulders seemed to ease. "And don't worry, I have no intention of asking you to marry me again." She grinned. "But it'll be nice to have you over to the house for dinner."

"Hey, you know how much I love your mother's cooking." Vaughn rubbed his belly. "I adored my mother and I appreciate everything she ever did for me. But that tuna casserole just didn't hit quite the same as your mamá's Sancocho de siete carnes." Vaughn made the chef's kiss gesture and seemed to be in heaven just thinking about the seven-meat deluxe Dominican version of the meat and root vegetable stew that was her mother's specialty. "Takes me back to my roots and reminds me of the delicious meals my birth mother used to make."

"That's right. She was from… Argentina, right?"

On Vaughn's sixteenth birthday, Mamá had gone all out helping Vaughn's mother prepare a traditional Argentinian asado. The elaborate barbecue was Argentina's national dish but was more like a social event. They'd invited half the town because his parents had wanted to cheer Vaughn up. He'd been missing his birth parents on the eve of such an important birthday.

"That's right." Vaughn grinned, seemingly pleased that Allie remembered. "Anyway, I just didn't want to be an inconvenience. I know there are a lot more people at your family's dinner table these days. But if you're really sure your parents don't mind, I look forward to dinner."

Vaughn looked at the time, then shoved the phone into his back pocket. "Speaking of food, let's pick out some tile so I can take you to lunch."

He slipped his hand into Allie's and tugged her toward the tile displays. Holding Vaughn's hand for the second time that day felt like the most natural thing in the world. Like her hand was made to fit in his.

Six

After a week in LA, Vaughn had returned to Willowvale Springs. While in LA, he'd met with the other members of Sin & Glory about possible replacements for Steven as the lead singer. They'd also discussed a new direction for the band's look and sound. The remaining members hadn't been able to come to a consensus on either point. And they'd been just as stalled in their efforts to get backing for the new album, given the way the group had imploded in the midst of a sold-out worldwide tour before. To say the plans had been frustrating would be a gross understatement.

But the entire week hadn't been a complete bust. He'd sat in on a few live sessions for small, intimate performances by Liza Jaymes—an old friend he'd dated before his marriage to Eva. Like Sin & Glory, Liza was trying to make a comeback. She'd looked and sounded better than ever after spending a few tough years in and out of rehab and terrible romantic and business relationships.

The performances were sold out and received rave reviews. It made him hopeful that Sin & Glory would get the same sort of reception from their fans once they could finally get all of the pieces into place.

It had felt a bit strange to be back in his house in LA. Normally, after time away, he looked forward to returning to his Hollywood Hills home. But instead, he'd found himself looking forward to his return to the little cabin in Willowvale Springs that had become his home away from home. More specifically, he'd found himself missing the bright smile and lovely face that always made him feel a sense of peace and joy.

He and Allie had spoken on the phone several times over the course of the week. Vaughn had called to get regular updates on the project and to run ideas past Allie about the second phase. And upon his return, once he'd put away his luggage, the first thing he'd done was walk over to the main building to check up on the progress of the project.

The possibility of getting studio backing seemed slimmer after his recent trip to LA. So it was a strong possibility that the resort would be funding the recording of the album. That only made Vaughn more anxious about getting the initial phases of the project completed quickly and on budget.

He'd been disappointed that while Allie's crew had made some progress in the week since he'd left, they weren't as far along as he'd hoped. He'd posed a variety of questions to the men he'd encountered working about the progress.

Vaughn returned to his cabin and sat on the front steps and surveyed the land around him. The old pool was just a few yards from his cabin. The heated pool was older than he was, but it was still functional and saw a lot more business than the resort did. Members of the community paid for a membership. So while he'd closed down the resort during the renovation, he'd agreed to keep the heated outdoor pool running. But in the next phase, they'd be doing both a functional and aesthetic remodeling including reconfiguring the pool's shape, updating the surface tile to something that felt more modern, and adding features that high-end guests would expect.

Vaughn pulled out his phone and jotted down a few notes about the pool to go over with Allie. He'd been so engrossed in typing his notes and looking at examples of pool renovations that he hadn't heard her approaching until she was a few steps away.

"Hey, Allie, I was just about to call you."

"Why does that not surprise me?" Allie sank onto the step beside him and leaned back on her elbows.

"Okay. I can see that you're a bit annoyed." Vaughn held up an open palm as Allie assessed him with narrowed eyes.

How is it that she managed to be gorgeous even when it looked as if flames might erupt from her ears?

"Whatever gave you that idea?" Allie asked incredulously as she hiked one perfectly arched eyebrow and pursed her full lips.

Vaughn tried not to laugh at the sarcastic remark, but he was doing a terrible job of hiding his amusement. "I know I've been calling about the project quite a bit. But I swear I'm not intentionally trying to be a pain in the ass."

"Okay, if you're not *trying* to be a pain in my ass, why is it that you're questioning my guys and calling me nearly every day that you were away to check up on me?"

"I'm not checking up on you per se…" He totally was, but just not in the sense she'd meant it. He wasn't checking up on Allie the interior decorator or contractor. He'd been checking in with the woman he'd started to look forward to chatting with nearly every day over coffee or lunch.

While he was away, yes, he'd been concerned about the project. But a part of him *needed* to hear Allie's voice. It was an instant balm that soothed him and brought a smile to his face in moments when it felt as if everything else was going wrong.

"I just want to make sure I'm doing whatever I can to speed the project along," he assured her.

"Well, it feels like you're undermining me with the guys. At the very least, you're causing confusion. In fact, I came here from another project because one of them called me. He said you weren't happy with our progress."

"That's not exactly what I said. I was just surprised that we aren't further along—"

"Before you left town you were gushing about how I get your aesthetic and seemed to know what you want. A week later you're questioning everything I do. Do you still not trust me?" Allie sounded hurt and there was a pained look in her dark eyes.

"That isn't it at all, Allie." Vaughn sat up straight, his arms folded over his knees as he assessed the beautiful woman seated beside him. "Of course, I trust you."

"It doesn't feel like it." Allie's voice was tight.

"I'm not questioning your abilities. I'm just very eager for this project to come out just as we envisioned it. Your designs are brilliant, Allie. I just—"

"Don't trust that *I* can execute them." Allie jabbed a thumb into her chest. "Not like Rey, or Manny, or my dad could. Or any member of my family who pees standing."

The searing disappointment in her dark eyes reminded Vaughn of when Allie was ten and he'd had to sit her down and tell her he couldn't marry her, and she needed to stop telling everyone that he would.

He'd broken her little heart then and he was pretty sure he'd disappointed her just as much now. Only this time, sneaking her a bag of her favorite Goetze Old-Fashioned Caramel Creams Candy probably wouldn't resolve the issue.

"This isn't about me not trusting you because you're a woman, Allie. If this were Rey, or Manny, or your dad, I'd be just as much of a stickler about the details because this project means a lot to me and to the town. And I don't take it lightly that Hank left me this *incredible* gift." He gestured to the land around them.

Allie didn't respond. She turned to look out at the pool. "You certainly didn't hover over Rey like this when he was renovating your parents' house." She glared at him accusingly.

"To be fair, Sin & Glory was on tour in Europe at the time. I had my assistant Cherry managing the renovation for me. She actually did pop into town and take photos," he said. "And believe me, I was as involved as possible from nearly five thousand miles away. Your brother was none too pleased about it at the time, I assure you." Vaughn chuckled. "I'm surprised he didn't tell you that."

"And admit that he's not perfect?" Allie snorted like she had when she was a kid. "There would be *zero* chance of that."

"You're being hard on your brother, aren't you?"

Despite considering the Prices family, Vaughn wasn't blood and had no right to interfere. But Rey was the closest thing he'd had to a brother. He couldn't not speak up if he could help smooth over whatever was going on between him and Allie.

"Well, Rey is hard on me." Allie folded her arms. "He doesn't trust that I can handle things on my own. And if I make a mistake, he *never* lets me forget it."

There was something in Allie's eyes. Something she wasn't saying. Vaughn wanted to know what it was, but he wouldn't press. He shifted the conversation back to her initial concerns.

"Look, Allie, about my hyper interest in this project… I know that I've been away a long time," Vaughn said. "But Willowvale Springs and this place—" he indicated the ground beneath him "—mean a lot to me. This town will *always* feel like home. A piece of my heart resides here." He pressed his palm to his chest.

"If Willowvale Springs, and presumably the people you left behind here, mean so much to you—" she studied his face "—why haven't you come back before now?"

Vaughn scratched at his beard and heaved a sigh. It wasn't that he didn't want to be forthcoming with Allie about why he hadn't returned to Willowvale Springs. It was more a matter of his own need to avoid dwelling on his reasons for staying away.

"If I'm being honest with myself, something I clearly don't enjoy—" Vaughn laughed bitterly "—I guess I've stayed away because the desire to avoid the sad memories has always been a hell of a lot stronger than the pull to revisit the happy ones."

"I'm sorry about your parents, Vaughn."

Allie's expression softened, and there was such genuine affection in her sweet tone. Tranquility and warmth spread through his chest as she placed a gentle hand on the tattoo on his right forearm.

It was an exact replica of the misshapen heart and names carved in the tree in the backyard of his adoptive parents' home. Vaughn had insisted that Rey and his crew keep the old tree—despite the landscaping nightmare it had caused.

Vaughn covered her hand with his much larger one.

"Thanks, Al." He squeezed her hand, then let go of it, afraid that if he didn't release it right away, he might not let go of it at all. "Like I said, I have a lot of good memories here. I'm lucky the Reeds saved me. That they loved me like I was their own flesh and blood. But before I met your brother and became an honorary member of your family... I was a pretty lonely kid," he admitted. "I would've done anything to have a house filled with siblings. Even annoying ones like Rey." He nudged her shoulder.

Allie huffed and raked her fingers through her glossy curls—a feature he'd always loved.

Yes, she was gorgeous with her straightened hair. But there was something about seeing her in those natural curls that made him want to sift his fingers through them. He'd spent more nights since his return than he cared to admit imagining those shiny, dark curls spread out on his pillow as he cradled her to his chest.

Allie tried her hardest to resist, but finally, she cracked a smile. She leaned back on her elbows again. "Okay, fine. Maybe I should appreciate my knucklehead brother more," she conceded. "After all, he did bring me my sister-in-law and two beautiful nieces—all of whom I adore—plus you." She nudged him this time, her smile widening. "I'm definitely grateful that because of Rey you were a big part of my life growing up. It took you long enough, but I'm glad you finally came back."

Her eyes twinkled and her lips had never looked more kissable than they did at that moment.

He swallowed hard and forced himself to look away from the mouth he'd been wanting to kiss from the moment she'd told him off.

"Maybe next time, don't be a stranger for so long."

Vaughn leaned back on his elbows, too, both of them staring up at the setting sun.

"I won't," he said. "Promise."

Allie stood and dusted off her bottom—a move Vaughn tried hard not to notice. But in a pair of fitted, black dress pants that clung to her sweet curves, not noticing them was a monumental ask of any single, straight man with a pulse.

"It's getting late. I should go," Allie said. There was almost a hint of reluctance in her voice. As if she wanted him to ask her to stay.

He wanted to. But if he was going to maintain his commitment to not crossing the line with Allie, it would be better if he didn't.

Vaughn stood, too. "I'll walk you to your car."

"That isn't necessary." Allie pulled her keys from the front pocket of her pants.

"Then humor me." Vaughn shrugged. "Besides, it'll give me a chance to tell you what I've been thinking about for the pool renovation."

"Not that you're micromanaging me." Allie rolled her eyes, then huffed. "Fine. Come on then. It's been a really long day and there's a tub surrounded by candles with my name on it."

Allie naked in a tub?

He stumbled over his own feet and nearly face-planted.

"Vaughn! Are you all right?" Allie reached out to steady him. She regarded him carefully, which made his skin flame.

"I'm fine." His cheeks and forehead were so hot they were probably glowing like Rudolph's nose. He started toward the lot for the main building where her car was parked. "So about the pool… I'd like to convert it to an indoor pool as part of the initial renovation rather than waiting for Phase Two."

"No objections here." Allie nodded thoughtfully. "But I thought you wanted this first phase to be quick and dirty." *Quick and dirty? Seriously?* Allie was *killing* him right now.

"And cost-efficient," he felt the need to add.

"Which is why I suggested it for phase two instead of phase one," she reminded him with a hint of amusement in her voice.

"I know. But if we want to start booking high-end guests off the rip, I figure we should go hard or go home, right?"

"Okay." Allie nodded. "Let me work up some numbers and talk to a few people to see what their availability is. But given that we're approaching the holiday season, I would temper my expectations on this. Understood?" She used the remote to unlock her car as they approached it.

Vaughn jogged ahead of Allie and opened the door for her.

Even at the end of a long workday wearing very little makeup and just a work shirt and some dress pants, Allie Price was absolutely stunning. When his gaze met hers, an impish grin curved one edge of her mouth.

Why did this feel more like the end of the night on a first date than saying goodbye to his interior decorator or his best friend's kid sister?

"Again, apologies if you feel like I didn't trust you. What I said at the granite yard… I meant it one hundred percent. You're an amazing designer and an organized, efficient project manager, Allie. And as you said the day you showed me that proposal, I'm lucky to be working with you."

Allie covered her face as if she was embarrassed. She shook her head. "I can't believe I actually said that to you and you still hired me."

They both laughed.

"It wasn't the kind of proposal I'm accustomed to," he admitted. "But you were right. So thanks for taking on this project on such short notice and for coming up with such an incredible plan. This is going be a fabulous venue and a financial boost to the town."

"Yes, it will." Allie nodded proudly as she glanced over at the main house.

Vaughn studied her profile as she took in the resort that was slowly being transformed. He sucked in a quiet breath and fought the growing desire to pull Allie into his arms and kiss her.

"Hank would be really proud of what you're doing here, Vaughn." Allie's voice and smile were soft and warm. "And so would your parents."

Allie wrapped her arms around him, her cheek pressed to his chest.

He permitted himself the luxury of indulging Allie's innocent gesture. He breathed in her sweet scent and the hint of vanilla wafting from her hair. Vaughn rested his chin atop her head.

"Thank you for saying that. I hope you're right."

"I usually am. Remember that next time we're selecting design materials, and you'll save yourself from having to spend the day traipsing through home improvement stores with me."

"Can I tell you a secret?" He smiled when she nodded. "I wouldn't have traded that trip for anything. It was one of the best days I've had in a really long time."

Allie pulled back, a bashful grin animating her gorgeous face. "I'm not sure if that's the sweetest thing I've ever heard or the saddest," she teased. "But it was a good day for me, too."

They stared at each other for a moment in silence, his heart thudding in his chest.

"Good night, Vaughn." Allie lifted onto her toes and kissed his cheek. "I'll see you at my parents' house on Sunday, right?"

"Wouldn't miss it for the world." Vaughn winked.

Allie slipped inside her Audi A5 Sportback and

drove off into the evening, leaving Vaughn wondering what might have been if Allie had been anyone in the world other than the sister of one of his closest friends.

He squeezed his eyes shut and shook the thought from his mind. Vaughn headed back to his cabin, reminding himself that this time around, he was too smart to make the same mistake. No matter how incredible a woman Allie Price had turned out to be.

Seven

Allie stood over the steaming pot of Sancocho de siete carnes. The flank beef, pork belly, pork ribs, chicken, goat, pork sausage and smoked hambones had been marinated in garlic, cilantro, salt and oregano, then cooked to tender, delicious perfection in a stew. Slices of corn on the cob and a variety of root vegetables like plantain, yam and cassava had been added later so as not to overcook them.

"¿Necesita más sal, mamá?" Allie ladled the fragrant stew onto a spoon and gave her mother a taste. She didn't want to go too heavy-handed with the salt for their guest, but she wanted the meal to be as good as Vaughn remembered when her mother had made it for him.

"No, es perfecto, princesa," her mother responded

proudly, looking like Allie's slightly older twin. A reality she'd finally made peace with in her midtwenties.

Her mother flashed her a knowing smile, her skin practically glowing as she stared at Allie.

"What is it, Mamá? There's something wrong, isn't there?" Allie asked, finally.

"No, sweetheart. The Sancocho es perfecto. It's your best yet." Her mother rinsed out a damp rag and wiped down the countertops while humming.

Allie stopped stirring and turned to her mother. "Then what is with that look you keep giving me?"

"Look? What look? I cannot look at mi hija and smile?" Her mother could barely contain her grin.

Allie hiked an eyebrow and her mother burst into laughter.

"Mamá!" Allie whined.

"Okay, okay." Dianelys Price stopped her cleaning and beamed at Allie with such a wide smile that her cheeks must've hurt. "Vaughn comes back home and you're spending all this time with him."

"Because I'm his interior decorator and the project manager for his very extensive renovation of Hank Carson's old resort. You know this, Mamá. It's not like I've been following the man around town like a lost puppy."

"The way you used to when you had such a crush on him?" Her mother grinned.

Allie chose to ignore that. "He is the most particular, hands-on client that I have ever worked with," she whispered, not wanting her brothers or father to overhear the conversation. "And after all of that, he usually ends up going with one of my suggestions anyway."

"Our little Vaughn has grown up to be an international rock star." Her mother beamed as proudly as if she'd given birth to the man and raised him herself. "He's a celebrity now. He's accustomed to calling the shots and having whatever…and *whomever*—" she met Allie's gaze with dancing eyes "—he wants."

"It's not like that, Mamá. Vaughn and I are just friends."

"First he's just a client, now he's just a friend." Her mother shrugged with a smile. "Things are moving muy rapido between you two, eh?"

Allie sighed and rubbed her forehead, her cheeks and neck suddenly hot and no doubt flushed.

Yes, she definitely had a thing for Vaughn. And not the same teenage crush she'd had. Her growing attraction to Vaughn Reed was based on the incredible man she'd been getting to know over the past few weeks. The man who'd permitted himself to be vulnerable with her by talking about his past and sharing stories he'd probably never even shared with her brother. But as long as they were working on this project together she needed to keep her head on straight.

Vaughn's renovation of the resort was the biggest and most profitable one she'd led or designed. She needed to think of her career first and how quickly things could go sideways if they crossed the line while still in the midst of the project.

Besides, she didn't want her father and brothers

worrying that every handsome, single client she handled might sweep her off of her feet. It had been hard enough to get them to acknowledge that she was capable of handling a project of this magnitude on her own. And if the rest of the team hadn't already been involved in other, ongoing projects, she doubted they would've given her this chance.

So she needed to knock it out of the park and prove her worth. That meant she couldn't have Mamá grinning at the dinner table and hinting that Allie still had a crush on Vaughn.

"He's my client and *our* friend." Allie gestured to everyone in the house. "And that's all. So please, Mamá, don't do that…that *thing* with your face." She indicated the grin that her mother was doing a horrible job of hiding. "You'll have Papá and the boys worried over nothing. And you know how they are with me. I don't want—"

"You're right, princesa." Her mother sighed, her expression sober. "I know that you get frustrated with your papá and your brothers, and I understand why. I'll keep talking to them about it. But try to remember, mija, they adore you, and they just want to keep you safe. All right?"

Allie nodded solemnly, then turned back to the large pot and stirred the Sancocho again.

"I will keep your little secret," her mother said quietly.

"There is no secret to keep, Mamá," Allie insisted.

Her mother folded her arms and cocked her head and one hip—a move Allie had adopted and perfected.

"You always complain when I ask you to make Sancocho with just three meats instead of one. But Vaughn is coming to dinner—which you cleverly persuaded your brother to arrange—and now you're voluntarily making it with all seven meats? Tu madre no es tonta, niña."

Irritation flickered in her mother's eyes at the thought that Allie was treating her as if she was too foolish to recognize that her daughter still had feelings for Vaughn.

Allie groaned quietly and set the spoon back in the trivet. She glanced around the kitchen to ensure they were alone, then placed her hands on her mother's shoulders and lowered her voice.

"Okay, maybe I like him a little. So what? As long as we are working together, nothing is going to happen. So I am *begging* you, Mamita, please, please don't make things weird and awkward for both of us. I just want Vaughn to be able to come here and enjoy a relaxing, home-cooked meal with the people who have always considered him family. I'm pretty sure he could really use a night like that right now."

Her mother's broad smile returned, her eyes bright and shiny as she cupped Allie's cheek. "You're in love with him, aren't you?"

"What? No, Mamá. I said I *like* him." Translation, she had nightly dreams of Vaughn Reed taking her over and over. Something she had no intention of sharing with her mother. "But as always, you go from zero to a full church wedding in sixty seconds flat."

"Hmm…" Her mother sniffed. "You don't realize

it yet, but I can see it in your eyes, princesa." Her mother smiled confidently. "You've always had a soft spot for him. Everyone knows this. Besides, Vaughn would make a very, *very* good son-in-law. Es dulce, guapo, en forma, viene de una buena familia y tiene mucho dinero." Her mother ticked each item off on her fingers.

"I know that Vaughn is sweet, handsome, fit, comes from a good family and has a lot of money, Mamá," Allie whispered harshly. "But I can take care of myself, muchas gracias. So would you *please* stop looking for a son-in-law beneath every rock? When I'm good and ready, I'm fully capable of finding my own man."

Her mother hiked an eyebrow and without saying a word, they both knew she was reminding Allie of the disastrous relationship she'd invested two years of her life into.

It'd been two years since that relationship had ended, and her family still wouldn't let her forget it.

"Anyone can find un hombre, princesa. But I am not talking about just any man. I'm talking about a man like your father and your brothers. Someone who will love you and treat you like una reina, because that, mija, is exactly what you are. Lo entiendes?"

"I understand, of course." Allie nodded.

And that was why she couldn't stay mad at her mother, despite her meddling. She wanted her to find a man who would treat her like a queen. How could she be angry with someone who loved her so much and only wanted the absolute best for her?

"But about dinner—"

"I will say nothing. I promise," her mother conceded. "Pero tu padre y tus hermanos tampoco son estúpidos," she warned.

Allie sighed at her mother's reminder that her father and brothers weren't stupid. Her brothers might be a lot of things, but oblivious certainly wasn't one of them. So she would heed her mother's warning. That meant none of her usual flirting with the dashing Vaughn Reed.

They were old friends and nothing more. No matter how much she wished things between her and Vaughn could be different. And while she'd admit to being in lust with the bad boy drummer, she certainly wasn't in love.

Even Mamá wasn't right about everything.

"Mrs. Price." Vaughn leaned down to hug Dianelys Price, who was a few inches shorter than her daughter who looked so much like her. "It's wonderful to see you again. Sorry I haven't made it over here sooner. I hope you can forgive my oversight."

Vaughn handed Allie's mother a crystal vase filled with two dozen white roses.

"Oh, mijo! They are so beautiful. Muchas gracias, Vaughn." The woman who'd practically been a third mother to him beamed. Tears shone in the dark eyes that were the spitting image of Allie's.

After all these years, hearing her call him *mijo*—the term of endearment she used with her own sons—made his heart swell. His gut knotted with guilt over not having come back to visit the Prices before now.

He'd kept in contact with Rey and always asked about the family and sent his love. But it wasn't the same as coming to visit them or, at the very least, picking up the phone and calling them.

"And I don't care how long you've been away," Mrs. Price said, as if she'd been privy to his thoughts. "You're still a member of this family. So call me mamá, just like always."

"Yes, Mamá." The guilt that tightened Vaughn's chest eased. He turned to the tall, barrel-chested man who approached.

Walter Price's full head of dark, curly hair was much thinner now. And what was left of it was salt-and-pepper gray—standing in stark contrast to his deep brown skin. He extended his large hand to Vaughn, then pulled him into a hug.

"Good to see you again, stranger." The old man's expression served as both a warm welcome and censure for staying away so long. "How's everything going with the renovation project?"

"Fantastic, sir," Vaughn said, mindful of Allie's concerns that her father and brothers were always looking over her shoulder. "The project is in good hands with Allie and her crew."

"Glad to hear it." The old man scratched his wiry beard. He leaned in and lowered his voice. "Thank you for being accommodating. Normally, Manny or Rey would've handled a project of that magnitude but—"

"Allie is doing an incredible job, sir. Honestly," Vaughn interrupted the man.

The hair on the back of Vaughn's neck bristled slightly. He didn't like the man's implication that Allie was essentially a third-string benchwarmer that he'd had to put into the game in a crunch.

"I'm lucky to be working with Al. Her designs are fresh and modern. She's creating *exactly* the kind of zen space I envisioned for the wellness center. And she's really good with the crew, too. She's tough but fair. They seem to love working for her, and they're doing a great job. In fact, I've been so impressed that I was talking to Allie the other day about going forward with the renovation of the pool."

"Is that right?" Walter rubbed his chin and studied him.

The way the old man was sizing him up, Vaughn wondered if he'd overplayed his hand. Not that everything he'd said about Allie wasn't true. It was. Every single word of it. But maybe he'd been a bit too effusive with the praise. Because now the man was looking at him less like a client and more like a man who'd come 'round to take his only daughter on a date.

"Well, I'm glad to hear it, son." Mr. Price stepped aside, gesturing for him to make his way through the house toward the large sun porch where the family often gathered. "C'mon in, and don't be shy."

He was greeted by Rey, Manny, Rafi, and their wives and children. Their youngest brother, Felix, was there with his girlfriend. But Allie was nowhere to be found.

Vaughn wanted to ask where she was but didn't want to bring attention to the fact that he was looking for her. So he played it cool instead.

"Don't worry. Allie is in the kitchen cooking. She'll be out in a minute," her mother said in a low voice that only he could hear. Her eyes danced and there was a knowing grin on her face.

Had he been that obvious?

Vaughn smiled and nodded, not quite sure how else to respond.

"Does Allie need help in the kitchen?" Vaughn asked.

Mamá's smile deepened. Rey, Manny and Walter eyed him as if he'd said something heretical.

"What?" Vaughn shrugged.

"Always the santurrón." Manny shook his head.

He'd just basically called him a Goody Two-shoes. But there were worse things a person could be.

"You just hang out with the boys." Manny's wife, Meera, elbowed him in the side and stood. She set their infant on her husband's lap. "We'll see if Allie needs anything else. C'mon, Yvette." Rey's wife handed their toddler off to him and followed her sister-in-law to the kitchen.

"Man, you've been here like five minutes, and you're already upsetting the status quo," Rey teased.

"If Allie's in the kitchen doing all the work while you four sit around and chill, maybe the status quo needs to change." Vaughn shrugged. "She works hard in the business just like all of you do."

"I love this man," Mamá said. "And he makes a very good point, doesn't he, mi amor?"

Walter hiked one of his wiry, gray eyebrows and stared daggers at Vaughn. He took a long, slow sip of his Corona before finally responding. "He sure does, sweetheart. So next Sunday, why don't you let the boys and I cook? We'll make my famous soul food feast. Right, fellas?"

Allie's four brothers muttered their agreement while glowering at Vaughn, and he couldn't help laughing.

"Glad you find it so funny, son," Walter said. "Since this was your idea, it's only right that you come back next week and join in on the fun."

"Umm...sure. I'd love to come for dinner again next Sunday," Vaughn said. "But I'm not much of a cook."

"I wouldn't be either if I had a chef and a house in Hollywood Hills," Felix said.

"That's all right. I'm gonna teach you everything you need to know. Just show up in something you don't mind getting sauce on and we're all good." Walter picked up one of his grandchildren who had toddled over and plopped her onto his lap.

"Yes, sir." Vaughn was distracted by the sound of Allie's laugh coming from the kitchen.

He glanced in the general direction of the sound, and when he looked back, Allie's mother was grinning at him again and her father was staring at him with that raised eyebrow.

Vaughn forced a smile and tried his best to relax.

But he really needed to work on his subtlety because at this rate, every single person in the Price family would know just how enamored he was with Allie.

Vaughn wasn't the only one who needed to work on being less obvious. Because her mother's less-than-subtle matchmaking efforts weren't lost on him or Allie. And while Manny, Rey and the rest of the family might've been oblivious to what was going on as they dealt with spouses and small children, Mr. Price certainly wasn't. Vaughn could feel the man's sense of concern heighten the longer the evening—and Mamá's efforts—went on.

Dianelys Price had done just about everything she could, short of saying the words, to indicate that she envisioned him and Allie together. First, she'd nearly shoved Felix's girlfriend—who was a Sin & Glory fan—out of the way when she'd tried to sit next to Vaughn. Then she'd insisted that Allie sit beside him instead. And Vaughn couldn't swear to it, but it felt like his and Allie's chairs were scooched a little closer than all the others. Close enough that their thighs kept touching and they barely had enough elbow room as they ate their meals.

Mamá had waited with bated breath as he'd tried each element of their meal. The mouthwatering Sancocho de siete carnes stew. The arroz blanco—simple white rice—and the avocado slices that accompanied it. The morir soñando—a surprisingly refreshing cocktail made with orange juice and milk. The delicious pudín de pan—a spiced bread pudding set in a bundt pan. Rich, decadent caramel flan that put to shame any other flan he tried during his travels around the world.

After he tried each item of food or drink and was quite obviously enjoying it, Mamá would say, "Es good, no? Princesa made it. She is such an amazing cook." Then she'd gush about some of the other meals Allie made from other Dominican and Caribbean favorites to a variety of soul foods and classic American cuisine.

Poor Allie's gorgeous, terra-cotta-colored skin would flush a deep red around her cheeks and forehead. He could sense the tension and heat coming off her body—so close to his—in waves. There was one moment when he was sure she was going to snap. Vaughn placed a subtle hand on her knee beneath the table and she inhaled deeply. Likely in surprise at the fairly intimate contact.

She snapped her head in his direction.

"Your mom loves you, and she means well. So don't worry," he said quietly.

Allie nodded; her sigh of relief audible. Her cheeks slowly returned to their usual color and her breathing slowed.

As they enjoyed dessert after their meal, Mamá bragged about how Allie updated the interior design of their home, which was quite lovely. Then she'd shown Vaughn before and after pictures of the cottage Allie had purchased and renovated a few years earlier.

He'd already known that Allie was a talented interior designer. But the transformation of her cottage was stunning. And she'd done wonders updating her old childhood home. He'd chimed in singing Allie's praises in relation to her work on the resort, which brought a huge smile to both Mamá and Allie's faces, but made Mr. Price regard him even more warily.

Between Mamá and Mr. Price seemingly analyzing every conversation and every gesture between him and Allie, Vaughn felt a bit self-conscious.

He was a well-known celebrity personality. He'd lived his life in a fishbowl for more than fifteen years. Still, it felt odd in this setting—seated at the Prices' dining room table and surrounded by the people who felt like the only family he had left in the world. A space that always made him feel safe and happy as a kid who hadn't always had those luxuries in the years between losing his parents and coming to live with the Reeds in Willowvale Springs.

When her infant granddaughter got fussy, Mamá insisted that Rey give the little girl to Allie. She seemed to calm down immediately. Then her mother pointed out what a good tita Allie was to her nieces and nephews and that she'd be an incredible mother someday.

When they'd settled back in the den, Mamá sat on one side of Vaughn and ensured that Allie was seated on the other side of him. When she left to grab the family photo album, Allie nudged him with her elbow and whispered, "Now's your chance. *Run*."

Vaughn broke into laughter. "And leave before I see embarrassing high school photos?" He rubbed his hands together. "You saw me in real-time at my awkward stage. There's no way I'm missing this. It's only fair, right?"

"I'll have you know that I was extremely cute in high school." Allie adjusted her sleeping niece on her shoulder and rubbed the little girl's back as she sucked her thumb in her sleep. "But seriously, this might be your last chance to escape. If I were you, I'd be running for the hills by now, determined to never, ever return."

Vaughn chuckled. "Well, that ship has sailed. Your father has already recruited me to come back next Sunday and help him and your brothers cook your dad's famous soul food feast."

"Papi is going to cook next week? He never cooks unless he's pissed off Mamá," she said. "How did that happen?"

"I might be slightly to blame for that." Vaughn rubbed his jaw. "I mentioned that you work as hard in the business as they all do, so maybe you shouldn't have been the only one in the kitchen cooking."

"Shit," Allie whispered, then immediately glanced at her niece to ensure she was still sleeping and that the word hadn't reached her little ears. "That and the fact that my mother is quite obviously trying to hook us up is why Papá keeps looking at you like you're my date to the prom or something." Allie heaved a quiet sigh. "I am so sorry about all of this. If I'd had any idea she was going to go into hyper-matchmaking mode, I would never have…" Her words trailed off. "I mean…"

"Wait…it wasn't Rey's bright idea to invite me to dinner, was it?" Vaughn studied Allie's face, her cheeks turning crimson again. It was all the confession he needed.

"Rey would've invited you eventually," Allie insisted. "It's just that with work and his family he hadn't thought of it. And maybe he didn't think his famous, rock star friend would be down for a night filled with crazy family and a basic meal when you're used to traveling the world, staying in five-star hotels and eating meals prepared by your private chef. So maybe I just hurried the process along." She shrugged one slim shoulder, exposed by the black, off-shoulder dress. The soft fabric hugged her delicious curves and the hem, which hovered just above her knees, had drifted upward while she was seated, showing off the gleaming, brown skin of her toned thighs.

Vaughn shifted his gaze from Allie's thigh and met Mr. Price's gaze. The man's frown deepened.

Vaughn swallowed hard, then returned his attention to Allie, continuing their whispered conversation while her mother was searching for family photo albums.

"I thought it would be nice for you to have a real meal made with love, surrounded by the people who've always considered you family," Allie continued. "I did not expect Mamá to be in such rare form with her heavy-handed attempt to hook a son-in-law. So seriously, no one would blame you if you took this opportunity to bounce before she gets back."

"Allie, it's fine. Like I said…" He resisted the urge

to place a hand on her knee again. Under the watchful eye of Walter Price, it would be an ill-advised move. "Your mom…she loves you and wants to see you happy. Who can fault her for that?"

"God, would you stop being so incredibly gracious and accommodating? You're making me feel even guiltier for arranging this whole mess." Allie gently rocked the baby—who'd been startled in her sleep—from side to side and rubbed her back.

Mamá appeared with a stack of family photo albums before Vaughn could respond.

"Here, let's trade." She handed the stack of photo albums to Vaughn, then took Allie's sleeping niece and propped the child—who'd been startled again by the transfer—onto her shoulder. "I'm going to lay this little one down upstairs."

Rey took one look at the photo albums and shot to his feet. "No, Mamá. We were just about to head out to get the kids home to bed."

"¿Tan temprano?" their mother objected, holding on to the child as if she was considering not giving her up.

"It's not that early, Mamá," Rey countered. "Besides, we've all got school and work in the morning. Dinner was great as always. But we really have to go." He reached for his young daughter.

The older woman clucked her tongue, then handed off the child reluctantly.

"We've got plenty of leftovers. I'll pack some up for you to take home." Allie started to stand, but her mother quickly objected.

"No, you stay. Show Vaughn the photos. And don't forget that year you won the Miss Willowvale Springs contest." Mamá beamed. "I'll pack the leftovers."

Rey shook his head and rubbed the back of his now fussy daughter. "Sorry, man. I had no idea my mom was on the hunt for a son-in-law. I'm sure you're probably dating some hot actress back in LA. So thanks for playing along and not bursting her bubble."

Allie seemed to bristle at Rey's insinuation that he was seeing someone.

Vaughn slapped Rey's outstretched palm. "No worries, man. Your parents are good people. And it's nice feeling like I'm with family again."

"You *are* family," Rey corrected him. "Always have been, always will be. No matter how long you're away or where you are in the world. But it's nice to have you home."

Vaughn's heart squeezed in his chest and he nodded. He stood and hugged his friend. "Thanks, man. I appreciate the invite. It feels good to be here again."

"You got us cooking next week, so your ass had better be here in the kitchen helping us slice sweet potatoes and prepare greens." Rey grinned. Then he rubbed his chin. "Since it looks like you're really going to be hanging around this time, if you're not busy on Saturday, you should come by the house. The fellas are hanging out, watching hoops and playing some billiards."

"I'd like that," Vaughn said.

"Cool. I'll text you the time and address." Rey bumped fists with Vaughn, then turned to his sister, who'd also stood to say goodbye. "Thanks for dinner, sis. It was incredible. Text us to let us know when you get home."

Allie nodded, then they said their goodbyes to her other brothers and their families since everyone seemed to be leaving.

Rey's words kept cycling through Vaughn's brain.

Since it looks like you're really going to be hanging around this time...

That explained why his old friend seemed a little standoffish.

Vaughn had expected that his friendship with Rey would pick up where they'd left off. But most of their conversations had been by phone and were about the project. Rey hadn't indicated that he'd wanted to connect socially. Vaughn figured that between work and family, Rey had been too busy to hang out. So he hadn't pushed. But now he understood.

His friend was more hurt by Vaughn taking off and not returning than he'd admitted.

Whether he'd been reluctant to truly reconnect because he was afraid Vaughn would simply abandon him again or he'd been freezing him out as a punitive measure, it seemed that Rey was finally willing to let him in.

Had dinner with Rey's family been some kind of test?

If it had, Vaughn had apparently passed to Rey's satisfaction.

But as for Mr. Price... He'd liked Vaughn just fine when he'd been a friend of his son's. Now that his wife had clearly set eyes on him as a possible suitor for his daughter…not so much.

Reluctantly, Mr. Price went to see off his grandchildren who weren't quite ready to leave their abuelito and abuelita. The older man gave Vaughn what could only be described as a warning glare before leaving the room. It was the first time he and Allie had been alone together all night.

They regarded each other for a moment.

Allie sank onto the couch and picked up one of the photo albums he'd set there. "We should go through these before Mamá comes back and insists on giving you the full, annotated version of every single photo. At least I can give you the quick and dirty version." Allie patted a space beside her on the sofa.

"Rey is wrong, by the way. I'm not seeing anyone." Vaughn wasn't sure why he felt compelled to make that clear again.

"Okay." Allie didn't look up from the album, but offered a ghost of a smile. She'd reapplied her gloss after dinner, drawing his attention to her pouty, shimmering lips. "But you don't owe me an explanation, Vaughn." She finally turned to look at him. "Despite Mamá's very obvious attempts to make it so, we're not together."

Vaughn fought the urge to lean in and kiss those full lips—as alluring as the call of the siren to the sea—before one of her parents, siblings, or rambunctious nieces came barreling through the door. He cleared his throat instead.

"Right. Still, I just thought you should know." He

managed to tear his gaze from her tantalizing lips and focused on the photo album spread open on her lap. "So let's get started."

Allie had shown him photos of her and her family throughout the years that Vaughn had been away. Far from being bored, he enjoyed catching up on the parts of their lives that he'd missed. And he couldn't help wishing he'd been there for it. Especially for the big moments like his friend's wedding and the births of his children. And he couldn't help wishing he'd been there in person to cheer Allie on when she'd won the town beauty pageant at seventeen.

The photo albums had been a walk through the lives of the only family he had left in the world.

During the years that Sin & Glory was together—even before they became famous—he'd taken solace in the found family he had with the band. But since their dissolution, he'd felt more alone than ever. His was an aching loneliness that he'd attempted to fill with material luxuries, travel, female companionship, and all manner of vices. Yet, nothing seemed to soothe the festering hole in his chest inflicted by the loss of not one but *two* sets of parents.

Having been surrounded by his friends all evening—people he'd once considered family—it felt as if that hole might finally be beginning to heal. And as he sat beside Allie, so close that their thighs touched, he was reminded of just how amazing it felt to be with someone whose very presence truly made him happy.

Allie was smart and incredibly beautiful. No one

had made him laugh as much as she had in ages. But as much as he wanted to kiss her and to tell her just how much he was feeling her, a small voice in the back of his head reminded him of his self-imposed rules. The rules meant to protect him from a repeat of the self-inflicted wound he'd suffered four years ago.

Don't think with your dick.

Never get involved with your best friend's sister.

Always consider your career first.

Never fall in love.

Vaughn sighed quietly as he recited the rules in his head again and again. Because right now, he was in danger of falling for the beautiful woman for whom his adoration was growing by leaps and bounds every day. The woman whose family meant so much to him. Coming back to Willowvale Springs reminded him of what was important in life. Love, family, community. The elements that had been sorely lacking in this life. He wouldn't jeopardize that. Even if it meant he'd never get the chance to be with Allie.

"Everything okay? You seemed far away for a moment there." Allie nudged him with her shoulder. "I'm sorry, I know this must all be incredibly boring to a man who has toured the world with the likes of The Rolling Stones and Imagine Dragons."

"No, it's not boring at all," Vaughn objected. "It's *normal* and comforting and wonderful." He placed a hand on her wrist, his eyes drawn to her expressive eyes. "Best night I've had in a really long time."

He stared at her for a moment, neither of them

speaking. A sense of longing seemed to build between them, as if she was hoping that he'd lean in and kiss her.

"Princess." Walter stood at the entrance of the den, a frown set firmly on his face. "Mamá and I are cleaning up. She sent me to ask if either of you would like café con leche or more dessert."

The old man seemed pained to have been sent to do his wife's matchmaking bidding when he was probably itching to plop down on the sofa and squeeze his girth between them.

"Your parents are cleaning up after all of us?" Vaughn turned to Allie.

"Usually, Mamá and I handle cleanup alone after the boys and their families are gone."

"Then we should help them. C'mon." Vaughn stood, then pulled Allie to her feet before turning to her father again. "We'll help with clean up. But if it's not too late when we're done, I'd love some coffee and more dessert."

The stoic expression chiseled on Mr. Price's face softened and his shoulders relaxed. "You're a guest, Vaughn. You don't have to—"

"I know," Vaughn said. "But I'd really like to. Besides, the meal and the company were outstanding. It's the very least I could do."

The old man nodded approvingly and gestured for them to follow him.

Vaughn and Allie helped her parents clean up the kitchen and dining room and straighten up the den. Then the four of them sat in the den and had café

con leche—espresso with steamed milk and sugar—
and what remained of the pudín de pan. It was a long
night, and he was tired, but Vaughn couldn't have
felt more at home.

At the end of the night, Vaughn walked Allie
to her car, hugged her and kissed her cheek, then
watched her drive off before going to his car and
doing the same.

On the drive back to the little cabin that would feel
cold, lonely, and bereft of the sounds and smells of
the Price's big, warm, cozy family home, he couldn't
help thinking of how desperately he'd wanted to take
Allie in his arms and kiss her. How he'd wanted to
invite her back to his place so he could get to know
every inch of her ruddy brown skin and become in-
timately acquainted with each of her curves. But at
some point, he needed to learn from his mistakes.

So despite it breaking his heart, he was determined not to do anything that might jeopardize his
chance to be part of a real family again.

Eight

Allie ran a hand down one of the freshly tiled bathrooms on the second floor of the resort. The elongated hexagon marble tiles with hints of cream, gold and gray were beautiful, and her team had laid them perfectly.

Everything was really coming together with the renovations at Hank's old resort. And she couldn't help wondering what the old man would think of the new look. But then, she also wondered what the resort's current owner would think.

Vaughn had come to her parents' place for dinner two weeks in a row, and his friendship with her brother had kicked up a notch since then. Vaughn had been hanging out with her brothers and their friends when he wasn't back in LA for one reason or another. But things between Vaughn and Allie had definitely cooled.

The anxious resort owner had stopped making random pop-in visits during the day to check out the progress of the renovations. His calls were far less frequent. When he did call, Vaughn kept things friendly but focused on the business at hand. There had been none of the teasing and flirting that had been common between them in the weeks prior to him coming to dinner. In fact, it was beginning to feel like Vaughn was intentionally avoiding her.

Had her dad or one of her brothers warned him off?

Allie completed her walk-through before locking the resort up. It was a Wednesday evening and her entire crew was gone. If she had to guess, most of them were probably trying to catch happy hour at the local watering hole. But they'd worked hard and certainly deserved it.

There had been a few setbacks, but they were back on schedule again. The walls had been painted. The hardwood flooring had been installed throughout the first floor and the tiling had been done in all of the bathrooms. Custom cabinets would be installed in the kitchen the next day.

It was an exciting stage. So after wanting to be involved every step of the way early in the process, it seemed odd that Vaughn suddenly seemed to have lost interest in the project. Or perhaps it was her that he'd lost interest in.

Allie couldn't help thinking of that first evening

Vaughn had come to her parents' house for dinner. It had been an amazing night—despite her mother's matchmaking shenanigans. But to say that Allie had been disappointed when Vaughn had passed on the chance to kiss her not once but *twice* that evening was like saying that the gray-haired, aging-like-fine-wine Chris Pine was just *a* man or that the incredible Denzel Washington was simply *an* actor.

She certainly hadn't prompted her brother to invite Vaughn Reed to their family dinner for the purpose of making out with him. But when they'd been alone in the den to go over the photo albums, the opportunity had presented itself. Then when Vaughn had walked Allie to her car at the end of the night, they'd stood together in the dim light cast by one of the outdoor lights. The way he'd looked at her, neither of them speaking for a moment, she'd been so sure that Vaughn would kiss her good night. But he hadn't.

Instead, Vaughn had given her a warm, friendly hug. Then he stepped back and waited patiently for her to get into her car and drive off. Twenty minutes later, Vaughn texted Allie to make sure she'd made it home okay. When she'd assured him she had, he texted back to say he'd had a great time with her family and then wished her a good night.

Allie had gone home frustrated and yet still giddy about having spent such a wonderful evening with Vaughn and with her family. But since then, she'd barely heard from him.

Still, he couldn't avoid her forever, and tonight she

needed to speak with him. They were at the point where they needed to make some decisions about the decor. So after she locked up the house, she walked the short path over to his cabin. His rental car was in the drive but when she knocked at the door, there was no answer, despite the front door being ajar. Allie knocked again, but then she noticed Vaughn over by the pool.

She walked over to the pool and joined him. He was wearing earbuds and seemed completely lost in thought as he stared into the water. Yet, when she walked up and stood beside him, he didn't seem startled.

Vaughn flashed her an almost shy smile.

"Hey." He pulled the buds from his ears and shoved them into the pockets of his classic B-3 style sheepskin leather bomber jacket in a cognac brown. Then he shoved his hands into the pockets of his dark jeans.

"Hey." Allie glanced around at the pool deck and waved a hand. "This is all going to look completely unrecognizable soon."

"I know." There was a hint of nostalgia and perhaps regret in Vaughn's voice.

Allie turned to him, concerned. There was definitely something going on with Vaughn.

"I thought you were excited about revamping the old pool? You said you wanted to make this the kind of indoor spa resort pool high-end guests would expect."

"It's what a spa of this caliber demands."

"Then why the long face?"

Vaughn stared at the steam rising from the heated pool in the crisp, fall Wyoming air. "Do you remember how it was a thing for local teens to sneak up here and take an unauthorized midnight swim in the pool?"

A faint smile curved Allie's mouth. She couldn't speak from experience, but she'd heard her older brothers talk about taking The Plunge.

"Sure. Why?"

"I never did." Vaughn kicked at a stone on the concrete deck with the toe of his black, Old Skool Vans sneakers. He had the shoes—with their classic white Sidestripe—in at least four or five different colors.

"You're kidding?" Allie folded her arms and cocked a hip. "Manny, Rey, and Rafi have done it lots of times. I just assumed you were with them on at least one of those adventures."

"I was." He rubbed his chin. "But after my time in foster care, I was terrified of doing anything that would make my parents want to send me away. I served as a lookout, but I wouldn't go onto the property. So the next few times the fellas went, they went without me." Vaughn shrugged. "I can't blame them. They thought I was being a santurrón." His pronunciation of the word was perfect.

"They thought you were being a holier than thou, Goody Two-shoes, when the truth was that you were terrified the Reeds would send you back." It broke Allie's heart to say the words aloud. "I'm so sorry, Vaughn. I know your mom and dad didn't do anything to make you feel that way, but still…no kid should live with that kind of constant pressure."

She squeezed his large hand with her gloved one.

But the gesture didn't ease the tension in Vaughn's shoulders. It seemed to heighten it.

Allie released his hand and tried not to take his reaction as an insult.

"If it makes you feel better, I never took The Plunge either," she said.

"That's surprising." Vaughn cocked his head. "Why?"

"Because you were a rebel and a badass. You were always pushing the limits to see what your parents and brothers would let you get away with." Vaughn rubbed his bearded chin.

His chin-length hair was pulled up into his preferred man bun. She resisted the urge to run her fingers along the buzzed sides of his head.

"I might've pushed the boundaries a little, but I wouldn't go straight to badass." Allie grinned.

"Well, you're definitely a badass now." His smile widened and his dark eyes twinkled. "You stand your ground with your dad, your brothers, even your mom when you need to. You haven't allowed any of them to dictate your personal life or your role in the business." Vaughn placed his large hands on her shoulders. "I'm proud of you for that, Allie."

His words made her heart swell, and her eyes stung a little. She wasn't sure why Vaughn's praise hit so hard, but it definitely felt like the thing she needed to hear right now.

"Thanks for saying that, Vaughn. I'm proud of you, too."

He dropped his hands from her shoulders and rubbed his chin again. "So why didn't you ever take The Plunge?"

"Honestly? I got into it enough with my parents back then. I didn't need the added grief of getting hauled in for trespassing. Just didn't seem like the risk was worth it." She shrugged. "But now you kind of have me feeling like I missed my moment, too."

They both stared at the water regretfully for a few moments, neither of them speaking.

Allie took off one glove and stooped down to slip her hand in the water. It was really warm while the temperature around them was in the mid-forties. No wonder there was so much steam coming off the water.

She stood, staring at Vaughn for a moment. She worried her teeth with her lower lip, her brain churning. Finally, Allie sucked in a deep breath, her eyes closed momentarily.

Allie was either going to break the ice that seemed to have formed between them in the past couple of weeks or she was going to make a complete fool of herself in a way she might never recover from. But it was Vaughn…so she had to try.

"We're standing here regretting not having taken The Plunge—a rite of passage for every kid that grew up here in Willowvale Springs," she said. "But the pool isn't gone yet. So it's not too late to take our place in the annals of town history." She offered a hopeful smile.

"Wait…you're talking right now?"

"Why not?" Allie asked.

"It's near freezing out," he noted in disbelief. "Besides, I'm pretty sure that neither of us brought a swimming suit."

"Neither did most of the kids who took The Plunge." She shrugged. "They just stripped down to their underwear and hopped in. So why can't we?"

"You're not serious," he said.

"Watch me." Allie grinned maniacally.

She unzipped her parka and tossed it into a nearby chair, followed by her sweater and the shirt she was wearing beneath it. The air was frigid, but she was too far in to turn back now. She kicked off her platform heel Doc Martens boots—a holdover from her emo period. Then she shrugged off the slim jeans that clung to her curves.

Allie danced from one foot to the other as she stood there on the concrete deck in her sports bra, a pair of boy shorts and her bare feet. She rubbed her arms.

"Don't tell me that the bad boy rock star is going to chicken out?" She raised an eyebrow, nearly biting her tongue from shivering.

"It's not considered chickening out when I never committed to doing this in the first place," he reminded her.

Technically true.

"C'mon, Vaughn. Two minutes ago you were commiserating about never having had your chance to do this. There's no one here but us. So here's your chance to correct that. What's wrong? Did you go commando today?" Allie poked him in the gut and laughed when his eyes widened. "If so, don't worry," she whispered loudly. "It won't be the first peen I've seen, and it definitely won't be the last. So relax."

Allie took a deep breath, stepped to the edge of the pool and jumped in. It was a shock to the system, but the water was soothing and warm. After a minute or so, she felt great. Now it was up to Vaughn whether he decided to join her or not.

It won't be the first peen I've seen, and it definitely won't be the last. So relax.

The first part of Allie's statement hadn't bothered him. She was a stunning, confident, thirty-year-old woman. It wasn't surprising that she'd had past relationships. He'd certainly had his share, including a marriage that had failed spectacularly.

It was the latter part of Allie's declaration that had snatched Vaughn by the throat and was currently squeezing the air out of his lungs.

It definitely won't be the last.

Why should that matter to him? He and Allie weren't involved. In fact, Vaughn had spent the weeks since he'd gone to dinner at the Prices' home trying to create distance between himself and the woman whose wit, charm and beauty had driven him to near obsession since his return.

He'd spent time hanging out with her brothers.

He'd made another brief trip to LA. And he'd forced himself not to check in on Allie or the project unless it was absolutely necessary. Instead, he'd waited until Allie and her crew had left for the day before he'd venture over to see how things were going. And he'd repeated the rules in his head many times since encountering the grown-ass woman version of the girl whose sincere marriage proposals he'd had to reject repeatedly.

Vaughn squeezed his eyes shut and silently recited the rules.

Don't think with your dick. Never get involved with your best friend's sister. Always consider your career first. Never fall in love.

But all of the warning bells that had helped Vaughn make good decisions thus far where his best friend's little sister was concerned currently seemed to be malfunctioning. Because the only voice he heard in his head now was Allie's. She was inviting him to join her with the promise that the water was fine. All while swimming in her lacy, black underwear—a vision he would probably never get out of his head—like she was an Afro-Latina version of legendary synchronized swimmer Esther Williams or Halle Bailey as *The Little Mermaid*.

"Are you praying or are you in the midst of a medical emergency right now?" Allie clung to the side of the pool and peered at him with a mixture of concern and amusement. "Blink twice if you can hear me," she added when he didn't respond.

He blinked twice because he could be as much of

a smart ass as she could. Then he rubbed his forehead and sighed. "The answer, by the way, is neither. I was just considering all the reasons this is a terrible idea."

Allie assessed him for a moment with her head cocked, as if she was trying to decide whether to say what she was thinking.

As much as he wanted to know, a part of him was equally hesitant to find out.

"What I'm hearing is that you really want to join me, but that part of your brain that is still conditioned not to disappoint people is interfering." She stated the words without judgment. "So if you're worried that my parents or my brothers won't approve, here's your reminder that I'm a thirty-year-old woman who has the right to do what she wants—regardless of whether my family approves of my choices."

Vaughn didn't respond, so Allie continued.

"If you're worried whether it's inappropriate for us to be in a whole ass swimming pool together wearing nothing but our underwear, I should tell you that my actual swimming suits are far more revealing than what I'm wearing now. And I'm pretty damn sure I've seen you in one of those candid celeb magazines wearing a Speedo that was like two sizes too small." Allie held up two fingers for emphasis. "So, like everyone else who saw that photo online, I've pretty much seen the goods."

"It was France, Allie. You literally cannot wear swim trunks to the pool there," Vaughn felt the need to point out.

"Why doesn't matter, Vaughn. The point is I've seen what you're working with." Allie winked, then swam away so gracefully it looked like she was born doing the backstroke. "You're not really going to make me do this alone, are you?"

Allie's toned arms and thighs sliced through the water as she lay on her back.

"Fuck it," Vaughn whispered under his breath. He shrugged out of his expensive coat, then stripped out of all the other layers of clothing meant to protect him from the frigid air, which was growing colder as evening descended.

He was probably going to die of pneumonia or suffer penile frostbite like Prince Harry. Either consequence he'd probably deserve because this was an awful idea and he knew it. Only he couldn't resist joining Allie in the pool. Partly, because she was right. He'd regret not taking The Plunge at least once before the old pool was demolished. But also because he seemed to have zero resistance when it came to Allie Price.

Vaughn had taken off everything except his black boxer briefs and his jewelry—a couple of rings and the sun, moon and stars necklace he wore almost constantly. He stepped to the edge of the pool, dismissed all the thoughts of how Mr. Price and Rey would both want to strangle him, then jumped into the water.

He'd gone from freezing to warm and now he was surrounded by a soothing heat as he tried to get oriented in the space. Vaughn blinked, wiping water from his eyes as his gaze swept the pool looking for Allie.

"You did it!" Allie wrapped her limbs around him like an octopus as she hugged his neck from behind, her lips pressed to his ear. "Didn't it feel amazing?"

Actually, what felt amazing was having Allie's full breasts smushed against the top of his back and the warm space between her thighs pressed just above his ass. But saying so didn't seem like a very good idea.

"It did," Vaughn said instead, still wiping water from his eyes.

"Race you?" Allie let go of him, and he missed her warmth and the heavenly feel of the curves he'd dreamed about most nights for the past few weeks.

By the time his brain seemed to be fully functioning again, Allie had taken off for one end of the pool. And instead of her smooth, fluid movements that barely disturbed the surface of the water, she employed big kicks that intentionally doused him, all while laughing her ass off.

Vaughn shook his head and took off after her, splashing as much water onto her as he could along the way, both of them laughing.

"Okay, now that we're both sufficiently wet—" Allie tightened her loosening ponytail "—here are the rules… We go all the way to that end and back. Whoever hits this wall—with any body part of your choosing, preferably not your head," she added. Likely because he'd done just that when he'd gone on a trip to Florida with her family when he was about fifteen and had nearly cracked his head open. "That person is the winner. Simple as that."

"And what exactly is it that we win?" Vaughn stretched his arms and shoulders in preparation for their impromptu race.

Allie considered his question. "How about we let the winner decide?"

"That sounds dangerous."

"We're both sensible people," Allie said. "I trust that you won't demand my car or a pro bono house build."

"Good point." Vaughn rubbed his hands together.

"I am not getting out of this water until it's time for us to leave." Allie seemed to shiver at the thought. "So how about we both place our feet against the wall?"

Vaughn nodded and placed one foot against the wall.

Allie counted them down, then they both took off as quickly as they could.

Vaughn had a little bit of a lead at first with his longer legs and arms. But by the time they'd reached the opposite wall, Allie had caught up with him, and by the time she'd hit the midway point of the final lap, she was well ahead of him. He managed to regain some ground, but Allie went into another gear and made a mad dash at the end. She touched the wall and shouted in triumph a few seconds ahead of him.

"You were toying with me that entire time, weren't you?" Vaughn dragged a hand down his face, wiping water from his eyes. "You could've left me in the dust and completely whipped my ass, couldn't you?"

Allie shrugged and gave him a sheepish smile. "If I'd beaten you too badly, you wouldn't have wanted to race again."

"Okay, that's it, kid." He shook a finger at her. "Best two out of three?"

"Why not?" Allie shrugged. "But are you sure you don't need a Bengay break first?"

"Oh, you're funny." Vaughn shifted an eyebrow and rubbed his hands together eagerly. "Go ahead. Talk your shit, little girl. I'm fueled by my haters. You ain't got nothin' on the Reasons I Hate Vaughn Reed manifesto created by VaughReedSucks382."

"People actually do things like that?" Allie's dark eyes filled with compassion. "God, that's awful. What kind of person does something like that?"

"A crappy one." Vaughn focused on the other end of the pool. Now wasn't the time to evaluate the level of misery that would make a person put that much time and effort into hating him. "This time, we go on my count. Ready, set, GO!"

Vaughn put every bit of effort into hitting that first wall first. Maybe he should've paced himself because his breathing was labored as he made his way back, and Allie started to gain on him. But as she closed in on him, he got another burst of energy, pushed hard and touched the wall a full half-length ahead of her.

Allie laughed at his celebratory jig. "Fine, you won. We're tied," she said. "That means this last one is for all the marbles. You need a breather, old man?"

"No." He did, but he wasn't about to admit that to

her when she looked like a goddess emerging from her watery kingdom. "Do you?"

"You're cute." Allie laughed, then patted his chest. She turned to face ahead, then angled her neck, as if trying to get out any kinks or stiffness. She stretched her arms above her head and arched her back, giving him an eye-popping view of the full breasts that were one stiff breeze shy of escaping the lacy, black sports bra.

Not fair, Allie. Not fair at all.

But he wouldn't admit that to her either.

Allie counted down and they took off, neck and neck for most of the race. At the tail end of the final stretch, he was exhausted, but trying to push forward. Allie seemed to sense as much. She surged forward with an outstretched hand and touched the wall just a fraction of a second before he managed to.

"Ha! I won. Take that," Allie raised a fist in victory as she bounced on her heels.

Vaughn couldn't help wondering how she managed to keep the girls contained in that lace bra. But the feat made her victory dance far more impressive than his. Moments like this—spent with Allie and her family—had been the most fun he'd had in a really long time.

Was it any wonder that he'd found every excuse he could possibly think of to extend his stay there in Willowvale Springs rather than just handing the project off to Allie, who was more than capable of handling it?

"Okay, fine. It was a close race, but you won it

fair and square." Vaughn chuckled. "So whatever
you want—"

"You." Allie's expression had gone from gloat-
ing and victorious to soft and demure as she stood
in front of him looking more vulnerable than he'd
ever seen her before. Allie wrapped her arms around
his shoulders, her eyes studying the shock evident in
his as their lower bodies pressed together.

"What happened to us being sensible people?"
Vaughn's arms instinctively circled Allie's waist,
tugging her even closer, his gaze not leaving hers.

"Who says we aren't being sensible?" Allie asked.
"This makes perfect sense to me." Her eyes drifted
closed as she leaned in closer.

Vaughn swallowed hard. His heartbeat raged in
his chest like Meg White's drum line in The White
Stripe's "Seven Nation Army."

Maybe Allie was right. Maybe the two of them
together did make sense and they just needed to convince everyone else in their collective world of that.

During the past two weeks, he'd been trying to
"be good" and get Allie out of his system. But he'd
felt an aching sense of loss without their daily interactions, which had become the highlight of his day.

And what if they couldn't convince Mr. Price,
Rey and the rest of Allie's brothers that the two of
them were a good fit?

It didn't matter. Because Vaughn was done fighting his growing feelings for Allie. He wanted her…
desperately. And he'd come to need her in his world

and in his life. Allie's family would just have to accept that.

Vaughn drew in a deep breath and closed the space between them, finally tasting the soft lips that had taunted him for weeks.

He lifted Allie, and she wrapped her legs around his waist. He backed her against the side of the pool, her soft curves pinned between the concrete wall and his hard body and growing length.

He ravaged the sweet mouth whose taste he'd imagined more times than he could remember. Allie Price was like a drug and he was sailing as high as a kite off of her taste, her warmth and the sweet little murmurs that increased in sound and intensity the longer they kissed. He swallowed the sensual sounds she made. Each one seemed to vibrate down his chest and go straight to his cock, making him increasingly desperate for her.

She broke their kiss and cradled his jaw. The moon was reflected in her dark eyes as she dragged a thumb across his lower lip. "I could really use a shower right now. Mind if I use yours?"

Vaughn froze, his mouth suddenly incapable of forming coherent words. His pulse raced and his dick strained against the thin layers of fabric between them. He swallowed hard and nodded clumsily. "Yes… I mean…no, I don't mind at all. I'll grab our things."

Allie grinned, then moved toward the stainless-steel ladder. As she climbed the three short steps to exit the pool, one cheek bearing his handprint had escaped her black boy shorts.

Vaughn sank his teeth into his lower lip and climbed out of the pool, his body aching for her, and filled with heat despite the chilliness in the air surrounding them.

This was going to be a night neither of them would ever forget.

Nine

Allie had barely gotten through the door of Vaughn's cabin before he'd dropped their things in a pile on a nearby chair, pulled her into his arms, pushed her up against the closed door and kissed her again.

Vaughn's fervent, hungry kisses filled her with intense heat. He kissed her like a man who'd been awaiting this moment as long as she had.

But he hadn't. Until a few weeks ago, Vaughn had probably only ever thought of her as Rey's annoying kid sister. But she'd been waiting for this moment since she was twelve years old and Vaughn had packed his things and moved to LA. She'd been as devastated by Vaughn leaving as Rey had—though her brother probably had never admitted as much to his best friend.

She'd eventually moved on. But the moment she and Vaughn sat down at that table to review her plans for the resort, those old feelings came creeping back.

In the weeks since then, they'd solidified into something that felt fully formed rather than the hazy fantasy of a little girl who had no real understanding of romantic relationships. She and Vaughn might never have what her parents had or what Manny, Rey and Rafi had found with their spouses. But she would take this…one night, one week, one month. Whatever it was that they could have before Vaughn returned to his life in LA and left her behind again.

Allie pressed her palms against Vaughn's chest, breaking their kiss. His damp skin was chilled. And now that she'd put a bit of space between them, she was shivering.

"You're freezing, baby." He regarded her with concern, his gaze hooded and his chest heaving. "Let me get you—"

"Hot shower," Allie finally managed to say, her teeth practically chattering.

"Of course." Vaughn rubbed up and down her arms, his dark brown eyes crinkling with concern. "There are plenty of fresh towels in the linen closet in my bathroom. You go ahead and shower while I get the fire started."

Vaughn pressed another kiss to her lips, then slapped her bottom as she walked past him, taking her by surprise.

Allie hesitated at the door, which led to the main

bedroom suite, her pulse racing. She turned back to Vaughn.

"Give me a few minutes, then join me?" She met his gaze hopefully.

"Be there as soon as I can." His reserved smile widened.

Allie sank her teeth into her lower lip and sighed quietly as her gaze skimmed the straining bulge in his black boxer briefs.

I am really going to enjoy that ride.

She turned and made her way through Vaughn's bedroom and into the dated old bathroom. The premium cabins were next on the project list once the main house renovations had been completed.

Allie turned the old porcelain knobs and allowed the water in the shower to heat up. The cramped space definitely didn't scream sexy, but it would serve its purpose just fine.

She wanted that chlorinated pool water off of her skin and out of her hair as soon as possible. Allie made a quick run to the bathroom and then washed her hands. She stared at herself in the mirror, her stomach tied in knots.

Allie wasn't having second thoughts about kissing Vaughn or about what she wanted from him tonight.

They were two unattached adults acting on their strong attraction to each other. They'd have an amazing night together. Then—whether they decided to do this again or not—at least they could maintain the friendship they'd been building since Vaughn had gotten to know her as a woman. Not as his best friend's kid sister. But no matter what, she wouldn't allow herself to get caught up in the belief that this relationship could be serious. Because Vaughn wasn't staying, and Allie wasn't leaving.

Yes, being Mrs. Vaughn Reed had once been the dream. But she'd matured since then. So she'd enjoy their night together for what it was rather than entertaining her teenage fantasy of a future with Vaughn.

Allie used Vaughn's designer brand shampoo and conditioner to wash the chlorine from her hair. Then she used Vaughn's lemon verbena-scented shower gel to scrub the pool water from every inch of her skin twice.

There was a tap at the bathroom door, which she'd left open just a crack. Allie sucked in a quiet breath, butterflies fluttering wildly in her stomach as she anticipated Vaughn joining her in the shower.

Once they crossed this line, there would be no going back. She was ready for it. Yet, a part of her understood the gravity of this moment—for both of them.

"Allie, is it okay if I come in?" Vaughn asked.

"Yes, of course." She was embarrassed that she'd been so in her head about this moment between them that she'd failed to respond to his initial knock. So maybe she was more nervous about this than she was willing to admit even to herself. "In fact, you'd better hurry before we run out of hot water. You know how these old water tanks are."

"I do." Vaughn chuckled, and she could hear the door close behind him.

When she peeked her head out of the shower curtain, Vaughn had stepped inside the room, but he was leaning against the door instead of making his way toward the shower.

"If you plan to join me, you'll need to lose those." She indicated his underwear.

"I suppose I do." A smirk lit his eyes. He shoved his underwear down his hips and his dick sprang free.

Impressive.

Those Speedos from that tabloid photo definitely hadn't told the entire story.

Allie tried not to stare or to lick her lips or to instantly get wet at just the sight of it. She failed miserably on all three fronts.

He kicked off his underwear, shoved the curtain aside, and stepped inside the old shower/tub combo.

Without thought, Allie stepped backward to make room for him in the small space. The old ceramic tiles were cold against her back.

Vaughn's gaze didn't roam her body—as hers had his. Instead, his gaze locked with hers as he pressed his hands to the walls on either side of her, boxing her in. He dropped a soft, sweet kiss on her lips, then another on her neck, followed by a kiss on her shoulder.

He lifted his head and met her gaze.

"You're sure about this?"

"I am." She tipped her chin defiantly, despite the fluttering in her belly. "Are you?"

Vaughn cocked his head, as if surprised that she'd

noticed his hesitancy. He rubbed the bearded chin that had abraded her skin as he kissed her neck and shoulder.

"No." He practically whispered the word. "I haven't been able to get you out of my head since the day you strutted into the resort in that sexy little skirt. And every moment we've spent together since then has only made me want you more. I've tried a million times to get you and the thought of us together out of my head, Allie. But no matter how hard I try... I just can't."

Vaughn lifted her chin and their connection seemed to intensify as she met his gaze again. "I want you in my bed, Allie. I want to spend the rest of the night showing you all the ways I can please you. Tasting every inch of your gorgeous brown skin. But if you have the slightest concern that—"

Allie didn't allow him to finish. She didn't want to permit him the space to talk them both out of the thing they wanted so badly: each other.

She looped her arms around his neck and pulled him down for a passionate kiss as she pressed her naked body to his, pinning his rock-hard length between them.

Vaughn angled his head as he took control of the kiss. His kiss was greedy and demanding, and she wanted more of it and more of him than the small space would permit. The water began to cool and Allie pulled back enough to meet his eyes, both of their chests still heaving.

"Does that answer your question?" She flashed

a smirk that made him smile, too. "Now, I need to rinse my hair, and you should get cleaned up before this becomes an ice-cold shower."

"Yes, ma'am." Vaughn chuckled.

She rinsed the conditioner from her hair and Vaughn scrubbed his skin before letting his hair down and washing and conditioning it, too. They stepped out of the shower, toweled off, then made their way into Vaughn's bedroom.

As she approached his bed, nerves seemed to grab hold of Allie again. But as soon as Vaughn slipped his arms around her waist and kissed her, she relaxed and got lost in his passionate kiss.

Vaughn lifted her onto the bed. He sucked in a quiet breath, his eyes trailing her skin and eventually landing on the hardened peaks of her breasts.

He went back to the bathroom, returning with a strip of condoms, which he tossed onto the nightstand after tearing one off and sheathing himself. Vaughn slipped under the cover and lay over Allie as he kissed her.

Her heels dug into the mattress as she spread her knees apart, making room for Vaughn between them. Allie loved the feel of his hard body pressed against hers. Loved how perfectly the two of them seemed to fit together. As if they were made for each other.

She pressed her fingers into his back, her nails scraping gently at his damp skin as his tongue glided against hers. When Vaughn trailed kisses down Allie's neck, then her chest—his beard scraping at her skin—her breath hitched. She pressed her palms to either side of her on the mattress and lay back, her chest rising and falling with each breath.

When he took one of the pebbled tips into his warm mouth, Allie gasped. The pleasure that had been slowly creeping down her spine—making her nipples tingle and her sex feel heavy—exploded in intensity.

Allie cursed softly as she swept Vaughn's damp hair aside to give her an unobstructed view of his mouth on her skin. When his eyes met hers, there was something wild in his heated gaze that made her tremble with her growing desire for him.

Vaughn moved to her other nipple, giving it the same treatment. Then suddenly, he was kissing his way down her body again. He placed delicate kisses on her belly, then on her mound. He pressed soft kisses to her inner thigh. Then finally, he pressed an open mouth kiss to the space between her thighs ravenous for his touch.

Allie cursed softly, her head dropping back onto the pillow behind her as Vaughn kissed and sucked her delicate, sensitive, swollen flesh. Until she was gasping and cursing and begging him for more.

When he delved inside her with his tongue, she shot up onto her elbows again as she looked down at him. Leaning on one elbow, she swept the hair from his face again as he tasted her again and again, the heat between them rising.

But when he stuck his fingers inside her and curved them, she gasped in response to the sensation. Vaughn grinned with a wicked glint in his eyes.

Then he sucked on her clit and she nearly screamed with pleasure.

Allie lay back on the bed and clutched the sheets as the sensation built, then rocketed through her body as she called Vaughn's name.

No, nothing between them would ever be the same. But she couldn't regret a single thing.

Vaughn watched as Allie fell apart, his name on her sweet tongue. Her chest rose and fell heavily. Conversely, her belly did, too.

He lay tender kisses on the flesh along her quivering, pink center, the taste of her on his tongue and the smell of soap and sex filling his nostrils.

Vaughn was pretty sure that he was already addicted to Allie's taste and to the sexy little sounds she'd made as he'd used his fingers and tongue to take her over the edge. To the way she shuddered as she cursed and called his name.

He lay between Allie's thighs, his head resting on her belly as she mindlessly raked her fingers through his hair. Vaughn had finally found his own personal Shangri-la, and he never, *ever* wanted to leave her or this bed.

Allie sighed softly, then kissed the top of his head.

Vaughn couldn't help smiling in response to the euphoric expression on Allie's face. He pressed a kiss to her hip. Then he climbed up the bed and lay on his side, facing her. "I didn't think it was possible, but you look even more gorgeous than usual."

"I'm completely blissed out." She sighed, a dreamy

look on her beautiful face as she stroked his cheek. "And I have the distinct feeling that my night is about to get even better."

"Oh yeah?" Vaughn chuckled. "And why is that?"

Allie kissed him passionately, her naked body cradled against his. She pulled back, nuzzling her nose against his. "You're not going to make me beg again, are you?"

"No, sweetheart, I won't."

Vaughn rolled Allie onto her back and hovered over her as he studied the face he saw in his dreams every night. The lips he'd imagined kissing more times than he could count. He knifed his fingers through her damp hair that smelled like his shampoo. Nuzzled the neck that smelled like his shower gel. Then he kissed her.

Allie looped her arms around his waist. As their kiss intensified, she held on to him tight, her nails digging into his skin as she clamored for more.

Finally, he gripped his shaft, pumping it before he began his torturously slow entry, permitting her body to adjust to his. Allie arched her back and cursed softly. Her chin tipped and her shoulders pressed back against the mattress as Vaughn began to glide his hips. He slowly pulled back, then went in again, going deeper this time.

Allie's eyes met his as she moved against him slowly at first. But then Vaughn's hips rocked in a small circle. He created friction against her sensitive clit, taking her higher and higher. Until she'd screamed, "Yes!" over and over again, punctuated by his name.

Vaughn kissed her neck and her shoulder as he moved inside her with more speed and intensity. Until his body stiffened, every muscle in his back suddenly tight as the most delicious sensation of bliss exploded inside him.

He lay beside Allie, pulling her into his arms.

"That was fucking amazing, babe." Vaughn kissed the top of her head.

"It was." She nuzzled her cheek against his chest. "You definitely won this round."

"I think we both won." Vaughn rubbed a hand up and down her back.

"You're not wrong there." Allie lifted her head. Her wide grin made his heart soar. "But next time, I'm definitely going for the win."

"God, you're competitive, woman."

"I can't help it. I have four brothers." Allie held up four of the manicured fingernails that had carved a trail down his back moments earlier.

"How about I scrape together something for dinner, then we go best two out of three?" Vaughn asked.

"Are you asking me to spend the night, Vaughn Reed?"

Vaughn hadn't even considered the need to formally ask Allie to spend the night with him. He'd just assumed that she'd want to stay as much as he'd wanted her there. But if he needed to formalize the request, he had no problem doing so.

"Sí. Quédate conmigo, esta noche, Alejandra."
He kissed the palm of her hand. "Por favor, cariña."

Allie cupped his cheek, her gaze softening. "I can't believe you retained that much of the Spanish you learned from growing up around my family."

"I've traveled the world for the past two decades, and I spent quite a bit of time in Buenos Aires and the Tortuguero National Park in Costa Rica. Helps to know the language. Pero no respondiste mi pregunta," he added, making it clear he was aware that she'd cleverly dodged his question.

"Sí, me encantaría quedarme contigo esta noche, Vaughn," she finally responded.

Yes, I would love to stay with you tonight, Vaughn.

He released a slow breath and smiled broadly his heart racing.

"But why don't I scrape together something for dinner while you move my car and grab my purse from the trunk? It probably isn't a good idea for me to leave it in a spot where it's visible from the street. Not unless we want the entire town to know I'm spending the night here." She kissed him, then climbed out of bed and headed toward the bathroom. "The keys are in my coat pocket."

"Yes, ma'am." Vaughn was mesmerized by watching Allie strut to the bathroom in nothing but the glorious brown skin she'd come into the world with.

She shut the door behind her.

Vaughn lay back with his arm folded behind his head and stared at the ceiling. When Allie's father and brothers learned there was something going on between them, all hell would probably break loose. But tonight, he was just going to marinate in the incredible bliss of having Allie Price in his arms and in his bed.

Ten

Vaughn had been all over the world. He'd awakened to fresh air in a hut nestled in the mountains of Tibet. To the demanding cries of howler monkeys in the rainforest in Costa Rica. To the sights and sounds of nearly every major city in North America and Europe. He awakened in palatial luxury suites and in a grass hut while volunteering on a mission in his birth mother's home country of Argentina. But he was pretty sure that he'd never awakened more content than he had that morning holding Allie in his arms.

He'd slipped from beneath the covers, gone to the bathroom and brushed his teeth before returning to bed. The moment his skin met hers, Allie wrapped herself around him again.

Allie's soft, warm curves were nestled against

him. Her cheek was pressed to his chest, and one arm and one leg were slung across his body as she breathed softly.

Her face was shielded by her wild, loose curls. And she wore one of his old Sin & Glory T-shirts and nothing else—since her bra and panties had been hand washed and were hanging in the bathroom to dry.

When Vaughn glided a hand up and down her back and kissed the top of her head, Allie stirred. She stretched and yawned, her face still pressed into his chest and hidden by her dark, silky strands.

He brushed her hair away and kissed her forehead. "Morning, beautiful."

Even seeing just half her face, the smile that slid across it made Vaughn's heart swell. She slowly opened her eyes and glanced up at him with a grin before burying her face in his chest again, distorting her words. "Good morning, handsome. What time is it anyway?"

Vaughn glanced at the bedside clock. "Six thirty."

She groaned. "I could lay here all day but—"

"Then stay." He cradled her against him. "You've only had four hours of sleep."

"I wish I could stay. But your custom cabinets are going in today, then we can finish laying the hardwood floor in the kitchen. Besides, if the crew arrives and sees my car, it won't take much of a leap for them to realize I spent the night here." She kissed his chest. "But I could stay again Saturday night, then I'll make a full spread for breakfast on Sunday morning."

Any disappointment he felt melted in the wake of her radiant smile and those glittering dark eyes that hinted at mischief.

"It's a date." He pressed a quick kiss to the soft, plump lips that he'd kissed so fervently the previous night. When he tried to slip his tongue between the seam of her lips, she immediately withdrew, pressing a hand to her mouth.

"Let me brush my teeth first." She scampered out of bed, grabbed her purse from a chair on the other side of the room, then ducked into the bathroom.

Vaughn chuckled as he stared at the ceiling with one arm behind his head. With the other hand, he ran his fingers over the charm around his neck. His mother would've really liked Allie. They both had bold personalities, vibrant smiles, an irreverent sense of humor and a contagious laugh.

Allie returned a few minutes later. She hovered over him, tucking her hair behind her ear. "So… where were we?"

Vaughn pulled her into bed and she let out the most delightful squeal of surprise, then she giggled. The sounds made his heart dance. He hovered over her, studying her gorgeous face, scrubbed free of all makeup. He thought about the little girl who'd asked him to marry her. Who would've believed that time and distance had brought them here?

Vaughn leaned down and nuzzled her neck, then pressed kisses to her ear.

"Your brothers are going to kill me," he whispered. "But I'll die one happy man."

Allie burst into laughter. She kissed him, then lay back with a gleam in her eyes. "Then it's a good thing your secret is safe with me."

Vaughn kissed her, his tongue exploring the minty taste of her mouth. Suddenly, her words hit him.

It's a good thing your secret is safe with me.

"Wait…what do you mean my *secret* is safe with you?" He studied her face. "Are you saying we need to hide our relationship from your family?"

"Okay…relationship is a strong word," Allie said with an uneasy, teasing-but-not-teasing smile. "We literally spent a night together, Vaughn. I don't think that's something I need to announce to my entire family."

Vaughn sat up and wedged a pillow between his back and the headboard. "I thought you said you didn't need your brothers' approval when it came to your love life?"

"I don't need my brothers' approval when it comes to my *sex life*." Allie sat up beside him. "But that doesn't mean I hop on the family group chat to announce every hookup I've ever had, either." Her tone was soft and teasing.

This was clearly no big deal to her. So why did it feel like one to him?

"So for you, last night was just a hookup?" Vaughn cringed inside just saying the words.

"Isn't that what this is for you?" Allie seemed genuinely puzzled. She pulled her knees to her chest and wrapped her arms around them as she studied his face. "I know we didn't discuss it, but I just assumed…" She raked her fingers through her hair and tugged it over her shoulder, then heaved a quiet sigh. "You're returning to LA once this project is done.

Allie furrowed her arched brows, her doe-like eyes assessing him carefully. When he still didn't respond, her gaze softened. He could swear there was a hint of pity in her eyes.

"Given the situation, what was I supposed to think?"

Her words cut deep, and Vaughn wasn't even sure why. He'd probably used every one of the lines Allie had just said.

Relationship is a strong word. We literally spent a night together. I'm returning to LA after the tour.

So this was how it felt to be on the other side of that conversation. Or maybe he felt different because it was Allie saying those words.

From the moment Allie Price had strutted through the front door of the resort and smiled at him, he'd been an absolute goner. Even before he'd realized who she was.

He'd spent the past few weeks fighting his attraction to her and vehemently denying his growing feelings for his best friend's kid sister. But Allie was all grown up now.

She was a brilliant, accomplished woman who was sweet and funny. Allie was confident in her abilities. She knew just what to say to set his world right again when it felt like things were going sideways. And she'd inspired him to write some of his best songs yet.

Suddenly, it was clear why things felt so different for him this time. He'd spent the past few weeks falling for Allie, despite his efforts to keep things between them platonic.

Vaughn cradled Allie's face and kissed her. When he pulled away, she stared at him, studying his gaze.

He grazed her cheekbone with his thumb. "Baby, do you really think I'd risk blowing up a lifelong friendship and my relationship with your entire family for a few nights together?"

Her throat worked as she swallowed hard. She opened her mouth, yet no words came out. He'd rendered the opinionated Allie Price speechless. Something that might never happen again.

Allie stared at Vaughn. Her heart raced, and she went through a variety of emotions in the blink of an eye. Shock. Guilt. Embarrassment. Affection. Flattery. More guilt.

She opened her mouth to speak, but her brain and her mouth suddenly seemed incapable of functioning. Allie sighed softly and squeezed her eyes shut as she leaned into the palm resting against her cheek. She opened her eyes and studied the face that had occupied her thoughts from the time she was a tween until she was twenty.

That was the summer Vaughn Reed had married the younger sister of the band's lead singer. Allie's heart had been broken, and she'd been forced to banish the notion that Vaughn Reed would one day return to Willowvale Springs, confess that he'd loved her all along and whisk her away to join him and his bandmates on Sin & Glory's latest tour.

Now it was ten years later, Vaughn Reed was back home, very single, and she'd just awakened in his bed.

Allie wasn't a little girl who fantasized about love and relationships anymore. She was a grown woman who'd known the heartbreak and humiliation of a relationship that had failed quite publicly. She'd learned to accept that not every connection was meant to last forever. Some were only meant to last a season—however long or short that season might be. She'd been loving her life since she'd learned that very painful lesson.

So no, she hadn't expected that Vaughn was interested in anything more than a spectacular one-night stand or perhaps a clandestine fling.

"Vaughn, last night was *incredible*," Allie finally managed to say, her pulse racing. "And we've already made a date for Saturday night."

"You mean we've made plans to *hook up* on Saturday night," he corrected her. One eyebrow shot up and his nostrils flared. He dropped his hand from her face, and she immediately missed his touch.

"I would happily spend every night with you for as long as you're here in Willowvale Springs." Allie kissed him and smiled. "I just didn't want to assume that's what you wanted."

"That's fair. But now you know that I *do* want to see you again." He toyed with a strand of her loose hair, his gaze not quite meeting hers. "So now what, Allie?"

Allie worried her lower lip with her teeth, her heart thudding in her chest. She took his hand in hers. "I'd still prefer we kept this between us."

The pained look in Vaughn's eyes made her chest ache. She had valid reasons for her concern, so why did she feel like such a terrible person?

"Being one of the bad boys of rock is part of your brand, Vaughn. People expect you to be in and out of relationships and have random one-night stands."

"Is that what's bothering you? My reputation in the tabloids?" Vaughn asked. "Because I'd think that by now you know I'm not the guy they portray me as for clickbait online."

"I do know you, Vaughn." Allie forced herself to meet his gaze. "But I have my life and reputation to worry about. If you and I had met under any other circumstances, I wouldn't hesitate to let my family know we were seeing each other. But you're a business client, Vaughn. Do you have any idea how long it was before my father and brothers trusted me alone on a job with the crew members or male clients?"

Vaughn sucked in an impatient breath, that one eyebrow cocked even higher. But he didn't respond.

"Three years." Allie held up three fingers. "One of them would always make an excuse about why they needed to come along or they'd suddenly pop in. I had to threaten to move to Salt Lake City or Vegas for them to start treating me like an adult. I don't want to go back to that because they're worried I'm going to be swept off my feet by every handsome, wealthy male client I encounter. Nor do I want the contractors I work with to think that this suddenly means they have a shot."

"I know how overprotective your dad and brothers are." Vaughn ran his thumb along the back of her hand. "And I don't want to make things difficult for you. But I don't want to play games either, Allie. Nor do I want to lie to my oldest friend about being with his sister."

"And why would you have to lie? It's not like Rey is going to randomly interrogate you about whether or not you've been banging me." Allie nudged Vaughn's arm playfully.

"There is such a thing as a lie of omission," Vaughn said. "I should know. My ex-wife was really good at it."

Allie threaded their fingers and leaned her head on Vaughn's shoulder. "I'm sorry about how things worked out with your ex and that it led to the dissolution of the band. But it sounds like she was holding back information you were entitled to as her life partner," Allie said. "My family isn't entitled to know who I'm sleeping with, Vaughn. It isn't the same thing. You see that, right?" She hoped so. Because she wanted to keep seeing Vaughn while he was in town.

"I do. So if you want to keep this between us, that's what we'll do," he said begrudgingly. "But I need to make something clear..." He lifted her chin. "I won't lie to your brother about us. Is that a gamble you're willing to take?"

After all her talk about how she was her own woman, she wasn't about to back down. Not if it meant walking away from Vaughn before either of them was ready.

"Deal." She extended a hand to him.

Vaughn didn't shake her hand.

"And what if this is just the beginning and we eventually want more?" Vaughn swept her hair from her shoulder and kissed her neck, then her ear. "Because when it comes to something I really want... I've never been a halfway kind of guy."

There were butterflies in Allie's stomach. Her childhood crush was actually worried that he might be falling for her. This night just didn't seem real.

After years of crushing on Vaughn, she'd finally come to the painful realization that her feelings for him had been a childish, one-sided, imaginary affair. That he'd never seen her as anything more than Rey's kid sister, and he never would. So despite her bravado in going after Vaughn, she was stunned by his question.

This can't possibly be real.

Allie was sure that any minute now she'd awake to discover that this was all some lust-induced dream and the hand that had taken her to such great heights had been her own.

A part of her was terrified to consider the possibility that Vaughn might actually be serious about her. That he might want more from her than some forbidden fling.

Allie shoved his shoulders back against the rickety old wooden headboard and climbed onto his lap, her sex positioned over the bulge in his boxer briefs.

She ground her hips and pressed her mouth to his, ending any objection he might've had to her evading his question.

Vaughn lifted the hem of the shirt, and she raised her arms to accommodate him. He tossed the shirt onto the floor and grazed her nipples with his thumbs, his eyes locked on to hers.

His gaze seemed to tell her that he knew exactly what she was doing, and he was choosing to let her get away with it.

Fair enough.

Vaughn dipped his head and took one of the pebbled tips into his mouth. Teased her with his tongue. Grazed her erect nipple with his teeth.

Allie dropped her head back, her hips moving more deliberately over his thick length. She murmured softly at the delicious friction provided by the now damp fabric encasing his erection as it made contact with her hardened clit.

Vaughn grabbed hold of Allie's waist, pulling her hard against him.

She cried out from the unexpected pleasure of the sudden move, her pulse racing.

The corners of his mouth lifted in a wicked smile. Vaughn lowered his hands, gripping her bottom so tightly she held back a small yelp. There was a hint of pain that only intensified the pleasure she was feeling. Then he repositioned her. She moved back and forth with increased fervor, chasing the high of the mind-blowing orgasms he'd given her last night. He pulled and pushed her, moving with her and increasing the friction for both of them. Until she came hard, calling his name so loudly again and again that her throat felt hoarse.

Vaughn flipped her over, then he reached for one of the remaining condoms and sheathed himself as she lay on her back looking up at him as she tried to catch her breath.

She whimpered softly at the sensation of him filling her until he'd reached bottom. Hands behind her knees, he'd lifted her legs, his hips gliding back and forth slowly at first. Then more quickly. He'd taken her over the edge again, her fingernails digging into his biceps as she called his name. Until he'd stiffened, his back arching as he'd emptied himself inside the condom.

He lay on his back beside her, both of them huffing, as they tried to catch their breath. Vaughn wrapped his arms around Allie and pulled her against him, dropping a kiss on her head.

Allie sighed quietly, her heart still racing as she held on to him. She squeezed her eyes shut, thinking about Vaughn's question.

What if this is only the beginning and we eventually want more?

It was too late for that.

She'd gone into this telling herself that her flirtation with Vaughn was only a bit of fun. A chance to bang her celebrity crush and check something a little wild off of her bucket list. Knowing that having anything real and long-term with Vaughn Reed was an impossibility because his life was in LA and hers was there in Willowvale Springs.

But now she wasn't so sure. Because that little voice in the back of her head that had always believed that she and Vaughn were meant to be together had grown louder. And she wanted to believe it, too.

Eleven

It was Vaughn's fourth consecutive Sunday evening at Allie's parents' home; the second since that night at the pool that had changed everything between him and Allie. Since then, they'd spent every evening together at his cabin and she'd spent nearly every night in his bed. He was in a state of utter bliss.

This was the happiest Vaughn had been in longer than he could remember. And it'd been an insanely creative period for him. He'd finished the rest of the songs for Extreme Overload's album and had started working on a few possible songs for Sin & Glory's comeback album.

Nearly every song was either inspired by Allie or centered around the ideas of coming home or reconnecting with friends and family.

Vaughn was in a great space mentally and physically—free of the stress and anxiety that had become his constant companions over the years. He was enjoying his life more than he had in a long time. But he was in a very different place in his life now. Nights of partying, hard-drinking, eating out every night, subsisting on minimal sleep, and living out of a suitcase didn't seem so appealing anymore. In fact, maybe they never really had been.

He'd found surprising contentment in the quiet nights he and Allie spent in front of the fireplace playing Uno Flip while a movie they'd both seen a dozen times like *Hitch*, *Groundhog Day*, or *Coming to America* played in the background, and in nights like the one he was currently spending with her family were his true idea of happiness.

A tug on his pant leg pulled him out of his temporary daze.

"You okay, Tío Vaughnie?" Stella—one of Rey's adorable little girls—looked up at him, her huge, doe eyes filled with concern.

"Of course, sweetheart." Vaughn put on his widest smile for the little girl who looked so much like her tía Allie. "But your abuelita and tía Allie fed me so much delicious food that my brain is a little fuzzy right now." He chuckled, prompting the little girl to dissolve into giggles.

"My tummy is full, too." Stella rubbed her tummy, her big smile showing off a recently lost tooth. She leaned in closer with one hand covering her mouth and whispered conspiratorially, "But I always have room for another slice of tres leches cake."

Vaughn ruffled the little girl's hair, worn in two long, curly ponytails that bounced with her every movement. Then Stella skipped off to play with her younger sister.

"The girls love their new tío Vaughnie." Rey handed Vaughn an opened beer, then sank onto the sofa. "And I have to admit, it's been good having you back." Rey sipped his beer.

Vaughn joined his friend on the sofa, abandoning his plans to find Allie and sneak in a hug or a quick kiss. He took a sip of his beer.

"It's been great reconnecting with you and your family," Vaughn said. "The other day, I visited my parents' gravesite for the first time since my mom was laid to rest there."

He'd stopped himself from adding that Allie had been standing beside him with her hand tucked in his and her head leaned against his shoulder. That her presence had infused him with her quiet strength and much-needed support.

There is such a thing as a lie of omission.

Vaughn tried to ignore the uneasiness in his gut.

"I hope it gave you some closure." Rey clapped a large hand on Vaughn's shoulder. "And I hope that being back here has been as beneficial for you as it has been for the town and for us."

Vaughn thought of his time with Allie at his cabin and their adventures exploring Shell Canyon together about an hour and a half away. "Being back home has been really good for me, too."

"Good. And look, I realize that my mother puts on the pressure for you to be here for dinner every week, but I know you have big plans for Sin & Glory. You can't make them happen when Mamá has you in the kitchen helping her and Allie slice plantain or clean collard greens." Rey chuckled, and Vaughn did, too. "Like I said, you're always welcome here. I just don't want you to feel obligated to stick around for us."

Rey was right. Vaughn had been focused on his songwriting and spending time with Allie and her family. Despite multiple nudges from Cherry and one from his agent, Vaughn hadn't pursued meetings with studio execs or taken the next steps in the search for a lead singer to replace Steven.

Had the choice been intentional? He wasn't sure. But thinking about everything he needed to do to set the album and a promotional tour in motion made his head spin and his chest ache. It was the very opposite of how he felt sheltered in the cocoon of family, friendship and deep affection that he was enjoying there in Willowvale Springs.

Vaughn had spent most of the evening chatting with Allie's brothers and her parents, entertaining her nieces and nephews, and playing a lively game of spades with Allie as his partner. She'd become his default partner for game night since every other adult in her family was either married or had a significant other. Later, they planned to watch a movie together—though they still hadn't settled on which one.

Vaughn relished the vibrancy of these Sunday night dinners filled with love and family. And he appreciated that Dianelys, Walter, and their extended family all seemed to go out of their way to make him feel like he was a part of it.

And despite being in a house overflowing with her family, he and Allie couldn't stop exchanging lingering glances and meaningful touches. They even managed to sneak in the occasional hug and kiss.

No, he definitely wasn't there out of a sense of obligation. He was there in Willowvale Springs and at the home of the Prices because he wanted to be. Because this place and the people in it had become his sanctuary.

"I know." Vaughn nodded. "But thank you for saying so."

Vaughn's phone buzzed in his pocket, despite being set to Do Not Disturb. Only three numbers were permitted through when his phone was set to that status: Cherry, his agent, and Allie. He was hoping it was Allie asking him to join her in the basement or the backyard for another quick kiss.

He pulled the phone from his pocket and his agent's face appeared. Vaughn sighed quietly. He held up his phone. "I should take this."

Vaughn excused himself and stepped into the kitchen, which was quiet for the moment—a rarity on these busy Sunday evenings. He put the call on speakerphone since he was alone.

"Hey, Hannah."

"Vaughn! There you are. I was beginning to think

that the rumors that you were retiring from the business were true," Hannah said, her voice raspy from years of smoking.

"I'm not retiring, Hannah," Vaughn assured her. "I've just been taking a little break to work on a very important project, spend some time in my hometown, get reacquainted with old friends. You know… have a life."

"A life, huh?" Hannah repeated the words as if they felt foreign on her tongue. "Oh, yes. I recall now. A life is that thing that *nonfamous* people get to have, sweetie. Famous badass rockers like you, Vaughn, have *careers*. Careers that require constant tending and watering. Which, of course, is why you have me," she concluded proudly.

Hannah wasn't wrong, so he didn't object.

"You know how much I love you and appreciate your relentless pursuit of my career, Hannah." Vaughn glanced around the kitchen, his impatience growing. "So I doubt that you called me on a Sunday evening to have your ego stroked. What's going on?"

"Well, since you asked so nicely…" Hannah chuckled bitterly. "My idea that you should start writing for other people is paying off *big time*. The nominations for the GRAMMY Awards are in and that power ballad you wrote for that pop princess was nominated for both pop song of the year and song of the year. So now what do you think about writing songs for 'baby artists'?" Hannah mocked his earlier complaint.

"You were right, as always." Vaughn grinned.

"That's really great news. Beckett's a good kid. I hope she wins."

"You mean you hope *we* win," Hannah corrected him. "After all, song of the year is a songwriter's award. The studio is throwing a fancy event for nominees this coming Saturday. I expect to see you there."

"I don't know, Hannah." Vaughn rubbed the back of his neck as he glanced around the space. "I'm kind of busy here. We'll be going into the next phase of the renovation of my resort soon. Besides, I'm not trying to poach Beckett's shine. She deserves this moment."

"And so do you," Hannah reminded him. "In fact, the head of Beckett's label called to personally extend you an invitation. He asked if you were still trying to make a Sin & Glory reunion happen, and I got the distinct feeling that they're open to financing the entire thing, so you won't need to rely on your little side hustle to fund the project."

"The wellness center is *not* just a side hustle." Vaughn dragged his hand through his hair, trying to remember that Hannah wasn't being intentionally insulting. She was a no-nonsense kind of woman, which is why he'd liked having her as his agent. She always gave him the news—good or bad—straight no chaser, the way he liked it. "But their interest in the band is intriguing. Maybe when the excitement of the nominations dies down they'll want to talk."

"Got a meeting for you with the head of the studio a couple days after the party!" Hannah squealed—which was unlike her—and it startled him.

"Great, thanks," he said. Though he wasn't sure how much he meant it. "I assume you'll be attending both events. So I guess I'll see you on Saturday night."

"Oh no," Hannah said. "We need time to work on our pitch, get you and your date fitted in designer clothing, work the promo circuit…you know the routine."

"Right." Vaughn heaved a quiet sigh. "What if I fly in on Thursday?"

"Make it Wednesday so we can get to work first thing Thursday morning," Hannah said, then made a kissing sound. "Congrats, sweetheart. You truly deserve this moment." She sounded like a proud mother for a moment, but then Hannah shifted back into cutthroat agent mode. "Now, let's milk it for everything it's worth and then some."

Vaughn couldn't help laughing. That was the Hannah he knew and loved. She could be as bristly as a cactus on the outside, but she always had his best interest—and the best interest of their collective bank account—in mind.

"I will. Thanks, Han. I'll see you on Thursday morning." Vaughn ended the call, still trying to process the fact that the song he'd written had been nominated for two Grammy awards. For some reason, this felt different from the songs he'd help write for Sin & Glory that had gone on to win awards. He felt good about the nomination and the studio exec's interest in producing a Sin & Glory reunion album. Still, he wasn't looking forward to leaving Allie to return to LA for what would probably be a week or more. Especially since he was already booked to spend two weeks in London immediately after that working with another young artist to write songs for their upcoming album.

"You won an award? This is so very exciting!" Vaughn turned to find Allie's mother hovering in the pantry.

"No, Mamá, I haven't won. At least not yet," Vaughn said. "A song I wrote for another artist was nominated for a couple of GRAMMY awards."

Mamá squealed almost as loudly as Hannah had, bringing half the family running. When they did, she turned to him, beaming. "Vaughn, you must tell them your good news."

Vaughn had wanted to share the news privately with Allie first and explain to her that he needed to return to LA for a week instead of spending the week before his trip to London with her as they'd planned. But Dianelys hadn't left him much of a choice.

"The song I wrote for Beckett…it was nominated for pop song of the year and song of the year," Vaughn shoved a hand into his pocket. As the entire family clamored excitedly, Vaughn turned to Dianelys and whispered, "Were you in the pantry the entire time I was on the phone?"

"I was organizing." She shrugged nonchalantly without making eye contact with him. "That is not the point. The point is that you need to return to LA to attend that fancy party and meet with those studio executives."

"What party? And what studio executives?" Allie demanded, one hip cocked. Her gaze shifting from his to her mother's. "And how is it that you know so much about this, Mamá?"

"I might have overheard him on the telephone," she admitted sheepishly. "But that is not the point," she repeated, seemingly annoyed that neither of them seemed to understand that.

Everyone congratulated him, hugging him and shaking his hand. Walter declared that this called for the good rum he kept in the cellar and more cake for the kiddos.

News of more cake made the children's mothers frown. Likely at the thought of dealing with their children's sugar rush right before bedtime when they had school the next day.

Before Vaughn and Allie could return to the dining room with everyone else, Mamá grabbed each of their wrists and held them back. She surveyed the space to ensure no one else was around. Then she whispered loudly, "Alejandra should go to California with you. She can be your date for this event."

Both Vaughn's and Allie's eyes widened.

"Date? Mamá, I told you—"

"Before you finish that sentence, princesa, I'm pretty sure it is a sin to lie to your mother." Dianelys narrowed her gaze and pointed at her daughter.

Allie snapped her mouth shut, then glanced back at the entry to the kitchen. "Mamá, I cannot just declare that I'm going to Cali to be Vaughn's date for this thing. Papá would have an absolute fit."

"If you say you are going there to be his date…
yes," Dianelys agreed. "But Vaughn has been saying for weeks that he wants to update his home in
LA with the thought of selling it, no? So Allie can go
there to assess the situation. Of course, you do not
have to hire her if you do not want to," her mother
added. "But your father certainly isn't going to turn
down a potential design contract of that magnitude, and it would give you an excuse to accom-
pany Vaughn to California."

Allie's mother folded her arms over her belly and
grinned proudly. "It's a good plan, no?"

"It's a brilliant plan." Vaughn turned to face her.
"That is…if Allie wants to go."

"A chance to finally see your place in person and
maybe tag along to a few Hollywood parties?" Allie
said. "Of course, I'd love to come."

"Perfecto." Allie's mother grinned, heading toward the door. She stopped and turned back to them.
"But maybe we don't mention this part of the plan
until the day before you leave."

"Everyone will be busy with the cake for a few
minutes." Her mother flashed them a knowing grin,
then disappeared from the kitchen.

"Your mom is a genius. We definitely don't tell
her that enough." Vaughn pulled Allie into his arms
and gave her a kiss. He released her reluctantly.

"Please don't tell her that. She'll be absolutely
insufferable." Allie grinned, slipping her hand into
his. A soft smile lit her gorgeous face. "And Mamá's
right. I'll bid out the job, but please don't feel any

obligation to hire me for it. I'm sure you'd prefer working with an established interior designer who's a household name in LA."

"I told you before, you'd be a hit in LA. This will give you the chance to see for yourself that you're more than ready for primetime." Vaughn kissed her again. "C'mon, we'd better head in there before your father sends out a search party."

Allie laughed, and they walked out of the kitchen and joined the rest of her smiling family, eager to celebrate Vaughn's latest accomplishment. Having Allie at his side and being surrounded by her family for such a pivotal moment in his life and career felt truly gratifying. And it pained him to think of ever leaving her or them behind again.

Twelve

The four days Allie had spent in LA with Vaughn had been absolute heaven. It had been her first time on a private plane and her first time in LA. She'd ridden through the streets of LA in the passenger seat of Vaughn's black Lamborghini Aventador. She was fascinated by everything from the palm trees synonymous with the town to the famous Hollywood Boulevard and Sunset Strip. They'd taken a short walk along the Hollywood Walk of Fame and had taken photos in front of the iconic Chinese Theater.

That first night, Vaughn had taken Allie on their first official date at Pace, a cozy Italian eatery with a warm, romantic vibe and impeccable service. He had the prime rib—grilled to perfection—and she had the Chilean sea bass. Both were delicious, as was their famous warm chocolate cake piled with whipped cream. It had been worth every bit of the wait. The wine and the overall ambiance had been perfect for what felt like such a special night. But what was most memorable about the evening was being on a proper date with Vaughn.

Allie hadn't realized just how badly she wanted a night like that with him. Or to be able to simply stroll down the sidewalk hand in hand or with his arm draped over her shoulder.

Vaughn was right. Whatever this was and for however long they were doing this, she didn't want to hide their relationship anymore. But it wasn't a conversation that should be had with her family over the phone. Nor did she want to potentially stress Vaughn out about it when he had so many other things on his mind.

Being nominated for his first solo songwriting award. Convincing the studio execs to finance Sin & Glory's comeback album and tour. The album he was working on with Extreme Overload. The trip he'd be taking to London to team up with a British singer to write her next album.

In the scheme of things, Allie being ready to tell her meddlesome but well-meaning family about them was small potatoes, and it could wait until he'd returned from London.

Now she stood in the main bedroom of Vaughn's gorgeous house in the Hollywood Hills that she'd fallen in love with the moment she'd seen it. It honestly broke her heart that he wanted to sell the place.

The contemporary architecture of the home was breathtaking, and the location provided stunning views of the ocean and LA Basin.

Allie looked out at the water and smiled softly.

She couldn't believe that she'd gotten to wake up to this view while wrapped in Vaughn's strong arms for the past three nights. It'd been like some crazy fever dream. A reality that exceeded any of the fantasies she'd had about being with Vaughn Reed. Except, in those fantasies, she and Vaughn would get their happily-ever-after.

Allie cared deeply for Vaughn. More so every single day. And she'd enjoyed spending time with him there in LA.

But while this glamorous world where one could encounter a movie star, sitcom actor, or rock legend at the local Starbucks was a great place for Allie to visit, it simply wasn't home. Yet, it was exactly where Vaughn belonged. More importantly, it was where he needed to be. He was staying in Willowvale Springs to be with her and with her family. She could see now that it was holding him back and stifling his career. She couldn't be the reason that his plans for Sin & Glory's comeback failed. Yet, the thought of ending something so beautiful broke her.

"Hey, sweetheart. Is everything okay?" Vaughn slipped his arms around her waist as he stood behind her staring at their reflections in the glass. He placed a gentle kiss on her neck. Vaughn had shaved his beard two days earlier. The stubble tickled her skin. "You aren't nervous about tonight, are you?

Because you look stunning, and you're gonna knock 'em dead."

Allie turned around and wrapped her arms around his waist beneath his black tuxedo jacket so she wouldn't wrinkle it.

"Thank you." She pressed a quick kiss to his lips, thankful the makeup artist had selected a non-transferable coral lip stain. "You clean up pretty nice yourself."

Vaughn looked incredibly handsome in the graphite-colored tuxedo jacket with gleaming, silver thread running through the fabric. The black, satin lapels of his jacket were affixed with a collection of silver pins. A burgundy shirt provided an unexpected splash of color. His hair had been trimmed and was worn loose and straight.

"And it only took an army of stylists to make it happen." Vaughn chuckled, then glanced around the room which was quiet again after it had been brimming with people for the past several hours. The same people who were waiting impatiently for them to emerge so they could see them off to the GRAMMYs and get lots of pics to share on their respective social media sites. "It's nice to at least have this room to ourselves again. But I can't wait to get you back here and out of that gorgeous dress once they're all gone."

A deep smile made her cheeks hurt. "Clearly, it pays to know people in high places."

Allie had no shortage of formal dresses. From bridesmaids' dresses to evening gowns worn to the quinceañeras of younger family members. But the dress she was wearing tonight was more than she could have ever expected. The café-au-lait-colored gown covered in hand-stitched, gold-sequined appliqués had a crisscross back and cutouts on either side of her waist.

Getting to wear the gorgeous loaner dress created by up-and-coming Afro-Latina designer Porsha Sanchez, whom Allie had gotten to meet, and having her hair and makeup done by legends in the business was like being in a surreal fairy tale. And later, she'd get to walk the red carpet on Vaughn's arm.

"You hungry?" Vaughn asked. "Because it's going to be a long night. I suggest you slip a few snack bars in that tiny purse of yours." He indicated the matching sequin clutch Porsha had gifted her.

They'd begun the day with a tremendous brunch at Chateau Marmont and she was still full.

"I can wait until dinner." Allie picked up her bag and took Vaughn's hand.

Vaughn put his hand on the doorknob, then stopped. He opened his mouth, but no words came out. Perhaps, he was more nervous about the pressure of the night than he was letting on.

"Hey, this isn't the actual award ceremony," Allie reminded him, hoping it would ease Vaughn's tension. "It's a party to celebrate the nominees, which has already netted you a meeting with studio execs. "Everything is going to be fine." She ran a hand down his chest, then kissed him. "So relax, okay?"

* * *

Vaughn forced a big smile and shook hands with yet another studio exec Hannah had introduced him to. He nodded along and tried his best to follow the conversation. But his attention kept drifting to the other side of the room where Allie was chatting with the partners and girlfriends of a few other industry guests. She was all smiles and looked gorgeous in her designer gown.

It had been adorable seeing the excitement on Allie's face as she encountered one celebrity or another and the way her wide eyes had lit up as they'd visited LA landmarks like the Hollywood sign, Griffith Park and the observatory.

Allie's genuine elation reminded him of how wide-eyed and naive he'd been when he'd first arrived in LA. He'd had a few rough years, but through a lot of hard work, a massive amount of determination and a little luck, eventually he'd made it to the top of his game. He'd done it before, and he could do it again. This time, with Sin & Glory's name and reputation behind him. But as he stood in the room filled with a who's who of the industry the hunger he'd once felt no longer seemed to be there. Instead, his only concern was when he could grab Allie's hand, make their way to the limo and retreat to his bed again.

This time, he would say the words that had gotten stuck in his throat earlier that afternoon. That he was in love with Allie, and he wanted more from this than a series of clandestine hookups. The realization had hit him the previous evening. He wanted to be able to take Allie out and spoil her as he had there in LA. And he'd wanted to be able to pull Allie onto his lap and kiss her at her parents' house as her brothers often did with their significant others.

Vaughn hated that he wouldn't be able to attend Sunday dinner at the Prices' home for the next few weeks.

And he missed the peace and solitude, fresh mountain air, and slower pace of life in Willowvale Springs where there was no traffic, smog, or relentless paparazzi.

He'd found creative inspiration again in his hometown. Or maybe he'd found it in the woman across the room who was wearing the hell out of that dress and smiling at him seductively. The festivities had yet to begin in earnest and he'd been toying with the idea of grabbing her by the hand, grabbing a to-go bag from his favorite greasy spoon dive eatery, and whisking her back to his place so he could spend the remainder of the evening worshipping every ounce of her golden-brown skin.

Hannah's pointy elbow brought him back to the conversation as one of the record execs gushed over his favorite Sin & Glory songs. Vaughn thanked the man and tried to get back into the right headspace for the evening. But as he tried to connect with the two men who might hold his band's future in the palm of their hands, Vaughn wasn't so sure that a future with Sin & Glory was what he wanted anymore.

Thirteen

Industry events like this one always felt interminably long. But tonight's event felt especially so. This was Vaughn's final night in LA with Allie before he put her on a plane headed back to Wyoming. Then, after his meeting with the execs, he would board a flight for London. So he didn't want to waste a moment of their remaining time together.

He'd ducked Hannah—who was probably still looking for him—and grabbed Allie's hand when she exited the ladies' room.

He escorted her to a quiet corner at the end of the hallway, pulled her into his arms and kissed her.

"And what did I do to deserve that?" Allie gazed up at him with the sweetest expression.

His heart thudded in his chest, the words, *I'm in love with you, Allie*, caught at the back of his throat.

"I just wanted to thank you for being here with me," Vaughn managed instead. He kissed her again. "Having you here means the world to me. But we only have a few hours left, and I'd much rather spend them back at my place, memorizing every inch of your skin and showing you how desperately I need you.

Allie's eyelashes fluttered. She sank her teeth into her lush, lower lip. "Sounds like a damn good plan. Let's go." She slipped her hand into his and they turned to leave.

A familiar figure slumped against the wall outside the bathroom. It was his friend, Liza Jaymes. Last he'd seen her, she'd looked amazing. But tonight, she looked...*rough*. Her eyes were red; her lipstick and mascara smudged.

"Liza?" Vaughn stopped. "What are you doing here?"

"Getting dumped, apparently." Liza laughed bitterly.

Vaughn dragged a hand through his hair and heaved a quiet sigh. Why had Liza chosen tonight, of all nights, to get completely trashed?

He turned to Allie and lowered his voice. "Al, this is an old friend of mine—"

"Liza Jaymes." Allie flashed a polite smile. "You two dated before you and Eva got together. But she's had a rough decade or so."

Vaughn raised an eyebrow. Allie always maintained that she'd been a big Sin & Glory fan. He just hadn't realized that she'd been versed on his complete dating life.

"What? The relationship was covered in all the celebrity magazines back then," Allie whispered. "I know you worked together recently, but I didn't realize you two were still friends."

"We've kept in touch over the years. That's why she asked me to sit in during her set here in LA a few weeks ago." Vaughn turned his back to Liza and lowered his voice so only Allie could hear him. "She looked and sounded amazing that night."

"Hi, I'm Liza."

They both turned to her and she waved, a giddy expression on her face.

"I got dumped tonight by a complete asshole." Liza pushed her signature wild, red hair away from her face. "He was supposed to help me rebuild my career but apparently, he's been promising that to a *lot* of second-rate, has-been artists." Liza's big, brown eyes filled with tears.

Vaughn squeezed Allie's hand. An unspoken apology for their plans going off the rails. With his free hand, he squeezed Liza's arm. "You are *not* a second-rate artist, Lize. You just need the right opportunity."

"That's really kind of you to say, Vaughn." Liza sniffled and placed a hand over his. She offered him a watery smile before turning her attention to the woman at his side. "And you must be… Allie. Vaughn told me all about you when he played my show. I'm pretty sure he loves you, but…shh…" She held a finger up to her mouth and whispered conspiratorially. "I'm not sure he knows it yet."

"Is that right?" Allie shifted her amused gaze to Vaughn momentarily before returning her attention to Liza. "Well, Vaughn couldn't stop talking about how amazing your sold-out shows were. He's excited for the music you'll make next, and so am I."

"He is?" Liza seemed happy about the compliment, but suddenly her expression crumbled, and tears slid down her cheeks. "Vaughn has always believed in me. But I'm always disappointing him, aren't I?"

"You aren't disappointing me, Liza," Vaughn said gently. "I just want you to be healthy and happy. You were in such a good place when I saw you a few weeks ago. But tonight—"

"God, I'm a mess," Liza blurted, then ducked through the bathroom door that swung open when another patron exited.

"Fuck, I'm so sorry about this, babe." Vaughn turned to Allie. "I wanted you to have an amazing night and—"

"I have," she assured him, wrapping her arms around his waist. "Encountering your inebriated ex doesn't change that. But what are you going to do now? You can't just leave her like this."

"I know." Vaughn groaned, rubbing his chin. "I wish I could whisk you away to the limo, take you back to my place, and finish what we started this morning. But if something happened to Lize, I'd never forgive myself."

"No, you wouldn't." Allie touched his cheek and smiled. "Because you're a genuinely good guy, Vaughn Reed." She lifted onto her toes and kissed him. "Go take care of your friend. I can find my way back to your house, and I remember the key code."

"Good. But you take the limo. I'll let Simon know that you'll be out front in ten minutes. I'll get back to the house as soon as I can." Vaughn pulled out his phone and shot off a quick text message to his limo driver.

Liza reemerged from the bathroom and leaned heavily against the wall before Vaughn could ask Allie to go in and check on her.

It looked like Liza was about to slide down the wall.

"It's okay, babe. I understand, and I'll be waiting for you," Allie squeezed his hand. "And if I see Hannah, I'll tell her something important came up and you had to leave."

Hannah. Crap. He'd completely forgotten about her.

"Thanks." Vaughn pulled Allie into his arms and kissed her long and hard before finally letting her go.

Vaughn called a car service, then he looped an arm around Liza's waist and guided her out of the hotel, trying to keep as low a profile as possible. They made their way to a coffee shop just up the road where he'd asked the car service to meet him. Vaughn bought a couple of bottles of water and a huge cup of black coffee.

They got in the car and began the drive to Liza's

townhouse in Studio City. He was worried about his old friend and would ensure that she made it home okay. But he couldn't stop thinking about Allie and what Liza had said about him. *I'm pretty sure he loves you, but I'm not sure he knows yet.*

Even drunk, Liza was perceptive. But she was only half right. Because Vaughn had become increasingly clear on his feelings for Allie. He just needed to find the right time to tell her how he felt. He only hoped that Allie could see a future for them, too.

Allie had tried her best to stay up and wait for Vaughn while watching movies. But when he'd called at 2:00 a.m. to say he'd be at least another hour, she'd tapped out and had fallen asleep. But she felt a kiss against her temple, smelled Vaughn's familiar scent and felt his beard scrape her skin.

"Hey, you're back," Allie muttered into the pillow, barely able to raise her head. "Is your friend okay?"

"I choose to believe that she will be." Vaughn pulled Allie into his arms and kissed the top of her head. "Thank you for being so understanding. Not many people would be, given our history."

Allie studied Vaughn's handsome face. She could see the concern for both his friend and for her feelings. The more she got to know Vaughn, the more thoughtful she realized he was. They lay on their sides facing each other and she cupped his cheek.

"You've never given me a reason not to trust you, Vaughn." She kissed him.

Vaughn ran his fingers through her hair, which

she'd released from the low bun she'd worn along with an expensive, jeweled barrette. Then he caressed her cheek with his thumb. "And I love you, Allie."

She smiled, her heart full and butterflies fluttering in her belly. Allie wanted so badly to tell Vaughn that she loved him, too. But part of her worried that she was rushing into this. That this was just the grown-up version of her teenage crush. That even if the two of them had fallen in love it couldn't survive the distance and their wildly different lives.

"Vaughn, I love the relationship we've been building and every moment we've spent together. But what about your life here?"

He drew in a quiet breath, as if it was a barrier he'd been considering, too. "You've had a good time in LA, right? You could move here. I'd even help you set up your own interior design practice if that's what you want," Vaughn said.

Allie sat up. "You're serious?"

Vaughn sat up in bed, too. "I am."

"LA is a fun place to visit. But my life…my family, my friends…they're all back in Willowvale Springs," she said gently as she threaded their fingers.

"Then I'll move to Willowvale Springs."

She was moved that he was willing to make such a big sacrifice for her. But she couldn't be the reason Vaughn gave up his dream of reuniting the band and traveling the world making the music that he loved.

"What about your songwriting, your session work,

and your plans to reunite the band? How will any of that work if you move back home?"

Vaughn sighed heavily but didn't answer.

Did his heart ache as badly as hers did at the realization that there was no good solution to their dilemma?

Allie forced a smile, though her heart was broken knowing that one day soon this fairytale would come to a painful and abrupt end.

"We only have a few hours until my flight. Let's not spend it mourning what we can't have. Let's focus on the moments we have left together before I return home and you go off to London."

"Then maybe reconsider coming to London with me?" Vaughn cupped her cheek.

She honestly wished she could. But it made her heart swell and her tummy flutter knowing that he wanted her to be there with him.

"I can't, babe." Allie kissed his palm and forced a smile. "But when you return to Willowvale Springs, if you still feel this way, we'll talk more about it. Okay?"

"Okay," he agreed reluctantly.

"Good." Allie forced a broad smile, despite her heart breaking. "Now, I think I remember you promising a night I'd never forget."

Allie sank beneath the covers, laughing, and Vaughn joined her. But as they made love a little voice in the back of her head couldn't help wondering if they'd ever be together like this again.

Fourteen

Allie had been back in Willowvale Springs for more than a week, and she missed Vaughn desperately. They'd spoken at least once each day. But because of the seven-hour time difference, they usually messaged each other. And despite having no clue how they were going to work things out, she couldn't wait for him to return. She missed having him there with her and waking up in his arms each morning.

Allie walked through the cabin she and Vaughn had been sharing the past few weeks. She'd wanted to surprise him. So she'd instructed her crew to begin updating it the day they left town. They'd sanded and polyurethaned the floors, repainted the walls, replaced the appliances and laid new carpeting in the bedrooms. The old furniture had been removed and the new furniture was being delivered that afternoon. She'd placed markers where each of the items should go to make the furniture delivery quick and efficient.

"My goodness. This looks like an entirely new place. Hank and Edith wouldn't believe what y'all have done with this old cabin." Barbara stood in the open doorway, marveling at the fresh new paint job and refinished flooring.

"And do you like it?" Allie couldn't help being a bit nervous about Ms. Barb's reaction to the more contemporary colors and decor.

"Like it? Sugar, I love it. You've truly outdone yourself on this project, Allie. The main building is absolutely stunning. With just some simple changes, you've completely transformed this cabin. This place is going to be booked all the time."

"That's certainly my hope." Allie smiled, glancing around the space.

Allie's phone buzzed in her pants pocket. She pulled the phone out and looked at the text. It was from Rey.

Urgent. Come to Mom and Dad's place. NOW.

Panic shot through Allie. She typed out a quick response.

Are they both okay?

Allie's heart raced as the three dots went into motion right away.

Physically? They're fine. But we need to talk. Let's save the questions for in-person.

Now that she knew her parents were okay she was irritated with her brother's tone.

"Everything okay, hon?"

She'd practically forgotten that Barb was there.

"I think so," Allie said. "But I have an important meeting to attend. I was hoping the furniture would've been delivered by now. I need to leave for an hour or so. Do you think you could—"

"Say no more. I'm on it." Barb waved a hand and grinned. "You go ahead and take care of whatever it is that you need to. I'll make sure everything is placed just where you want it."

"Thanks, Ms. Barb. You're a lifesaver. And please, examine each piece before they bring it in. Make sure there are no cuts, no marks and no funny odors. You'd be surprised how hard it is to get them to take away a damaged piece once you let them bring it inside."

"Yes, ma'am. Will do." Barb saluted as if they'd just exchanged sentinel duty. "And I'll lock the place up when they're done"

"Thanks, Ms. Barb." Allie hugged the older woman, then made her way to her car and drove to her parents' house hoping everything was okay.

"Mamá! Papá!" Allie called as she walked through her parents' house.

In the kitchen, her mother had been in the midst

of peeling potatoes and cutting up vegetables, but it looked as if she'd suddenly abandoned the task.

She walked into the den and her parents were seated on the sofa, her father comforting her mother who dabbed tears from her eyes.

"¿Qué pasa, Mamá?" Allie hurried to her mother's side and held the hand her mother wasn't using to dab her face with a tattered napkin.

"I thought that Vaughn was tu novio, princesa." Her mother sniffled.

Every muscle in Allie's body stiffened. She glanced around the room at her father and brother, who both seemed angry.

What the hell is going on?

"I never said Vaughn was my boyfriend, Mamá. In fact, I've always maintained that Vaughn and I were just friends," Allie said carefully. "But why does it matter?"

"This is why." Her mother produced folded, wrinkled pieces of paper and handed them to her.

Mamá had printed what looked like a webpage from a gossip blog. The headline read: *Sin & Glory's Bad Boy Drummer Is Up to His Same Old Tricks*. The story had what were undoubtedly paparazzi photos of Vaughn with various women.

Him hugging Liza Jaymes on stage at her show. Vaughn carrying Liza into her town house. Vaughn "creeping out of" Liza's place hours later. Red carpet photos of Vaughn and Beckett. Photos of Vaughn and Allie on the red carpet and candid shots of them stealing kisses later in the evening. A photo

of Vaughn and the young British singer he was writing an album with boarding the plane for 'a long,
cozy flight to London.'

Allie's heart thumped inside her chest, her pulse
was racing, and her face and chest were hot with
embarrassment. It felt like she was back to that day
when her mother read the engagement announce-
ments only to discover that her 'boyfriend' of two
years had gotten engaged to someone else who was
much older and much wealthier.

She closed her eyes and heaved a quiet sigh, then
handed the pages back to her mother. "No puedes
creer todo lo que lees, mamá."

"I do not believe everything I read," her mother
protested angrily. "But I do believe what my own
eyes see, Alejandra. I would never have suggested
you go to LA with Vaughn if I knew that he was not
exclusively committed to you, princesa."

"This isn't what you think, Mamá." Allie shot to
her feet and paced the floor.

"Well, explain it to us, baby girl," her father finally
spoke through gritted teeth. "Because this doesn't
look good." He gestured to the wrinkled pieces of
paper in her mother's hands. "This article makes it
seem like—"

"Vaughn is taking advantage of my sister and
the kindness and generosity our family has always
shown to him." Rey's tone dripped with outrage.
"What were you thinking, Alejandra? Vaughn is a
business client. We do *not* date clients."

"Don't yell at your sister." Her mother sniffled.

"Felix is literally dating a former client's daughter, and they started seeing each other *during* the project!" Allie yelled back, then took a breath and sighed. "And Vaughn isn't just a client. He's a friend."

"Yes, *my* friend." Rey slapped his chest. "Not yours. Besides, he's too old for you."

"It's nine years, Rey. Which was a big deal when I was ten. But not now that I'm thirty. You're six years older than your wife. And no one batted a single eyelash about that," Allie noted. "So you can stop it with the double standard bullshit."

"Alejandra!" her parents both said.

She folded her arms and cocked a hip.

"Dammit, Al. Why must you always be so stubborn? We're only trying to protect you. And when you don't listen, look at what happens," Rey said.

"I'm a freaking adult, Reynaldo Price. I don't *have* to listen to any of you." Allie gestured to all three of them, and her parents' eyes widened and they both looked insulted.

"I realize that in this context the photos look quite damning. But this isn't a news article. It's gossip and lies. Vaughn would never behave as they're implying he has."

"So you two *are* seeing each other." There was disappointment in her father's voice.

"Yes," Allie admitted. "Vaughn thought we should tell all of you, but I asked him not to."

"Why, princesa?" Her mother sounded truly hurt, and guilt churned in Allie's gut.

She sank onto the sofa opposite her parents. "Papá

and the boys already watch my every move and treat me like a child."

"So to prove that you're not a child, you behave as one, hiding your relationship with Vaughn rather than being honest about it?" Her father hiked one of his furry eyebrows as he tapped the edge of the sofa.

Yikes. Point for Dad.

She didn't have a good response for that one, so she didn't even attempt it.

"Vaughn isn't staying, Dad. I figured that if you all knew about us it would upset you and Rey for nothing and Mamá would needlessly get her hopes up."

"Translation: the two of you were just hooking up, so you didn't want the rest of us to know about it." Rey rubbed his jaw.

Allie glared at her brother but decided against throwing a shoe at him. She ignored him instead.

"Like I said…each of these photos is quite innocent." She moved to the other side of the room and took the paper from her mother. "Here Vaughn is congratulating a friend on a great performance. Here, he's escorting that same friend home when she got drunk after getting dumped rather cruelly—which I happen to think was quite admirable of him. The photos of us are self-explanatory." She quickly cleared her throat. "This is Diva Divine—the British R&B singer Vaughn is collaborating with to write songs for her next album. She was one of the *ten* passengers on that private flight to London."

Allie handed the pages back to her mother.

"I'm disappointed that you all would believe this

of Vaughn. The man adores this family. That's why he was so reluctant to give in when *I* pursued *him*," she said. "He was worried about losing your friendship—" she nodded toward Rey "—and he didn't want to disappoint either of you and risk his place at your dinner table." She gestured toward her parents. "Because we're the only family he has left."

Allie glared at the three of them, none of them meeting her gaze.

"Too bad none of you hold him in the same regard. Because he would never have thought the worst of any of you." Allie huffed. "I need to go. We're putting the finishing touches on Vaughn's cabin this week."

"You mean your little hookup shack," Rey said.

Allie was beyond caring what any of them thought at the moment.

"You wanna call it that? *Fine.* But it beats your old hookup spot—the bed of your old pickup truck—any day of the week." Allie glared at her brother.

Rey's face flushed as their mother stared at him with widened eyes and their father frowned at him.

Her father cleared his throat. "Allie, Rafi's project is winding down. Maybe it would be better if—"

"*No*, Papá," she said firmly. "I plan to see this project through from start to finish, and I need to go back to it." She kissed her parents' cheeks, then glared at her brother again on her way out of the den.

Allie got in her car and drove back toward the resort.

She'd fiercely defended Vaughn, and she believed

every word that she'd said to them. But as she sat in the quiet of her thoughts, the pain and humiliation of the words of that blog post, which would likely get picked up on lots of gossip shows, burned her chest and made her eyes sting.

What that post had intimated about Vaughn's relationship with those other women might not have been true. But now that the accusation was out in the world, people would always regard her as the poor little pathetic girl who "thought she was special."

Vaughn hadn't done anything wrong. Yet, she'd ended up humiliated and fodder for the gossip circuit. She loved Vaughn, even if she hadn't been ready to tell him so that day. But if this was what she'd have to endure for them to be together…was it worth it?

Allie wiped the warm tears from her cheeks and sniffled. She needed some time and space to figure that out.

Vaughn stepped out of the London studio after seeing a 9-1-1 message from Cherry. He called his assistant as quickly as he could.

"Hey, Cherry. What's going on? Is everything okay?"

"No, I'm afraid it isn't. Have you been looking at the Google alerts I set up for your name?"

"No. Sorry." Vaughn stretched, his neck, shoulders and back stiff from long hours seated in the studio. "We've been going hard at this for the past week. In fact, we're pretty close to being done," he said. "Why? Is there something I should see?"

"Yes," she said after a long pause.

His phone dinged with another text message from Cherry. When he clicked on the link she'd sent, his blood started to boil.

"Shit! Have any other networks or podcasts picked up this story?"

Another pause. "I'm afraid so, Vaughn. I've already contacted Hannah about getting the PR team on it, but she thinks it's best to just let a story like this peter out on its own. You know Hannah's philosophy. All PR is good PR."

"And you know mine, Cherry. Especially when these lies are hurting the person I love," he said without hesitation.

"I do." There was a softness in Cherry's voice. "That's why I drew up a response for you to review. I just sent it to your email address. Review it. Tweak it. Scrap it and write your own. Whatever works for you."

"Thank you, Cherry," he said. "I need to call Allie before she sees this."

"It might already be too late for that," she said. "But may I suggest that before you put out this denial you check with Allie first. If she's seen this, I can only imagine how distressed she must be feeling, whether she believes it or not. When something like this happens, you feel powerless. So maybe let her have a say in how you respond to it. She might also prefer that we let this story die out rather than putting her at the center of it and garnering more press."

He heaved a sigh. "You're right. Let's not do anything until I speak with Allie." Vaughn ended the call and dialed Allie's number. But the call rolled over to voice mail. He called again and the call went to voice mail immediately. Vaughn sent a text message.

Sweetheart, I just saw that blog post. You know none of that is true, right?

Three dots indicated that Allie was typing. But they started and stopped several times with no response coming through.

Vaughn paced the hallway outside of the studio as he awaited Allie's response. Finally, her two-word response came.

I know.

There was more typing.

My mother saw it first. I explained about the photos, but it's a lot for everyone to process. I just need a little time and space. We'll talk when you're back in town.

Vaughn swallowed hard, his chest aching. His gut told him that Allie wanted to end things, but that she had the decency to want to end it to his face. But if there was even the smallest chance in hell that he could convince Allie that he loved her and wanted to be with her, he had to take it.

Fifteen

Vaughn had barely put his rental car in Park beside Allie's car in the cabin's short drive before turning off the engine and hopping out. He jogged up the front steps and made his way inside.

His gaze swept the space, his heart thumping furiously. She wasn't there. But when he sucked in a deep breath, Allie's subtle, sweet, signature scent tickled his nostrils.

"Allie, babe, are you here?" Vaughn called out, but there was no answer.

He froze, listening carefully. A soft smile curved his mouth as Allie belted out the chorus to "With You or Without You" in that awful singing voice that he'd come to adore.

His heart swelled. Because even in a moment

when this woman was probably furious with him, she'd resorted to singing a song he'd written and on which his drum play loomed large right alongside Beckett's vocals.

Vaughn made his way into the bedroom where Allie was wearing her AirPods and singing her heart out as she placed pillows on the brand-new bed. He glanced around the space. The entire room was freshly painted and had new decor. He'd been so focused on seeing Allie, he'd hardly noticed any of it. And with her headset on and the music blasting, she obviously hadn't heard him, either.

He placed a gentle hand on Allie's shoulder and she nearly jumped out of her skin, then immediately went into a karate stance that would've made Bruce Lee proud.

"It's just me, sweetheart." Vaughn held up his palms.

"Don't ever sneak up on me like that! You nearly got kneed in the nuts just now." Allie ripped the earphones from her ears, her hands shaking slightly. She shoved the AirPods into the pockets of her gray, plaid skirt and stared at him

"What are you doing here? You're supposed to be in London."

"I called you, but you couldn't hear me," he said. "And as for why I'm not in London… You wanted to talk in person instead of over the phone, so I'm here."

"You flew all the way to Wyoming in the middle of writing Diva Divine's next album?" she asked incredulously.

Dear Reader,

Your opinions are important to us. So if you'll participate in our fast and free "One Minute" Survey, YOU can pick up to four wonderful books that WE pay for when you try the Harlequin Reader Service!

As a leading publisher of women's fiction, we'd love to hear from you. That's why we promise to reward you for completing our survey.

IMPORTANT: Please complete the survey and return it. We'll send your Free Books and a Free Mystery Gift right away. And we pay for shipping and handling too! ← *We pay for EVERYTHING!*

Try **Harlequin® Desire** and get 2 books featuring the worlds of the American elite with juicy plot twists, delicious sensuality and intriguing scandal.

Try **Harlequin Presents® Larger-Print** and get 2 books featuring the glamourous lives of royals and billionaires in a world of exotic locations, where passion knows no bounds.

Or TRY BOTH!

Thank you again for participating in our "One Minute" Survey. It really takes just a minute (or less) to complete the survey… and your free books and gift will be well worth it!

If you continue with your subscription, you can look forward to curated monthly shipments of brand-new books from your selected series, always at a discount off the cover price! Plus you can cancel any time. So don't miss out, return your One Minute Survey today to get your Free books.

Pam Powers

"One Minute" Survey

GET YOUR FREE BOOKS AND A FREE GIFT!
✓ Complete this Survey ✓ Return this survey

1 Do you try to find time to read every day?
☐ YES ☐ NO

2 Do you prefer stories with happy endings?
☐ YES ☐ NO

3 Do you enjoy having books delivered to your home?
☐ YES ☐ NO

4 Do you share your favorite books with friends?
☐ YES ☐ NO

YES! I have completed the above "One Minute" Survey. Please send me r Free Books and a Free Mystery Gift (worth over $20 retail). I understand that I a under no obligation to buy anything, as explained on the back of this card.

☐ **Harlequin Desire®**
225/326 CTI G2AF

☐ **Harlequin Presents® Larger-Print**
176/376 CTI G2AF

☐ **BOTH**
(225/326 & 176/376)
CTI G2AG

FIRST NAME

LAST NAME

ADDRESS

APT.#

CITY

STATE/PROV.

ZIP/POSTAL CODE

EMAIL ☐ Please check this box if you would like to receive newsletters and promotional emails from Harlequin Enterprises ULC and its affiliates. You can unsubscribe anytime.

HD/HP-1123-OM

"I needed to make sure you knew that story isn't true. I would never treat you that way, sweetheart." He took a tentative step closer.

"I know." Allie's perfectly arched brows furrowed as she dropped her gaze.

"Then why wouldn't you talk to me?" Vaughn was genuinely confused by Allie's response. He gently lifted her chin, forcing her gaze to meet his. "Babe, I've been worried sick about you."

"I didn't mean to worry you, Vaughn. I just..." Allie heaved a quiet sigh and frowned deeply. "This whole ordeal has been so heart-wrenching and humiliating. I hadn't even had a chance to tell my family about us. That's my fault, I know," she added. "But having the story come out that way... It was awful. Every single person in town knew and had some opinion. I needed some space. A chance to pretend none of it was really happening."

Allie slid out of Vaughn's grip and his gut knotted.

He felt like he was losing her. The warmth and light that had emanated from her every pore seemed dim. Her eyes were filled with a pain Vaughn would do *anything* to take away. She'd done nothing but bring love and joy into his life, and he repaid her with humiliation and anguish.

"Sweetheart, I'm so sorry." His throat clogged with emotion. "I would never do anything to hurt you. I should've seen this coming. I should've known that—"

"There's no way you could've known that the paparazzi was cooking this story up, Vaughn. She squeezed his arm. A comforting touch despite her own pain. "And I know you didn't do what that article intimated. That you have no desire to get back with your ex. Still…"

Allie's eyes became watery and her frown deepened. But when he reached for her, she turned her back to him, walking a few paces away. The heels of her knee-high boots clicked against the beautifully refinished wood floor.

Vaughn wanted to take Allie into his arms and convince her of how truly sorry he was that this had happened. That he'd have done anything to prevent this ordeal. To tell her that his publicist had already issued a statement denying the lies in the article. That he loved her. But Allie clearly needed the space to express her feelings about what had happened.

He wouldn't deny her that.

Vaughn held onto the gold sun and moon pendant hanging around his neck that was all he had left of his birth parents. He'd always hoped it would bring him the unparalleled love it brought them but none of the tragedy and pain.

Allie finally turned to face him. She tipped her chin and looked him squarely in the eye.

"We've always known this relationship would end sooner than later, Vaughn." Allie shrugged. "The first phase of the renovations is complete." She gestured toward the space around them. "It feels like a good place to end things, you know?"

"No, baby, I don't." Vaughn took a few steps forward and gently gripped her elbow, his eyes stinging at the thought of losing her. Hers were filled with unshed tears, which only made his heart ache more. "I thought things were good between us. Would I have invited you to come to London with me if I felt otherwise?"

"I know. I did, too. I was on Cloud 9 the entire time we were in LA. And I'd been walking around here grinning like an idiot because I was so incredibly happy." She laughed bitterly. "Then… BAM. Everything blew up." Allie swiped a finger of her free hand beneath her eyes and sniffled. She cleared her throat and then flashed a pained smile. "I don't blame you for any of this Vaughn. But it gave me a glimpse of what publicly dating you would be like. I don't think I'm strong enough to handle that."

"Alejandra Price…" He used the perfect pronunciation of her name—rolling the *R* on his tongue like she'd taught him those nights they'd lain together in the bed just a few steps away. "You are one of the strongest, most confident women I have ever known." Vaughn's voice wavered slightly. "So don't tell me you can't handle it. Tell me you don't want to."

He dropped his hand from her elbow and raked his fingers against his scalp in frustration.

"You have every right to feel that way, Allie. But unfortunately, in this business, even the most beloved celebrity couples have to endure the lies and the bullshit—no matter how solid their relationships are. No matter how adored they are. And there's nothing I can do that will change that. I don't want this to end. But I won't lie to you either, sweetheart. I can only promise you that I will always be honest with you and that I will always love you, Allie."

Her gaze shot to his. She swallowed hard. "I believe that you have feelings for me, Vaughn. But I need you to be honest with me and with yourself about whether you're in love with me or with my family."

Allie's shoulders were tense as her dark eyes carefully assessed him. He hated that she'd felt the need to ask, but he could understand why.

"Easiest question ever. Both." Vaughn laughed when Allie's eyes widened with confusion. He pulled her into his arms and stared down at her. "I know it sounds like I'm evading your question, but it's true. I've loved your family since I was a kid. I used to dream of being a Price. But Allie, sweetheart, this—" he gestured between them "—isn't about my admiration for your family. It's about the brilliant, funny, badass woman who captured my heart. Baby, I do love your family. But if I had to choose between you and them, I would choose you…every single time. Maybe that seems impossible because it's only been a couple of months. But what I feel for you, Allie…"

Vaughn smiled, his chest bursting with all of the emotions he was feeling at that moment.

"I've never felt this kind of deep connection and frantic need for anyone. I know you probably don't believe that—"

"I do, Vaughn. Because I'm in love with you, too."

A sad smile lifted the corners of her mouth. Tears slid down Allie's cheeks. She swiped angrily at them. "But there are so many other factors to consider. Your life is in LA. Your career takes you all over the world. And I love that for you. But my life and career are here in Willowvale Springs. I can't give up the place and the people who mean so much to me."

"I'd never ask you to give up all of the things that make you *you*, Allie." Vaughn cradled her damp cheek and smiled. His heart leaped with joy at the possibility that the two of them could move forward. That Allie just might be willing to give this a chance. "I'll stay here in Willowvale Springs and sell my place in LA."

"You can't do that." Allie pressed her hands to his chest as she gazed up at him sincerely. "You're far too talented a drummer and a songwriter to give up everything you worked so hard for. Then there's your dream of reuniting Sin & Glory… You're so close to having everything you've ever wanted again, especially with all the attention your recent nomination is garnering. You can't give that up."

"But I wouldn't have you." Vaughn stroked Allie's cheek. "And for you, sweetheart, I'd give up the house in LA, the car, the reunion with the band."

"You'd be miserable," she protested. "Eventually, you'd regret giving up the things you've worked so hard for. You'd resent me for making you choose between everything you've ever wanted and me."

"What I have always wanted, Allie, is to feel like I truly belonged. To have the love and sense of family

I've been chasing since my birth parents died. To be with someone who would be a true partner in love and in life. And baby, I believe with everything in my heart that I've finally found that in you."

Vaughn stared into the depths of Allie's shimmering, dark eyes, hoping she felt the same.

Allie could barely speak. In fact, she could barely breathe. First, Vaughn had flown in from London just to make sure she was okay. Then he'd confessed his love for her, prompting her to admit that she felt the same. But now, Vaughn was actually willing to give up life in LA and his dream of reuniting the band just to be with her?

After years of fantasizing about Vaughn falling for her and them finding their happily-ever-after… was it possible that she would get just that?

None of it felt real.

Allie was sure she was in some fever dream. Any minute now, she'd awaken to discover she'd gotten lost in some all too real fantasy like Dorothy in *The Wizard of Oz* or Alice in *Alice in Wonderland*.

Vaughn kissed her, his hands gliding around her waist as he pulled her closer, heat building between them.

Finally, she broke their kiss, taking a step back. Her head was spinning, and butterflies fluttered in her belly.

"Vaughn, you're not serious," she said, finally.

"I am." He threaded their fingers and led her over to the bed where they both sat.

She rested her head on Vaughn's shoulder, melting into him. They'd spent little more than a week apart. Yet, she missed him desperately. She'd missed his warmth, his touch, his smile. The way he'd been so supportive and encouraging of her career. The way he listened when she needed him to. How he made her laugh. The way he'd stood up for her to her family. His gift for making her feel like she was the most important person in his world.

But as much as she wanted the happily ever after she'd long dreamed of, she could never be happy knowing it had meant Vaughn sacrificing his dreams.

"You've been fighting so hard to get Sin & Glory back together. Doing all of this…" Allie lifted her head and cradled his stubbled cheek, needing to see his face. "How can you just give up everything you've worked for, Vaughn?"

He pressed a kiss to the palm of her hand, then met her gaze again. "The money, the fame…yeah, it was great. But I'm not that same twenty-year-old kid who was desperate for those things. I understand now how high the price can be, and that they don't necessarily bring happiness. I realize now that there are far more important things in life."

Vaughn turned toward her with one leg folded on the bed. He held her hands in his, and his expression exuded such genuine warmth and affection that it felt as if her heart might burst.

"I had a lot of time to think on that flight to London," he said. "And I realized that the reason I wasn't excited about meeting with the record execs was because what I was really chasing was the sense of belonging and community I felt as part of the band. We were a dysfunctional family, but we were a family nevertheless, and I'd missed that since the band broke up. I felt alone the way I did when my birth parents died and then again when my adoptive parents died. I was trying to recreate that sense of family. But being back here in Willowvale Springs, getting reacquainted with everyone, feeling like a part of your family again, and falling for you... I've never been clearer about what I want, Allie. And what I want is to be here...with you."

Allie couldn't stop the tears of joy from falling, and she wouldn't even try. She kissed the generous, loving, accomplished man she'd fallen in love with. The man who'd brought her so much joy and happiness.

"And you're really okay with making this your home base?"

"There will be times when I'll need to be in LA or London or New York," Vaughn conceded. "But I want Willowvale Springs—the place where everyone feels like family, and the woman I adore is waiting for me—to be the place I call home."

He dropped a sweet kiss on her lips and it practically took her breath away.

"I don't want to expose you to ridicule like this tabloid article. But I won't hide what we have either. Not from your family, and not from the world. All right?"

"Okay." She nodded. "But what if I said that as

open and progressive as I am about love and relationships that one day I'd like to be a wife and a mother?" Allie held her breath as she gauged Vaughn's genuine reaction to the words she hadn't been willing to speak aloud again since the implosion of her previous relationship.

Vaughn's eyes widened, and a look of pure joy animated his handsome face. His eyes were misty. He pressed a soft, sweet kiss to her lips, then pulled back and studied her. "Then I'd say that I can't wait until the day that I get to make you Mrs. Alejandra Price-Reed or the day that we get to welcome our first child into the world."

Allie's heart felt so full, it felt like it had grown too big to fit into her chest. A smile spread across her face.

"Then if we're really doing this, I know that together we can face anything, Vaughn. My family will come around. As for anyone else…it's us against the world. And baby, that's enough for me."

Vaughn pulled Allie into his arms, his lips crashing against hers. His tongue met hers as he glided his fingers into her hair and tilted her head to deepen their kiss.

Allie had missed Vaughn's touch, his taste and the panty-melting kisses that left her dreamy and reeling long after they'd gone their separate ways.

She fumbled with the buttons on his shirt, and within a flash, their clothing was strewn on the floor and they'd burrowed beneath the covers of the bed she'd made so meticulously just minutes before Vaughn's arrival.

Allie didn't care. All that mattered was that she would get to have this beautiful, caring, brilliant, talented soul in her life every single day for the rest of her life.

Epilogue

Three Years Later

Vaughn glanced over at Allie, seated beside him. She was stunning in a slinky, red, backless gown with a high slit and embellished with crystals. Her dark hair cascaded onto her bare shoulders in beachy waves, and the platinum and diamond barrette gave her look an old Hollywood feel. They'd been together for three years and married for a year and a half, but when Allie flashed that magnificent smile his heart danced and his breath caught every single time. As the nominees for Song of the Year GRAMMY were listed, the only tell of her intense nervousness was how tightly she gripped his hand. Her bright red nails nearly broke his skin.

He lifted her hand to his mouth and gently kissed the back of it, hoping to calm her nerves. Her grip loosened and the tension in her shoulders seemed to ease.

"Regardless of whose name is in that envelope, I've already won." His lips brushed her skin as he whispered in her ear.

"I should say so, Mr. Songwriter of the Year." Allie's dark eyes twinkled. "After tonight, we're going to need a proper, lighted trophy display case."

The night had already been long and incredibly surreal. Like the realization of a dream he'd never even had the audacity to imagine. At the Grammy Premiere Ceremony—the hours-long show that happened before the televised one—Vaughn had received the Songwriter of the Year award. Projects he'd written songs for had already taken home the awards for Best Rock Album and Best Pop Solo Performance. Songs he'd played drums on had been nominated in the Rock and Rap categories. And earlier that evening, he'd been reunited on stage with the four other original members of Sin & Glory—including lead singer Steven Iverson—for their first performance together in seven years. They'd performed a medley of their biggest hits in celebration of the twentieth anniversary of their debut album. And in a few weeks, they'd be heading into the studio to record a reunion album.

"I'm not talking about the awards, babe. I'm talking about us. About our family." He placed a hand over her belly. She was six months pregnant with their first child and he'd been bursting with joy from the moment Allie had shown him the positive pregnancy test. "Being with you...it's been such a remarkable gift. I honestly couldn't want for anything more."

Allie's eyes flooded with tears. She cupped his cheek and pressed a kiss to his lips, just as his name was being called along with the two members of Extreme Overload he'd worked with to write their latest album. There was thunderous applause all around them as the members of the band headed to the stage and beckoned him to join them.

Vaughn sat, stunned as he glanced around the room at industry professionals he'd admired his entire life climbing to their feet and applauding him.

"Congratulations, baby. You deserve this." Allie kissed him again, then lumbered to her feet, standing and applauding with the rest of the crowd as he rose to his feet and joined his fellow songwriters.

Vaughn stood on stage, clutching his Song of the Year GRAMMY as the two members of Extreme Overload talked about the difficult journey of making the album and how they'd dedicated it to the band member they'd lost. When it was Vaughn's turn at the mic, all the noise and sounds seem to fall away. His focus was on the woman he adored.

Alejandra Price had come into Vaughn's life again, prompting him to break every single one of his self-imposed rules. Rules he'd put in place to protect his heart. But instead of being hurt again, Vaughn was happier than he'd ever been.

His songwriting and session drummer careers were soaring. They'd broken ground on the final building for Vaughn's summer music camp for kids in foster care or underserved communities which would be opening in Willowvale Springs that summer. He had good friends, an amazing extended family, and a brilliant, loving, supportive partner with whom he was so damn lucky to share his life. And in just a few months, they'd be starting a family of their own.

Vaughn fingered the sun, moon, and stars hanging around his neck, then placed a quick hand over the tattoo on his forearm, hidden beneath his clothing, before reaching inside his breast pocket and pulling out the 'just-in-case' speech he'd written at Allie's insistence.

Vaughn swallowed hard, his eyes stinging and his vision blurry. He wished his parents had lived to witness his achievements. That they could share in the joy and happiness he felt tonight. One of the last things his birth mother had said to him is that she and his dad would always be there watching over him. That even when things got bad, he should never ever lose faith because better times were ahead.

Maybe his parents couldn't be there with him tonight, but they guided him to Allie and her family. And for that, he would forever be grateful.

* * * * *

USA TODAY bestselling author **Jules Bennett** has published over sixty books and never tires of writing happy endings. Writing strong heroines and alpha heroes is Jules's favorite way to spend her workdays. Jules hosts weekly contests on her Facebook fan page and loves chatting with readers on Twitter, Facebook and via email through her website. Stay up-to-date by signing up for her newsletter at julesbennett.com.

Books by Jules Bennett

Harlequin Desire

The Rancher's Heirs

Twin Secrets
Claimed by the Rancher
Taming the Texan
A Texan for Christmas

Angel's Share

When the Lights Go Out...
Second Chance Vows
Snowed In Secrets

Dynasties: Willowvale

A Bet Between Friends
Their White-Hot Christmas

Visit the Author Profile page
at Harlequin.com for more titles.

You can also Jules Bennett on Facebook,
along with other Harlequin Desire authors,
at Facebook.com/HarlequinDesireAuthors!

Dear Reader,

This is it! The final installment in the Willowvale Springs series. Reese and I so hope you have enjoyed our characters and this adorable little town tucked in Wyoming. I love a good cozy Christmas story—don't you?

Pax's and Kira's worlds collide when she's on a forced getaway to a dude ranch and Pax has just come in to claim his inheritance—one he doesn't really want nor know what to do with. Seeing as they're both at the ranch temporarily and it's the holidays, a little fling ensues, bringing both of them closer than they ever anticipated. These two couldn't be more opposite, yet they balance each other beautifully.

In my final Dear Reader letter for Harlequin Desire, I just want to say *thank you* to all of you amazing, loyal readers for showing me so much love over the years! I love, love, love the Harlequin Desire family and couldn't have been more blessed to be part of this creative, supportive world. I can't wait to share what is next for me, but until then, keep reading and keep dreaming.

Much love,

Jules

THEIR WHITE-HOT CHRISTMAS

Jules Bennett

There are so many people to give my love
to here, so I will just say if you are in my life
and have been on this journey with me
at any point, thank you. I love you all.

One

"Come on, you big ugly thing."

Kira Lee grunted and tugged at the obscenely hideous tree she'd just purchased from the cutest Christmas Tree Farm here in Willowvale Springs. Unfortunately, this close to the holiday, the pickings were slim. But she'd bought enough garland and ornaments to tuck into the holes of this pathetic excuse of a tree, and she was only using it in her tiny rental for a few weeks.

The workers at the farm loaded it on top of her small SUV, and she didn't take into account her height, or lack thereof, or how to get this beast inside the cabin.

"Who's winning the fight?"

A masculine voice startled her, and she couldn't see

the other side of her car for all the evergreen blocking the view.

"I'm going to win," she insisted with another hard pull. "You could be a gentleman and help."

Normally she'd have better manners, but the frigid Wyoming air made her rush to get inside by her cozy, crackling fire. The altitude was a bit different here than Portland.

"I never said I was a gentleman," the faceless man scoffed.

Wow. She'd only been in town less than a day for her forced vacation from her bestie and she was already agitated. But this situation was her own fault. She'd wanted her bland cabin to be a little spruced up for the holidays. She couldn't believe the owners of this dude ranch didn't go all out with festive decor.

Kira gave another jerk of the burlap sack between the tree and the top of her car. She tumbled backward when the bundle shifted. Finally. She might actually make it inside before dark.

"Let me get that before you hurt yourself."

The voice drew closer and Kira glanced over to see the hunkiest cowboy she'd encountered since she'd gotten to town. Okay, maybe he was a little short on the sweet side, but he more than made up for it with his looks. Tanned skin, black hat, black wool coat, dark jeans, and boots? He probably had a black, menacing horse somewhere close by and a gaggle of women just swooning at his feet.

Well, all she wanted was help with her tree. Nothing else. But she wasn't opposed to taking in the view for the time being.

With a strength she didn't expect, the guy hoisted the tree off her vehicle and over his shoulder, then motioned toward her cabin.

"Can you at least get the door?" he grumbled.

Kira offered her sweetest smile, then turned on her heel to head up the steps to her door. "Someone is in a festive mood."

She punched in the code and opened the door wide for him to enter ahead of her. Once he maneuvered the tree through the opening and managed to dodge the steps, he turned toward the open living/kitchen combo.

"Where's the bucket?" he asked.

Kira stilled. "Bucket?"

"To put the tree in."

He swung around to face her, giving her the first good look at his chiseled face. If the man actually smiled, he might be considered lethal. Those dark eyes resting beneath thick, black brows could mesmerize a woman into forgetting her own name.

"You do have something to put this in, right?" he added.

Oops.

"Didn't think that far ahead, but I did get some gorgeous decorations," she snickered, but she seemed to be the only one to find that amusing.

The stranger walked toward the fireplace and carefully laid the wrapped tree on the rug. When he stood, her eyes traveled up to take in his impressive height.

"You didn't plan this out very well, did you?" he asked.

Before she could answer, he muttered something about being right back. He marched out the door, leaving it open for the cold air to rush in.

Kira glanced out and watched as he drove off in his ominous black truck… But of course, what else would he have?

She closed the door, pushing out the wintry wind. When she turned to the sad tree lying on her floor, she felt like joining it. She was positive there were some similarities between her and this half-dead tree.

Kira tried to concentrate on this adorable getaway her bestie had set up for her instead of the disaster her life had become through no fault of her own. Between the immediate loss of her condo and her mother planning her fourth—yes, fourth—wedding and the burnout from her demanding career, she needed a break.

Kira had always had a mundane, boring life. She'd been perfectly fine with that. Structure and planning down to the final detail worked just fine for her. So all of this upheaval had nearly caused a panic attack and total meltdown. Thankfully, Delia recognized Kira's state of mind and found this quaint dude ranch in Wyoming, far away from the issues back in Oregon.

Maybe the tree she'd found was hideous, but something about it made her smile. Maybe just because something was damaged didn't mean it had to be destroyed…much like her life. She could rebuild and shift her focus, just as soon as she allowed herself the time to decompress and stop worrying about everyone else's problems—her clients, her mother, her landlord. She had to switch the attention to herself for once—or so Delilah said.

No doubt her bestie would have been all over that sexy, brooding cowboy, but Kira wasn't here for antics or flings. She had to figure out what to do with her life, namely where to live and how to get a hold of this career burnout that was a very real problem.

She didn't think Mr. Tall Dark and Grouchy would be any help.

Paxton Hart didn't have time to set up the saddest excuse for a Christmas tree he'd ever seen. Hell, he didn't even want to be on this dude ranch.

Unfortunately, he couldn't go anywhere for the time being. For reasons that he still didn't understand, Hank Carson thought it would be a good idea to leave his ranches, farms, house, and resorts to a group of guys who had worked for him over the summers years ago. Pax hadn't seen ole Hank in over a decade, but apparently Pax had left an impression on the farmer's life.

Mason, Kahlil, and Vaughn all inherited Hank Carson's properties over the past six months along with Pax. The other guys came back with every intention of selling and leaving, getting back to their busy lives, but fate had other plans. Each of them had worked for Hank as teens and each of them had vowed to achieve bigger and better things. They'd become successful in their own fields with lucrative, fulfilling careers, yet now they were all back. Pax had assisted his old pals in trying to sell their properties, but for one reason or another, the men had opted to stay and hold on to their inheritance.

The main reason, though, was that they had all fallen in love and planned to settle now in Willowvale. The three guys were either engaged or married, which scared the hell out of Pax. He didn't come back to town to fall in love or whatever those guys thought they felt. Pax had a full schedule and a checklist of career goals—namely that new start-up real estate agency in Spain. Spending time in Willowvale Springs didn't make the cut on any of his lists.

By the time Pax grabbed a good-sized bucket from the closest barn, he still hadn't shaken the fact that the new guest in one of the rental cabins was one of the most adorably petite women he'd ever laid eyes on. He wasn't sure if he was agitated that he had to take time out of his schedule to prop up an ugly-ass tree, or if he was annoyed at how she'd affected him.

Both. Definitely both.

He followed the old familiar path back to the row of cabins. This dude ranch used to thrive with visitors from all over the country and even some international guests. Now, well, according to the recent records, the average was about half the capacity. He supposed that was a good thing, considering he had no clue how to run a dude ranch and a good bit of the staff had left. The manager stayed on after Hank passed, but mainly because he had nowhere else to go and he'd just started a few months prior to Hank's death.

Pax might have worked here over several summers back in his teen years, but what did he know about running a dude ranch? His life revolved around buying and selling real estate. He'd already dominated the US market, and now, fingers crossed, he'd be opening his new location in Spain in the next few months.

Which was why he didn't have time for this dude ranch or the sexy tenant in Cabin Five.

He pulled to a stop just behind her small SUV. With bucket in hand, he stomped up the steps to knock the snow off his boots. Pax tapped his knuckles on the door, even though he'd told her he'd be right back. He still respected her privacy, and they were strangers.

The sturdy wooden door swung wide and another punch of lust to his gut caught him off guard. The petite woman with her adorable high ponytail, fitted red sweater, and body-hugging jeans shouldn't be getting to him. Had to be all this frigid air making him lose his mind and all common sense.

"Where do you want it?" he asked, hoping to make this quick and painless.

She glanced around the room and pointed to the corner near the fireplace.

"That's perfect."

Pax stepped over the half-dead tree and set the bucket in the empty spot. When he turned, he nearly ran into her. She startled and took a step back.

"Sorry." She offered a smile and wrinkled her nose. "Do you think it will look good there?"

Pax resisted the urge to just flee. He didn't care where she put the tree because this wasn't his cabin and likely when he went to move it, the needles would fall off.

"If that's what you want," he replied.

She seemed to think for a minute, which was about fifty seconds longer than his patience allowed. He thrived on efficiency. Wasted time did nothing but stall progress. No matter what the situation might be.

Finally, she nodded.

"Yeah, let's do there. It will look great with a crackling fire and a stocking."

"You are aware Christmas is in just a few days, right?"

A smile spread across her face as her gaze shifted back to his. "Which is why we need to get this tree up."

She started to bend down, but straightened. "Wait. I don't even know your name."

"Does it matter, when all you need is my help to put the tree in the bucket?" he countered.

"Scrooge it is." She held out her hand for him to shake. "I'm Kira."

He eyed her, then the extended hand, and there was no way he was touching her. His stomach had balled up in knots just from looking—who knew how he'd react with a simple touch. No attachments of any kind. He'd vowed that to himself long ago.

"I have more things to get," he told her, easing around her to head back out to his truck.

He picked up the pace, gathering the bag of sand and getting back inside. He didn't want to be here a minute longer than necessary. For one thing, he had an online meeting in an hour that he couldn't miss, regarding this new development in Barcelona, and for another, well…he just couldn't be here with Kira.

Even her name sounded adorable. Everything about her seemed adorable, from her girl-next-door hairstyle to her petite frame to her bubbly personality. Adorable wasn't his typical type. He preferred someone almost high-maintenance, more glam, over-the-top, because that way he wouldn't get attached and he could walk away easily.

But this trifecta before had him focusing on setting the tree as straight as possible in the bucket with sand, and now she'd already gotten under his skin.

"Hold that steady," he told her as he continued to shift the sand around and adjust the trunk.

"Doesn't this need water, too?" she asked from above him.

"It needs dumped somewhere and put out of its misery," he muttered.

Once he figured the thing was as good as it was going to get, he eased back out from beneath the tree. He'd come back home to Willowvale Springs to figure out the best way to sell this unwanted, inherited property, not frolic and help the guests.

"Wait until you see it decorated," Kira stated, smiling up at the tree like she could already see the image in her mind.

"I'll take your word for it."

She glanced over to him, and her dark brows drew in. "You have something better to do than decorate a Christmas tree? I bet you don't even have one up."

"You'd win that bet."

"Are you always so surly?" she asked, propping her hands on her hips.

"Are you always this chatty with a stranger?" he countered.

Kira shrugged. "Occupational hazard."

Don't ask. Don't ask.

"And what is it you do?"

Clearly he didn't take his own advice, but seriously, what career did someone have that could make them so…perky.

"You're a wedding coordinator," he guessed.

Kira laughed and rolled her eyes. That laugh warmed something inside him—something he hadn't even known had chilled. This whole situation was utterly ridiculous.

"Not hardly," she replied. "I'm a Life Coach."

Pax snorted and waited on her to laugh, but she continued to stare.

"Oh, you're serious?"

"Why wouldn't I be?" she volleyed back.

She reached up and grabbed her hair in two spots, gave a pull, and tightened her ponytail. He knew that maneuver. It was like some battle-ready move women did when someone pissed them off. Clearly he was that someone.

"What exactly do you do?" he asked, not sure why he insisted on staying when he had a call and literally anything else he should and could be doing.

"At the moment, trying to figure out why you won't give me your name, you seem to get angry over Christmas trees, and how I can fix you."

Offended, Pax crossed his arms over his chest and widened his stance. "Fix me?" he repeated. "What do you believe needs fixed?"

"Your attitude for one thing, though you did help me with the tree, so thank you."

She moved over to a stash of bags she'd set on the sofa and started pulling out garland, boxes of lights, and ornaments. Pax wondered when the items would stop coming out of bags and where the hell she thought she could put all of that when the branches were so sparse.

"Did your wife put up a tree at your house?" she asked, still sorting through her things.

"You dodged my question, and that wasn't a subtle way of asking if I'm single."

She tossed a saucy grin over her shoulder. "I'm not answering your question and I don't care if you're single. I assume there's no way you'd put up a tree on your own so I'm assuming if there's one in your home, then your wife did it."

"I'm not married and I don't have a tree."

She pursed her lips and turned with a box of lights in hand. "You live here on the ranch?"

"Something like that," he muttered.

Passing through didn't count as living, but considering he was staying in the main guesthouse, he'd just keep his response vague. He wasn't here to make friends, just to sell off this dude ranch and turn over a nice profit. He'd moved on from this small town long ago and looking back had never been on his to-do list.

"I'm going to guess you're into something depressing and stuffy like accounting. Is that why you're angry? Because if I had to do math all day, I'd be a grouch, too."

Where did this chatty woman come from?

"Are you here alone?" he asked.

The words slipped out before he could stop himself.

"Forced vacation," she told him with a half grin. "My best friend booked this for me after some…we'll call them issues back home."

Issues? He sure as hell didn't want anyone's issues to deal with, not when he had more than enough of his own.

His cell vibrated in his pocket, pulling him from the moment. Pax reached in and cringed. He'd been standing here talking so long and this was the call he'd been waiting on.

"I have to take this. Enjoy the decorating."

He started for the door, sliding his finger across the screen to answer at the same time.

"Let me know when you need help with yours," she called after him.

Pax cursed himself for finding her amusing, but even more so for letting her distract him from one of the most important calls of his career. Damn it. He needed to be back in his office in a professional setting with his notes and his laptop.

He answered the call and drove away from Cabin Five, making a mental note to let the property manager deal with any more of Kira's needs.

Two

Kira pinched the bridge of her nose and closed her eyes as her mother's voice echoed through the cozy cabin. She'd called twenty minutes ago to run over some wedding plans, and that was the last thing Kira wanted to discuss on her "relaxing" getaway.

Did a fourth wedding really need planned?

"I'm on the fence about a destination wedding," her mother went on. "I already have a dress, but it doesn't go with a beach theme. More like a rustic cabin, boho theme. But I could always buy another."

Sure, why not? Another dress…another husband. You can never have too many apparently. Was it any wonder Kira was still single? She didn't even know what romance or true love looked like…or if they even existed.

"Honey, you seem distracted," her mother added. "Are you listening?"

Diane Morton Lee Frasure, and soon-to-be Leith, typically never paid attention if anyone listened or not. If anyone was within earshot, she took that as akin to open mic night. She loved talking, mostly about herself, so usually Kira could put the phone on Speaker and go about her business, occasionally chiming in with a *hmm* or *uh-huh* for added flare.

"I'm here," Kira replied. "Just decorating for the holidays."

"The holiday that's in a couple days?" her mother laughed. "Oh, honey. You really need to find time for better things. Where are you again? Utah? Montana? Maybe hit a local hot spot and see if you find anyone single."

Here we go.

"Mom, I like being single. Some people don't care if they get married and have kids."

"You always were so odd, but I love you."

Kira sighed. Her mother did love her, and maybe Kira was odd, but she was happy...or she used to be, which was why she'd gone into her career of helping other people fulfill their lives. Clearly having a spouse wasn't the ticket to happiness. If that was the case, her mother wouldn't keep searching for the next one.

"I'm in Wyoming," Kira tacked on, but her mother started talking again at the same time, so Kira went about adjusting the beaded garland she'd draped over the mantel.

"I've chosen a lovely shade of lavender for you to wear, since we're doing a March wedding," Diane stated. "I went with a halter-style top, since you're so flat. I thought that might give you more of a shape."

Yes, please, bring up all the flaws. Flat chest, single, spending the holidays alone.

Why did she let her mom pull her mood down? She'd been perfectly happy moments ago with a helpful, albeit moody stranger. He might have growled a bit, but he wasn't completely rude. He did help, so there was some type of redeeming quality inside him.

"I can find my own dress, but why don't you and Tim just run off and elope?"

"Tom. Your new step-father's name is Tom."

Did it matter? Tim? Tom? He wouldn't be around this time next year.

"I really need to go, Mom. Just text me if you need me for anything else. Love you."

Kira disconnected the call before her mother could say anything else. The number one Kira always gave her clients was to remove the negativity from their lives. While she couldn't exactly remove her mother entirely, she could impose limits and boundaries.

Part of her felt a little like an imposter for always doling out advice to others about living their best life and how to fill themselves with happiness, when she clearly didn't have things figured out in her own life. Especially at this point, there wasn't one solid and her entire world seemed to be up in the air.

For the next three weeks, Kira fully intended to

embrace the vacation. She had plenty of books to read, podcasts to listen to, and new recipes to try. Stepping from the city to the country definitely left her no choice but to slow down the pace she'd been keeping up. Her clients completely understood her break, but she'd also left them with things to work on in her absence so they'd still feel like she was there.

Kira took a step back and examined her decorative skills. The tree leaned a bit toward the window, but hopefully it wouldn't fall over. The ornaments and variety of twigs she'd purchased helped hide the holes from missing branches. But honestly, she loved how imperfect this tree seemed. There was enough perfection plastered all over social media; she didn't want it in her real life.

Although, social media was job security for her. Aside from her own posts pulling in clients, she also found people who had lost their joy because they were too busy comparing themselves to others… which was where her number one rule came from. If something is causing you negativity, remove it.

But this little cabin and her festive vibe was bringing her pure joy. She cranked her holiday tunes up as she moved toward the tiny kitchen. She'd sent a message to the property manager requesting someone to come start the fire. She should've asked Scrooge to show her how. She only had a gas insert in her condo back in Portland, so working an actual wood fireplace was certainly not in her wheelhouse. Hopefully someone would show up soon. She couldn't wait for a crackling fire while she watched the snow fall and the aroma of fresh baked bread filled her cozy space.

First, though, she had to get started on this cranberry bread with orange glaze. She might not be the best cook, but she enjoyed trying, and this trip was all about finding joy.

Kira opened the few cabinets until she found the bowls and measuring cups she'd need. Just as she was heating up the oven, a knock on the door boomed above her music. Kira startled as she turned toward the entryway as if she could see beyond the large wooden door. There were windows on either side, but she couldn't see who was out there. She'd seen just one other guest since she arrived last night. She had to assume her visitor was the Firestarter.

When she reached the door, she peered out the side window and blinked. Scrooge stared right back at her. She offered a smile, but unsurprisingly he didn't return the gesture.

Oh well. If he could start a fire, she didn't care if he scowled the entire time. Maybe the warmth would thaw his cold heart.

Kira flicked the lock and eased the door open. "I hope the property manager sent you because I'm dying for a fire."

"I should have asked earlier."

Scrooge stepped inside and came to a halt. She followed the path of his stare and landed on the festive area she'd just decorated. From the frown, she assumed he wasn't a fan of her gold garland and twinkly lights. Perhaps he was a colored light man? No matter which side of the light battle he landed on.

"Don't you love it?" She clasped her hands together, totally proud of what she'd done in a short amount of time. "I would have still been wrestling the tree off the car if you hadn't stopped by."

"I have a feeling you're persistent enough to have gotten it all on your own."

"Without a doubt, but you still saved time and energy."

The man, still with a name she didn't know, went to the fireplace and bent down. She stood back and tried to see what all he did to get this going so she didn't have to call someone else again. Granted that was one of the services provided, but she'd rather be self-sufficient.

"How long have you worked here?" she asked, mostly because she couldn't stand the silence and she just had a curiosity.

He stacked a couple of logs and adjusted them to form a point. "Not long."

A man of few words. She wondered what made him so mysterious and moody. Or maybe not moody. Maybe he had issues he was dealing with in his life just like she did. Maybe the last thing he wanted to do was leave his living quarters and come start a fire for the woman who made him wrestle a decrepit tree into her cabin.

She worked with people who had a variety of different personalities and temperaments. She always had to adjust her wording, and even her actions, for whatever type of person she was dealing with. Granted, she didn't know this stranger at all, but she had always been excellent at reading people and honing in on what made them tick.

Clearly, holidays weren't his thing.

The timer from the kitchen chimed through the tiny space, pulling her from her thoughts. The guy glanced over his shoulder at the sound.

"Dinnertime?"

Those piercing dark eyes landed on her and sent a shiver down her spine. She didn't even know his name and he certainly wasn't flirting, but that didn't diminish the potency of the man who'd come to her rescue twice in the span of a few hours.

"Just the oven preheating. I'm making bread. Cranberry with an orange glaze."

A hint of a smile pulled at the corner of his lips, but was gone before she could fully appreciate the unexpected act.

"Reminds me of someone else," he muttered before turning his focus back to start the fire.

He struck a match and tossed it in, then came to his feet. With his hands propped on his narrow hips, he stared into the opening, waiting on the flames to take hold.

Even with his bulky coat on, the man had a sexy frame. His height, his broad shoulders, the dark hair, and lack of emotion shouldn't keep capturing her attention and making her lose her train of thought... but she was human, and he was striking. Nothing wrong with admiring the view while he was here.

"I'll have plenty if you'd like to come back."

Why did she say that? She didn't even know this man, and he never gave off any vibe that he wanted company or to socialize. When her friend had scheduled this forced vacation, Kira had never thought ahead to the fact she'd be alone. Not that she minded, but she also figured she could take advantage of the fact he was here now.

"I'm busy the rest of the day."

Flames licked over the wood, turning the brown to black. Scrooge shifted around to face her and held her in place with that bold stare.

"Thanks, though."

"Oh, you do have manners," she joked. "I was wondering if you just did good deeds because you were forced."

"Nobody forces me to do anything."

That low, sultry tone didn't help her growing attraction. She didn't know if it was the life coach within her that found him so interesting or the female. While she always wanted to know what made people tick because of her career, she didn't think her instant fascination had anything to do with work.

"Thanks for getting that," she replied. "I'll try to do it myself next time."

"You ever started a fire?" he asked.

"Does the pilot light on my gas logs count?"

The muscle in his jaw jumped, drawing her attention to yet another sexy aspect.

"City girl," he murmured.

"Guilty, but I can appreciate the beauty of the

country. I just don't get out of Portland very often. Work keeps me pretty grounded and I love where I live."

"Can't you work from anywhere?"

"I can," she confirmed, surprised he'd asked about her personal life. "But I have several clients in and around my area, so I do like some face-to-face time every now and then. I think it's important to step out from behind the screen and do some old-school interaction."

"Interesting. Most people want to be remote with everything."

She shrugged and leaned against the sofa. "I'm not like most people. Maybe that's why I have such a successful business."

He stared for another minute before adjusting the collar on his coat and taking a step toward the door. "Let us know if there's anything else you need."

"Just one more thing."

With his hand on the doorknob, he glanced over his shoulder and quirked a dark brow.

"What's your name?" she asked.

"Pax."

And with that nugget of information, he let himself out the door.

Pax. Of course he had a short, unique name. That suited him, but she would bet it was a nickname. He wouldn't offer any more information without being prompted, no doubt, but something about him made her want to persist.

She headed straight to the kitchen with an extra

pep in her step. Delilah would warn her against getting tangled up with some stranger working on a dude ranch, but Delilah also wanted her to relax and have fun. Kira intended to do just that.

Three

"This doesn't even make any sense."

Pax had muttered that to himself with each flip of the page. He'd gotten Hank's financials for the past five years, and for reasons Pax couldn't comprehend, the dude ranch had consistently lost money. Willowvale Springs might be a hidden gem, but at one time, this place thrived and raked in millions per year. Had Hank just given up? The robust, powerful man in the town had been a staple. He'd been the one constant in Pax's life, and many others here. The jobs he'd provided had kept everything running.

Hank had demanded loyalty and respect, and that's why everyone wanted him as an employer. He might have been old and somewhat crabby at times, but he was fair and just.

The fact the dude ranch started spiraling downhill just didn't sound like the Hank that Pax remembered.

He curled his fingers around the tumbler of bourbon he'd poured. He hadn't taken a sip. Each time he reached, he saw something else in the numbers that pulled his attention from the amber liquid.

He'd just picked up the glass when the chime from the main door echoed down the hall.

Pax opted to stay in the main house, where Hank had living quarters and a study in the back. The entire front part was the guest check-in, but since the one other guest checked out a couple hours ago and nobody else was scheduled to arrive until after the new year, that meant either the one employee left had come in or Cabin Five had just entered.

He pulled in a deep breath and rounded the old, scarred desk as he headed for the corridor. As he made his way to the front, Pax had to put himself on high alert. This woman could be trouble. She was too sweet, too adorable, too…everything.

He'd fallen for sweet and adorable once before. That mistake had nearly cost him a portion of his savings and his heart. He'd never make that mistake again. His heart and his money were all his, and he had no interest in sharing either. He'd worked damn hard to protect his professional and personal life, so no distractions would throw him off course.

Pax didn't want this guest in his headspace and he didn't want to think about her any more than necessary. He had a business to decide to sell or restore and keep. Neither option appealed to him because he didn't want to be here. Didn't have the time, either.

The moment he reached the open two-story lobby, there she stood all wrapped up in her coat, scarf, hat, with dark hair tumbling down around her shoulders…and a foil-wrapped package in the exact shape of a loaf of bread.

"I wasn't sure if you'd be up here or not, but I was going to leave this here for you at the front desk," she told him with one of those wide smiles that shouldn't affect him…but did on every primal level.

Little did she know, *he* was the front desk right now. The very few employees he had left were doing other things. He could run the main quarters. What he couldn't do was clean up after guests and provide the snacks in the lobby. Thankfully, Kira's package for her stay didn't include the extra amenities other than, apparently, fire starting. He did see on her preference sheet that she might want to see the stables and possibly ride a horse, weather permitting.

He'd have to hand that off to their lead ranch hand, because the last thing Pax had time for was to give this city girl the lay of the land. While she was incredibly adorable and sexy, and part of him wanted to give in to his primal urges, he had no intention of being her bestie during her stay here.

"You didn't have to come all the way up here," he told her. "But I won't turn down homemade bread."

She crossed the open lobby area and headed toward him with that wide, megawatt smile spread across her face. The closer she came, the more his heart kicked up. Just because they were essentially alone in the place didn't mean anything. They were strangers and adults. He needed to remember that as well as all the tasks on his priority list…none of which involved a fling with a guest.

"You might want to hold the compliments until you try it," she warned, handing the package over. "I've never tried this recipe before."

"I'm sure it's fine."

He took the loaf and sat it on the live-edge check-in counter. She'd come all this way. He felt like he should offer her a drink or something, but she wasn't a guest in his home, she was a guest at the ranch. His ranch, now.

"Do you live here on the grounds?" she asked.

Pax nodded, not really wanting to get into the current status of his life. He was simply passing through, not wanting to stay any longer than necessary. He'd been in Spain when the letter had come to his office about the inheritance. He should have known Hank had left him something, mainly because of the other guys who had been left substantial properties from their old employer.

"I'd love to see more of it if you ever have the time," she added. "Just the drive from the cabins to here is gorgeous. But I'm sure you're busy with your family and all with the holidays."

Family? He had no family. The only family he had was a set of divorced parents who were so miserable in life, he tried to steer clear as much as possible. He worked his business from the ground up and refused to allow negativity into his life to ruin what he'd built.

"I'll be spending the holidays alone," he found himself saying, then wished he'd kept his mouth shut.

"Well, you're more than welcome to come to the cabin for Christmas dinner," she offered. "I have the kitchen fully stocked for my stay, and I do have something special planned for that day."

"You planned something special for a day alone?" he asked.

Kira shrugged and slid her hands into the pockets of her long puffy coat. "Why not? I have to eat and it's Christmas, so I might as well make it fun. You in?"

Hell, he shouldn't be. He really shouldn't agree to this.

"Sure."

But he couldn't stop himself. One meal wouldn't hurt, right?

If possible, her smile beamed even more, warming something deep inside him he hadn't even known had chilled. What had he just gotten himself into? He hadn't even tried to resist.

"I should let you get back to work," she told him. "Thanks again for the fire earlier. The cabin is so nice and warm. Just what I imagined when coming here for a remote getaway. I am surprised you don't have more guests right now."

Yeah, that made two of them.

"We're undergoing some transitions at the moment," he explained, trying to keep any and all replies about the business vague. "The ranch is normally booked to capacity."

Or it had been back in the day, and if he had his say, it would be again. No matter if he kept ownership or sold it off, he fully intended to get this ranch back to the way Hank had it when everything thrived. The man had always had a big vision, which was part of what shaped Pax into the real estate mogul he was today. Hank had instilled a strong work ethic and fast drive. As much as Pax didn't want to be here, or have the time to undertake another project, he owed everything to Hank.

And still couldn't believe the man who seemed larger than life was truly gone. Nobody before or since had shown Pax such love. There was a hole Pax hadn't counted on and a void that might never be filled with love again.

"You okay?"

Pax shook away from the past and the impending decisions he had to make and wondered what look he'd had on his face to warrant that concerned tone from Kira.

"Perfectly fine," he replied with a firm nod. "Just lost in thought."

"Well, let me know if you liked the bread. And if you don't, just throw it out."

He'd never be that rude.

"It will be fine. I don't know the last time anyone gave me something homemade before, so I appreciate the gesture."

"It's the least I could do. Besides, I might need

to call on you for another fire in case I can't figure it out."

"Happy to help."

Kira turned to leave, then glanced back over her shoulder. "If you get bored, you know where to find me."

Then she slipped out the double doors and down the steps, leaving him with what he knew was a blatant invitation. He didn't need to get involved, he needed to get the business sorted out and employees back on the payroll. In order to do that, he had to get business back on this dwindling ranch. He'd come to town for one reason and one reason only. Figure out what to do with his inheritance and get back to Spain.

But the very masculine part of him wanted to explore Kira's offering and maybe take a page from her book and relax. When was the last time he did something that didn't involve work or making money?

Years, if he had to guess. Maybe even a decade. There was nothing wrong with enjoying the company of a woman…that didn't mean anything other than a little conversation and a meal.

Right?

"Your stuff is in a storage unit right now."

Kira rubbed her temple and attempted to concentrate on the sweet aroma coming from the oven and the crackling fire. Thinking about the mess back in Portland really didn't help her sanity or her calm retreat.

But the entire situation was out of her hands, and

she couldn't change the fact she was essentially home-less. Why did her stupid landlord have to have an undisclosed gambling problem, owe back taxes, and have all of his properties seized? None of that was her problem, yet his lack of financial common sense had trickled down into her own life, and now she had to find a place to live. Portland had grown so much, yet the housing market still wasn't as broad as she'd like. So far, all she could find were condos or apart-ments outside of town or something well beyond the monthly allowance she'd given herself for housing.

And she could only stay in Wyoming through the second week of January, so time definitely wasn't on her side. Still, she had to believe that everything would fall into place as it was meant to be.

"Kira, are you still there?"

She focused back on Delilah and the phone lying on the old wood coffee table.

"I'm here," Kira sighed. "I'm just thinking. Thanks for making sure my stuff is safe."

"Nothing you wouldn't have done for me," her friend replied. "I only paid for a month and I've got some local agents looking for a place for you. If noth-ing else, you can stay with me until something be-comes available."

Kira shook her head no, even though her friend couldn't see her. "You have a new baby and a de-manding job. I won't shack up, but thanks for the offer and thanks for the storage unit. I'll send you money as soon as we hang up."

"I'm not worried about getting paid back. I'm worried about my homeless friend."

Kira laughed…because what else could she do at this point?

"I'm not homeless. I'm in a lovely cabin right now that I decorated, got a fire going, and I'm currently making turtle brownies."

"Wow, I'm impressed. Any hunky cowboys out there?"

Pax instantly came to mind. With that brooding gaze beneath a wide-brim, black hat and the firm lips and strong jawline, how could she not find him hunky? Beneath the gruff exterior, he did have manners…somewhat.

"I'll take that silence as a yes." Delilah snickered. "Good for you. I hope you're having the best time. You deserve it."

Yeah, she did, but nothing too crazy was happening here. Just a decorated dead tree and wedding planning for her mother's fourth walk down the aisle.

Sometimes the people-pleasing aspect of her career spilled over into her personal life, and she had a difficult time expressing how she truly felt. She didn't like conflict of any kind and perhaps that's why she thrived in her field.

"I'm not having some hot affair, D." Kira laughed as she went to the kitchen. She peeked through the oven door and closed it back up. "The ranch is pretty vacant for the holidays, but the property manager did help me bring in my Christmas tree, so I made him a loaf of bread. He's a bit grouchy, but he's coming around."

"Oh no. Don't make him a temporary client. You're supposed to be taking a break from everything, including work."

"I don't know any other way." Kira leaned against the counter, waiting on the cookies to finish baking as she watched more snow fall outside the back window. "I just want to help people."

"And that's why I love you."

Kira smiled. All she ever wanted out of life was to make people happy. Since being little and seeing her mother's own happiness ebb and flow, Kira had always wanted to fill in those gaps when her mom seemed down. Of course, looking back now, Kira could see that nothing could make her mom happy, not even hunting for a new man.

But since Kira had started working on filling voids when she was little, that just spilled over into every aspect of her life, and she'd been smart enough to make a career out of her knack for people-pleasing.

"Just make sure you're still doing your own self-care," Delilah scolded. "This trip is all about putting you first. Got it?"

"Yes, ma'am."

Kira tapped the screen and ended the call, then grabbed a pot holder to get the cookies from the oven. She'd just set the pan on the stovetop when her cell vibrated on the counter. Kira glanced to see a text from her mother.

Do you think personalized coasters for each guest is too much?

Too much what? Money or over-the-top? Because Kira thought yes to both. Did a fourth wedding really require party favors? That whole concept was ridiculous anyway in her opinion. Why did weddings have to get so outrageous with everyone trying to outdo others and compete from what they'd seen on social media?

Just another reason Kira needed the break. Trying to keep up with millions of lives and make her clients see that they shouldn't live that way was getting even more stressful. She just wanted to make a living to support herself and help others. Was that too much to ask?

Kira opted to not answer right now.

The turtle cookies smelled amazing, and Kira was so glad she'd brought her cozy elastic waist leggings and sweat pants. Didn't everyone gain a few pounds over the holidays? Weight never mattered to her. That was another aspect she tried to instill in her clients who struggled. Being healthy was a great thing, but being on a constant diet for the sake of the reflection in the mirror was a surefire way to be miserable.

Self-confidence could be found in so many other areas of life, and Kira happily would show them the way.

Kira slid her spatula beneath each hot cookie and transferred it to a cooling rack. She really didn't know what she'd do with two dozen cookies, but she loved baking, and since that brought her joy, she'd just go with it. She'd make another run to the main house and drop off some goodies again. Or she could make a little bundle of this and other goods and gift it to him when he came for Christmas dinner.

Why did the thought of him coming here for that make her stomach curl with anticipation and excitement? They weren't doing anything other than eating and chatting. Maybe she could dig into his mind a bit more and peel back another layer.

Just because she found him attractive and invited him for dinner didn't mean anything. She had to keep telling herself that. The man hadn't even shown interest or flirted with her. Hell, she didn't even know his last name.

But Delilah did tell her to do something for herself, and maybe getting to know Pax a little better was just what she needed during her temporary stay.

Four

"Cheers."

"It's been a hell of a year."

Pax raised his beer stein and tapped his glass to the other guys he'd met at The Getaway. The local pub off the beaten path catered to all the regulars. The wings and beers on tap were legendary in Willowvale Springs.

Of course Mason raised his glass of soda in his own toast to the hellish year. As a Major League Baseball player, he'd gotten a career-ending head injury. Now, coupled with his medication, any type of alcohol was prohibited. But he didn't mind anyone else enjoying a beer, and the man had gone and fallen in love, so right now, nothing seemed to faze him.

And not just him, but Kahlil and Vaughn as well.

Out of the four of them that had inherited Hank's properties, three had lost their damn minds.

But Pax was happy for them. If that was the path they wanted and they were living their best life, who was he to judge? He could support them and still stay faraway from whatever water they were drinking.

While he was thrilled to see his old pals so content and settled with their lives, Pax was perfectly fine being the lone wolf here. What they'd found with each of their significant others had to be special enough to get these guys to stay here in Willowvale Springs after being gone for so long.

"I can't believe you all are staying here," Pax mumbled. "I mean…why?"

Vaughn shrugged. "With the group disbanded, I can pretty much write from anywhere. Plus the recording studio at the ranch is done, so I'm perfectly fine staying."

"I can't imagine being anywhere else," Kahlil chimed in, reaching for his buffalo wings. "Andraya and I are finally settling in and just acquired two more quarter horses. No way do I want to go back to my old life."

Mason nudged Pax with his elbow. "You better watch it. You'll fall in love and stay here, too."

"With who?" Pax chuckled.

But a flash of Miss Perky assaulted his mind and an image of her delivering that damn loaf of bread followed. He seriously couldn't remember the last time someone gifted him something from the heart or without wanting something in return. In his line of work, he was schmoozed by billionaires wanting to get their listings out front and center. He was given lavish presents in the hopes of selling properties for top dollar and never failing.

But a damn loaf of bread had touched him and made him feel foolish for loving the gesture as much as he did.

The music and bustling crowd around them pulled Pax from his thoughts of his one and only guest back at the ranch. Rolling her over and over in his mind wasn't going to help him figure out where to go from here or how to grow his company.

"You never know who you'll find," Vaughn replied. "I never intended on staying, let alone connecting with Allie, but here we are."

"I've got too much on my plate." Pax shifted in the booth and set his mug back on the scarred-top table. "I'm in the middle of opening my first agency overseas and nothing can get in the way. I've worked too damn hard to break into that market."

"Hopefully you're tapping into someplace tropical." Kahlil met his gaze across the table. "I love Wyoming, but damn these winters can be brutal."

"I'm pushing into Barcelona and I've already put some feelers out in Costa Rica."

"And what about the dude ranch?" Mason asked. "You keeping it or selling it off?"

Pax sighed and leaned back in the cushioned booth. "My very first instinct is always to sell, but I can't bring myself to pull the trigger just yet. Even if I keep it under the umbrella of my agency, I won't be living here. I just want to make sure I do right by Hank in the end. I'm just not sure what that answer is quite yet."

"I think we all are in agreement there," Kahlil stated. "Hank left a lasting impression on everyone in this town. I still can't figure out what made him choose the four of us."

"Plus Mabel," Vaughn laughed. "That woman has been the ruler of Hanks's General Store for decades."

Mason nodded. "Nobody else could take that place. She's the staple there."

"Mabel has the store?" Pax asked. "I had no idea. I didn't even think about that, but it makes sense. But what about us? What made us so special?"

"According to the letter with the will, he thought I was successful and powerful enough for the undertaking," Kahlil replied. "I assume that since we all went on to bigger and better things, he took pride in our journeys. Maybe he wanted us all back here for a reason or perhaps he just thought we were the best ones to take over and resurrect his failing properties."

"The dude ranch is a financial nightmare," Pax ground out, reaching for his beer. "I can't wrap my head around how everything seemed to just go downhill so damn fast."

"When Edith passed, Hank seemed to lose a piece of himself," Kahlil explained, his dark stare meeting Pax. "People said he just gave up. He became a shell of the man he used to be. It just goes to prove that even the strongest men have a vulnerable spot. His was Edith."

Yeah, Pax couldn't imagine being that invested in someone that he gave up the will for anything once that person was gone. He'd never let anyone have that much power and control over him or his life. He hadn't gotten this far by letting others make decisions for him.

"I really needed this." Vaughn pulled a paper towel from the holder on the table and wiped his hands. "I'm still not used to all this downtime since my traveling days are behind me. I wondered how I would adjust, but this is pretty damn nice."

"It's definitely good to see you all again," Pax admitted. "I can't believe we're all back in the same town at the same time after all these years."

"I still say Hank intended for this very thing to happen," Mason stated, poking his ice with his straw. "Maybe he wanted to form some mini reunion."

"I don't mind it," Kahlil replied. "What are you all doing for Christmas?"

Pax listened as the guys discussed plans with family and friends. No way in hell was he admitting that he was having a dinner with Cabin Five. These guys would latch on to that kernel of information and never let him live it down. Then they'd get some delusions of grandeur in their mind that something intimate was taking place, when clearly there was nothing. Absolutely nothing.

Just because he found her extremely sexy, not to mention a sweet woman with a knack for baking, did not mean he had time or wanted to enter into some temporary fling. He had a life to get to, and obviously so did she.

Thankfully the conversation turned to upcoming weddings for the guys, and Pax could enjoy his beer and wings without chiming in. Of course, they all extended an invite to him, and he promised if he was in town, he'd be there. But he hoped to be long gone. He'd have to make a point to return, though. He did miss seeing these guys. They'd all changed so much since they'd been here last. Catching up was good for the soul.

And maybe sharing a festive dinner with an attractive woman would be good for his soul as well. But that's all they could share. Nothing could distract him from his goals, and an emotional attachment was absolutely out of the question.

Kira tugged on the tie of her green wrap shirt. She hadn't packed anything too fancy, but she did have a couple nice tops and jeans. She turned side to side in the oversize floor mirror in the main bedroom. Would Pax think she looked good?

Why did she care? She shouldn't hinge her outfit or her mood on someone else's opinion of her.

But yet, she wondered.

"So silly," she muttered to herself as she stepped from the bedroom.

Just as Kira moved into the kitchen, a knock on the door sounded through the open space. She shouldn't be nervous. For pity's sake, the man had seen her at her most ridiculous moment wrestling a tree from her car. This was nothing.

She flicked the lock and opened the door, nearly stumbling over her own feet as she backed away to let Pax enter. She hadn't prepared herself for how he might look, but all in black with a darker shadow of beard over his jaw and matching black hat really went a long way to making her heart beat much faster than it should.

The oven timer chirped and she blinked away the fantasy that started to build over her guest.

"Just in time," she informed him. "Come on in and hang up your coat."

She turned away to go focus on the food. If she burned everything, then she'd have to explain why, and she imagined Pax had enough women falling all over themselves trying to capture his attention.

"Whatever you're making smells amazing."

She pulled out the dressing balls, ham, and rolls and set them on the stovetop.

"It's not a ton because I wasn't expecting company, but I did also whip up a chocolate cake. Hope that's okay."

"Who doesn't love chocolate?"

"It's a simple meal, but... Merry Christmas."

He came to stand on the other side of the island separating the kitchen from the living area and set a bottle of Pinot Noir on the counter. She'd been so mesmerized by him, she'd totally missed the fact he had a bottle in his hands.

"You didn't have to bring anything," she told him. "But I won't turn down a bottle of wine."

"I have no idea if this is good or not," he confessed, taking a seat on the stool. "My friend's fiancé recommended it, so I just went with that."

"Not too many wines I would turn away," she joked.

Even sitting down, Pax had a broad, commanding presence. She realized just how small this cabin was, now that their interaction seemed more intimate than before.

Just dinner. That's all. Calm down.

"Here. You come sit and I'll serve."

Kira stilled. "Excuse me?"

He came to his feet and circled the island. Reaching across her, he grabbed a spoon from the decorative holder and leaned back. His gaze caught hers and she held her breath. His coal-like eyes could be seen as harsh to some, but she only saw warmth... and maybe even a little interest.

Well, well, well.

She smiled, knowing full well that would likely drive him crazy. Good. He'd been driving her crazy for two days now.

"Pour some wine," he demanded.

Had his tone gotten even huskier than before? This dinner might be more interesting than she originally thought. So much for a lonely holiday.

Kira took a step back and broke the unexpected moment as she went in search of wineglasses and a bottle opener.

"I wouldn't have taken you for a wine guy."

Pax grabbed a couple of plates from the open shelves above the stove and started plating their dinner.

"You've put thought into what I drink?" he asked without looking up from the task.

Her grip on the bottle nearly slipped, but she thankfully remained composed. So what if she'd thought about him? She didn't think it was too vain to believe she'd run through his mind at least once. He wouldn't be here otherwise.

"I just assumed you took shots of whiskey at the end of a long day of chewing up your enemies and spitting them out."

His rich, robust laughter filled the tiny cabin. Something new and even warmer spiraled through her.

"Oh, you can laugh," she stated, shifting her attention his way. "I had no idea."

"So you think about my drinks and my laugh? Good to know."

He set their plates on the side of the island where the stools were and glanced her way. That black stare held her in place.

"Anything else about me that's crossed your mind?"

Captivated and utterly out of her element, Kira shrugged. "Your last name. What brought you to Wyoming or if you've lived here your entire life. What made you want to run a dude ranch. The basics. And maybe why you seem irritated most of the time, but you appear to be coming out of your shell, even though that seems to be difficult for you."

Thick, dark brows drew inward. "My shell?"

"Ah, there he is. The brooding man I'm used to. What makes you so serious all the time?"

He stared at her, whether thinking of an answer— or trying to figure her out, she didn't know. But she'd never met anyone like him. Granted, she'd only been around him for two days, but she still couldn't get a feel for his personality. Normally she excelled at her skills, which was why she had become so successful with her career. She'd always prided herself on reading people, but Pax kept that steely wall up and she wanted to know why. Of course he wouldn't willingly open up, but that didn't mean she couldn't place some very sneaky questions throughout their conversation.

"Hart. My last name is Hart."

Well, that was a start.

She circled the island and set his wine in front of his plate before taking a seat on the iron-back stool.

"Did you grow up here?"

He dug into his meal without answering for a minute, but she waited. She had a feeling everything with Pax was calculated. He'd be the type to take his time and be methodical about each move, each word.

"I did," he finally answered. "You're not trying to get inside my head, are you?"

Kira went straight for a sip of wine before her food. "Maybe. I imagine you don't let a lot of people in there."

"You'd be right."

She dropped the topic for now, wanting him to feel

comfortable here. Typically people opened up to her, but she couldn't figure out what made him so closed off. As much as she wanted to push sometimes, her client always had the control.

But Pax wasn't a client, was he? He was just a stranger passing through on this blip of time in her life. She had no idea what these next few weeks would bring, but she fully intended to get to know him quite a bit better…on whatever level they ended up.

Five

He should've left by now. But dinner rolled into dessert and that spilled into opening another bottle of wine.

Now he'd shed his jacket, hung his hat on the back of the barstool, and toed off his boots. He reclined on the couch and didn't remember being this relaxed in a long time.

Kira had peppered him with questions for the past hour, and he'd either been extremely vague or dodged them altogether. Being a life coach, something he still didn't understand, clearly left her quite inquisitive.

She sat in front of the fireplace on a large floor pillow, swirling her glass of Pinot. She'd pulled her hair up into some messy knot on top of her head and he couldn't tell if the sexy hair around her shoulders or her overall laid-back style appealed more to him. Nothing about this guest should be drawing him in, but Kira had a knack for making him feel comfortable and at home.

Willowvale Springs was no longer his home. He would come and go and still had an office in town, but Brandon Littlefoot ran that branch. Pax preferred his home in Vail or his penthouse in Manhattan overlooking Central Park. His bungalow in the Keys wasn't too shabby, either.

Being in Willowvale brought back too many memories. Memories of working on this dude ranch, catering to tourists who wanted overnight trips into the valley for the whole cowboy experience. That lost teen barely existed inside him anymore. With the back-and-forth toss he got from his divorced parents, Pax had vowed never to put a child through that. He also promised himself not to fall into a marriage trap, because that rarely ended well enough to take the risk. He didn't have the time, nor did he care about feeding a relationship long enough to worry about forever. He never wanted to go through that pain ever again.

"You've picked at me long enough," he told her after she tossed another personal question his way. "I'm turning the tables."

Her perfectly arched brows rose. "I'm anxious to hear this."

Yeah, so was he. He wasn't confident in his questions like she seemed to be with hers. Granted, her career stemmed from learning her clients' minds and souls. His career only worried about his clients' bank accounts. Oh, he had to wine and dine clients, but any relationships he'd built were purely surface level.

"You have a condo in Portland," he started. "You either have a cat or a bird. Something that's low maintenance and can be left alone for periods of time."

Her lips pursed. "I don't have either at the time. No condo, and my cat actually died last year. I can't bring myself to get another just yet."

"You have an apartment? Something with a courtyard."

"Wrong again." She shook her head and tipped back her glass for another sip. "I'm currently homeless."

Her statement startled him. Even though he was in the real estate business, he didn't come across homeless people. His clients had millions if not billions. They demanded that level far above perfection. Homeless? How the hell was she homeless?

"Maybe the wine is getting to me," she murmured, staring at the contents in her glass before setting it on the hearth. "I try not to discuss my personal life."

"Ironic, don't you think?"

Kira stretched her legs out in front of her and crossed her ankles. She leaned against the leather chair behind her and continued to hold his gaze. The tension between them didn't seem at all awkward, but almost…calming. When was the last time he didn't feel pressured or rushed or in demand from someone? Kira asked nothing of him other than to spend the holiday and share a dinner that she had graciously made.

"I'm not often asked," she replied. "I mean, when I meet with clients, we're discussing them and their needs or goals."

He should stay out of this world of hers. He had no reason to dive any deeper. Focusing on his own state of affairs made more sense than trying to figure out hers. Attaching himself to her on any level could cause a domino effect of falling into that trap with others—and that was something he shouldn't allow.

But he couldn't help himself.

"So how long have you been homeless?" he asked, unable to help himself.

"Since last week. It's a long story."

Which should be his cue to leave. He had financials to look over; he had emails to read. Even on Christmas, Pax still had work that needed his attention. Resting and taking breaks would only put him behind. He didn't get this far by taking days off.

Hank had taught him that. Nobody had a work ethic like that man, and Pax owed his success to working on this ranch all of his teenage years. Which was precisely why he needed to do right by him and make sure this ranch was run by someone who would take care of the property, just like Hank would want.

Silence settled heavy in the room. The fire sparked and cracked. Orange and red flames slid over the charred logs. Pax should put on his gear and head back to the house. He kept telling himself to stand up and thank her for dinner.

But there was something about her normally exuberant attitude that had a chink in it. Maybe it was that tired tone her voice had taken on, or perhaps the sadness that crept through her gaze for the briefest of moments. He wasn't sure, but he knew whatever she was dealing with was getting to her.

"So where will you live when you get back?" he asked, already thinking of contacts he had in Portland.

She pursed her painted pink lips as she mulled over her response. Did she not have anyone who could assist her? Family or friends? One of her clients she'd made friends with over the years?

Perhaps Kira had too much pride to ask for help, but where did that leave her?

Again, he needed to distance himself, but that would only make him a jerk. This ranch had been his refuge when he'd been growing up. Hank and Edith had taken a young, bratty teen and turned his life around. Oh, he'd had a home to go to, but with no support and a dad who cared more about his gambling than his own son, Pax knew that feeling of despair.

"I'm confident something will fall into place," she replied. "You don't happen to have a spare condo in Portland, do you?"

Her sweet laugh seemed to mask that pain he'd heard lacing her tone earlier.

The woman made her living off positivity and happiness. Of course she wouldn't let her facade crack…at least not intentionally and in front of a virtual stranger.

"I don't have a spare condo lying around, no."

Leaning forward and crisscrossing her legs, Kira let out a deep sigh. "My best friend, the one who forced me on a vacation here, offered a room at her place until I found something, but she just had a baby and there's no way any of us would be happy with that setup."

Pax cringed at the idea of trying to live with a newborn, but he never wanted children, so that just seemed like a nightmare.

"No family in the area?" he asked.

"I only have my mom…well, and her soon-to-be fourth husband, but they live in Washington."

"I'm sorry, did you say—"

"Fourth," she confirmed with a nod. "Some people collect stamps. My mother collects husbands and ex-husbands. I don't look for this one to last any longer than the others."

Interesting. Clearly Kira didn't have much stability in her life, either. Her career and goals were all on her own shoulders, much like him. And Pax really didn't care for all these similarities that continued to pull him even closer to her and her world. He had his own world he was quite content with, not to mention his schedule was beyond full.

Yet here he sat, trying to solve the problems of a woman he'd known all of two days.

"I admit I was surprised to see you were traveling alone and staying through the New Year," he told her. "That's pretty rare."

"I'm rare," she volleyed back with another adorable laugh. "I do love the holidays, but I don't hang much around family traditions. I guess I'd have to have them to begin with."

Family traditions? Yeah, he didn't even know that concept himself. Hank and Edith would always host a large gathering around the holidays for any staff who wanted to attend. He never missed. For one, he didn't really care about spending those days with his father, and his father wasn't exactly whipping up anything grand. For another thing, Pax's respect for the Carsons wouldn't allow him anything else other than joining them for a meal they'd prepared in appreciation.

"I take it you don't have much family."

Her statement had him shifting his focus from the past to the present.

"My dad is alive, but I haven't spoken to him in years."

"So we're both just a couple of outcasts?" she asked, reaching for her wineglass.

Outcasts. He never thought of himself that way, but she wasn't far from the truth. He and Kira had both made their way through life and to their goals without support or assistance from family. He appreciated a strong woman and one who wasn't afraid to take charge of her life…or travel alone for a new adventure.

Kira stared at her empty glass and frowned. "That went fast."

Pax couldn't help but chuckle. Not that he was a heavy drinker by any means, but this petite thing was clearly a lightweight. She wasn't drunk, but she was very likely feeling good.

Which was definitely his cue to leave.

He came to his feet and stretched the stiffness from his shoulders and back. He wasn't used to sitting in one place for so long.

"You rushing off?" she asked, her wide eyes staring up at him.

He didn't want to rush off. He wanted to stay, to explore this undeniable, indescribable pull toward her. Ignoring the pull seemed careless. He'd always honed in on his emotions and followed his gut.

But he also had common sense and an intimate setting coupled with too much wine was not a good combo.

"It's getting late."

He assumed. He'd actually lost track of time, which he never did. For once, he wasn't looking at his watch or his phone. He'd enjoyed the evening and the woman.

Kira extended her hand, a silent request for him to assist her up.

Pax gripped her delicate hand in his and gave a slight tug. She popped up to her feet with a wide smile that punched him directly in the gut with a need he didn't want, but couldn't ignore. She didn't pull her hand away and he didn't let go.

"You're not as grouchy as I first thought," she murmured, her eyes exploring his. "You're just lonely."

Like me. Those two unspoken words hovered between them just the same as if she'd said them out loud. He'd entered so far into a dangerous territory with Kira, he wasn't sure he even knew the way out at this point.

And he wasn't lonely. He'd had a thriving social life back in Spain just weeks ago. He'd leased a temporary penthouse while working on his start-up company. He wanted nothing more than to get back and finish things. Losing his momentum there could be the end of his firm, and he refused to admit defeat. He'd worked too hard for this next step.

But the woman standing before him with a silent invitation in her eyes threatened to distract him in the most intriguing way.

She inched closer, keeping that wide gaze locked in on his. His gut tightened in both anticipation and arousal. He hadn't been with a woman in quite some time. While his social calendar remained full, he'd been too busy obsessing over his latest development.

But seducing a woman half-intoxicated wasn't on his to-do list, either.

Then her lips grazed his and Pax pulled up every ounce of willpower he possessed to resist temptation. But when her lips parted and covered his in the softest, sweetest gesture, he nearly snapped. He clenched his fists at his sides, but returned the kiss. His lips fit hers a little too perfectly, and the sweet taste of wine had him wanting even more.

Kira let out a soft moan as she eased back and looked up at him once more. A flirty smile danced around her mouth, and Pax felt he deserved some award for how well he'd handled himself. But he wasn't out of here yet. The snow fell outside in the dark of night, the fire provided a warm, intimate atmosphere, and there wasn't a soul around to stop them.

"I shouldn't have done that," she told him. "But I'm not sorry."

He should say something, do something, but she kept him on his toes and so damn confused. He needed to go before he forgot all the reasons this was a bad idea.

"Thanks for dinner," he told her before moving toward the door. He slid into his boots, pulled on his coat, and plucked his hat from the hook. Curling the brim in his hands, he turned to glance over his shoulder. With Kira's hair framing her petite face and that inviting mouth he'd just experienced, he had a hard time leaving her standing here by herself, just to go back to the main house to spend the evening alone.

Sometimes life provided impossible forks in the road. No matter which way he went, he'd wonder if he made the right decision. And maybe if she hadn't had wine and he knew her head was in the right place, just maybe he'd stick around. But that wasn't the case.

"I'm not sorry, either."

He left her with those words as he stepped out into the bitter cold and headed out to finish the rest of the night alone.

Six

To say Kira had grown restless would be a vast understatement. Since having Pax for Christmas dinner last night, all she could think of was that kiss. He said he wasn't sorry, but did that mean he enjoyed it? She'd never had a man kiss her back without touching her anywhere else…although she felt the passion from the softness of his lips throughout her entire body.

She'd woken early and made waffles with berries and tidied up in the small space. Now she just really wished she had something else to do besides baking. She could read or dig back into the Portland housing market, but none of that sounded appealing right now. She wanted out of the cabin, but she wasn't sure where to go or what to do.

With the sun shining bright on a new blanket of pristine snow, she figured she could bundle up and set out toward the barns. Perhaps a stable hand would be in, and she could see the horses. If she was lucky, maybe she could ask for a ride. She'd never ridden a horse before, but since she was on a totally new adventure, she might as well give that a shot, too.

Kira quickly layered up her clothing to ward off the Wyoming elements and left her phone charging on her bedside table. She wanted to completely unplug from the world for now and she couldn't do that when she was tied to a demanding device.

Once she felt like she wouldn't turn into a popsicle, she waddled out onto the porch and inhaled the fresh, crisp air. She smiled at nothing in particular other than the beauty surrounding her. The snow-covered mountain peaks seemed to reach all the way up to the clear blue sky. The land stretched as far as she could see. The row of wood and stone cabins exactly like hers went off in either direction, making a perfect line. The biggest barn was maybe thirty yards away and, according to the booklet of information in her rental, that's where the horses were kept and riding available on certain days and times. She hoped someone was in there today. With it being the day after Christmas, Pax might have given the employees some time off.

Every thought she had seemed to circle back to him, and when she thought of him, she thought of that brief, yet effective kiss. She shouldn't have been so bold, but she meant it when she'd told him she wasn't sorry. The whole point of her trip was to relax and put herself first, right? Well, the wine relaxed her, and kissing him had been a completely selfish choice. But she'd do it all over again if given the same circumstances.

Kira made her way down the cleared path from the cabins toward the barn. She huddled deeper into her coat and kept her gloved hands inside her pockets. The knitted cap on her head had been pulled down enough to keep her ears warm. She hated the cold, but she couldn't hate the beauty of this dude ranch.

She wondered what made the place start to slide downhill. She couldn't imagine someone ever letting such a stunning piece of land go unattended. Pax had hinted that he was working on restoring everything, but how had he come into such a problem that it needed restored? Did he have a financial issue that prevented him from running the ranch properly? Had he been manager and then taken over? Or maybe he was merely a stable hand put in charge for a while and had ideas of how to make this place prosper again. She had quite a variety of questions and figured he still would remain close-lipped about his personal business.

Perhaps that's what made him so irritable at times. Worry over a business or personal life could take hold of someone's emotions and send them into a roller-coaster tailspin. Maybe she could distract him...

Maybe they could distract each other.

The snow crunched beneath her boots as she made her way toward the open end of the barn. She stepped inside and was instantly enveloped by the warmth from the overhead heaters. The stalls lined either side of the wide concrete path. The walkway was completely clean of any straw or hay. The aroma of horses and other farm scents that weren't entirely pleasant hit her. She supposed being on a ranch wasn't all beauty and scented candles, even if it was Christmastime.

She walked a little further in, hoping to see someone who could assist her or let her ride. She had no clue what she was doing or even if animals came out in the winter like this. But hopefully she could learn something and get her mind off Pax for at least a few minutes.

A gorgeous spotted horse poked his head from over the half door. She didn't know types or even if this was a boy or a girl, but she knew loveliness when she saw it.

"Hey, buddy." She eased her way over, not sure if she could touch or not, so she kept her hands in her pockets. "You're a big guy and so pretty. What's your name?"

"Thunder."

Kira jumped and spun around toward the doorway she'd just come through. Her heart beat faster than seconds ago, at both the fact she thought she was alone and because Pax strode through just as casual as you please.

"I didn't know if anyone was here or not," she

stated, trying to relax her breathing after being startled. "Do you do everything around here?"

Pax made his way closer, his old boots scuffing along the concrete floors.

"Seems like it, but no." He stopped just before her. "I was on my way down here when I saw you leaving the cabin."

She turned her attention back to Thunder. He tipped his nose up and down and let out a neigh.

"He wants you to rub his nose," Pax told her as he came to stand beside her.

"I wasn't sure if I was allowed." Kira pulled her hands from her pockets and removed her gloves. She clutched them in one hand and reached for the horse with the other. "Like this?"

She slid her fingertips up and down the space between his eyes.

"Just like that," he confirmed. "Thunder has been here about a year, but he's quite a flirt."

She tossed Pax a glance and a grin. "Unlike his owner."

Pax's brow quirked. "You think I don't flirt?"

"Not with me."

He reached up and took her hand, pulling her from the horse. She turned to face him and let out a sigh.

"I'm not looking for a compliment or to rehash the kiss."

"No?"

His strong hold warmed her hand where he still held on. Now her heart beat faster for an entirely different reason. While she didn't mind the fact they were alone, she did wonder where a stable hand was, and why there weren't more workers for such a vast ranch.

But any thoughts of employees or day-to-day operations here vanished as Pax inched closer, obliterating that gap between them. She didn't recognize that look in his eyes and she hadn't seen it before. Desire? Intrigue?

She'd obviously dated before, but everything about this interesting, almost mysterious man had her fully believing she might just be out of her element…and she really wasn't mad about it. He gave her a zing of thrill that she'd never experienced and if nothing else came from this trip, he'd awakened something deep inside her.

"Are you going to kiss me again?" she asked, feeling bolder than ever.

His lips quirked. "I didn't kiss you the first time. You kissed me."

Semantics. Did it matter?

"Are you complaining?" she retorted. "Because you didn't really touch me when I kissed you and I'd had wine, not enough to affect my thinking. I wanted to kiss you, but after you left I worried—"

His mouth covered hers, cutting off any words or thoughts she had. And he didn't just touch her with his lips. No, he gripped her waist with his strong hands and tugged her toward him. Kira sank into his warmth and let him take the lead. Today she had a clearer head, not that she didn't appreciate the brief encounter last night. But now? This moment was a game changer.

Pax eased his mouth from hers just slightly, but didn't release his hold on her body.

"I didn't touch you last night because it didn't seem right. And if I had touched you, I didn't know where to stop, or if that's really what you wanted."

Kira attempted to unpack all he'd just said. Once his words rolled through her mind for a minute, she couldn't help but laugh.

"Well, you're quite chatty. Had I known a kiss would have made you open up, I would have kissed you on day one."

"I haven't opened up, but I wasn't going to do anything after you'd had a bottle of wine."

"And what about now that I've only had a cup of coffee?" she countered.

Those dark eyes held hers for a moment. The muscle in his jaw ticked, but he released her and took the slightest step back, leaving her confused and wanting more.

"I don't know what the hell I'm going to do," he muttered, almost as if frustrated with himself. "I didn't plan on finding a guest attractive."

"Yet here I am."

His lips twitched as if he wanted to smile, and she knew without a doubt she was getting to him. Honestly, she hadn't expected this, either. Oh, her bestie had hinted more than once, and not so subtly, that Kira should find a cowboy and have a hot, holiday fling, but that hadn't been Kira's intention when agreeing to this trip. The overwhelming demands from clients, the high-maintenance mother, and the landlord from hell had nearly driven her out of her mind. Her only goal on this trip was to escape reality and now that she looked into Pax's coal-like eyes, she realized she'd far surpassed even her own expectations.

"What brought you to the barn?" he asked, pulling her from her thoughts and any idea that he might kiss her again.

Fine. She could pace herself and let the anticipation build. She had no idea what would happen between them, if anything, but she could enjoy the few weeks she had here and maybe learn a bit more about the man and the ranch.

This mindset was completely out of character for her, but so was a spur-of-the-moment trip alone to a brand-new area. There was something thrilling and exhilarating about experiencing all of this in a place where nobody knew her. She could be anyone she wanted, and if that was a woman who wanted to have a heated fling with a sexy cowboy, then that's who she'd be while she was here.

"I was hoping to see the horses and maybe ride," she told him, turning back to face Thunder. "But I wasn't sure who all was working or if you gave them time off after the holidays or even if horses can go out in this weather."

"I take it you know nothing about horses," he snorted. "Yes, they can go out."

She glanced over her shoulder. "It's not a 'must

have' on my list, but maybe before I go back to Portland, we could ride? I'm not sure you want a rookie on the back of a horse, but I could ride with one of the stable hands."

"You'll ride with me."

Kira blinked at the adamant statement he delivered without hesitation. Well, that was even better than she'd anticipated.

"I won't turn that down," she replied with a wink.

She reached once again and stroked Thunder's nose. Animals fascinated her, but she didn't even own one. She didn't have time to care for one with her schedule and having one cooped up in her condo wouldn't be fair to the pet. Of course, she didn't have a condo anymore, so...

"Are you the only one here today, too?" she asked.

Pax leaned against the edge of the stall and adjusted his hat. "I'm the only one here through the first of the year."

A flutter of excitement zinged through her, but she still had so many questions.

"I'm just surprised this place isn't booked," she told him, thinking out loud. "I know you said you were going through some changes, and I'm assuming that's why my friend got the price so low, but still. It's so peaceful and beautiful here. What all are you changing?"

Something dark glazed over his stare, but not a darkness that worried or scared her. No, this seemed to be more of a sadness she hadn't seen from him before. Did the owner die and now Pax was left to run this sprawling place alone? Is that why he sent the employees home? Did he not have the funds to keep the dude ranch running?

"All of that is still up in the air," he replied, offering no more information.

As much as Kira wanted to pry and learn more, she also had to respect his boundaries. Just because she'd gotten chatty last night after a few glasses of bubbly, didn't mean he wanted to share his entire life story.

"So what are your plans for the day?" she asked, wondering if that would give her any more insight to his life outside of ranching.

"I have a meeting at noon in town and then some other business to tend to this afternoon. You plan on baking, or what are you doing?"

Baking. Oh my word. She'd totally forgotten his gift last night.

"I can't believe it," she muttered.

"What?"

"I had a gift for you when you came over for dinner, and it slipped my mind."

He jerked like he'd been slapped. "A gift? What for?"

"Christmas, obviously. You know, yesterday *was* a holiday."

"Well, yeah, but I didn't think gifts were a thing between total strangers."

The man didn't gift anything? Or receive? Did he have absolutely nobody in his life?

A low level of dread settled in her belly. What if

this ranch had belonged to like his grandfather and that was the only person he'd had in his life and now he was gone, leaving Pax to tend to everything?

Mercy, she read too many books. Her imagination wanted to run wild. But in her defense, what else should she think? She had nothing to go on, and the man was so tight-lipped about everything…except the fact he liked kissing her.

"You didn't have to get me anything," he told her.

Kira stepped back from Thunder and turned to focus fully on Pax. The dark hat and coat with fitted jeans and worn black boots were a lethal combination to her hormones. No man should look this good, and no man dressed like this back in Portland. Perhaps that was just another of the many draws she had toward him. He was different in the most infatuating type of way. He didn't want anything from her, except maybe another kiss, and he wasn't nosy. The man was just trying to figure out how to make this ranch run again, and maybe she was just that distraction he needed. She didn't mind if that's the category he wanted to put her in. She wasn't looking for anything long-term, either. Hell, she couldn't even take time for a cat, let alone trying to feed into a relationship.

Pax didn't seem like a forever type of guy. He seemed like he'd take a few extremely lucky lovers, letting them know well in advance that he wasn't emotionally available for more. He'd keep his circle small, clearly if the idea of a Christmas present shocked him. He wouldn't share his worries with anyone, he'd want to handle them on his own.

"Why are you looking at me like that?" he asked, his dark brows drawing inward.

Kira blinked. "Like what?"

"Like I'm being dissected."

She shrugged. "Just admiring the view."

He continued to stare at her with a gaze that she couldn't quite read. He knew what he looked like. There was no need to stroke his ego anymore, but she also wasn't going to lie or pretend like she wasn't attracted. She'd already kissed him, so…

"You want to get off the property for a bit?" he asked.

Kira blinked and jolted at his abrupt invitation.

"Yeah, I surprised myself, too," he added with another adjust of his hat. "I have a lunch meeting you can't sit in on, but there's shops and a coffee place in town you might enjoy."

Kira clapped her gloved hands together. "Count me in. I'll meet you at my cabin. I just need my phone and purse."

She took off out of there, thrilled to see more of this adorable town, but even more excited that he'd thought to ask her. This trip had just taken a turn she hadn't expected, but certainly welcomed.

Seven

"Your best bet would be to renovate like you were going to live there. Make it state-of-the-art everything. This area is growing like crazy, man. You'll get a bidding war going."

Pax listened to Brandon Littlefoot give his best business and real estate advice. There was no one else Pax trusted more in this industry than Brandon. Not only was he the lead in this Willowvale Springs office, but he also had been with Pax since the beginning. He knew the values in the area, and he also knew Pax better than just about anyone…at least as far as business went.

They'd met in high school when Brandon had been new to the area. He and Pax seemed to hit it off because Brandon also guarded himself with relationships. The two seemed to jibe when it came to business sense, so when Pax needed a right-hand man, so to speak, Brandon was the only choice.

Laughter from the café filtered toward him and Pax stiffened, his shoulders taut. He knew that sound. He'd tried like hell to ignore the fact Kira sat behind him in a booth. She'd brought her laptop and said she had some work to do, which he figured meant she was still on the house hunt.

Pax had told the barista to put anything Kira ordered on his tab, but he hadn't let Kira know that. He didn't know why he felt the need to protect her or suddenly come to her aid. He had enough on his plate without some destitute traveler. She didn't seem upset about her situation, so why should he?

Or was she trying to play off just how dire her current state actually was? Something about her stubborn independence coupled with a layer of vulnerability made him want to intervene.

"Pax?"

He blinked and focused back on Brandon and not the woman behind him, who'd obviously made a friend.

"Yeah. Just thinking."

Brandon's dark brows rose. "Thinking about the woman you walked in with, who is back there talking with some guy?"

He would not turn around to see what Brandon could see. He had no ties to Kira, nor she to him. He'd invited her so she could see the town and get off the property for a bit. He was surprised how busy the café was today, but perhaps people were over the family gatherings and needed out of their own houses.

"She's just a guest at the ranch," Pax defended. He reached for his mocha and curled his hand around the warm mug. "Figured she could use a change of scenery since she's the only one there right now."

"Is that so?"

If possible, Brandon's brows rose even higher.

Pax set his mug back down and sighed. "Relax. I'm just playing the dutiful owner, although she thinks I'm a stable hand."

Brandon chuckled and eased back in the booth. "And you don't see the need to correct her?"

He could straighten her out, but why? His whole life since becoming successful involved people wanting something from him. So many people sought him out looking for a backer for their business deals. They wanted advice on real estate, always wanting something from him for nothing. Women who tried to date him were especially attracted to the money and the power. Being around Kira was quite refreshing and a nice change. Between her and the extremely slow-paced lifestyle of Willowvale Springs, he didn't hate his return trip as much as he thought he would. The timing could certainly be better, but this dude ranch had to be restored and resurrected better than ever.

"She's not staying long and we'll never see each other again," Pax replied. "It sounds arrogant to tell her I'm the owner."

"Or maybe it's embarrassing, considering the place has gone to hell," Brandon retorted. "I mean, to a new person coming in, the grounds are still beautiful and so are the cabins. You can't beat the Wyoming scenery. But the amenities aren't what they used to be, and the added touches Edith insisted upon are gone."

Yeah. Edith and Hank had been such a dynamic duo when it came to knowing exactly how to run a business. Hank was a shark when it came to finances, but none of that ever mattered to Edith. She homed in on the people, their hearts, and that is what made their employees so loyal. Everything they touched in town had exceeded success, and Pax refused to see that dude ranch be anything less.

"I'm not embarrassed." Pax stretched his arm along the back of the booth. "I'm frustrated and can't figure out where to start."

"Because your mind is preoccupied with Spain and your new guest."

He ground his teeth together. There were draw-backs to having such a close associate.

"My mind is definitely on Spain," Pax agreed, dodging the topic of Kira altogether. "We're so close to the opening and I've still got agents to interview, not to mention trying to oversee the final designs of the building. It will be worth it once I'm up and running, but it would be a hell of a lot easier if I was there in person."

Brandon's eyes moved from Pax to just over his shoulder and then he got the widest smile on his face.

"Good afternoon."

Pax didn't even have to turn. He knew who'd come up to their table. If Brandon's flirty smile didn't give away their visitor, the familiar scent of floral perfume wafting around him certainly did.

Pax resisted the urge to kick his buddy beneath the table.

He had to get it together. The sudden burst of jealousy had no room here. Brandon could flirt all he wanted. Kira was a free woman, not to mention just passing through.

"Hey. So sorry to interrupt."

Now Pax did glance to Kira, who offered one of her sweetest grins as she darted her attention between the two guys. She clutched her shoulder bag and motioned toward the door.

"I'm going to head to the boutique next door and then I'll be back," she told Pax. "Take your time. I'm just checking things out."

Brandon eased from the booth and extended his hand. His long, black braid hung down his back as he turned on his charm. Pax wanted to laugh, but he also wanted to swat that hand out of the way. Being jealous was beyond ridiculous. He'd shared a kiss with her and a few stolen glances and one evening. That didn't bind them together.

"I'm Brandon Littlefoot." He extended his hand and shook Darcy's. "I'm an associate of Pax. Do you want to join us?"

Darcy's smile widened as she continued to clutch Brandon's hand. "Oh, that's sweet, but I'll let you guys finish your meeting and I'll get some shopping done."

She pulled her hand back and gripped the bag on her shoulder. Pax remained seated, but kept his eyes locked on her. Did she captivate everyone she came in contact with? He'd been no different, even though he'd tried to avoid her charms and appeal. There was just something about her positivity and the way her whole face lit up when she smiled. If he could use one word to describe Kira, it would be *refreshing*.

"Well, it was nice to meet you," Brandon told her with a nod. "We'll be right here if you change your mind."

Kira shot them both her signature megawatt smile before turning on her booted heel and striding through the café toward the exit.

Brandon stared down the path she'd taken, still with some dumbass smile on his face.

"Would you sit down," Pax growled. "You look like a damn fool."

His friend shifted his focus back around as he slid back into the booth.

"Well, well, well."

Brandon let out a chuckle that grated on Pax's nerves. He ground his teeth and toyed with the handle of his mug. He'd let his emotions take over and now he was the one that looked like the fool.

"Don't start," Pax muttered.

"Why not? This is great." Brandon couldn't seem to stop laughing as he shook his head. "I've never seen you infatuated with a woman before."

"Infatuated?" Pax scoffed, annoyed that Brandon might just be hitting too close to the truth. "I'm not sixteen and I'm sure as hell not infatuated. She's a guest at the ranch. My *only* guest, I might add, which is concerning, considering that place used to be booked up months, if not a year, in advance."

There. Let Brandon chew on that nugget of information. The man loved solving business crises, which is why Pax brought him on years ago.

"We can circle back to Kira in a bit," Brandon stated, shifting in his seat to lean forward. "You need to zero in on what your plans are for the ranch. Do you want to stay? Let's start there."

Stay? No. That had never been on his radar. How could he remain in Willowvale Springs when he had a new company in its infancy in Spain? He'd need to be there for quite a while to set a solid foundation and make sure he had the right crew to take over and make sure the company soared. Remaining in Willowvale for too long would be too risky. Getting involved or attached would only go against everything he'd vowed to distance himself from.

"I don't see how that's possible unless you want to go to Spain," Pax joked.

Brandon would never leave Willowvale Springs. Even though he hadn't lived on the reservation with the rest of his family, he wouldn't want to be that far from his family.

"Okay, so you're not staying," Brandon replied. "So you need to do some updating and then find a hell of a property manager to breathe new life back into that place. It would have to be someone lively and social, but also have a good business mindset."

Kira instantly came to mind. Lively? Check. Good business sense? Check...at least from what he could deduce. But he couldn't ask her to stay here. Hell, he didn't even know her. She could be a smart business-woman because she was a scammer for all he knew.

Pax blew out a sigh and rubbed the back of his neck. Unfortunately, this dude ranch was just like any business that needed time, attention, and funds. He had the funds, that was never the issue. The time and attention? He didn't have either of those to invest. But Hank had trusted him with this inheritance, for reasons Pax still didn't understand. As much as Pax wanted to up and leave and wish some new owner or manager the best of luck, he couldn't do that. He owed everything in his life to Hank and Edith. With-out them, Pax wouldn't have near the work ethic he did. They'd always been more than just his em-ployer...they'd been like family.

"There's no quick solution," Pax finally stated. "I keep waiting on some miracle to fall into my lap."

"You know that's not going to happen."

No, it wasn't. He'd have to carve out the time to get this dude ranch up and running. So what did he do with Spain? Virtual appointments were okay with an already established business, but that's not how he ran things or ever wanted to start up.

"I'll go to Spain."

Pax jerked and focused on his friend. "Excuse me?"

"Not long-term," Brandon amended. "But I can

take a few months and get things up and running. I mean, if you trust me with that process."

Trust him? There wouldn't be anyone else Pax would trust with this vital step in the Agency expanding overseas.

"Man, if you're serious—"

"I am."

A weight seemed to lift from Pax's shoulders that at least one of his issues had sorted itself out. Maybe a miracle had fallen into his lap.

"Let me know where everything stands," Brandon went on. "The prospects for interviews, the building itself and renovations—I'll need it all."

"You'll have it," Pax confirmed. "Let me know when you can go and I'll change the interviews from video to in-person. I trust you to make the right decisions."

"No pressure," Brandon chuckled.

"There shouldn't be. You're the only man I'd put in this position, and I'm positive you'd make the same decision I would if I was there."

Brandon nodded, and Pax mentally ran through all of the pertinent information he'd need to send over. There were several applicants, potential listings already on the docket, finalizing office structure and design. There was a great deal left for the initial foundation, but having Brandon there to spearhead that part while Pax figured out the dude ranch was the perfect solution. While Pax would have liked to have been the one to launch everything, he'd rather this than to push out any date for opening.

"Now, let's get back to your guest."

Pax reached for his coffee at Brandon's statement. Of course the man wouldn't let that go, and Pax was about to bring this little lunch meeting to an abrupt close.

Eight

"Okay. Talk to you later."

Kira tapped her screen to end the call with her mother. The third phone call of the day regarding dresses for the wedding. Still with the dresses.

Honestly, Kira didn't care. Maybe that sounded harsh, but…well, it was the truth.

She tossed the cell onto the cushion of the couch beside her and reached for her laptop on the table. She might as well look up these dresses and text her mother or she'd just get another phone call.

Part of Kira wondered if her mother had an addiction to weddings. Did she love being in them over and over? Did she love the planning or did she truly fall in love this often? Was it any wonder Kira remained reserved when it came to her heart and her feelings? Love shouldn't be so easy to fall into…at least that was Kira's opinion. She'd never been in love, and her mother had supposedly found it four times.

Kira pulled up one of the websites just as a knock on her door interrupted the silence of her cabin. Her heart always kicked up a beat, because no one else would be knocking except for Pax. She hadn't seen him since he'd dropped her off back here after his meeting and her shopping. She'd found quite a few adorable things from the local boutiques and vowed to check them out once again before leaving. After-season sales were the best time to stock up on all the goodies like cozy sweaters and fuzzy socks. She'd even grabbed a pair of cute cowgirl boots. Hey, when in Wyoming…

She padded to the door in one of her new warm socks and peeked out the side window. Not Pax. Some old, rugged, authentic-looking cowboy with a scraggy gray beard, worn brown hat, and a thick coat up around his ears. He stared at the door as if waiting on it to open.

Confused and a little unsettled, she glanced to make sure the door was indeed locked and went back to the table to grab her cell. She was dialing Pax when the voice boomed from the other side.

"I'm just checking to see if you need anything," the man called. "I'm Tate. The ranch hand."

Hadn't Pax let the employees go for the holidays? He wasn't picking up the call, so she hung up.

"I'm good, but thanks," she yelled back, still unsure if he was telling the truth.

But who would randomly come onto a dude ranch and seek out lonely women. Still, she wasn't opening the door for him.

"Okay. Well, Mr. Hart had to run into town on an emergency and called me in, so if you need anything, just ring the main line. I'll get ya."

An emergency? And Pax wasn't answering his phone. What the hell was going on?

"Thank you."

She at least remembered her manners as worry took over. Was he hurt? Did he need someone to help him? Who did he have in his life besides staff? As the manager, or whatever he was here, he seemed to be spread thin. No wonder he'd been so surly when she'd first met him. The man needed a break and some help.

Heavy footsteps moved away from her door and Kira felt ridiculous for overreacting. But as a woman traveling alone, she'd rather overreact than to take any chances.

As much as she wanted to call Pax again, she didn't want to bother him if he was dealing with a crisis. But every single part of her flooded with worry and fear. She couldn't concentrate on anything until she heard from him. She did shoot him a quick text to call when he could and that she wanted to know he was okay.

What could have happened in the hour since he'd dropped her off until now? If he was alone and could call Tate, then he was likely okay. Kira had to calm her mind and think rationally now. Maybe a friend of his had a problem and he just went to assist.

She went to the kitchen and looked at what was left of her baking ingredients. She couldn't focus on dresses at her mother's request right now. She needed to stay busy and focus on something else. She scrolled through her phone at some of the saved recipes and landed on a chocolate chip dip she'd been wanting to try and have around to snack on. That's what she'd do. Then if Pax stopped over, she'd have something ready.

Mercy. She sounded like an old country woman, always needing something on the counter in case guests dropped in unannounced. She loved reading those Southern fiction books, and maybe a little bit of that influence had spilled over into her vacation. Back home, she didn't have guests that popped in, and she never made the time to bake or cook. She rather liked this laid-back atmosphere and slower pace. She had wondered how she'd do on this forced retreat, but she wasn't sorry she came. In fact, she had every intention of coming back one day.

Maybe Pax had a hand in that decision, but she also loved the gorgeous mountain scenery and the serenity she didn't get back in Portland.

She laid her cell on the counter and went about making the dip, glancing to her device about every minute. She could have asked Tate what happened, but honestly, this wasn't any of her business. Their friendship, if this could be called that, and a couple of kisses didn't give her a window into his life.

Once the dip was done, she slid it into the fridge and cleaned up her work area on the small counter space. She washed up her dirty utensils and bowls and had just dried her hands when her cell lit up.

She rushed to grab it, only to find a message from her mother asking if she'd looked at the dresses. On a sigh, Kira moved back to her living room and her laptop. She wasn't in a dress mood or anything else other than finding out if Pax was okay or what tore him away from the ranch in such a hurry.

Kira had just brought her laptop back to life when another knock pounded on the door. She jumped, putting her computer back on the table and heading over to the entryway. She peeked out the window fully expecting to see Tate again, but a familiar dark gaze met hers.

With a quick flick of the lock, Kira threw open the door.

"What happened? Are you alright? Get in here. I have been worried sick."

She grabbed his hand and practically hauled him inside the warm cabin and out of the frigid elements.

"Relax," he told her as he took off his hat and hung it on the hook next to the door. "I'm perfectly fine. Just an issue with one of our mares, and I had to go over to the Amish community and bring back a balm for a cut."

Relief spread through her that the emergency was with an animal, and not one that was life-threatening.

Pax hung his coat next to his hat and Kira blinked at the simple gesture, realizing he'd come in and done those simple tasks just like he belonged here...with her. Which was positively silly. He was the manager, or something, of the dude ranch. Of course he belonged here. She was the outsider and had no ties to him or this place. But she was also human and could readily admit she cared for him.

"Tate came by to check on me."

Pax propped his hands on his hips and sighed. "I've no doubt he did. He knew a pretty lady was in the cabin. While he certainly would have done anything for you, he likely wanted a peek as well."

Kira crossed her arms over her chest, tipped her head, and smiled. "And how did he know a pretty lady was here?"

Those dark eyes held her in place with a tingle that was just as potent and powerful as a solid touch.

"I told him we had a female traveling alone."

"And he deduced I was pretty?"

Pax shrugged. "He asked what you looked like. I told him."

"And what adjectives did you use?"

His lips pursed. "Are you trying to get a compliment?"

"Just trying to get the facts."

Pax widened his stance, making him appear even more menacing and broad. Not in a scary way at all, but in the sexiest commanding manner she'd ever encountered. She hadn't planned on finding a real-life cowboy, but here he stood in her cabin and he seemed just as intrigued with her as she with him.

"The facts are you're gorgeous and sexy, but I didn't share that with him."

Pax's bold statement combined with his heavy-lidded stare moved something inside of her she hadn't even known existed. How could anyone have such a strong hold over her emotions and moods after only knowing them a handful of days? She couldn't imagine how she would feel if she were to stick around longer and truly get to know him. They'd likely form a fast friendship and perhaps even more. No doubt more, actually, if that bedroom gaze and the fact he found her sexy were any indicators.

"Well, it's good to know where I stand," she replied.

"If you've ever looked in a mirror, I'd say you already knew."

The crackling tension in the tiny cabin seemed to envelop them and she should feel somewhat awkward, yet all that filled her was a zing of arousal. She'd never in her life felt a zing before and just the fact that was the first word that came to mind seemed…well, perfect.

"So, what are you doing here?" she asked. "Not that I mind. I'm just curious."

"Checking in on you. Seeing if the dead tree needs to come out yet."

Kira glanced over her shoulder to the tree in question. A few more needles had fallen, the green faded, and some had gone straight brown.

"That's staying up as long as I'm here." She turned back to face him with a smile. "You can hardly see the ugly for the decorations."

"Your decorations are going to fall to the floor when those needles go," he grumbled.

She took a step forward and reached up to pat his bearded jaw. "Aw, there's that sweet Christmassy spirit I'm used to."

In a bold, swift move she didn't see coming, Pax covered her hand with his, holding her firmly in place. He closed the gap between them, never taking his midnight eyes from hers. Kira's heart raced, her breath caught in her throat as anticipation curled through her.

"It's not Christmas anymore."

His low, husky tone sent a warm shiver down her spine. She'd completely forgotten they were talking about a tree. The coarse hair of his beard beneath her palm, the heat from his broad body so close to hers, and the desire staring back at her sent her entire body into overdrive. The sexual awareness at this point couldn't be ignored, nor did she even want to try. He'd come here for a reason. Was it just to see her? Or was there something more? She didn't take Pax for someone who played games. He'd get what he wanted, when he wanted.

"Are you staying?" she murmured.

"That's up to you."

Putting the control back onto her only made him even sexier. He knew his full power and potency, but he also had manners. The fact he didn't even hesitate only proved that while he had a surly side, he also had gentlemanly qualities.

"So...is this going to be a temporary fling?"

She had to know where he stood and what this was. She'd never done anything like this in her life, so she had no clue about the rules. Maybe he didn't, either. If they both left this open and casual, they'd ultimately go their separate ways. Just like her trip, any type of fling would only be a blip in time.

But she didn't really want to think about another woman with Pax right now. An unexpected surge of jealousy threatened to slide into her euphoric moment, and she refused to allow that. She would take hold of her happiness and cling tight, because right now, that's what kept her motivated and looking toward her unknown future.

"Is that what you want?" he retorted. "A short-term fling?"

"I mean, I'm not staying here," she murmured.

"Yeah, me n—"

He stopped short and Kira blinked. He wasn't staying? Or what had he been about to say? She'd almost gotten a glimpse into his mind, something she'd been wanting more of. But if everything between them was truly going to be short-lived, then maybe diving too deep wasn't the smartest decision.

Instead of saying anything else, Pax slid their hands from his face and settled them between their chests.

"Let's focus on tonight and pretend tomorrow doesn't exist."

That throaty tone sent a ribbon of arousal spiraling through her belly. Awareness, anticipation, and attraction catapulted into a higher gear. The awareness of the privacy, with no one to bother them and nothing surrounding them but the night and the crackling fire. Regardless of the need to keep everything superficial and physical with no emotions involved, even she couldn't deny the charge of romance enveloping them.

Without another word, Kira went up onto her toes and captured his lips. Another taste, a stepping stone to more, had her entire body heating up. Pax released her hands and slid his around to cup her backside. He lifted her body against his and turned toward the short hallway leading to the only bedroom. This take-charge attitude of his only fueled her desire. She looped her legs and arms around him, never once breaking that sweet kiss.

With master skills, Pax maneuvered them into the bedroom and turned, trapping her between the wall and his hard body. His hands came around and found the hem of her shirt. The second his fingertips feathered across her bare skin, she pulled from the kiss and gasped. She hadn't even realized how much she'd craved his touch until this very second.

Pax slid his hand down into her leggings and immediately found her core. Kira pressed into his touch, closing her eyes and letting the moment consume her. When was the last time she'd been intimate? Way too long ago and she wanted to enjoy every single second of this.

He stroked her with an expert touch, at the same time he grazed his lips along her neck until he found the sensitive spot just behind her ear. He murmured something to her she couldn't understand, mostly because she was too busy concentrating on her body's euphoria.

When he eased his hand away, her eyes darted open. Pax's heavy-lidded gaze and sexy smirk stared back at her.

"You better not be done with me," she warned.

"Darlin', I've just gotten started."

Oh, that Southern drawl of his must only get stronger when he was turned on. She wanted more of that sexy talk, more of the man.

He reached for the button on his jeans and quickly maneuvered his pants down as she hoisted her legs as high as she could to allow him the space. Then he wasted no time in jerking her pants down, but when they got caught on her hips, Kira laughed as she reached to help. Somehow, they managed to get the material dangling from one of her ankles amidst a flurry of hands and laughter.

And then he was there…right where she ached for him most.

"I'm on birth control," she told him. "But I didn't pack anything else. I wasn't expecting…"

The muscle clenched in his jaw as his eyes grew even darker than before.

"If we need to stop—"

"No," he ground out. "I don't have anything with

me, either. But I'm clean and I trust you. So, it's your call here."

Kira slid her hands over his chest and curled her fingertips slightly into his bare skin. The coarse hair tickled her palms, adding to the pleasure that she could no longer deny for herself. She wanted him and she was going to have him.

In lieu of an answer, she tipped her hips, silently pleading for him to join their bodies.

And the moment he did, they both stilled, allowing a second for their bodies to adjust. But Kira couldn't take it. She needed more, so she arched into him and jerked her body just enough to set the motion. Pax obliged and flattened one hand on the wall next to her head and with the other hand he gripped the back of one of her thighs as he set the perfect rhythm.

Kira gripped the back of his neck and eased his mouth to hers. She wanted to be utterly consumed by him for as long as possible. She wanted to feel him, to *experience* him in every way possible.

Pax captured her lips and didn't miss a beat with his body. As much as she wanted the night to last, there was no way she was going to make it much longer. Her entire body climbed toward climax and she wasn't about to deny herself.

"That's it," he murmured against her lips. "Let go."

How had he known? How could the man, still somewhat of a stranger, know her body so well?

Kira didn't dwell on that, instead she let him take her exactly where she wanted to be…right over the edge between reality and a dream.

Her head tipped back against the wall as her body jerked. The warmth spread through her as she pressed her knees into his body, allowing the wave of sensations to wash over her. Pax moved faster now, clearly heading to his own oblivion. The second his body tightened, he covered her mouth with his once again. Their bodies rose together and formed a bond she just knew would be more than physical.

But she couldn't think about that right now.

As the exhilaration gave way to a host of postcoital tingles, Kira kept her eyes closed. She didn't want to risk seeing anything in his eyes that signaled he was done after this one time, or worse…regret.

For now, everything was perfect and she just needed to lock that happiness in for as long as possible.

Nine

Pax gripped the poker and stoked the embers in Kira's fireplace. The orange glow burst to life as the heat took hold of the new logs he'd just added. The sun still hadn't come up and the only light in the cabin came from the fire and the ridiculous tree in the corner.

He didn't know why he'd stayed the whole night—he hadn't done that in years with a woman. There was something about Kira that made staying hard nearly impossible. Not only that, but he'd come here because he'd been eaten up with jealousy over that harmless encounter between her and Brandon. The man flirted with everyone, but the flashy smile toward Kira had really agitated Pax in a manner that was both unhealthy and unexpected.

He propped the poker against the stone and took a step back. Rubbing a hand down his bare chest, Pax contemplated getting dressed and heading back to his own space. Sleeping over and encountering the whole morning after never held any appeal to him. Purposely putting himself in an awkward situation that could give off the wrong impression could only lead to a disaster for both parties. But considering Kira wasn't staying and she'd already labeled this a temporary fling, he hadn't been able to pull himself away...so he didn't.

Pax quietly made his way to the kitchen and figured he'd at least start some coffee. He hadn't been able to sleep much, not with his mind working on overdrive trying to figure out the plans for the ranch. Plans that most certainly never included a certain sexy traveler, but he couldn't be sorry for the distraction. As much as he thrived on working 24/7, there had to be time for other activities, and he'd just encountered some of the best of his life.

Kira had all the personality and charm and charisma outside of the bedroom, but inside... Well, who knew that sultry vixen lurked beneath the surface?

Pax found coffee filters and a dark roast bag from the local coffee shop. At least she had good taste in coffee, not that he was looking for or wanted to find similarities in their lives. He'd managed to temporarily unload a heavy portion of his worry onto Brandon and needed to remain in control and focused on the ranch. He couldn't mentally afford to let Kira take up too much real estate in his head.

Thankfully they were in agreement as to what this was and wasn't. He didn't do messy, complicated, or long-term.

Pax glanced to the closed bedroom door and wondered how late she slept. Did he wait on her so he didn't look like a jerk by just disappearing? Or would the pot of coffee and a note be sufficient for their morning after?

Once the pot had nearly filled, Pax poured himself a cup. He might as well drink one while he figured out the gentlemanly thing to do here. He hadn't taken a lover in nearly a year and even that had been casual…yet nothing compared to what he'd experienced last night with Kira.

Was that only because he'd gone so long without? He couldn't count on his thoughts right now. His mind had never been more vulnerable, and trusting any type of personal emotions wasn't smart at this stage.

Hank had entrusted Pax with the dude ranch, and that's the only thing he needed to be pouring his energy into.

Pax curled his hand around the warm mug and crossed the old hardwood until he came to the large area rug in the living room. The warmth from the fire and the coffee soothed something inside of him as he stared at the dancing flames. He couldn't recall a recent time in his life when he'd felt any type of contentment or peace. Something with his career or growing business always seemed to be up in the air and at times, precarious. Making deals and never losing or backing down was the only way he'd climbed to the top in his field, and he didn't intend to stop now. The ranch just gave him a very minor setback, but thanks to Brandon, this wouldn't be an issue. He could get this ranch up and running again and launch his Spanish agency, all within a smooth, efficient process.

He rolled over in his mind where to start with the ranch. Definitely he'd have to start with a long talk with Tate. The old stable hand had been around for years and knew more than Pax in regards to this property. Pax hadn't worked any type of ranch or farm work since he'd been a teen here in Willowvale Springs. Not that he couldn't remember what all he'd done, but there were so many details that went into running not only a ranch, but a successful business. He assumed he and Tate would have to be on the same page here, but ultimately, Pax would have the final say. He just wanted to keep the valued, trusted employee on hand because he wasn't staying a minute beyond the time it took to set some plans into motion here.

He took a sip of the hot, black coffee just as a floorboard creaked behind him. His gut tightened in an instant as he glanced over his shoulder. The sudden impact of desire hit him once again, harder and more intense than last night.

Kira stood just outside the bedroom door wearing only the comforter draped around her shoulders. One bare leg and bare feet stuck out the bottom with one creamy shoulder on display. Her long, dark hair still tousled, evidence of their passionate night together. The picture only thrust him back to those erotic images.

"You stayed."

Her soft statement sliced right through the silence and the moment. Pax fully turned to face her as he nodded, his breath still caught in his throat, making him unable to speak. The sensual sight of her made all thoughts vanish. How could he want her so soon? No, not want...*crave.*

"I thought you'd be gone," she added as she made her way closer.

Yeah, he thought he'd be gone, too, but now he was damn glad he opted to hang around.

When she got about two steps away, she released the blanket, then took those final steps. Without glancing around, Pax reached behind him to set his mug on the mantel, not giving a damn if the thing crashed to the floor. He'd clean it up later.

Kira went into his arms. Her bare chest pressing against his had his body tightening up once more. Arousal and desire pumped through him as her delicate hands ran up and down his back.

"You stayed and you made coffee." She tipped her head back to stare up at him and those dark eyes held both need and joy. "I might make you stay here until I leave."

The idea of staying here for two more weeks should send him into a panic...yet it didn't. Yeah, he had a business to get back into shape, but damn it, that seemed not near as important as the naked, willing woman in his arms.

He gripped her backside and lifted her until her ankles locked around his waist. They weren't going to make it back to the bedroom. Pax covered her mouth as he carefully maneuvered to the sofa. He turned and eased down, adjusting her so she straddled his lap. In a lighting move, she started working on his elastic pants, and he tipped from side to side until they were low enough. She curled her fingers around his shoulders as she rose up onto her knees. Her eyes held his as she sank down, joining their bodies.

Damn. They'd barely been back in the same room, maybe a whole minute, and they were both primed and ready to go. What the hell did that say about this dynamic chemistry?

He didn't care. All he cared about was her and how amazing she made him feel.

Her hips rocked against his as she arched her sweet body into his and tossed her head back. Pax kept one hand on the small of her back, urging her closer, while he cupped her breast with the other. She cried out the moment his lips covered her nipple.

Bringing Kira to her climax might just be his favorite new hobby.

Her entire body moved faster, with more intensity and drive than anything they'd shared last night. He released her breast to look up at her face. He didn't want to miss one single bit of ecstasy.

With her eyes squeezed tight, her mouth open as she let out those soft pants, and all of that bare skin flushed with arousal, watching her come completely undone also sent him over the edge. Pax continued to let her control the pace, but he didn't even try to hold back. His fingertips dug into her hips as he let himself go.

He had no clue how to stop this roller coaster of emotions he'd started with her, but he did know one thing…he wasn't in a hurry to stop anytime soon.

"You're getting married?" Pax exclaimed, his tone a mix of shock and irritation.

Kira glanced toward the living room as she wiped her hands on the kitchen towel.

"Married?" she snorted. "Not anytime soon."

Pax pointed to her open laptop and she remembered the screen she'd had pulled up. She shook her head and tossed the towel back onto the counter. Pax had offered to make breakfast, but the moment he started burning the pancakes, she took over and kicked him to the living room. She'd served up fluffy, golden pancakes and bacon along with the coffee he'd made before they got distracted. He'd offered to clean, but she really didn't want him in her space…at least not this space. He didn't seem too comfortable or confident in the kitchen, but she did give him bonus points for offering and trying.

"My mother is, remember?" she reminded him as she made her way around the small peninsula separating the living area and kitchen. "I mentioned that the other day."

He stood with his hands on his hips, his eyes boring into hers. While she couldn't exactly put a label on that stare, she had a feeling he'd gotten jealous. She thought she'd seen a sliver of that back at the café yesterday when she'd been talking to Brandon, but Pax had remained quiet.

Surely she'd been seeing things that weren't actually there. Pax had no reason whatsoever to be jealous. For one thing, they were just having fun. A holiday affair. Second, they had no ties to each other and had made no promises. But she did have a feeling that Pax would expect his lovers, no matter how temporary, to be loyal.

"I've never cheated in my life," she told him. "And I sure as hell wouldn't be married, traveling on my own, and hooking up with some hunky cowboy behind my husband's back."

"Hunky cowboy?"

"Yeah. That's you."

"I'm not a cowboy."

Kira stopped and blinked. While she'd thrown on a comfy, oversize sweater and leggings, Pax had thrown on his jeans and left them unbuttoned and forgone his shirt. She certainly wasn't complaining about the view, but she was startled by his statement.

"No?" she laughed. "Yet you work on a ranch, you have the swagger and the hat. If you're not a cowboy, then what are you?"

He stared another minute before he let out the most robust laughter she'd ever heard. Kira crossed her arms over her chest as she waited on him to calm himself and stop chuckling at her expense. She hadn't even been aware that the man had that much humor living inside and the raw emotion really struck something in her that seemed to just click. While she never liked being on the receiving end of a joke, she did enjoy hearing his deep laugh.

"I really don't know what's so funny," she stated after he still hadn't composed himself.

"A hat and a swagger?" he asked. "That's what makes a cowboy? And what the hell is a swagger? You're saying I walk like I'm off a horse?"

Kira shrugged, now feeling a little silly. "Listen, I'm from a city. I don't know the lingo here. I just know you look, walk, and act like a cowboy."

Some dark wave of emotions seemed to come across his face, but was gone in an instant. She wasn't sure what to make of the gesture or what thoughts rolled through his mind or what she'd even said that triggered his reaction. Despite being intimate multiple times, he still kept his feelings guarded and close to his chest.

She could appreciate that and respect him for it, but a sliver of her wished he'd just open up a little and let her in. This all might be temporary, but she wanted to feel like she wasn't sleeping with a stranger.

"I'm actually into real estate," he offered.

"Real estate?"

Well, she'd wanted him to open up, but she never would have guessed real estate.

"I'm sure that keeps you busy with trying to work here, too," she offered, maneuvering around the sofa to take a seat. She curled her feet up on the cushion beside her and stared up at him as he remained by the roaring fire. "Which one do you love more?"

He rested an arm along the mantel and stared out the side patio doors. She tried to focus on their conversation and not the excellent masculine form he'd just put completely on display. He likely didn't even have a clue how delicious he looked right this very minute.

"I haven't thought about it," he told her, but kept his attention focused on the snowy view out the double doors. "Real estate is just ingrained in me."

"Interesting," she murmured, resting her arm on the edge of the couch. "You just seem like you were made for this life. The love and care you have for the horses, the way you tend to the land and want to get the business back up and running. You clearly have a special place in your heart for the ranch. But is the real estate what you have to do for money? Because that's totally understandable. Most people have a true passion, but they can't turn that into a career."

There it went again, that flash of something she couldn't put her finger on, but now that she'd seen the heaviness of whatever he was feeling, she'd have to say there was some sadness or almost regret or remorse.

"Did someone in your family own this land?" she asked before she could stop herself. "Your grandfather or something?"

Pax's focus whipped around to her. "My grandfather?"

"I'm just curious why you seem almost protective when we talk about the ranch. You close in on yourself like your mind is racing and you're not sure what to say."

He dropped his arm and sighed, then stared up at the ceiling and let out a humorless laugh.

"Do you ever turn off your work mode?" he asked, moving his gaze back to her. "Or do you study everyone to zero in on their happiness?"

Kira didn't want the conversation turned back to her. She felt like they were always discussing her. Either he wanted to get to know her or he was a master deflector...she firmly believed the latter.

"It's a habit," she explained. "But I love my job, so most of the time, I don't feel like I'm working."

"And that's how you know you're in the right profession?" he asked, crossing his arms over that perfectly chiseled bare chest spattered with dark hair. "What if you can't live off the pay of something you love? What if you have to bust your ass doing something that's profitable over your happiness?"

Kira swung her legs around to rest her feet on the plush rug. "I realize that not everyone can turn their passion into profit, but sometimes you can get creative and combine the two worlds. Besides, money isn't everything."

"That's usually what people say who grew up with money," he countered.

A sliver of irritation slid through her as she came to her feet. Her sweater fell off one shoulder in her abrupt move and she didn't miss the way Pax's eyes darted to her bare skin. Good. At least everything they'd shared had affected him just as much as her.

"I grew up with a mother always seeking her next sugar daddy and clearly she's still on the hunt again," Kira told him, a little more heat in her tone than she'd intended. "I don't give a damn about money, but I do care about character and loyalty."

"Is that what you're looking for in a man or people in general?" he asked.

Kira snorted. "I'm not looking for a man."

She didn't want to appear weak or needy because sometimes that's how her mother came across. Kira wanted to stand on her own two feet at all times.

"Yet here I am," he stated, spreading his arms wide.

"I wasn't looking for you."

His hands dropped to his sides as he took two steps to eliminate the space between them. He stood as close as possible to her without touching, but with his impressive height, Kira had to tip her head back to meet his intense gaze.

"I wasn't looking for you, either," he murmured, reaching to sweep her hair away from her.

That slightest graze of his fingertips along her cheek and neck sent a rapid tingle shooting through her. No matter the power behind his touch—light or demanding—her body responded without hesitation.

"So…we're just riding this out for the next couple weeks?" she asked.

"Looks like it, but we're making a few changes."

Kira jerked. "Is that so? What changes? And don't say my tree."

A grin flirted around his mouth. "We can address that once all the needles are gone…which should be soon."

"Then what is it?"

"We'd have more space and be more comfortable at the main house."

The main house? Like, move in with him for the rest of her stay? That seemed like jumping from fling to family and not only did she not want that, she was utterly shocked that he'd even mentioned the idea.

"Don't read anything into this," he added, as if reading her thoughts. "This is strictly for convenience for me and more space for both of us. There's plenty of room if you'd still like your own space. Or you can stay here. The choice is totally yours."

He'd put the proverbial ball in her court and she wasn't sure what to do with it now. But she had two weeks left with this man and she fully intended to make the most of every single second.

Ten

Pax scrolled through past reviews on the web page for the ranch…a site that needed updating about five years ago. He'd get his web designer right on that as soon as he figured out what he wanted done.

But he needed to know what worked and didn't work when the place was up and running, so he'd been reading these comments for the past hour while making notes and rolling ideas through his head.

The general consensus was that the property itself was perfect; many even described the place as majestic. The tall mountains around the perimeter of the town just seemed to envelop everyone and protect the tight-knit community. That was another positive mention he'd seen—the close proximity to the town for local shops and cute restaurants was a nice draw.

But Pax knew it wasn't the setting or Willowvale Springs that caused the problems and present downfall of the ranch. From everything Mason, Kahlil, and Vaughn had said, Hank had started a quick decline when his sweet Edith had passed away. He'd stopped caring because they'd been a team. Even a man as strong and robust and take-charge as Hank had a vulnerable spot in his life, and that was his wife.

Word was after she was gone, Hank decided nothing was worth working for anymore and all of his businesses and homes started to suffer. The man lived a few years longer, but he'd been just a shell of who he used to be.

Pax regretted not returning sooner, and not being there for Hank during his time of mourning. But Pax was here now, and all he could do was move forward, not look into the past and stare down the face of remorse.

So first order of business was to get the site updated with a banner across the top about initiatives coming soon and new changes and exciting package deals. If he could get that going, it would buy some time until he had those exact details figured out.

What he needed was a team. He knew real estate and what made people comfortable and want to stay, but he could admit there were areas to running a dude ranch that were simply out of his wheelhouse.

The light tap on the office door pulled his attention toward the doorway. He fully expected to see Kira, even though she still hadn't made up her mind to come here for the duration of her stay. He'd proposed that earlier today, but ended up leaving to come do some work and to let her think over his offer.

But Vaughn Reed, with his wildly curly hair and long, lean build, stood in the doorway.

"Bad time?" his friend asked.

"Oh, just trying to figure out how the hell to turn this place into a profit." Pax pushed his chair back and came to his feet. "Come on in."

"You should've had that done by lunch," Vaughn laughed. "Anything I can help with?"

"I might need Allie to come in and help with freshening up the cabins and the main house and dining area," Pax stated. "But I'm not quite there yet."

Vaughn moved further into the room and rested his hands on the high-back leather chair. "We can do anything you need," his friend confirmed with a nod. "Just name it."

"'preciate that. So, what's up?"

"Allie and I want to invite you to our New Year's Eve party at the resort. I know it's kind of last-minute, but if you're free, we'd love to have you."

"I'll be there. I'm anxious to see what you guys have done with the place," Pax stated.

Vaughn and Allie had fallen in love when Vaughn inherited Hank's resort spa and ranch on the other side of town. She'd been brought on to help redesign the area for resale, but fate had other plans. Now Allie and Vaughn were engaged and had jumped headfirst into making a go of the ranch resort.

What did a relationship of that nature even look like? Pax honestly had no clue, but he couldn't be happier for them. They seemed to have found their common ground and stood strongly together.

"You're more than welcome to bring a date," Vaughn added. "You know…your cabin guest."

Hell. He didn't think they were at the point in their relationship to be attending parties arm in arm. Then again…they weren't in a relationship, and he had invited her to stay here with him. That had been a bold, rash move, which even surprised him. But he hated holing up in that cabin. He wanted space and didn't want to keep going down to the guest cabin for Tate to see the truck when he'd be heading back to the stables. Tate wasn't a gossiper, but the man wasn't stupid.

"Are you trying to think of a way to tell me to mind my business?" Vaughn chuckled. "I would, but if I don't bring Allie back some kernel of information, she's going to come here and demand to know if you've got a woman you're not sharing."

Pax groaned and raked a hand down his jawline. He needed to shave or at least knock this beard down, but he'd been a little preoccupied this morning.

"You can tell Allie that Kira is a guest at the ranch and nothing more."

Vaughn's intense stare didn't waver as he crossed his arms over his chest. "So you'll bring her. It's settled."

"What's settled? She's a guest."

"And there's more going on between you two,"

Vaughn fired back. "You don't have to say it, I can see it. Hell, I lived it not long ago. So bring her. Our place at six. We have everything catered, so don't bring anything but your date."

"We're not dating," Pax insisted, but the argument fell on deaf ears as Vaughn has already moved on.

"How about I have Allie swing by in the next day or two just to give some ideas on the design?" he suggested. "Then she can start working on a timeline and budget for you."

"I don't really care about the cost so long as it's quick and perfect."

"Quick, perfect, and pricey. Got it."

Pax wanted to be done with this as fast as possible, mostly so he could relieve Brandon from Spain. But the idea of leaving Willowvale Springs didn't feel as right as it had just a week ago. Something akin to remorse niggled at his soul and he wasn't quite sure why. He wasn't getting attached to the place… or the woman. Getting attached to her would be absurd, because she had no reason to stay here, either.

"Send her by whenever," Pax replied. "I'm always here lately."

"Well, I meant it when I said I could help with anything. Just give me a yell. I'll see you in a few days."

Vaughn turned to head toward the door, but stopped and glanced back over his shoulder.

"Don't forget Kira or I'll extend the invite myself."

Pax shook his head and sighed as his buddy let

himself out. He didn't doubt that Vaughn, or worse, Allie, would get in touch with Kira and tell her about the party. But it was just one party with friends. He and Kira were friends…right? No reason he should go and just leave her here to spend that monumental holiday by herself.

But he'd have to word it just right so she didn't think he was asking for more than just one night out. He already freaked her out with the suggestion she spend the rest of her weeks here. Maybe he should've just kept his mouth shut, but he hadn't been able to and now all he could do was wait for her to answer him.

He hated waiting and he hated not being in control. But since he'd met her, he really didn't know when he had the control in his possession or when Kira was subconsciously taking the lead. Pax had never met anyone so sneakily charming. She had a way to get under your skin without your knowledge until it was too late. He actually enjoyed her company, found himself thinking about her when she wasn't with him, and hated this damn time limit on their fling. What if he wasn't done in two weeks? What if he wanted her to stick around longer?

He wouldn't ask. Pax never asked for anything. If he wanted something, he found a way to make it his, but Kira wasn't property to obtain and she had to make her own decisions. Perhaps that's what pissed him off the most. He couldn't just order her to do what he wanted like his employees. Part of him found he didn't want to. He liked her mind and respected everything he knew about her.

He also worried where she'd go once she returned. He wanted to get to the bottom of the fact she didn't have a place to stay and he'd sent out some messages to his contacts in Portland but hadn't heard anything back yet. Even though his own plate was full, he had to stay on top of Kira's housing situation. He wouldn't let her leave here without a solid plan to secure her future.

But first, he had to ask her to a party before his well-meaning, nosy buddy extended the invitation. The last thing he needed was for any of those women to get an idea that Kira was a long-term girl sticking around. There was a deadline and it was fast approaching.

Kira stepped into the stables and didn't know if she should be nervous or excited. Pax had shot her a text to meet him here and to wear warm layers and boots. After he'd dropped the bomb of her moving into the main house with him, he'd left, and she'd had all day to think about that notion. The giddy part of her had mentally already packed her suitcase, but the logistical side of her forced herself to take a step back and think before jumping straight in.

She didn't see any harm in moving forward and in with him for now. They both knew she wouldn't be staying and they had both vocalized that this fling was nothing more than a fun, temporary arrangement.

But she didn't want to look desperate, so she'd tell

him later that she'd be coming on up. Let him stew on it a bit longer.

Kira moved down the walkway between the stalls. She was sure there would be a proper name, but she didn't have a clue what it would be. This was her first time on a ranch, around horses, in a stable...all of it. She did love just the snippets she'd seen and experienced. She had to think that Pax was taking her out on the horses today with meeting here and telling her to dress in layers. While the snow had stopped falling, the air was still brisk and wintery.

One beautiful brown head popped out of his stall as she drew closer. This was a different one than the other day and on the opposite side.

"Hey, buddy. Did you hear me coming?"

She stopped just outside the stall and reached to pet just like Pax had explained. Even with her gloves on, she could tell the animal was soft and so sweet. A little spot warmed in her heart at how amazing these creatures were. The whole lifestyle here in Wyoming and on the ranch was such a juxtaposition from her own life back in Portland. Even the air was different. Crisp and refreshing and relaxing, if that made sense.

Of course, the great sex also helped that whole relaxation process. She couldn't think about Pax without allowing every single touch and taste to roll through her head like the most erotic movie she'd ever seen. She didn't often take a lover, and never one with an expiration date, but she had to admit, this was the most fun she'd ever had with one, and she'd hate to see everything come to an end.

Which was why she had to enjoy herself while she was here and fully embrace their new living arrangements…once she let him in on her answer, of course.

"Sorry I'm late."

Kira dropped her hand and turned as Pax came striding through the stable. Yeah, there was that strut she'd mentioned to him. The swagger, the sexy walk…whatever it was called, he had it and she couldn't tear her eyes away.

Dark denim covered those long, lean legs. Black boots, a dark coat buttoned up, and his black hat pulled low over his head all summed up the cowboy she'd taken a serious interest in. If she had time to stay and the mental bandwidth to feed a relationship, she wouldn't mind exploring more. But he'd made it perfectly clear he had a full plate, what with trying to get this business up and running to its full potential. She made a mental note to come back once that was all done and see the place, and the man, in the future.

"You're not late," she told him, sliding her hands into her coat pockets. "I've only been here about a minute. I was late, too. I just put an offer in on a town house back home and I got caught up in looking at pictures and submitting my price. I had to come in low, so I'm hoping the seller is motivated and there's no other offers."

Pax came to stand in front of her; his dark eyes seemed to study her like usual. She'd gotten used to that familiar stare that could easily be misconstrued as cantankerous or closed off, but she was starting to get a better idea behind the man with the coal-like stare. Something kept him guarded, which was another reason she wanted to move into the main house and his quarters with him until her time here was up. She wanted to continue to peel back those layers and uncover more of what made him the intriguing man she'd gotten to know.

"Do you have an agent?" he asked.

"One of my clients is an agent. She's just getting started so maybe this will help her grow her business."

Pax's lips thinned. "You need to get someone experienced so you're getting the best deal and you feel confident with how a contract is written up."

"Everyone has to start somewhere," she stated. "You had your first sale and hopefully I'll be Tammy's first sale."

"Keep me posted on every step of this process," he commanded in full business mode.

Kira gave a mock salute and she thought she might have seen a fraction of a smile.

"So, did you call me here to ridicule my choice of real estate agents back home? Or are you giving me that horseback riding lesson?"

"You're not getting a lesson, but you're getting a ride." He reached up and patted the horse's head. "Colter and I will be taking you together."

Kira couldn't help but smile as anticipation and giddiness filled her. "Really? I'll be riding with you? Is there a weight limit on him?"

Pax laughed. "We're good with the weight. He's not going to break down. But there is a process that we have to go through before riding, so that's what you'll learn first. Everything on the ranch revolves around safety both for the people and the animals."

Oh, he transitioned from businessman to cowboy in a blink and both sides of him were pretty sexy. She wasn't sure if he had to hold two jobs to make ends meet, but she didn't care. He seemed to have a genuine heart and anyone who treated animals so sweet and with a tender touch had to have an authentic soul.

"Show me what to do," she told him. "I'm ready to learn."

"I need to check on Sebastian real quick and see if he needs more balm put on his leg."

Kira waited and stood back while Pax moved to another stall and tended to the wounded horse. He murmured something softly as he checked the animal. This delicate side wasn't something she'd seen from him. She'd experienced the surly, the passionate, the stern Pax, but this new layer he'd just revealed left her with a whole other wave of emotions.

Feeling something this strong, this fast after meeting him seemed risky. She shouldn't be trusting her deeper sensations right now, not when her mind and world were too vulnerable. But she also had to wonder if Pax had come into her life at precisely the right time to help her heal.

Pax continued to speak to the animal in the sweetest tone while he applied more balm to the slight cut near the hoof. Once he was done, he stood and patted the horse on the back before stepping from the stall. He slid the door back into place and clicked the latch closed.

"How did he get hurt?" she asked.

Pax moved toward the small bath and set the balm on the counter before washing his hands. Kira followed, but remained outside the door.

"Tate had him out in the ring trying to work with him getting used to a saddle. He got scared and ended up scratching himself on the fence. It was definitely a freak accident, but I want to keep an eye on this so it doesn't get infected."

"And the Amish supply you with medicines?"

He wiped his hands on the towel and turned to face her once again. "There is a vet for the ranch, but for something like this, Tate always uses the Amish for their natural healing products."

"So, are you Tate's boss, or is he your boss?"

Pax laughed as he stepped from the bathroom. "There's days I'm not sure."

He motioned for her to follow him to a side room where there were blankets, large boxes, saddles, and other equipment she had no clue what she was looking at. She had no idea so much went into a ranch or stables, but she really was eager to learn.

Of course Kira couldn't wait to get on that horse and wrap her arms around Pax for a snowy ride. Maybe have more chats about the property and dig a little deeper into his mind. Physically, he had no flaws, and she'd never been more attracted to anyone in her life. Mentally, she still wanted more. And a wintry ride through the snow-covered ranch had all the makings for something even more intimate than sex. Talk about romantic. She hadn't come to Willowvale Springs looking for romance, but romance had found her nonetheless.

Still, part of her felt Pax was holding back. She wanted to know more about him, because their connection went beyond sex.

And now she had to decide exactly how to proceed, because she could see herself falling for this man and she didn't want to leave here with a lifetime of memories and a broken heart.

Eleven

Pax grabbed a blanket, then put it back and searched for another. He hadn't been in this room in years, but this certainly wasn't the same way Hank had set everything up. Pax shuffled things around on the shelving unit until he found the bridle he wanted. He should have come in here before thinking to take Kira out for a short ride. Now he looked incompetent, but getting a horse ready to ride wasn't difficult, and he'd done this exact thing countless times when he'd worked here before. One of his duties had actually been to get the horses ready for the guests.

Now he only had one guest he wanted to impress.

Kira stood in the doorway and he tugged out a different blanket and handed it over. "Hold on to this," he grumbled as he went back to find the right bridle.

"You sure we're good to go?" she asked. "It's no biggie if we can't."

Oh, they were going, and he was going to make a note to put Tate in this tack room and purge anything that was old and worn out, then make a list of anything that needed replaced.

"We're fine," Pax insisted. "Let me get one more thing."

Finally he found one that was in good shape and wondered why these were just thrown in here in a haphazard manner anyway. He'd definitely be talking to Tate at the first chance he got.

"First we're going to put his blanket on because that goes under the saddle," Pax explained as he led her from the room.

He led her through the steps and found the proper saddle. Thankfully there was one in great shape, but that was something else that would have to be gone over. He wanted every single item in this stable to be new and worthy of a Hank Carson ranch.

"Hold on to the reins." Pax handed over the leather straps and motioned toward the alley. "Bring him out here. I haven't been on him, but Tate assured me he's the gentlest giant and perfect for a beginner."

"Why haven't you ridden him?" she asked, holding on tightly. "I figured you'd have ridden each one."

Pax thought over his answer. Kira still wasn't aware that he owned the place, and honestly, he wasn't purposely trying to keep it from her, it was just that he didn't want to get too personal. He didn't want to answer a bunch of questions that he wasn't sure he'd have the answers to. Besides, none of this was Kira's problem. And knowing her giving heart, she'd try to find a way to fix things and then she wouldn't be fulfilling her friend's request to relax and enjoy her break.

"I don't get much time to ride," he answered honestly. "So I'm using you as my excuse and we both get to have a fun day. We might even follow this up with a little surprise back at the main house."

Her smile widened as she held the leather in one hand and reached to rub Colter's nose with the other. "A surprise? Like hot chocolate or something better?"

Pax stared for a moment and then laughed. "The best surprise you could think of was hot chocolate?"

She shrugged and he figured anything he did would be an upgrade to what she requested. But he did pull out his cell and fire off a text to one of the few remaining staff he had other than Tate. He sent a sizable grocery list to be delivered before evening. He wanted everything ready and everyone gone by the time he and Kira returned.

"Ready?" he asked, pocketing his cell.

"I'm so excited."

Her radiant smile beamed and he wanted to press the issue of her coming to his place, but at the same time, he respected her privacy and her right to decide. Not to mention, the main house wasn't *his space*. He simply had to borrow the place while he was in town.

"Let's walk him out." Pax gestured toward the opening at the other end that led out to the fields. "Then I'll get on and help you."

"I'm nervous," she stated as she led the horse out.

"Nothing to be nervous about. I'm right here and Colter has a gentle side."

As soon as they reached the field, Pax took the reins from her and mounted the horse. Damn, this felt good. The view from atop a saddle was something he hadn't seen for years and the instant his butt settled onto the leather... Hell, he couldn't explain it. Something familiar and warm and soothing settled deep in his chest.

Pax glanced around the snowy land that glistened with the late afternoon sun. Was it any wonder Hank was so possessive of this place? Why he wanted everything to be perfect and top-notch? There was a serenity that couldn't be bought and a peacefulness that couldn't be described.

"Pax?"

He blinked and glanced over to Kira. He extended his hand for her to take hold.

"Put your left foot in the stirrup and swing your right leg over."

She hoisted herself right up with ease as if she'd done it so many times before.

"You're a natural already," he praised. "You can either hold on to me or wherever your hands are comfortable. We won't be going fast."

In an instant, her arms circled his waist and she inched closer as her thighs framed his. Another mental click seemed to lock into place, like this was what he was meant to be doing. That whole idea was absurd, though. He'd only known Kira a week and he hadn't been on this ranch in years. A stranger and an inheritance couldn't completely transform his life from what he'd climbed and clawed to create. He simply basked in the newness of everything, that's all. He didn't want this life. None of this was on his career plan—short or long-term.

Kira's chin rested on his shoulder, her head bumped his hat slightly, but he didn't mind. Having her warmth press so solidly against him was just an added bonus and he wasn't about to make her move.

"How far are we riding?" she murmured as he kicked his heel into Colter's side.

"However far you want." He led the horse toward the back of the land to an area he always loved. "Are you comfortable?"

Her grip on him tightened and the arousal in his gut grew.

"More than I thought I could be," she stated.

The gentle rocking of their bodies from the stallion's gait didn't help his growing desires. This ride was supposed to be about fulfilling one of Kira's goals and giving her an experience she'd never had. Not to try to turn everything about their relationship into sex.

But that's what it was, wasn't it? They'd agreed on a short-term fling, but something about that seemed so cheap and almost, well, dirty. Kira deserved better than something cheap and dirty. Who did she have to go back to once she returned home? A bunch of clients that only used her for her services, but didn't get to know the actual woman? She had a friend who had forced her on this trip, and she had her mother who obviously was too self-absorbed in her own life.

She still had no home, but she did have a prospect. That made him feel a little better about her returning to Portland. But he fully intended to have a host of options for her as well, because deals fell through all the time and she was using a rooky agent. He didn't want to just throw his power around, but he would if that meant she would get the best housing option. He had no idea about her budget, but he'd work around that as well.

"You're pretty quiet."

Her soft words and warm breath on his cheek pulled him from his thoughts.

"Just enjoying the moment," he replied.

"I can't imagine living here. I don't know that I would ever want to do anything else but ride horses and explore the beauty."

That's exactly how he'd felt as a teen. He thought he'd always be here, but then his home life wasn't getting any better and he wanted, no *needed*, some distance. He'd never felt like his home had been a safe place for him with the way his parents were always arguing. One would move out, then come back. Then the fighting and cycle would start all over again. Real estate had been a draw for him because he wanted people to feel like they had a safe place to land.

And maybe that's why he was so protective of Kira right now. He wanted her to have a place to go to when she returned where she felt safe and right at home. He had no clue how a sexual relationship turned him into some crazy version of a Fairy Godmother, but here he was.

"How often do you get to ride?" she asked.

"Not often enough."

A niggle of guilt speared his heart. He should tell her the truth about the land and his status. He didn't take her as the type to be a money-hungry woman, but there was that part of him that appreciated his privacy. He valued his space and keeping to himself and he didn't want her to look at him any differently.

But then, if she went to the party at Vaughn and Allie's she'd have to know the full truth because she'd hear chatter and he wouldn't put her in a position to look foolish in front of a crowd.

"We're going to a party on New Year's Eve," he told her.

"Oh, we are? Was that an invitation or demand?"

Yeah, his delivery did need some work.

"Will you come with me?" he amended, steering the stallion toward the right and around the frozen pond. "It's a friend of mine hosting. Well, he and his fiancée."

"Do they expect you to bring someone? I understand if you need a night with friends. I'm not holding you hostage every evening."

The idea of going without her seemed to be the best choice to save himself a whole host of questions from the ladies, but on the other hand, attending alone seemed wrong. From the little he knew about

Mason, Vaughn, and Kahlil's ladies, Kira would very likely fit right in.

And he wasn't so sure if that was a good thing or a bad thing.

"The choice is yours," he informed her. "I hate the idea of you ringing in the New Year with your dead tree and stack of books."

She swatted his chest and let out the sweetest laughter in his ear.

"I'll have you know my stack of books has gotten me through some difficult days. There's nothing wrong with escaping reality when you want or need to."

"Then escape reality and come to the party with me."

"I don't have any party clothes to wear."

He'd buy her anything she wanted because he realized just how much he wanted her to be on his arm.

"We can fix that," he stated.

They rode a bit further in silence and Kira tipped her head to rest her cheek on his back. Everything in him went completely primal. A week ago they were strangers and now she trusted him to protect her on this new journey. His heart swelled and he cursed himself for even allowing such an emotion to creep in. He couldn't let his heart get involved. He hadn't opened up his life to anyone outside of business since Hank. That man had really made a world of difference in Pax's life. Having unloving, distracted parents made the very act of loving anyone difficult. He didn't have much to base his feelings on.

Hank and Edith had always welcomed him like a son, and he had adored them both. When he'd left town, those were the two faces he'd missed the most.

And now he was back and neither one of them were here. He knew death was part of life, but that hurt more than the absence of his own parents.

"Do you want to give me a hint as to the surprise when we get back?" she asked.

"Not really. That wouldn't make it a surprise anymore."

"Is it food?" she asked.

He said nothing as he made his way toward the old path he used to ride with guests.

"Is it an actual present or something you want to show me?" she went on. "Did you bake a cake? Put up a real Christmas tree?"

"Why would I do that when it's after Christmas now?" he countered, amused that she was relentless in her guessing.

"Because they're festive and fun."

"No. There's no tree, festive or dead."

"Hmmm… You got me a new stack of books? I saw a little bookstore in town, but didn't get a chance to pop in."

"No books."

But he'd make a note to get her there so she could buy all she wanted.

"Then what could it be?" she cried. "You're driving me crazy."

"Well you've been driving me crazy since you got here, so I guess we're both even."

Her hold on him tightened, but she said nothing else. There. Let her think about that nugget of information. He hadn't meant to say that, but he wasn't sorry for his outburst. She deserved to know the hold she had on him.

She nestled deeper against his back as he continued to steer Colter along the snowy paths. He'd thought of explaining everything to Kira, but the silence and beauty of the day seemed to be enough for both of them. He'd done more talking with her than he had any other woman outside of work. He'd also said more than enough. He'd exposed a little too much and now he had to keep calm. He didn't want more than what they already shared, but he wasn't in a hurry to see things end, either.

He didn't know where that left them in the end, but the inevitable date was approaching. Soon she'd be just a cluster of memories and the thought of her leaving already left a void he couldn't explain.

Twelve

Kira glanced around the living area in the back of the main house. With the check-in and lobby out front and the public dining room taking up a majority of the left side of the building, she was surprised at how much living space was in the back.

She was also surprised at how none of this seemed to match Pax's personality. The furniture and decor appeared rather dated, like his grandmother had lived here. The floral wallpaper coupled with the worn yellow sofa really didn't feel like a ranch, but rather a setup for a tea party. There was no way Pax had a hand in any of this.

Which made her wonder what his role truly was here. Did he get free housing in exchange for running the ranch? With their temporary arrangement, she didn't feel like prying was her place. Pax had a variety of locked compartments and she wasn't so sure she had the time to discover each one. If he wanted to divulge more about his life, he would.

"Have a seat," he offered, gesturing to the sofa. "I just need to do a couple things."

"For this surprise? You're making that hot chocolate now, aren't you?" she joked, crossing the old worn rug. "I like mine with extra marshmallows."

Pax muttered a curse and shook his head. "You're relentless. Give me a minute."

He slipped from the room and down the hallway. Kira figured if she was going to learn anything about him, now might be her only opportunity. Oh, she knew basics. He was complicated but compassionate, surly yet sweet. He was loyal or he wouldn't be here trying to revive a dying business and he had a love for animals and those in his close circle.

Instead of having a seat, Kira walked around the room. The built-ins on either side of the stone fireplace drew her in. Various books were stacked, but she didn't pay attention to the titles on the spines. Her attention shifted to the photographs in various sizes and frames. An elderly couple standing on the porch of a home she'd never seen stared back at her. The black-and-white image seemed to be from long ago, but one thing stood out. They were in love. The young man had an arm wrapped around the woman's waist as he leaned in for a kiss on her cheek. The lady was laughing and something about that image seemed to come to life. She had to assume those were the people who lived here at one time. Grandparents, perhaps, but Kira saw absolutely no resemblance between this couple and Pax. Was he adopted? Or did this couple help raise him?

The more things she uncovered, the more questions she had.

Her gaze scanned from picture to picture, then she moved to the other side of the fireplace to look at more. This couple seemed to grow older before her eyes, some of the images had even yellowed. There was something so normalizing about seeing them and wondering what impact they had on Pax's life. She wanted to know, she wanted to ask him about them, and maybe she would. Maybe he'd want to share who these people were to him. He didn't owe her anything, but she wanted him to want to let her in, if that made sense.

"Everything is ready."

Kira turned at the boom of Pax's voice. She'd gotten so wrapped up in the displays, she'd lost herself in her thoughts.

He had nothing in his hands, but he did have on some long robe and had one in his hand.

"Go get changed."

Kira snorted. "Into a robe? What are we doing? Having a spa day? A couple's massage?"

"We're going to the hot tub, where your hot chocolate with extra marshmallows will be waiting."

Kira squealed and did a jump that should have embarrassed her, but it didn't. "Are you serious? A hot tub and a sweet treat? But, I have no swimsuit."

"Neither do I," he retorted. "That's why we're wearing the robe to get outside, so we don't freeze before we can get into the water."

A surge of excitement and arousal overcame her as she raced across the room and snatched the robe from his hand. She started from the room, but whirled back around, laughing at his amused face and smirk.

"I have no idea where to go."

He pointed. "Down the hall, second room on the left is my bedroom. Leave your clothes in there. Then head toward the back of the house. You can't miss the double doors leading out to the patio."

Kira sprinted toward the bedroom, not a bit surprised to find it also outdated and nearly bare. One king-size bed with a simple white comforter and two pillows. One large chest of drawers with only an old antique clock on top. An attached bath and a door that was likely a closet. The only sign of life in here was Pax's cowboy boots at the end of the bed. And the entire room smelled deliciously like him with that woodsy cologne of his.

She quickly changed and slid into the plush gray robe. After a few hours of riding, she was both sore and still chilled. Soaking in a hot tub sounded absolutely amazing and knowing Pax was out there waiting for her, wearing nothing but the moonlight, had her removing her clothes in record time.

The jets on his back soothed his tired muscles. Since coming back to the ranch, he hadn't realized how tight he'd been. Stress over launching a global company would do that.

Finding new ways to relax sure as hell wasn't on his to-do list when he'd arrived back at Hank's dude ranch. He'd fully intended to come here, put the place up for sale, and head back to Spain, where he could get on with the next phase of his career. The plan in his head seemed flawless and perfect, the execution on the other hand...

The patio door slid open and the landscape lights set off a glow that put Kira in some romantic lighting.

Kira was another part of this journey he certainly hadn't planned on. Nor did he expect any type of romance, especially with someone so opposite.

He couldn't deny that's the phase they'd entered into. What started as fast and physical had somehow flipped to romantic and caring. She had a zest for life that he found refreshing and he could easily see why clients wanted her in their corner. He wanted her in his corner as well.

"It's freezing," she gasped as she eased out of her robe and hung it on the hook on the post of the patio.

She raced for the steps of the hot tub and groaned the moment her toes hit the warmth of the bubbling water. She sank down across from him and extended her legs, instantly intertwining with his. If this was any other fling in his past, he'd make quick use of the fact they were alone and naked, but she'd changed something inside of him. He wasn't in such a hurry and he found that he wanted more than just her body.

He wanted inside her mind and he wanted to solve her problems if at all possible.

"You need one of these for every single cabin."

She sighed and dropped her head back against the cushioned pillow and closed her eyes. The water rolled in waves over the swell of her breasts and Pax had a difficult time concentrating on staying on his side of the hot tub. What the hell had happened to him? Now all of a sudden he wanted to talk?

He turned and reached for the mug he'd made for her. He'd brought two hot chocolates out and placed them on the wraparound table edge that Hank had built along the perimeter of the tub.

"Your drink," he stated, extending the mug.

She lifted her gaze to his and reached for the handle. Her eyes lit up when she glanced inside to see the heaping pile of marshmallows.

"You did good," she declared as she took her first sip. "Oh my word. I haven't had this in so long. A cold night with a hot drink under the stars and a naked man in a hot tub... Doesn't get much better than this."

Pax took a careful sip of his own drink, sans marshmallows, and he'd added a shot of bourbon to his.

"I was with you until you got to the naked man part," he murmured around the steaming mug. "I'd prefer a naked woman, but not any woman."

He preferred her, but he had to be careful how he worded things or his statements could come out as needy or clingy.

"I mean, there's no one else I'd want to spend this

night with," he amended. "I didn't know I needed this-any of this—until you got here."

A wide smile spread across her face. "I didn't expect this, either. I saw nothing on the website about being this pampered and catered to."

"Yeah, well, you definitely are getting a unique experience."

"I should hope so." She took another sip and removed the foam from her top lip with one sexy sweep of the tip of her tongue.

"I don't strike you as the type to enter into flings with all the beautiful women that come through."

He wouldn't know who came through since he'd only been here a short time. Not to mention, he couldn't remember the last time anyone had intrigued him enough to pull him away from his work and have him so damn distracted. Actually, no woman had ever kept his mind so preoccupied that he couldn't solely focus on work. He'd always been an excellent multitasker...until Kira.

He wasn't sure what that meant for the long term. Would he be able to just switch gears once she was gone and devote every waking minute back to this property and business? He didn't want to think about when she'd be gone; he wanted to enjoy this moment beneath the starry Wyoming sky with the woman who had turned his world upside down and inside out.

"Tell me about this place you put an offer on," he stated.

Kira's hands cupped her mug as she shifted in her seat. "Well, it's a little smaller than where I was, but it's a better location and the views overlooking the park are amazing. It's just outside Portland, so a little quieter. I'm finding I like the laid-back lifestyle."

Yeah, so was he, which was not a good mode to get into, considering his fast-paced line of work. He couldn't mentally afford to be lax in his career. He'd worked too hard to get away from his mundane life here, from the parents who were more concerned with fighting than raising their son in a loving, co-parenting manner.

He'd always thought bickering at home was just a way of life until he'd been at the General Store one day and heard Hank talking about needing help on the dude ranch. Pax jumped at the chance to learn about horses and make money over the summer. That day changed his life when Hank and Edith showed him what love was about, what family meant, and that loyalty coupled with hard work could take you anywhere. Then he couldn't save up his money and leave home fast enough when he'd graduated.

So he had to stay here, no matter what else happened with his businesses, he had to stay until he could see the ranch up and running the way Hank and Edith had. No, he wanted to do even better. Maybe that was to prove to himself that he was worthy of this inheritance, or maybe to prove to them that they'd entrusted the right man for the job.

"What are you thinking?"

Kira's soft question pulled him from his thoughts. He blinked and set his mug on the table ledge.

"You seemed sad for a minute," she added.

"Sometimes I drift back to my childhood," he confessed. "It's not the happiest place to settle into."

"Tell me about it."

Pax sighed and tapped the jets to turn down a notch. "That's not the prettiest time of my life."

"Life isn't always pretty." Her legs entangled with his once again as she shifted to the seat closest to him. "Maybe I want to hear the bad side, too. Maybe I want to know what makes you the man you are today."

For the first time in his life, he found that he wanted to share that piece of him. Kira made it so easy to open up, to have a shoulder to lean on. He'd never wanted to lean on anyone before, but having a personal sounding board and someone who had nothing to gain by his admissions was an invigorating point in his life.

"My parents made a hobby out of arguing," he found himself admitting. "They decided to devote every waking minute to making each other's lives miserable, which made mine miserable. I really thought that's just how family dynamics worked until I would go visit friends. Then I came to work on this farm when I was a teen to escape and make some money."

"You've been here since you were a teenager?" she gasped. "No wonder this place is so special."

Tell her everything.

"Not exactly," he went on. "I got into real estate and that took me away for a while."

"But you're back now and you seem to love it here."

"I do," he murmured, realizing that he loved this place more than he'd originally thought.

"There's something to be said for having a job that brings you peace." Kira turned sideways to face him fully. "And there's a reason people say money can't buy you happiness. Happiness lives within you and it's your job to find it and bring that emotion to the surface. Then you have to wrap yourself in that feeling and use it as a hedge of protection so the evil and ugly can't penetrate back in."

Her words slid like a balm over his bruised soul. He'd never been so vulnerable or exposed...and that had nothing to do with their state of undress. Maybe this was the perfect time to reveal himself and his past wounded heart. He couldn't run and he trusted Kira with everything he'd said.

But there was still that kernel of information he hadn't revealed. She was nothing like his ex, yet that fear still held him back from being completely honest.

"Do you think you'll come back here to visit?" he found himself asking, because the idea of never seeing her again was simply not an option.

"You getting hot tubs put in every cabin?" she countered with a smirk.

Pax turned and came to kneel in front of her, bracing his hands on either side of her head against the edge of the tub. Her smile widened as she looked up into his eyes.

"When you come back, you won't be staying in the cabins," he growled. "You'll be with me."

"Then I'm definitely coming back."

He covered her mouth with his, more than ready to be done talking and make use of the fact neither of them had suits. Talking about the future in such a personal manner had always made him twitchy, so he couldn't explain why discussing it with Kira only left him wanting more.

Thirteen

Kira tipped back her last drop of coffee and placed her mug in the sink. She had a fun day planned of book and dress shopping in the quaint little town. Apparently she needed something for this New Year's Eve party, where she would know absolutely nobody except Pax. Which was fine, she didn't shy away from meeting new people. She just didn't want anyone to get the wrong impression of the relationship she and Pax had.

She had no idea what to wear, and he'd been absolutely no help because he told her she looked good in everything and he planned on ripping it off of her as soon as they returned from the party.

So, she was clearly on her own. All she knew was the party was a small gathering of friends at a resort ranch in Willowvale Springs. She did look up the resort online just to get a feel for the atmosphere and the place was absolutely gorgeous. Rustic yet contemporary. Whoever the designer had been had done an amazing job and had an extraordinary eye for detail. Kira actually couldn't wait to see the place in person.

She unplugged her cell from where it lay charging on the kitchen counter and started to turn toward the door. The tree in the corner caught her eye and, sad as that thing looked, she still smiled. More needles had fallen to the floor, her garland now sagged, and her topper leaned nearly on its side. She wouldn't change one single thing about it. That tree brought her and Pax together; they'd shared some laughs over it and she couldn't help but feel the poor thing paralleled the rose in *Beauty and the Beast*. When that last needle fell, would her time be up here?

Her smile fell as her heart clenched. She didn't want to think about her end date. She was too busy enjoying the now, so she turned toward the door and grabbed her purse from the hook. She had some shopping to do if she wanted to impress Pax and his host of friends in a couple of days.

Honestly, she didn't even care about impressing the strangers. She wanted to wow Pax. She wanted his mouth to drop open, his eyes to widen, and his breath to catch in his throat. She wanted to dazzle him and make him want her the entire night they were out. She fully intended to grab that perfect outfit that would induce emotional foreplay and drive him out of his mind.

With an extra giddiness in her step, she headed out of her cabin, locking the door behind her. As she made her way down the shoveled path to her car, she noticed two large black trucks over at the main stables and paused. Had more workers come back? Was there a problem with the horses?

Concern filled her, but this wasn't her property or her place to butt her nose in where she wasn't needed. Maybe Pax would talk to her later if there was a problem.

Kira slid behind the wheel of her car and immediately turned on her heated seat. She hated this ghastly cold weather when she first arrived, but now she was growing more and more used to it. The beauty of the snowcapped mountains and the winding country roads, the tall evergreens around the property, and the livestock all made this place feel so cozy and inviting. The log cabins mimicked the main house, just on a smaller scale. Everything about this ranch had the solid foundation for a prosperous business, and with Pax's drive and determination, she had no doubt he'd get everything up and running soon.

The drive into town was just as picturesque as being on the ranch itself. Not a cloud in the bright blue sky and the mountains seemed to just follow her. The actual town itself had that small, relaxing vibe, and she could easily see why people flocked to Willowvale Springs. There wasn't a building on the main streets that wasn't occupied with some type of business from boutiques to bookstores, cafés to convenience. She could easily blow a good chunk of her savings here, but she was all for supporting small businesses.

She found a spot to park just in front of the bookstore and killed the engine. Pulling the collar of her coat up around her neck, she grabbed her bag and stepped out onto the snowy street. She hustled across the salt-covered sidewalk and into the store, thankful for the blast of warmth as she entered.

"Good morning."

Kira glanced up to the worker up on a sliding ladder pulling a book from one of the built-in shelves along the wall. The middle-aged woman with cropped silver hair smiled back down.

"Anything I can help you find?" she offered.

Kira shook her head. "I have no expectations, but plan to leave with no less than five books."

With a soft laugh, the lady climbed down the ladder and cradled a hardback book against her chest. "Well, I can certainly help you with that as soon as I fill this order. Do you have a favorite author or genre?"

Kira's eyes scanned the adorable shop. The cozy reading circle directly in the middle with a plush rug and cozy worn leather sofas was so inviting. She could easily lose herself in here for hours, and she just might.

"I love anything set in a small town," Kira stated. "Romance, mystery, fiction."

"Oh, then you have to check out one of our local authors. Give me one minute and I'll pull some for you. I'm Celeste, by the way."

"Kira."

The lady froze as a wide grin slowly emerged. "Kira. Well, it's lovely to meet you. I have orders to start a tab for you."

"A tab? What is this, a bar?" Kira laughed. "And who gave these orders? As if I don't already know."

"Mr. Hart was quite adamant for you to choose anything you wanted. That man is a keeper, that's for sure. Any man who will give you an endless budget on books is one you'll want to rush to the aisle with."

Kira nearly laughed again at the thought of rushing to the aisle with Pax. She wasn't looking for marriage—her mother had that area good and covered multiple times over. But she also wasn't turning down the gift of books. She'd let him buy one or two, she wouldn't want to wound his pride or bruise his ego, but she also didn't plan on letting him pay for things like they were dating or a real couple. They were just...

At this point, she didn't know. They were more than a fling, and she couldn't even lie to herself anymore because part of her was falling for him. The good thing was she'd be leaving in about ten more days. Surely she wouldn't fall completely in love before that. She just needed to pace her emotions and make sure she remained fully in control until she could get home. Then she'd shift her focus onto the new chapter with her home and live with the most amazing memories she'd ever made.

"Okay," Celeste stated as she came back with a few books in hand. "Check these out and see what you think. This is the local lady I was telling you about. She actually does signings here a few times a year and all of these copies are also signed."

Signed copies? Kira had never had an author sign a book before. Of course she'd have to get them all. She took the stack and settled into the reading area. She read the back covers and before she knew it, she had started in on the first chapter of one that especially caught her attention. An hour later, she found herself with an even bigger stack at the checkout, and Celeste ended up giving Kira a large canvas tote with the bookstore logo printed on the front.

"I hope you'll be able to make it to the signing in February," Celeste told her as she handed over the tote bag. "She has a new release, so we're really playing up Valentine's Day."

A portion of Kira's heart clenched at the idea of life in this little town just moving on without her. But of course it would. She was simply passing through and had a life to get back to. Granted, a life in upheaval with her belongings in storage and no home at the moment, which was all the more reason she needed to get back and regroup.

"I'm afraid I'm leaving next week," Kira replied with a smile. "But I'll be back. Hopefully in the summer. This is my first trip to Willowvale Springs, but I'm keeping it on my regular travel rotation."

"Well, I have a site and do shipping, so check me out when you need more books," Celeste told her.

"I definitely will."

Kira headed out of the bookstore and put her

heavy tote in her car before moving on down the row of shops to the cutest boutique. This was one she hadn't popped into the other day and the adorable sparkly outfits with paired accessories in the window seemed fitting for a New Year's Eve party. That holiday just seemed to call for extra bling.

The door chimed as she stepped in and the scent of something festive and cinnamon hit her, reminding her of her favorite holiday and the coziness of her cabin. Whatever that candle was, she'd love to have one to take back to Portland so she could light it and reminisce.

The soft instrumental music sounded through the store. A modern mix, but classical tone was just what Kira loved to listen to while working.

"Good morning."

The cheerful woman putting up a new wall display welcomed Kira into the shop, and Kira returned the smile. The lady might be in her midforties, with her hair in an adorable bun, a sparkly headband, and a fitted black dress with sleeves, and booties. Chic and classy, yet modern and elegant. Yes, this is the person who could guide Kira in the right direction for her party wear.

"Morning," Kira replied.

"What can I help you find?"

Kira sighed as she tried to glance around at all the displays at once, but she realized this might be more overwhelming than she first thought. She truly had no idea what to prepare for.

"I need a party outfit, but I have no idea if the

party is casual or dressy, and I only know one person attending the party." Kira scrunched her nose and shrugged. "I'm clearly going to need your help."

The woman pursed her lips while she scanned the store. Kira waited, hoping something sparked the woman's inspiration.

"How about you show me some pieces you like and we worry about matching your style instead?" she suggested. "Then you'll feel confident, like it's the absolute best outfit you could ever wear."

Kira nodded. "I like you already," she laughed.

"Well, thank you." The lady gave a mock bow. "I'm Stella. Would you like a mimosa while we look?"

"That would be wonderful."

Just as Stella turned toward the back, where Kira noticed the mimosa and pastry station, the front door chimed once again and laughter and chatter filtered in from the street. Kira glanced over her shoulder to discover three ladies piling in. Clearly they were on a girls' day out. How fun to have girlfriends to spend the entire day with. She hadn't spent a whole day with her bestie in so long. Kira made a mental note to do just that when she returned to Portland.

"Hey, ladies." Stella returned and handed Kira her mimosa. "You guys are just in time. We need to help Kira find the perfect party outfit."

Kira took the mimosa and smiled at the trio of ladies. They were each uniquely gorgeous and stylish and obviously frequent shoppers here or friends with Stella.

"We're here for party outfits, too," one of them stated. "This will be fun."

"This is Kira," Stella told the new crew.

Kira moved toward the ladies. "Hi. Sorry to interrupt your girls' day, but I'm new in town and going to a party where I have no clue how to dress or the people in attendance. I was just invited by a guy I know."

A guy I know?

How ridiculous did she sound right now? But boyfriend or bedmate didn't quite fit the bill, either, so...

"Do you know where the party is?" another one of the ladies asked.

"I think some ranch resort." Kira took a sip of her mimosa. "I looked it up online and it's gorgeous, but I don't know how everyone else will be dressed."

The three women exchanged a glance, then immediately moved toward Kira.

"I believe you're coming to my house," one of them said with a gleam in her eye. "I'm Allie Price. My fiancé Vaughn and I are hosting. And these are my friends, Darcy and Dray. Their fiancés will also be there. It's a small gathering, but it will be fun. I'm so glad Pax is bringing a date."

Kira's mind started spinning. She tried to log the names of the ladies. Allie had the most flawless dark skin and the widest smile that instantly put Kira at ease. The lady named Darcy had that small-town, girl next door vibe going with tortoiseshell glasses and her hair in a high ponytail. And Dray had such striking dark eyes and perfectly applied makeup, Kira wondered if she'd give her some tips.

"Are you sure you don't mind helping?" Kira asked. "I'm sure you guys didn't set out today to take on a charity case."

"Oh, please." Darcy waved a hand in the air, dismissing Kira's comment. "We're all having mimosas and picking out the best outfits, shoes, and accessories to drive our men wild."

Our men. Perhaps Kira should set the record straight, but the women immediately seemed to start talking and scattering toward racks while Stella served up more mimosas. In record time, Kira had a variety of outfits, shoes included, in a dressing room behind a thick, white drape.

"Are we ready?" Darcy asked. "We should all model together."

"Agree," Dray nodded. "Let's go. We're all going to look amazing."

"And you're so damn cute, you're going to look adorable in everything," Allie stated, pointing to Kira.

Kira smiled. "Well, thanks, but I've been a bit envious and self-conscious with three gorgeous women here."

"Stop that now," Dray scolded as she finished off her mimosa. "We're all beautiful, strong women. Now get your ass in there and try on that sparkly fitted dress first. I just know that's the one for you."

Kira found herself getting swept up in the excitement and instant connection with these women. She'd never felt so welcomed or loved as she did since coming to Willowvale Springs. Each stranger she'd encountered in the town had treated her like family. The shop owners, the ladies helping her with clothes, literally every single person had made Kira feel like she belonged…like she was part of something bigger than she'd ever imagined.

And then there was Pax. He'd told her he wasn't looking for anything when she'd dropped into his life. Well, she hadn't been looking, either, but now she wasn't so sure she could look anywhere else. She didn't want to get hurt, nobody set out for heartache, but at the same time, she had to believe she'd met him at this point in her life for a reason.

Was he worth taking a risk on? Could she stay a bit longer and see where things went? Would Pax even want that, or was he looking ahead to the date she left? Maybe he had a life to get back to and work to focus on. Maybe she'd just been a necessary distraction, but she truly didn't believe he felt that way.

"Is everyone dressed?" Allie called from one of the fitting rooms.

Kira tugged the short sequin dress and wondered how she'd let these women talk her into this. If she didn't have a proper coat, her nether regions would have icicles hanging.

"I'm not so sure about this dress," Kira stated, easing her curtain aside and stepping out to the area with a wall of mirrors.

Allie popped out first, wearing a silver sequin halter pantsuit with sexy strappy heels. Dray eased her curtain aside and showed off a red crop shirt with gold pants and Darcy stepped out wearing a body-hugging floor-length white gown that accentuated every curve.

"Well damn," Dray laughed. "We look good."

"I think I need to put the four of you in my front window and remove the mannequins." Stella clasped her hands together as her eyes roamed over each woman. Kira continued to tug at the hem of her dress.

"Would you stop that," Allie scolded as she came to stand behind Kira. Their reflections caught in the mirror. "You look amazing and Pax is going to text Vaughn and give some lame excuse as to why you all are late to the party. He's not letting you out of the house in that dress."

Kira's body tingled at the thought of Pax removing this dress and doing every single thing she wanted to her body. She'd wanted something to wow him, but damn it was cold out.

"I'll freeze," Kira murmured.

"It's a short walk from the drive to the house," Allie promised. "A little cold won't kill you. If I had your body, I'd be wearing that dress and those stilettos, too."

Kira dropped her gaze to the strappy silver heels and her pink toes. She'd want to change that up to red or something. If she was going to go all out with a dress like this, she had to step up her polish, hair, and makeup.

"I'm not used to dressing like this," she admitted. "Are you guys sure?"

A resounding, echoing yes from all the ladies had

Kira pulling in a deep breath. She did another glance at herself in the mirror and found all eyes on her.

"If you all say so. But, someone is going to have to do my hair and makeup. I have no clue what I'm doing there."

"Why would you need to know?" Darcy asked. "You're naturally perfect."

That's it. Kira wasn't leaving. She'd found her people, her group, her cheer section. Women supporting women, not threatened by others' beauty or success, really made Kira feel more confident than ever. Maybe she should make a point to keep in touch with these women when she got back home. Even a life coach needed a boost every now and then.

"Okay, let's try on our other things," Darcy stated as she moved toward her dressing room. "And then I want to get the dish on what's going on with you and Pax. He's so private. I love that he's bringing a woman with him."

"And one so fun," Dray chimed in as she closed her curtain behind her. "Kira, we're headed to lunch after this. You have to join."

Kira took a seat on the plush velvet bench in her dressing room and slid out of her shoes. "I'd love to."

Maybe she'd have to really consider sticking around a bit longer after all.

Fourteen

Pax might be chilled to the bone, but for the first time since arriving back in Willowvale Springs, he had a good feeling about the projection of the ranch. At least, the livestock he'd just inquired about. They needed more horses and a few updates to the current stables before having a grand reopening. The next guest wasn't due to arrive until February, and even though that was just over a month away, Pax had every intention of getting as much done before then as possible. He needed to get Allie here to check the cabins to see what she thought about updates. He truly didn't think a renovation needed done, but revamping the decor and very likely getting those hot tubs put in on the back patios would be the next move. Of course there would need to be some privacy dividers between the cabins as well. Even though there was plenty of space between each one, Pax knew from recent experience that couples wanted their privacy.

He hung his coat inside the back door and headed down the hallway toward the living quarters. He didn't have to stay here at the ranch. He had a penthouse in Cheyenne, but he'd allowed a long-term renter to use it because he'd thought he'd be in Spain much longer. The idea of living here on the property where the usual staff lived seemed odd at first. But now that he'd been here a bit, he didn't find the place too bad. Ugly, but livable.

As he reached the small living room in the back, he glanced at the two suitcases sitting by the worn sofa. Kira stepped from one of the bedrooms, not his, and leaned against the door jamb.

"Moving in?" he asked, thrilled she'd finally made the decision, but confused why she hadn't unpacked. So he remained where he stood until he knew what she was thinking.

"I was," she sighed. "I mean, I am. Sorry. I had the absolute best day shopping and lunch with your friends' girlfriends, which was the most unexpected amazing surprise, but I just got off the phone with my Realtor. The deal fell through on the place I wanted. Someone else made a better offer and the seller took it and I didn't get time to counter."

Damn it. This was why he didn't want her going with a rookie agent. Yes, everyone had to start somewhere, but he wanted better for her.

Pax didn't want to focus on the negative right now. There was nothing that could be done now that the house she wanted was gone. So he crossed the room and gripped her shoulders, giving the gentlest squeeze until her sad eyes met his. This might be the first time he'd seen her deflated.

"I don't need to tell you that another place will come along," he stated. "Something you like even more. It always happens in this industry."

"In the next few weeks?" she asked. "The last thing I want to do is head home and have to find someone's couch to sleep on. How pathetic is that? It's a good thing before that call I had halfway decided to stick around for another week or two."

A complete sense of satisfaction filled him. He hadn't even realized he'd inwardly wanted her to stay longer. He didn't even think that was an option.

"What made you decide that?" he asked.

She shrugged beneath his hands. "I have nothing to go back to right now," she snorted. "Especially now. I can video my clients and message them to get everyone back on track by the original date I told them. I'd rather continue to rent the cabin or a room here with you than to be homeless in Portland."

No way in hell was she paying to stay longer. And she certainly wasn't going to be in the guest cottage. If she'd already put her suitcases up here, then this is where she'd stay.

"I would have brought your things up," he told her.

"I know, but I was frustrated after the call and

threw everything into my luggage and just came up. I do still have groceries down there. And my tree."

"That tree isn't coming here."

A smile tugged at the corners of her mouth. "No, I don't imagine it would survive the trip."

"Honey, it didn't survive to Christmas."

Her eyes widened. "Say that again."

"Say what?"

"You called me honey. I'm not used to that from anyone, let alone you. I liked it."

Damn it. He hadn't even noticed—which just told him that she'd come to mean more than he thought if his default mode was to refer to her as an endearment in lieu of her name.

"Nobody's ever called you honey?"

Kira snorted. "Like who? It's not like I have a throng of men lining up out my door. I honestly don't recall the last date I went on."

The completely primal male side of him loved hearing that, but then he hated knowing she didn't have many people in her corner. What a lonely world that must be…

Similar to his. Who did he have besides associates? He didn't go out much, didn't want to take the time to feed into a relationship if it didn't further his career goals. For the first time in…well, since his relationship with Hank and Edith, Pax finally found someone who made him think of someone other than himself and of something other than work.

And she was staying just a bit longer until she figured out her housing situation back in Portland.

Kira rested her head against his chest and groaned. "I so wanted that town house," she murmured. "I hate this. I don't like feeling out of control or having no solid plan. That's what I stress to my clients."

She lifted her head to look back up at him. "I stress how important control over your life is to secure your happiness. I look like a failure at this point."

"Nobody has to know your personal business." He framed her face with his hands. "And housing deals fall through all the time."

"I bet you don't lose a deal," she sighed.

No, he didn't. But he did at the start of his career, which only made him hunger for success even more.

"I don't like to lose anything," he replied. "And you're the furthest thing from failure. Hell, you won't even give up on a dead tree."

Her soft laugh warmed another piece of his soul and he found that each time she offered that sweet sound, he readily soaked it all in.

"I don't give up on anything," she insisted. "Not when I want something."

Just another way they were so, so similar. He didn't know how to feel about all of this and the way their worlds collided, but little by little, he found that this fact didn't scare him...he was rather excited to see where their journey would take them. He didn't believe once she left that would be the end of them.

At first, he'd been adamant their fling would be just that...a fling. He had no expectations of anything beyond these few weeks. Now, though, he couldn't imagine this place without her.

"I need to get back online and start the search again." Kira took a step back and reached up to adjust her ponytail as she let out a frustrated sigh. "I really have no clue what else is out there that I could afford and in a neighborhood that I feel safe. Living alone as a single woman is something I have to take into consideration."

And he absolutely hated that. The fact that any woman had to worry about her housing simply because she had no partner was unsettling. This wasn't a new problem, but this issue hit too close to home for him. He wanted her safe and happy at all times. He wanted to be the one to provide all of that for her, no matter how this relationship worked or didn't work. Kira had implanted herself so deeply into his life, he knew they had no end in sight.

That revelation hit him hard and there was a portion of him that was absolutely terrified at the fact. But the majority of him had a newfound excitement he hadn't felt in…well, ever. What did this mean for him? For his future and his career? He'd never wanted to enter into something permanent.

Is that what he wanted? Did he want her to stay? Or…hell. He had no idea, so until he figured it out, he had better keep his thoughts to himself.

But he did need to tell her about his actual status here. That he wasn't a worker struggling to make ends meet and hopefully not lose the ranch. He'd never lose this place; it was more a matter of if he would stay or ultimately leave the business for someone else to run. Kira deserved to know the truth. She wasn't like his ex and she clearly didn't care about money. Her heart was pure and transparent. She deserved nothing less in return.

"Kira—"

She stepped back and pulled her cell from her pocket. On a groan, she tipped her head back before glancing back to the screen.

"Sorry. I should take this," she told him. "Hold your thought and tell me in a minute. It's my mother and I've dodged her calls all day because I was dealing with the housing nightmare."

"Go." He moved aside. "I won't forget what I wanted to say."

Pax took this chance to grab her luggage and take everything into the room he'd been using. Everything about this setup seemed like a sham. None of this was his stuff, except the personal items he'd brought with him. But the furniture, the decor…nothing.

Or perhaps it was. His name was on the deed now, so legally every bit of this was his. He needed to make a decision as to where he wanted to land. Yes, he'd made progress on where he wanted the ranch to go, but he hadn't made progress on his personal life. Before coming here, he had everything laid out in a perfect plan. Now, since Kira and the inheritance, he had no clue where the hell to go or what to do next.

All he knew for sure was that he wasn't ready to let Kira go, and he couldn't be sure what to do with her if she stayed.

* * *

Kira sank onto the worn sofa and pinched the bridge of her nose. Her mother continued to cry into the phone and list all the reasons why this wedding was a no-go.

"Can you believe that?" her mother went on in between tears and hiccups. "He actually thought we'd both move to Kansas? My home is here in California, not to mention I think he has already found someone else."

In Kansas, no doubt.

Kira kept all comments to herself. She didn't point out the obvious—that her mother had only known this particular man a few months and had already decided to jump into marriage. Who did that? Not to mention, shouldn't living arrangements be discussed at the early stage of a serious commitment?

Oh, who was she to judge anyone? Kira fell back against the cushions as she stretched her legs and propped her feet on the scarred coffee table. She'd started falling for a man who had no intention of taking their status from fling to relationship. She'd known him far less time than her mother had known her fiancé, so why was Kira so frustrated?

More importantly, was she just like her mother? Could she trust her feelings? She didn't know any other way than how her mom had raised her, not to mention Kira had come to Wyoming at one of the most vulnerable times in her life. So trusting her emotions right now seemed like a rocky place to land.

Still, she couldn't ignore how she felt. She was a

grown woman and she wasn't stupid or naive. She'd gone into this physical relationship with no expectations…and somehow gained more than she'd bargained for.

"Are you listening?" her mother scolded.

"Yes, Mom. I'm here. Just taking it all in."

For years Kira had listened to her mother complain about one man after another, but now she realized her mother just wanted love. Kira felt sorry for the woman and found her heart softening.

"I'm sorry your marriage isn't going to work out," Kira found herself saying. "What can I do to help?"

Silence filled the other end of the line. Kira pulled her phone away to glance at the screen to see if the call was still on.

"Mom?"

"Sorry, honey." Her mother sniffed once again. "I've just never had that reaction from you."

Yeah, well maybe it was past time for some compassion. Instead of Kira thinking how this all affected her, perhaps she should think how one failed relationship after another had affected her mother.

"Is there anything I can do? I want to help if there's something you need."

"Just a listening ear is good for now."

As her mother went on, not sounding nearly as upset now, Kira also realized that perhaps their relationship would take time. Starting off trying to understand each other was the only way to move forward.

Pax stepped from the bedroom and into the open

living area situated between the other bedrooms. He mouthed "you good" and when she nodded, he moved toward the front of the main house where the check-in area and offices were located. She'd never been with anyone, short or long-term, who showed her so much care. He wasn't with her just for the intimacy. Oh, of course that's exactly how they'd started and what she'd insisted on. But they'd moved so far beyond physical. Pax had worked his way into her soul and her heart. He didn't seem to freak out when she mentioned staying a bit longer, so did that mean he wanted her to?

And what had he been about to tell her?

She had so many questions, and with each passing day, she only added more instead of finding the answers she so desperately needed in order to make a decision about her future.

Kira spent the next hour on the phone with her mother and by the end, Kira had a new, warm feeling in her heart and a promise to show her mother Wyoming one day. And why not? Kira loved this place and wanted to share. Maybe a mother-daughter bonding trip would be another step on their road to forging a bond.

For the first time in a long time, Kira had a sliver of hope in her heart that she and her mom might actually come together.

Now, if she could figure out her housing and this up in the air unsureness with Pax, she'd be all set to a solid plan. But she had no home and no idea where Pax's heart was in all this...if his heart was even invested. She truly hoped he was because there wasn't a doubt in her mind she'd be leaving here with a shattered heart if he wasn't.

Fifteen

"So what are we doing today?"

Kira fit perfectly in the crook of Pax's arm as he trailed his fingertips up and down her bare side. That dip in her waist was an area that couldn't be explored enough.

"I have to go to the stables and meet Tate to go over the new plans," he told her. "I talked with some guys yesterday about getting more horses. Can't have a dude ranch without better stables and more horses."

"I could go get the rest of the things from the cabin and get it all cleaned up since I'm staying here."

Pax jerked and shifted so he could look her in the eye. "You'll do nothing. I'll get your things and we have someone to clean. You think I'd expect you to do anything like that?"

"I didn't say you expected me to, but I'm offering to help where I can."

She rose up onto her elbows, holding his gaze the entire time. Like hell he'd let her lift a finger around here. She'd come to the ranch as a guest and turned into far more. No way would she be putting in any type of work while he was in charge.

"We've got it under control," he assured her, placing a kiss on the tip of her nose. "Why don't you take a ride or read one of your books."

A smile spread across her face. "Yes, the books. I don't expect you to pay for my things while I'm here, but that was the sweetest gesture anyone has ever done for me."

"Seriously?" Why wasn't he surprised? "You've dated some assholes."

Kira's sweet laughter filled the foreign room. He wanted her in his place, with his things, on his turf. He knew she'd fit right in with his house. He could easily see her there, her books on the coffee table, some ugly ass tree in the corner with her variety of decor, and her trying out all those new recipes in his state-of-the-art kitchen. She'd love his home secluded in the mountains of Wyoming, and he found the more he thought of her there, the more anxious he was to show off his real life.

He'd tell her everything tonight and ask if she wanted to take all of her things there after the first of the year and the New Year's party. Maybe spend a few weeks there and explore what they'd started.

"What are you thinking?" she asked, her brows

drawn in. "You've got a weird look on your face. Does this have anything to do with what you wanted to tell me last night?"

"Yeah, we got distracted."

Distracted seemed to be the theme surrounding their entire relationship. He hadn't been himself since the day he'd seen her wrestling that pathetic excuse for a tree off the top of her car. He'd never once let anything come between him and his career, and he still had his goals lined up. He just might take a different path to get to everything he wanted for his future.

"Do you want to talk now?" she asked.

"Tonight," he promised. "It's something important and I don't want to rush before I have to meet Tate."

She sat up and the sheet fell away from her breasts and puddled at her waist. He couldn't help where his eyes roamed. All of that silky skin on display and he knew each and every place to touch her to make her surrender to anything and everything he wanted.

"How soon do you have to meet him?" she asked, stretching her arms high above her head with a soft, sultry sigh. "You're not leaving me just yet, are you?"

In a fast move, he had his hands around her waist and flipped her so he was on his back and she straddled him.

"Take what you need," he offered, gripping her hips. "Tate isn't going anywhere."

There was nothing more important than proving to Kira that she had become a priority in his life. He didn't know the next steps here and he had to tread lightly because the last thing he wanted was for either of them to wind up hurt.

The moment her body started to move, Pax lost all thoughts and let himself get lost in the moment. He'd worry about next steps later...much later.

Kira pulled her knit cap lower over her ears as she stepped into the stables. After she and Pax had quickly, yet effectively distracted one another, he'd gotten a phone call from Brandon that he needed to take. Kira offered to head on down to let Tate know he'd be right there.

And she wouldn't mind getting another chance at petting these beautiful horses again. Once Pax got here, she'd head to her cabin and finish getting the rest of her things and the groceries. Despite what he said, she could pitch in and clean. This might have started as a vacation, but quickly turned into so much more. She felt invested in this property now.

"Hey, Miss Lee." Tate stepped from the tack room and tipped his brown hat to her. "Warming up out there, isn't it?"

Warming up? Her nether regions were still frozen, so no.

"I've been warmer," she chuckled. "Pax will be down soon. He had a quick call he had to take."

"No worries. Always plenty of work to keep me busy here."

He grabbed a pitchfork from the wall where several tools hung and started toward one of the empty stalls.

"It's nice having you here." Tate moved into the

stall and stabbed a pile of hay with the metal tines. "Mr. Hart deserves some happiness in his life. Since being pulled back here after Hank's death and then the inheritance… It's been rough on all of us."

Hank. He must be the grandfather. That would explain a good bit. Kira couldn't imagine inheriting a dying business and then trying to breathe new life into it.

"Still not sure what Hank was thinking," Tate went on as he continued to scoop the hay into a wheelbarrow. "Leaving all of his ranches and homes to successful men who don't even live here. Calling all those guys back to Willowvale Springs, uprooting their lives. Hank must've seen that they had the money and potential to get his places where they used to be. I'm just glad I can hang around and help Pax."

Money? Pax had money to fix this place up? And who were all of these successful men? Likely Pax's friends she was going to meet at the party. But just how much about Pax did she not know?

"I'm new to all of this." She tried to play like she knew a little, but she realized she knew nothing. She wanted more info without seeming like she was digging. "Will a dude ranch be really expensive to get going fully again?"

"I believe Pax said he'd use about a million to start and then see where things went."

Another shovel into the barrow while Kira leaned against the frame, completely blindsided by the staggering number she'd just heard. A million dollars? Pax wasn't just wealthy, the man was rich. She'd had no idea, not that it mattered, but she sure as hell wished he'd trusted her with his personal life and opened up to her. Money never meant anything to her—hadn't she already told him that?

"I guess the question is now whether Pax will stay or head back to Spain," Tate went on, clearly just thinking out loud. "That man needs to slow down and enjoy life before he works himself to death. He was always like that when he worked here as a teen. I'm not surprised he's still the same. He was destined for bigger things than a small town."

Kira's knees weakened and she wished she could take a seat. All of this information flooding her, and not from Pax himself, had her list of questions growing even more.

While they'd never said they owed each other anything, she couldn't help but wonder why she'd felt so comfortable spilling her heart to him while he'd kept his closed and guarded. Perhaps that's what he'd been wanting to tell her last night and today. He could see she'd gotten fully invested and he was not. He was trying to break it to her easy.

Well, she wouldn't beg for any man to want to be with her, to trust her with his secrets and his fear, or hope he had the same level of feelings she did.

"Spain is a far cry from Wyoming," she murmured.

Tate snorted. "There's nowhere else I'd want to be than right here. I just hope like hell if he does leave, he finds the right property manager."

Tate continued to express his concerns if Pax ended up back in Spain, but Kira didn't even know

Spain was on the table. Here she was worried about going back to Portland and all this time Pax was considering going across the globe.

Obviously what she assumed was a growing relationship was clearly one-sided.

Her chest tightened, her throat clogged with the impending emotion that only led to tears. She had no one to blame but herself. He'd never promised her anything, he'd never alluded to the fact he wanted more. She'd just assumed...

"Sorry I was late."

That voice behind her had Kira pulling in a deep, albeit shaky breath, and squaring her shoulders.

"Got plenty to do," Tate stated, never breaking stride with his work. "Miss Lee has been keeping me company."

Pax's boots shuffled along the concrete floor, but she couldn't turn around. She wasn't ready to face him just yet and had no idea the look she'd have on her face.

"Is that so?" Pax asked as he came to stand beside her. "Nice to have a pretty woman around, isn't it?"

The first time he'd mentioned her being pretty to Tate, Kira had gotten all those silly butterflies like a teenager with a crush. How ridiculous she felt now.

"I was just telling Miss Lee how you're really invested in this ranch," Tate stated, resting his arm on top of the pitchfork as he faced them. "Not just anyone who inherited this mess would be so willing to sink their time and money into making it whole again. Nice to see you kept your humble roots once you got successful."

Pax's swift intake of breath had Kira blinking up at him. His eyes moved from Tate to her and that muscle clenched in his jaw.

"Yeah," she murmured. "That's nice you're donating your own money. A million? That's really amazing, Pax."

"Kira—"

"I need to get back to the house and make some calls." Like finding a new house ASAP. "I'll see you guys later."

Pax said her name again, but she kept moving. Fixing her eyes on the opening of the stable, she put one foot in front of the other, cursing herself when her vision blurred and a lone tear slid down her cheek.

Sixteen

As much as Pax wanted to run back to the main house, he took his time. He'd cut his meeting short with Tate, making some lame excuse about not feeling well. If Tate knew anything was up, he was wise enough to keep his comments to himself.

The look on Kira's face had absolutely gutted him. He should have told her when he thought of letting her in. He shouldn't have waited, because now she didn't trust him, or she thought he didn't trust her. Either way, he'd damaged something with her and that was the absolute last thing he ever wanted to do.

Now he had to hope like hell he hadn't screwed up anything they'd started building. Maybe he didn't know what he wanted or even if this would lead anywhere, but he sure as hell knew that he respected

Kira and wanted to keep her heart protected. She'd come here to escape pain and the stress of her life back home, and what did he do? He'd kept the truth about his personal life to himself for fear of being hurt. That decision only made him selfish and a complete jerk.

The snow crunched beneath his boots and he crossed the yard toward the back door. He stepped onto the covered patio and stomped off the chunks of snow as his eyes landed on the hot tub. Was there any part of this ranch Kira hadn't touched? How could he make this right? *Could* he make this right?

As he stepped through the back doors, he wasn't quite sure what to say, but he assumed starting with an apology might go a long way in getting back into her good graces.

And it wasn't so much that he wanted to be in good standing, but more that he wanted her pain-free and able to trust him again.

He went straight to the room they'd shared last night only to find the sheets still rumpled and her suitcases gone. He poked his head into the adjoining bath and none of her bottles were on the vanity. His heart sank. Had she gone back to the cabin or left the ranch for good? He'd only been about thirty minutes with Tate, but obviously enough time for her to load her car and get away from him. He didn't blame her. She'd been nothing but transparent with him since she arrived, while he'd been guarded for fear of getting too involved.

Too late. He'd gotten deeper with her than anyone

else in his entire life, so keeping his secrets and true identity had only backfired.

He cursed as he headed out the back and to his truck. She deserved to know the truth from him, even if his defense seemed lame at this point. He had to try to make her understand his point of view. Maybe that wouldn't make a difference, but he had to take a chance that his words would change her outlook.

A sliver of relief trickled down his spine as he spotted her car in front of the cabin. She'd stayed… for now. But her absence at the house spoke volumes of the wedge he'd driven between them.

Taking a deep breath, he parked behind her and killed the engine. His only hope at this point was that she didn't slam the door in his face and gave him two minutes to apologize.

Just as Pax stepped up onto the porch, the door flew open. Kira's dark gaze stared back at him and beneath the anger, he noticed the hurt. She crossed her arms over her chest, blocking the entrance and obviously giving him the answer about whether or not he'd be welcome inside.

"We really have nothing left to say," she informed him, her tone cold and closed off.

"You might not, but I have plenty to say, and I want you to listen."

She scoffed and shook her head. "Is that so? Well, I wanted honesty, so here we are."

"I have my reasons."

"You don't owe me an explanation, Pax. We were nothing more than a fling—you've said so yourself.

So take your guilt and go on back to work or whatever it is you need to be doing."

He took a step closer to the threshold. "I'm not leaving until I explain myself."

Her stare lasted about five seconds before she dropped her hands and turned to walk further into the cabin. Considering she didn't slam the door, he took that as a silent invitation to enter.

Pax stepped over the threshold and closed the door behind him. Kira kept her back to him as she started removing mantel decor from Christmas. Seeing all of that stuff come down hit him harder than he'd thought. He'd never been one to decorate for the holidays, but her style and all the lights and garland had gotten to him. Ridiculous, really, but now he didn't want to see the cabin bare again.

"I looked you up, you know."

She started talking before he could, all while plucking gold decor from her greenery. He slid his hands into the pockets of his coat and let her speak.

"I had no idea you were a billionaire." She tossed a glance over her shoulder and eyed him. "You don't look it, so nice acting job."

"I wasn't acting."

She shrugged and turned back to her task. "Anyway, you seem to have really made a name for yourself, which will be good for the dude ranch. I'm sure once you sink that money into the property, people will flock here once again. It truly is a magnificent setting."

"All of this is what I tried to tell you last night and what I was going to explain tonight."

She dumped the items into a tote at her feet he hadn't seen before now. Then she turned and propped her hands on her hips.

"Like I said, you don't owe me an explanation, and I'll get over being hurt and bitter. But since you walked in here, you're going to be the target of my wrath."

"I deserve that," he agreed.

Kira pulled in a breath as she glanced around the cabin, then back to him. "Well, go ahead and say what you need. I have plenty to do here before I head out."

"Stay." The word slipped out before he could stop himself. "At least stay in the cabin, but don't rush back to Portland. You don't have a place to go."

"I put an urgent request in to my agent. I told her to look for rentals as well, at least that would buy me some time."

"If you're insistent, let me find something out there for you. Don't go until you have a safe, secure place to land."

A humorless laugh escaped her. "And this is safe and secure? I thought we had something. Yes, we started out fast and physical, but in my mind, we were building something. Then you asked me to move up to the house with you, I was sure it wasn't one-sided."

"This isn't one-sided," he insisted.

"Your actions prove otherwise."

Yes, they did, which was why he had to make her see his reasoning.

"I worked on this ranch as a teen," he started. He moved toward the counter separating the living room and the kitchen and took a seat at the barstool. "Hank and Edith became like my parents as well as my employer. My parents were... Well, they were definitely in their own world with making each other's lives miserable and it wasn't much of a homelife. So I poured every bit of my time into this place. I didn't do it for the money, but because I felt like I belonged and was making a difference. Then when I graduated, I knew I wanted more and something clicked with real estate. I never wanted anyone to feel like they didn't have a safe place to call home."

Kira's shoulders sagged just a bit and he wondered if his words were making an impact. He didn't want her pity, but more her understanding. If she still hated him at the end of all of this, he obviously only had himself to blame, but at least he could say he tried.

When she said nothing, but he knew he still had her attention, he went on.

"I was engaged a few years ago."

Saying that sounded so odd. He couldn't even recall why he'd wanted to get married looking back, and he sure as hell wasn't in love.

"All of my associates would bring their wives to functions, and I guess I thought I always needed someone on my arm. Someone consistent," he corrected. "I found out too late that she didn't care for me one bit, just my bank account. Days before the wedding I caught her trying to steal from me. I was completely blindsided and vowed to never let anyone get that close again."

Silence settled in the small space and he didn't know what else he could say or do to make her understand his situation. Considering her silence, she was either taking it all in or waiting on him to have a better reasoning.

"This was nothing against you," he added. "I had to stay true to myself and trust my gut. I never wanted more than a fling."

"Yes, that's apparent and absolutely my fault for reading more into our situation. You were up front with me from the beginning." Kira took a step toward him and wrapped her arms around her waist. "But you have to see my point of view. When you invited me to stay in the house for the rest of my time here, you can understand where I'd be confused."

Pax nodded. "I can. I wanted you with me for the time you were here. I didn't want to go back and forth, and I thought you'd be more comfortable in a bigger place."

"Again, this was all about your needs. I get it."

Damn it. His words sounded logical in his head, but the execution was going all to hell.

"I had to guard myself first," he insisted. "Everything between us happened so fast and every bit was unexpected. Then I wanted to find the right time and that never seemed to happen."

He paused and thought for a second before adding, "Did the girls not say anything about me when you guys were shopping and at lunch?"

"We were too busy having fun and trying to find the perfect outfits," she explained. "Then they wanted to get to know me, so no. They never revealed who you were or your status. They said something about you trying to build up the ranch like it used to be and how their guys were good friends with you and they couldn't wait for us all to be together at the party."

A sadness swept over her as she glanced down and chewed the inside of her cheek. She took a moment before bringing her attention back to him.

"I'll text them and let them know I had to leave town," she told him.

"You don't have to leave."

"Yes. I do."

Those three whispered words sliced right through him. He didn't know what to say to get her to stay, but clearly her mind was made up. He'd done all he could and he wasn't going to beg. At least he had to hang on to his pride.

"There's no need to rush back to Portland." He held up his hands when she opened her mouth, no doubt to argue. "Hear me out. Stay here in the cabin. I promise not to bother you and I'll give you Tate's number if you need anything. Stay as long as you need until you find a place back home."

"I can't do that," she argued, but the conviction had left her tone. She sounded defeated and broken. "I should go and try to…"

She blew out a sigh and turned back to her mantel,

muttering words he couldn't make out. He came to his feet and started to take a step, but stopped himself. Everything in him wanted to go to her, to comfort her, but how ridiculous would that be? He was the one who'd caused the pain. Did he truly believe she'd just willingly go into his arms?

She'd shut him out, shut him down, and now she'd turned her back. There was no better cue to leave than that. He'd barely took a step when her words stopped him.

"Did you see anything beyond these few weeks?" she murmured, keeping her back to him.

Of all the times in his life, now his honesty counted more than ever.

"I don't know what I saw beyond that," he told her. "I'm not even sure if I'm staying here long-term."

She merely nodded and carefully folded the greenery and placed in the tote. He wanted to tell her more, but how could he when he wasn't even sure himself? It wouldn't be fair to ask her to stay, to give them time to figure things out. The truth was, he might very well end up back in Spain. Asking her for anything would only be selfish and could still end in heartache.

So maybe this ending was the best for both of them. He'd explained his stance, she'd listened, there was nothing else to say or do at this point.

But that didn't mean he didn't care.

"I'll let Tate know you might be here and give him your number," Pax told her as he made his way toward the door. "Any communication while you're here can be done through him, though you know where to find me if you need anything."

She didn't reply, didn't even act like she heard him or she cared. The lump of guilt and remorse settled so weighty in his throat, he had a difficult time pulling in a solid breath. He had to get out of here.

Seventeen

"You look like hell."

Pax glared at Mason over the rim of his beer stein. The guys had invited Pax to lunch at The Getaway while the girls got ready for the party tonight.

The party Pax would be going to stag.

"I've been better," he admitted after a long pull of his favorite craft beer.

"What's going on?" Kahlil asked, easing forward in the large, round corner booth. "Something with the ranch?"

He wished it was something that simple. If the ranch was the issue, he could throw money at the problem and make it disappear. Unfortunately, handling hearts was out of his wheelhouse and nothing he could pay to fix.

"Ranch is good." He set his frosted mug down and leaned back against the leather seat. "On track to open fully in the spring with new livestock, updates to the stables and cabins, and I'm bringing in any of the old staff who wants their positions back."

"That's great." Mason nodded. "So why do you look like you'd rather be anywhere else than here."

Pax didn't know if his old buddy meant here at The Getaway or here in Willowvale Springs. Regardless, Pax did want to be anywhere else. Someplace away from the pain and guilt that consumed him here. He'd left remorse and sadness here once before when he'd been a teen outrunning his family's drama.

But this ache in his chest was nothing compared to anything he'd ever felt in the past. How had Kira gotten so deep into his life in such a short amount of time? She'd impacted him in a way he never thought possible, yet he still couldn't tell her what she wanted to hear. He didn't know if he wanted a commitment and honestly had no idea what the hell that even looked like.

"Women issues," Vaughn muttered. "We all had the same look not long ago."

"I don't have woman issues," Pax all but growled.

"Damn." Mason patted the table with his hand. "The girls really love Kira. Are you telling me you guys had a falling-out?"

Falling-out? Out of what? They weren't in love and they hadn't professed anything toward each other, so there was nothing to fall *out* of.

"What the hell happened?" Vaughn demanded. "Allie won't like hearing this. I know the girls were all excited to decorate and get ready for the party tonight. They seemed to form a fast friendship with your woman. I was looking forward to meeting her."

Yeah, well, he'd been looking forward to having her on his arm. He'd wanted to introduce her to his friends and see how well they all interacted together. Having her integrate further into his world hadn't been part of any plan, but everything with them just seemed to keep clicking into place.

Until he broke that bond of trust.

"She's probably leaving town now," he told them, staring at the half-empty glass. "Or tomorrow. Hell, I don't know when. She's done with me."

"I'd make a joke, but you look like you can't get any lower," Kahlil muttered. "What happened?"

"I screwed up."

No need in sugarcoating it or trying to save his pride. He'd messed up anything he'd had with Kira and the last thing he worried about now was his ego.

"Then fix it instead of moping around."

Pax jerked his attention to Mason, who nursed a soda. The former celebrity baseball player returned his gaze with one of command.

"Fix it?" Pax snarked. "Why didn't I think of that?"

Kahlil shifted in the booth to face Pax a bit better and look around Vaughn.

"What our well-meaning friend means to say is, we've all been there and if you want her, you have to fight for her."

Silence settled between them, but the bustle of the pub carried on. Music pumped from the hidden speakers, patrons laughed and chatted, happy in their own little worlds while his continued to crumble.

"Do you want her back?" Mason asked after a bit.

That heavy ball of guilt seemed to grow inside Pax's chest. He'd not wanted their time together to come to an end, but he hadn't thought beyond that. He'd always vowed not to let his heart get involved or to let anyone have such power over him that he dropped so low emotionally.

Somehow, he'd lied to himself and allowed all of that to happen.

"Does she look as miserable as you?" Vaughn asked.

Pax shrugged and glanced to his friend. "I honestly have no idea. I know I hurt her, but that wasn't my intent. I just… I couldn't tell her what she wanted to hear."

"Will you ever be ready?" Mason asked. "Because if not, then you have to let her go."

"I don't want to let her go," Pax insisted without hesitation.

"Then you have your answer." Kahlil stretched his arm along the back of the booth and smiled. "Now what are you going to do about it?"

Did he have his answer? Could things be as simple, yet as complicated, as that? Just because he wanted her didn't mean she'd return the feelings. He'd left a bruise on their relationship, so even if he went back to her, that pain still lingered.

"I promised her I wouldn't bother her if she stayed," Pax explained.

"Listen." Mason smacked Pax on the shoulder. "You've given yourself the pity party you needed. I get it. But now you have to man up and go get what you want. If that's Kira, then get off your ass and do something."

Vaughn and Kahlil raised their beers in mock cheers at Mason's demand. They were right, and if the tables were reversed, he'd be telling them the same thing. Stop feeling sorry for yourself and go after what you want. Isn't that how he handled every business transaction in his career? Only this was the most important "deal" of his life. He had to know exactly what to say and how to deliver the message. But he couldn't do it alone.

"I'm going to need your help."

Every one of his buddies nodded, and he only hoped with them having his back, that he could convince Kira to stay.

"I don't know why I let you all talk me into this."

Kira smoothed out the gold tablecloth and turned to her new friends...friends she likely wouldn't see again once she left Willowvale Springs. Well, unless they came to Portland to see her. She highly doubted she'd be back. She loved the town, but returning would only run the risk of seeing Pax again and she couldn't take that chance.

"Because we promise Pax isn't coming now," Allie stated as she brought over a clear vase with white roses for the table. "According to the guys, he's moping and not in the mood for company."

That sounded like him. Moping. That's exactly how he was when she'd met him. Looking back now, she realized the stress he'd been under with inheriting the ranch, having a guest, trying to keep his businesses growing and going global.

He'd had so much on his plate and clearly too much to feed into any type of permanent relationship...which is what he'd told her and she'd still ignored those red flags and fallen too hard, too fast.

"I'm not sure I'm the best company, either," she admitted, turning to face Darcy and Dray as they continued to set up the champagne bar along the exposed brick wall of the resort great room.

"Being alone will only make you feel worse," Dray stated, turning the bottles around with the labels out. "At least you can ring in the New Year with people who adore you and we'll pamper you with food and drinks."

Kira couldn't be in a bad mood with these amazing ladies. They'd each texted her and insisted she come help them decorate while the guys finished their lunch. Kira had to admit, she was thrilled to see this amazing resort Vaughn and Allie had transformed. The grand room had an entire wall of windows that overlooked the patio area with a vast pool perfect for a summer lounging area. But it was the surrounding snowy mountains that stole the show for the view. Everywhere she looked, there were tall evergreens and mountain peaks. Nature seemed to paint the perfect backdrop for any event held here at the ranch resort.

Like weddings.

Goodness. Why did her mind go straight to a wedding? It wasn't like she was walking down the aisle anytime soon. Maybe it was just the whole idea of love that she'd been surrounded with the past couple days. The women she'd met and instantly clicked with were all headed toward their own 'I do's' soon and nothing was more romantic than a snowy setting and the holidays. Love just seemed to be in the air. Not the air she was breathing, but still.

"You know you have to come because you looked too good in that outfit," Darcy stated as she adjusted her glasses. "This is going to be a memorable night. I promise."

Kira nodded. "Well, I am glad I was still invited, but I couldn't have come if Pax was going to be here."

"We can see him anytime." Allie clasped her hands together and glanced around the spacious room as if figuring out what to do next. "We need to soak in all the time you're here."

"When are you leaving?" Dray asked. "Not that we're in a rush to see you go, but we'll need at least one more get together before you go."

Kira pulled out the white chair and took a seat. She was both mentally and physically exhausted and just wanted a short break. She was glad the girls invited her to decorate, this beat sitting in her cabin staring out at the snow and wondering what Pax was doing.

"I was going to leave today, but I might stay a few more days. Pax said I could stay as long as I wanted in the cabin and he'd leave me be, but I don't know."

"I'm sure he's miserable," Allie added. "You two have something."

Kira shook her head and rested her arm on the back of the chair as she crossed her legs. "Had. Or at least, I thought we had something. Now I just look foolish and desperate."

The ladies all shared a look and Kira glanced between them. She had no clue what silent language they all spoke. Clearly their years of friendship had given them a deeper bond.

"You're not foolish or desperate," Dray scolded. "We've all fallen in love and it just leaves you in a vulnerable spot and you feel exposed to the world. I swear, we get it."

Kira sat straight up in her seat. "I never said I was in love."

Silence settled over the room, then the women burst into laughter.

"You can try lying to yourself, but we've all recently been through the highs and lows of love." Allie crossed the room and stood before Kira. "There's nothing to be ashamed of, but if Pax is as miserable as you are, I have a feeling this will all work out."

Kira opened her mouth to argue that statement, but Allie held up her hand.

"No arguing," she demanded. "I'm just saying that if an opportunity presents itself, don't turn away a second chance."

Before Kira could ask what that even meant, Allie reached for her hands and tugged her to her feet.

"Let's finish this room so we can start on our make-overs. We need to look our absolute best tonight."

Maybe this distraction would help Kira at least think of something else for the day. She wasn't really in a festive mood, but at the same time, the idea of ringing in the New Year with only her new books—books that Pax had bought her—really didn't hold any appeal, either. So getting her hair and makeup done, plus putting on an outfit that made her feel sexy and confident and beautiful was definitely the better option.

She had no doubt she'd look fantastic on the outside, but how did she gloss over the ugly she held on to inside?

Eighteen

If this entire plan backfired, Pax had no idea what the hell he'd do. He'd never been so far out of his comfort zone or defenseless, but he'd also never been so miserable, knowing he'd let someone go that he should've held on to.

Everything had happened so fast—the fling, the falling, the breakup. He wanted time, so much more time with Kira than he'd been given. How could he let her walk away, thinking he didn't want more?

He adjusted the brim of his hat as he stepped through the open double doors leading into the grand room of the newly renovated resort. They hadn't fully opened to the public yet, but this time next year, no doubt the place would be hopping with a spectacular party and full of life and tourists. Pax could appreciate all of the decor and changes later, right now his heart was beating way too hard and his nerves were on edge.

The music blared through the speakers, something modern and upbeat. The whole crew stood over near the two-story floor-to-ceiling windows that overlooked the property and the mountains. Twinkling lights from the heated patio area sparkled, making the outside look just as festive as the inside. The gold decor on the tables combined with the white roses in vases and gold balloons with the year printed all over them filled the space. The women had really gone all out.

But there was only one woman he was interested in seeing, and he scanned the small group until Kahlil stepped aside and Pax spotted her. Even with her back to him, especially with her back to him, he took in the jaw-dropping sight of whatever magical thing those sequins were doing to her petite frame. The length, or lack thereof, should be illegal. Those legs all on display had his gut tightening with arousal, but he had to focus...which was damn hard when she took a step back in those silver stilettos and turned.

Her eyes shifted and landed directly on him. Even from this distance, he saw her grip tighten on her champagne flute. He'd told the guys to have their ladies get Kira here any way they could. Pax had purposely arrived late so she'd get comfortable and hopefully let her guard down a little. He had to use every trick to get her to forgive him and he'd had to put his pride aside in order to get this whole crew in his corner.

Pax waited to see what she would do, but then she turned around, giving him her back once again. While his heart sank, he also knew this wasn't going to be easy, and he honestly didn't want it to be. He wanted to show her he'd fight for her. He wanted to prove to her that she was worthy of someone fighting.

Vaughn caught his attention next, and he nudged Allie. One by one, his friends made their way from Kira, and Pax knew this was his one and only chance. While Allie gave him a thumbs-up, the other two women seemed to be giving him a glare as if warning him he better not hurt their new friend.

Too late for that, but he hoped like hell he could repair the damage he'd done and more than make up for the pain he'd caused.

Pax came to stand beside her as Kira took her last sip of champagne. She kept her gaze on the starry night.

"Did every one of them lie to me about you not being here?" she asked without even looking his way.

"Don't be upset with them. I needed backup."

She handed him her glass. "And I'll need a refill."

He reached for the glass, but curled his fingers around hers, holding on until she glanced his way.

"I messed up," he admitted, keeping his hand on hers. "I can't remember a time in my life when I apologized, or at least did so and actually meant it, but damn it. I'm sorry, Kira. I wasn't completely up front with you when I had chances. All I can say is that the only real relationship I've ever had was with Hank and Edith and coming back here made me even more protective of what we shared and all I had with them. It was nothing personal at first with keeping my true identity to myself because I thought you were leaving before anything serious could develop."

She pulled her hand away with her empty glass. "I am."

"No, you're not."

When she turned to look back to the window, he stepped in front of her so all she could see was him.

"You're not running back to Portland to a life you don't even want."

"You don't know what I want."

He smiled. "I do. You want happiness, you want festivities all the time, and a big kitchen to bake in. You want ugly trees and cozy fires. You want hot tub nights under the stars. You want a family to call your own. And you want love."

Her eyes widened as her mouth dropped into a perfect O. Those pink painted lips begged him to take what he wanted, but he had to wait. There was something much more important and much deeper than physical. He wanted that next level of intimacy, and he knew she did, too, or she wouldn't be so agitated and upset with him.

"You said yourself you don't know what you can give me," she murmured. "I deserve better and I deserve someone who knows my worth."

He couldn't stand another second without touching her. He framed her face and made sure to lock his gaze with hers.

"I know your worth and I know I made you feel less than that earlier. I'll have to live with that forever." And that gutted him. "But the thought of you leaving here, of not being with you again seems like the worst thing that could ever happen to me. I don't know how you got to me like no one else ever came close, but I can't live without you, Kira. And if you give me another chance, I swear, you can put your ugly trees in every room of our house next Christmas."

A corner of her mouth twitched. He'd seen that before. She wanted to smile, but she refused to let herself. Good. He was breaking through.

"If you want to stay in the cabin, I'm okay with that," he went on. "Just please, don't leave. Let's work on us."

Now her lips spread into a soft smile and his heart warmed a little more. Maybe they would get that second chance they deserved.

"Us," she repeated. "You've never said that before, like we are a unit."

He dropped his hands from her face and held on to her arms as he stepped into her. The empty champagne glass wedged between their chests.

"We are a unit if you'll give me another chance," he explained. "I've never groveled in my life, if that tells you anything about how bad I want you here with me. I know that's asking for more than I deserve, and you do have friends and a life in Portland, but—"

"No house," she joked. "I couldn't even focus on looking again."

"Good. That means you missed me."

She rolled her eyes. "It means I was angry with you and couldn't think straight."

"And now?" he asked.

"I'm still angry," she muttered, then shrugged. "But I appreciate you humbling yourself and getting all your friends to trick me. I'm sure your ego took a hit."

"You have no idea."

Kira tipped her head back just a bit more and quirked a perfectly arched brow. "If I stay, what does that mean for us?"

"What do you want it to mean?" he countered. "I want you in my house, but it's not close to the ranch. We can commute or we can build something on the land. We can renovate a better living quarters in the main house if you want. I swear, I don't care where we are if you'll just stay with me. I need to be here for the ranch, for all that Hank did for me, I feel Willowvale Springs is my home. *You're* my home."

Her gasp and the tears welling in her eyes were all good signs he'd said the right thing. But he hadn't just been saying the words. He'd meant each one.

"I've fallen in love with this place," she admitted. "I can't imagine staying here and calling this home."

"I hope you will because I've fallen in love with you."

Her mouth dropped once again. "You have?"

Damn, those words felt good to let out.

"Of course I have, I just didn't recognize it until the threat of you leaving was shoved in my face."

She reached up with her free hand and slid her palm along his cheek. "I fell for you, too, so I guess I'm staying."

She held up her glass and wiggled it. "I think we need to toast to this."

"Is that my cue for the refill you wanted?"

"And we should probably tell the gang that your little plan worked."

He reached around and cupped her backside, hauling her against him. "I want to know why the hell nobody warned me you'd be wearing this damn dress to drive me crazy. It's like you did this on purpose."

She smirked. "I did, but at the time I had planned on getting ready with you where you could enjoy this a little before the actual party."

"Oh, I'm enjoying the hell out of this right now," he growled. "It's like visual foreplay."

"Good." She patted his cheek. "You deserve to suffer a little."

He covered her lips with his, finally taking what he'd been craving since he walked away from that closed cabin door.

"Does this mean we can celebrate?" Mason called.

Pax pulled away from Kira and glanced up to six eager people staring at them from a few feet away. Kira laughed and wrapped her arm around his waist as she tucked against his side.

"Yes, we can officially celebrate and ring in the

New Year properly," she told them. "I'm staying at the ranch."

"We had no doubt this would all work out." Darcy beamed. "I can't wait to see what you all do there."

"I'd say this all calls for an early toast," Vaughn stated. "We can't wait until midnight to celebrate all of this great news."

Kahlil wrapped his arm around Dray and pulled her against his side. "Can you imagine if Hank and Edith were here to see all of this? They'd never believe they got all four of us back home and back on the ranches we busted our asses at as teenagers."

"I think they'd be proud of each of us," Mason agreed. "And I'm sure Edith would love knowing each of these women will have an impact on the properties. It's like a whole new generation taking over."

"Which is exactly what he wanted when he put us in his will, I'm sure," Vaughn stated. "This past year knocked us all for a loop, but we're getting our footing now."

Pax cupped his hand over the curve of Kira's hip. "This next year is going to be our best one yet. For all of us."

Darcy and Dray moved toward the table with drinks and refilled the flutes, making sure to put sparkling water in one for Mason. They came back and passed out the drinks.

Pax raised his glass. "To fresh starts and lasting friendships."

Vaughn raised his. "To Hank and Edith."

"Most definitely," Kahlil agreed.

A chorus of cheers resounded as they all clinked their glasses together. Before Pax took a sip, he leaned down to Kira's ear.

"We're not going to make it home," he whispered. "We're going to sneak to a private room. Meet me in five minutes."

She tipped her head back and smiled, a naughty gleam in her eye. "Make that two minutes and there's a storage closet second door on the right if you take that first hallway inside the main door."

He smacked a kiss on her lips. "I do love a woman who plans ahead."

"I love you, too."

* * * * *

COMING NEXT MONTH FROM

DESIRE

PATERNITY PAYBACK & THE TEXAN'S SECRETS
PATERNITY PAYBACK
Texas Cattleman's Club: Diamonds and Dating Apps
by Sophia Singh Sasson

Journalist Willa St. Germaine's interview with her ex, rancher Jack Chowdhry, is the perfect chance to settle the score. But their "professional" reunion reveals untamed desires—and Willa's secret daughter...

THE TEXAN'S SECRETS
Texas Cattleman's Club: Diamonds and Dating Apps
by Barbara Dunlop

Computer hacker Emilia Scott just scored her best hack yet—matching herself with handsome, enigmatic "Nick" on the K!smet dating app. She doesn't know he's successful CEO Nico Law, a man with secrets as complex as her own...

MIAMI MARRIAGE PACT & OVERNIGHT INHERITANCE
MIAMI MARRIAGE PACT
Miami Famous • by Nadine Gonzalez

Gigi Garcia will do anything to save her struggling film production—even marry to ensure her inheritance. Restaurateur Myles Paris is the perfect fictional fiancé, if she can seduce the sexy, stubborn chef into agreeing with her plan.

OVERNIGHT INHERITANCE
Marriages and Mergers • by Rachel Bailey

An unexpected inheritance thrusts Australian schoolteacher Mae Dunstan into the world of single father Sebastian Newport, her business rival...and now her secret lover. Will sharing his New York City office, and his bed, end in heartache?

FALLING FOR THE ENEMY &
STRANDED WITH THE RUNAWAY BRIDE
FALLING FOR THE ENEMY
The Gilbert Curse • by Katherine Garbera

After losing years to a coma, Rory Gilbert wants all life has to offer, including a steamy romp with Kitt Orr Palmer. Little does Rory know, she's the sister of Kitt's enemy—forcing him to choose between his desire for Rory and revenge.

STRANDED WITH THE RUNAWAY BRIDE
by Yvonne Lindsey

When wedding planner turned runaway bride Georgia O'Connor is stranded with loner Sawyer Roberts, they never expected attraction to turn into a heated affair. But when reality intrudes, can he let her go?

You can find more information on upcoming Harlequin titles,
free excerpts and more at Harlequin.com.

HD2in1CNM1123

Get 3 FREE REWARDS!

We'll send you 2 FREE Books plus a FREE Mystery Gift.

FREE Value Over **$20**

Both the **Harlequin® Desire** and **Harlequin Presents®** series feature compelling novels filled with passion, sensuality and intriguing scandals.

YES! Please send me 2 FREE novels from the Harlequin Desire or Harlequin Presents series and my FREE gift (gift is worth about $10 retail). After receiving them, if I don't wish to receive any more books, I can return the shipping statement marked "cancel." If I don't cancel, I will receive 6 brand-new Harlequin Presents Larger-Print books every month and be billed just $6.30 each in the U.S. or $6.49 each in Canada, a savings of at least 10% off the cover price, or 3 Harlequin Desire books (2-in-1 story editions) every month and be billed just $7.83 each in the U.S. or $8.43 each in Canada, a savings of at least 12% off the cover price. It's quite a bargain! Shipping and handling is just 50¢ per book in the U.S. and $1.25 per book in Canada.* I understand that accepting the 2 free books and gift places me under no obligation to buy anything. I can always return a shipment and cancel at any time by calling the number below. The free books and gift are mine to keep no matter what I decide.

Choose one: ☐ **Harlequin Desire**
(225/326 BPA GRNA)

☐ **Harlequin Presents**
Larger-Print
(176/376 BPA GRNA)

☐ **Or Try Both!**
(225/326 & 176/376 BPA GRQP)

Name (please print)

Address   Apt. #

City   State/Province   Zip/Postal Code

Email: Please check this box ☐ if you would like to receive newsletters and promotional emails from Harlequin Enterprises ULC and its affiliates. You can unsubscribe anytime.

Mail to the Harlequin Reader Service:
IN U.S.A.: P.O. Box 1341, Buffalo, NY 14240-8531
IN CANADA: P.O. Box 603, Fort Erie, Ontario L2A 5X3

Want to try 2 free books from another series? Call 1-800-873-8635 or visit www.ReaderService.com.

HDHP23

HARLEQUIN
PLUS

Try the best multimedia subscription service for romance readers like you!

Read, Watch and Play.

Experience the easiest way to get the romance content you crave.

Start your **FREE TRIAL** at
www.harlequinplus.com/freetrial.